I Have Seen Him
IN THE **WATCHFIRES**

I Have Seen Him
IN THE **WATCHFIRES**

CATHY GOHLKE

MOODY PUBLISHERS
CHICAGO

© 2008 by
CATHY GOHLKE

Editor: Cheryl Dunlop
Interior Design: Ragont Design
Cover Design: Chris Gilbert, Studio Gearbox
Cover Images: Image of two boys, Phillip Behr, i-stock;
 Image of horse, Jupiter Images

Library of Congress Cataloging-in-Publication Data

Gohlke, Cathy.
 I have seen him in the watchfires / Cathy Gohlke.
  p. cm.
 ISBN: 978-0-8024-8774-2
  1. Teenage boys—Fiction 2. United States—History—Civil War,
 1861-1865—Fiction. I. Title.

PS3607.O3448I15 2008
813'.6—dc22

                                                        2008013224

We hope you enjoy this book from Moody Publishers. Our goal is to provide high-quality, thought-provoking books and products that connect truth
to your real needs and challenges. For more information on other books and
products written and produced from a biblical perspective, go to www.
moodypublishers.com or write to:

Moody Publishers
820 N. LaSalle Boulevard
Chicago, IL 60610

1 3 5 7 9 10 8 6 4 2

Printed in the United States of America

~In loving memory of my grandparents,
Who prayerfully sowed seeds of faith within their families,
Then tended our gardens in hope~

Bertie Dunnagan and Mack McKinley Goforth Sr.
and
Olive Florence Dubock and Homer Milton Lounsbury

Acknowledgments

*T*hank you to all the readers of *William Henry Is a Fine Name* who asked that Robert's story continue. Your enthusiasm inspired me.

Warmest thanks to my mother, Gloria Bernice Goforth Lemons, my families of origin and marriage, friends, church family of Elkton United Methodist Church, and colleagues, who daily encourage, share, and pray for this writing journey. You mean the world to me.

Thank you to Andrew McGuire, my editor at Moody Publishers, for believing in this new author, and for working with me to make this book the best it can be.

Thank you to Cheryl Dunlop, my copy editor, who challenges my every wayward literary turn, and is severe in all the ways I love.

Many thanks to Lori Wenzinger and Randall Payleitner, and all at Moody Publishers who work so diligently to place my stories in the hands of many.

Special thanks to the wonderful team who carefully critiqued this manuscript, helped me laugh when things got too serious, and kept me on the straight and narrow: My sister,

Gloria Delk; my brother, Dan Lounsbury; my pastor, Rev. Karen Bunnell; my friends and colleagues: Tracy Leinberger-Leonardi, Carrie Turansky, and Ivan P. Mehosky, who guided me in all things military.

For rousing discussions and historical enthusiasm that knows no bounds I thank my brother-in-law, Ron Delk, Jake Jacobs, and all those who have shared family and regional stories, historical details, old books, diaries, heirlooms, and photographs. I gleaned a sense of time and place that I could not have found alone.

For help in researching historical details that brought this book to life I thank historians Milt Diggins, Mike Dixon, and the staff and volunteers of the Cecil County Historical Society; David Healy, for his class on The Civil War in Cecil County; Fort Delaware historians George Contant, Martha Bennett, and Daniel Citron, Historic Site Manager; the librarians of the Cecil County Public Library in Elkton, Maryland, and of the North Carolina Room of the Forsyth County Public Library in Winston-Salem, North Carolina; the volunteer tour guides at Mendenhall Plantation, Jamestown, North Carolina; historians and staff of Old Salem Museums and Gardens, MESDA, the living history staff in Old Salem, North Carolina, and the men and women who serve each year at Old Salem's Moravian Candle Tea—a treasured memory of my childhood and a pilgrimage I make each year.

Thank you, again, Uncle Wilbur, for reminding me that a sure way to know if I'm working in the will of God is to ask, "Do I have joy? Is this yoke easy? Is this burden light?"

Last but never least, I thank Dan, Elisabeth, and Daniel, my beloved family, for your love, encouragement, and patience with my passion.

Prologue

Ma left us to go south and live with Grandfather Ashton a full year before the Confederacy fired on Fort Sumter. When President Lincoln called for 75,000 Union troops to squelch the rebellion, Pa telegraphed Ma that North Carolina wasn't safe, that he was coming to get her to bring her home to Maryland, to Laurelea. Ma shot back, "Ashland is my home. I'll defend it with my last breath. I am proud of our men who will do the same on the battlefield. Do not come unless you come to enlist with them. I will not go with you."

I wanted Ma to be proud of me too—more than anything. And I was itching to fight, like every boy I knew, but not for the Confederacy.

I'd cast my lot with Pa and the Henrys, and with Mr. Heath, their employer, in running Laurelea as a station—a safe house, part of the Underground Railroad. I'd run escaped slaves north on the freedom train, beginning with Grandfather Ashton's son, born of a slave woman—the boy he'd planned to sell. I'd buried my best friend, William Henry, who'd died protecting us all for the same cause.

I could not fight for states that bought and sold human

beings. But with Ma and all her kin in the South, how could I carry a gun to her door?

Pa made me promise that whatever I decided, I'd stay at Laurelea to help Mr. Heath and the Henrys with the farm and the Underground Railroad, that I'd wait to enlist until I turned eighteen. "Then think long and hard," he said, "before you agree to shoot one of your countrymen—or kin—between the eyes."

It was a promise I sometimes regretted, but kept true, until the spring of 1864, until the day Emily's letter came.

One

Late May, 1864

Our worst spring storm broke on the edge of midnight, a river thrown from the sky. By dawn the Laurel Run had overflowed its banks and was busy stripping the lower fields clean. I knew it even as I lay in my bed, listening to the downpour.

Maybe it was the wind and thunder, or maybe my mind so bent on worry for our new crop, but I never heard the parcel thrust inside the parlor door, never heard so much as a knock or footfall. When at first light I found it, battered and beaten, bound by twine, I knew that the messenger had taken care to keep it dry. But the seal on Emily's letter was broken, proof that somebody knew our business.

It wasn't that violation that made the heat creep up my neck as I tore open the letter. It was the first words Emily'd ever penned me: "Dearest Cousin Robert." She'd written on Christmas Day—five long months before. Still, it was a miracle that it had come at all, the mail from the South being what it was.

"Yesterday," she wrote, "I was visited by Lt. Col. Stuart Copeland, of the 11th North Carolina, lately a prisoner, exchanged from Fort Delaware, Pea Patch Island. Lt. Col. Copeland informed me that Papa—Col. Albert Mitchell—there, I've written his precious name—was chest wounded, and captured at the battle of Gettysburg, Pennsylvania, 3rd July, along with his remaining men from the 26th North Carolina. He said that Papa, like so many prisoners at Fort Delaware, suffers gravely from smallpox."

It was the first news she'd had of him in more than a year, and she was desperate to know if he lived . . . "I beg you, by all the love of family we have ever known, to forget the estrangement of this maddening war and do all you can for Papa."

I raked my fingers through my hair. It was a hard request. I'd turn the world over for Emily, if given the chance, but Cousin Albert was another matter. I figured him to be the reason, or a good part of the reason, Ma never came home.

"Gladly would I go myself," she wrote, "but the railroads are a shambles, and Uncle Marcus is not well. I do not know if he will see the spring." I couldn't imagine Ashland without Grandfather, or Ma without him—and why was all this left to Emily's care? She was no older than me. I took up the letter again.

"I would send Alex, but Papa sent him to school in England for the duration of the war, and we have heard nothing from him in two years. The blockades prevent all such communication."

I felt my jaw tighten, remembering Emily's younger brother. Alex's first priority was always Alex. I couldn't imagine him risking life and limb to help anyone, his father included, if it meant he'd inherit Mitchell House, and possibly Ashland, sooner. That was his life's goal, even before his voice began to squeak.

"As you can imagine, this horrible war has taken its toll on us all, especially your dear mother. I promise that Cousin Caroline will want for nothing that I can provide in this life as long as I live and am able to care for her. If there is any way you or Cousin Charles can come to her aid, I urge you to do so. But I beg you to see about Papa first."

My heart raced to think of going to Emily, and to Ma, that they might need me, might want me. It was the first news I'd heard of Ma in months. I tried to conjure their faces, but they wouldn't come. I remembered that Emily was a younger, darker version of Ma, that Ma's eyes were blue and Emily's brown. But four long years had passed since Ma'd left, it had been longer still since I'd seen Emily, and there was not so much as a tintype to remind me. I forced myself back to the letter.

"With this letter I enclose a parcel of comforts for Papa. I have no hope that they would reach him if I sent them directly to the prison. We have heard such stories of the prison guards. . . ."

I set the letter on the parlor table and counted the days since the battle of Gettysburg. After ten months, stuck in a Union prison—chest wounded, and with smallpox—I couldn't hope that Cousin Albert lived. But for Emily's sake, and for all she'd done and bound herself to do for Ma, I vowed to heed her plea, to go and see and do my best by him.

As soon as I'd seen to Cousin Albert I'd head for North Carolina, no matter that Grandfather had disowned me and forbidden Pa or me to set foot on Ashland. Grandfather couldn't keep me from Ma if she needed Pa or me. And Pa was gone south more than a year now, drawing maps of back roads and terrain for the Union, though no one was to know.

Pa'd gone as a civilian, not willing to carry a gun. He said he wanted to help secure the Union's power to settle the slavery issue, but he wouldn't fire on his countrymen. It didn't seem to me that the secessionists, the secesh, were our countrymen anymore. But Pa figured it was the politicians that seceded from the Union, that the Southern people weren't our enemy. He'd long ago decided he'd not take the life of another man. It angered me that Pa would not protect himself, that he'd march into enemy territory without a gun. It was the only thing in life that stood between us. I didn't know if he was still alive.

So it was up to me. I'd bring Ma home—Emily and Grandfather too, if they'd come. But it must be done quickly. My eighteenth birthday was in two months, and I wouldn't wait one more day to enlist. I wanted Ma and Emily out of the South before then. It would put to rest every worry I carried over fighting the Confederacy.

I packed my bag before walking up to Mr. Heath's to tell him and the Henrys I'd be going. I almost packed Pa's heavy black Bible, the one from the mantle that we'd always used for the evening read, then set it back. I wanted it to be here, to be waiting when Pa and I returned. I'd kept that read all the months Pa'd been gone, every night. I could never make the words stand up and sing like he did. I didn't know whether I'd ever draw the faith or strength from the Word, same as him. But I knew that reading it was a path to life, and that you never reach a thing without setting your feet straight and walking toward it. Leaving it seemed a pledge that I'd make it home, that we'd all be together again.

I set my bag in the parlor, by the front door, and picked up Emily's letter. I stopped the pendulum of the mantle clock. Already the house felt empty. But it wouldn't be empty long.

When the rain had stopped, and the wind died to a stiff breeze, I walked the lane to Laurelea's Big House, straddling the puddles. I pulled my collar high, tight around my neck, and bent my head to my thinking.

I knocked on Mr. Heath's open study door. He'd been snoring in his chair by the fire, though I don't think he wanted me to know. When I gave him Emily's letter he pushed his lap rug aside, pulled his spectacles over his ears, and carried the letter to the window, catching the late afternoon light to read.

Aunt Sassy walked in, balancing a tray of steaming sassafras tea and fresh molasses cookies. My mouth watered at the sight, the smell.

"You'll leave soon?" Mr. Heath asked.

"First light. I'll do all I can for Cousin Albert—if he's still at the fort—still alive. Then I'll leave straight for Ashland, and Ma." I didn't say, "and Emily."

"Ashland?" Aunt Sassy's bronzed face jerked toward mine. She sloshed tea across the tray.

Mr. Heath didn't answer, but nodded, handing the letter back to me. "That he's a colonel should help him. They generally treat officers better than enlisted men." His brow furrowed. "I only wish Charles were here."

"But he's not, and Emily said Ma needs me." I wouldn't back down. "I know I promised to stay till I was eighteen, but it's only two months, and I—"

Mr. Heath waved his hand. "I understand that. I know you must go, but you're nearly of age now. It won't be so simple to pass through the South out of uniform."

Aunt Sassy teetered. "What about our crop? You can't leave Mr. Heath with no crop!"

"The crop doesn't matter, Sassy," Mr. Heath interrupted. We'll replant what we can when we can. We have enough workers. Robert has to go."

15

"They shoot you for a spy." She trembled, and the pot of tea slipped, crashing to the floor. "They shoot you and not know who you are or where to send your dead body."

"Sassy, that's enough," Mr. Heath warned her gently. "Robert has no choice if Caroline needs him."

"Miz Caroline got along fine without you these past four years." Aunt Sassy'd never spoken against Ma. "Don't be taking off. Don't leave us, Robert."

I bent to pick up the broken pot, to mop the floor with her tea towel. I wouldn't look in her eyes.

Aunt Sassy and her husband, Joseph Henry, were slaves when Mr. Isaac and Miz Laura Heath freed them the year before I was born. Aunt Sassy had cooked for the Heaths for as long as I could remember, and Aunt Sassy'd nursed Miz Heath—Miz Laura—through her long illness, till the day she died. Two days later the Henrys' only son—my best friend, William Henry—was killed, hit by a train. Those losses shadowed her every day.

"I'll be back with Ma, and maybe Emily and Grandfather if they'll come, before my birthday, Aunt Sassy. I promise." I didn't look at her, didn't say I'd be going off again, enlisting for the Union right away. But they knew my plans, had known them all along.

Her mouth set, grim. She swayed, taking that in, rocking back and forth softly.

I finished mopping the tea and set the broken pot pieces on the tray.

"You be needing this, then." She pulled a small, round tin from her pinner pocket. "Mama brought it up here this morning, said to give it to you, make sure you take it along."

I reached for the tin. "What is it?"

16

"Salve. Some kind of salve she concocted. Said it's for rope burns, that you be needing it."

I swallowed. I didn't want to ask how Granny Struthers, Aunt Sassy's ma, knew I'd be needing a salve for rope burns, what that meant, or how she knew I'd be going off. Granny Struthers was an old midwife and herb doctor, black as the crow that flies, small and ancient, bent and gnarled like an old apple tree. She knew things before they were spoken and understood what went on inside people's four walls—even in their heads—long before they did. The salve wasn't a good sign.

Mr. Heath squeezed my shoulder. "Robert, your times, like every one of ours, are in God's hands."

"Yes, sir," I said, knowing Pa would've said the same. But Granny Struthers' salve made it hard not to wonder.

Aunt Sassy cooked my favorite meal that night, a feast of roast chicken and hot dandelion greens poured over potatoes. She baked apple dumplings, cinnamon and molasses oozing out the tops, and brought out the last of the coffee. "You be thinking on this cooking when you're off half-starved, and come on home."

"Yes, ma'am." I grinned. "Fast as I can." Since Miz Laura and William Henry had died, since Ma and then Pa left, the four of us—Mr. Heath, Aunt Sassy, Joseph Henry, and me—took our meals together at Mr. Heath's table. We made a family, two black, two white, bound by missing those we loved most.

"Be careful visiting that prison. They's sickness of every kind there, and no secesh, kin or no, is worth you dying for," Aunt Sassy fussed as she heaped another ladle of sweet cream over my dumpling.

"Sassy, don't be filling this boy's head with your bitterness." Joseph Henry shook his head at his wife.

"I want this boy back to this table, safe and sound!" Aunt Sassy shook her dripping spoon. "I won't lose him too!" And then the brewing storm broke. Joseph Henry looked away. I stood and cradled her in my arms. The Henrys should've had a whole passel of kids to spread their love and worry over.

"You'll write as soon as you know anything about Albert, before you leave for Ashland?" Mr. Heath tried to steer the talk away.

"Yes, sir. As soon as I find him, or if I don't."

That night, once the lights of Laurelea were snuffed, I stole away to the colored cemetery, to William Henry's grave, and set a blanket next to his marker. It was a peaceful place, a place that kept the world and its troubles outside the gate. I talked things over with William Henry there, just like I'd done all my life, and his. Only more and more I'd start talking to William Henry and end up talking to God. I wondered if sometimes the Lord thought kindly of that roundabout prayer, but figured mostly He'd understand.

"I guess you know about Emily's letter. I've got to go, William Henry—you know I do. And I want to! I want Ma to come home . . . I'm glad Pa's not here. I want to be the one to go." I dug the twig I carried into the ground, worrying it back and forth. "Maybe she'll come with me, where she wouldn't come with him . . . I just hope we can get back through the lines . . . I promised your ma I'll be back for my birthday." I rubbed circles in my temple and sighed. "I'm tired of sitting home while every boy I know is off fighting the secesh. You'd feel the same. I know you would . . . I just didn't figure my first trip out would be to a Union prison." The twig snapped.

It was late, but I sat long, listening to the lonesome call of the hoot owl and the baying of a far-off hound, watching the old man move across the sky.

I leaned back against William Henry's marker and looked up at the stars dancing, winking in their constellations. Cousin Albert had taught me their names. I remembered how we'd wondered if the Pleiades was really the home of God, like it said in Job. Those four years seemed so long ago. Now he was an officer—a colonel—and my country's enemy, locked in a Union prison. He was also my blood kin, and except that I resented that Ma had gone south to live near him, near all of them, I knew he was a good and decent man.

"But his view of slavery." My voice in the night prickled me. "He treats his slaves better than most, but it's still buying and selling, owning people." And Cousin Albert was willing to fight and die for the right to do it. I didn't understand that.

I didn't know what I'd find at Fort Delaware. I dreaded not finding him—for Emily's sake. Emily. My heart picked up a beat. I felt the heat travel up my neck at the memory of her, and tried to squelch the rising hope in my chest.

I hadn't seen Cousin Albert or Emily or her brother, Alex, or even my Grandfather Marcus Ashton since Christmas Eve 1859. That night, as they sang in church, then danced a midnight ball at Mitchell House, I'd run north with Jeremiah, Grandfather's son by a slave woman.

I could not abide that Grandfather'd planned to sell his own son, like he'd sold Jeremiah's ma, Ruby. So together we stole away. We were both thirteen at the time. It set my feet on a path, and I've never looked back, never been sorry, but for the loss of Emily's friendship and for wondering if things could have turned out different with Ma.

"Show me the straight path, Lord. Watch over Pa, wherever

he is, and Ma, and bring us home again." I knew God heard me. I also knew His will sometimes ran a mystery to mine.

I traced the letters of William Henry's name across his marker. "I'll be back, William Henry. God willing, I'll be back."

Two

I rode before first light, not wanting to say more good-byes, not wanting Aunt Sassy's tear-stained face to be my last memory of home. Loaded down by my bag and Mr. Heath's gifts of blankets, a set of clothes, spirits, and all the food I could carry, I still made good time.

We'd long heard that Northern prisons ran cold, and prisoners north and south near starved. Fort Delaware's pox epidemic had killed more than 150 Confederate prisoners, even some Union soldiers. I carried all the supplies I could, but it was little enough.

I reached Elkton as the sun's rays warmed my face, and made Delaware City long before the light waned. I searched the docks, eager to find a boat to take me across the river to Fort Delaware, Pea Patch Island. The pier bustled with fishing and supply boats, all pulling in.

"You'll have to wait till morning, son. Nobody's putting out this time o' day." The brawny fisherman looked me over, tossing his torn net ashore. "Fort Delaware, you say?" I nodded. He glanced up and down the pier. "You can likely go over first thing with Tom Ames," he said, jerking his head toward a boat just pulling in. "He supplies the fort every day or two. I don't think the *Jenny* was over today. He'll probably put out tomorrow or the next." I thanked him and was about to walk away. "Most people try to get out o' that fort, not into it."

"My cousin's there. I've come to see about him," I answered.

"Union or secesh? That'll make the difference, you know." He eyed my bundle, then squinted his suspicion toward the river.

I felt my heat rise. "He's a prisoner, my ma's people. But I'm Union, through and through."

"You ain't in uniform." He spit to the water, then turned and eyed me hard. "And you ain't from around here. I 'spect I know every family up and down this river." His mate stood beside him then, and the look between them turned me cold.

"I will be. Soon as I'm of age." I walked away, feeling the shame I'd felt when boys from church had signed up and left with their regiment, ladies cheering and handkerchiefs waving—the shame and threat I'd felt when I'd returned to our buckboard one Sunday to find the seat tarred and chicken-feathered. Lots of boys had lied about their age to join early. I wished again that I'd not promised Pa I'd wait. I thought hard of him for asking such a thing during war, especially when the Union needed more troops. Well, I'd get there, and soon.

"Mr. Ames?" I called to the gray-haired man climbing ashore from the *Jenny*. "Captain Ames?" I ran after him.

"No catch today, son. See us tomorrow." He threw up his hand behind him and shuffled up the pier.

"I'm not wanting fish, sir," I called, stepping up behind him. "I've come to see if you'll take me across to Fort Delaware."

He stopped short and eyed me over his spectacles. "Fort Delaware? Why? Why do you want to go?"

I thought about lying to make it easier, but I was no good at that. My face'd heat up like a smithy's fire. "I need to find my ma's cousin. He's a prisoner there."

"How long?"

"Ten months."

"Ten months." He paused. "Gettysburg?" I nodded, and his face softened. "It was a hard time. A lot of those men didn't make it. You from around here, son?"

"Below Elkton."

"But he's your family? Your people?" I nodded again. "Well, a lot of folks have people down south. Different sympathies." He waited, but I didn't answer. "He'll be grateful for the company." He stroked his beard. "I'd take him food, if I was you."

"Yes, sir. Will you take me?"

His eyes bored mine, then looked away, as if he tried to decide something.

"First light. Be on the *Jenny* at first light."

"Thank you. Thank you, sir!" I stood while he limped, one leg shorter than the other, up the pier. Halfway he paused, and limped back.

"You have a place to stay, boy?"

"Not yet. I came straight to the docks."

"You might have a speck of trouble if folks know you're going to the fort for kin."

I figured he spoke true. "I'll get my horse and sleep outside town."

"Wouldn't do that if I were you." His eyes traveled to the two at the end of the pier, the two who'd eyed me hard ever since I'd told them I was going to the fort. "There's a storm brewing and you'll not want to be caught in it." He turned his back on the men and took out a paper, scribbling an address with the stump of a pencil. "There's a boarding house two blocks west from the dock. Couple by the name of Maynard. They'll take you in and be glad of the business. Got money, do you?"

"A little," I admitted.

"Don't advertise where you're staying. Walk off this pier with me, get on your horse, and don't look back. There's a stable at the boarding house. Go to the back door. Tell Ida Maynard to send me one of her apple pies." He shook hands, placing the paper in mine, tipped his cap, and walked away.

I followed on his heels, mounted my horse, and rode off, just as he'd said. A block from the dock I opened the paper. I checked and rechecked the address, then found the house as the first lamps were lit.

"Certainly you'll stay with us, young man!" The landlady pulled me into the kitchen, calling her husband to stable my horse. I offered to see to him myself, uneasy about turning Mr. Heath's horse over to a stranger. Mr. Maynard took that in stride and showed me the stable, offering anything I needed.

The Maynards made me welcome, and over supper I felt free to tell my story—at least the part about Cousin Albert and Emily. I could tell from their talk they had a son volunteering for the Confederacy in Virginia. That explained why I was their only boarder. Try as I might, it was hard not to think of them and their son as traitors.

"As you can imagine, we are no longer held in high regard by our neighbors, nor welcome in our church." Mrs. Maynard spoke quietly. "If they could only realize that we are in as much anxiety and fear for our Stephen as they are for their sons."

"But they can't, my dear. War makes everyone shortsighted." Mr. Maynard lit his pipe. "But you, young man, will be a welcome sight to your cousin. If you think they'll let you take food, we'll be glad to send whatever we can—for your cousin or anyone else. We've heard those boys are in a sorry state."

"Thank you, sir. I've brought a fair load of supplies, myself. I don't know what they'll allow."

The Maynards exchanged a look I didn't understand. I put it down to the hard times they'd had with neighbors.

That night, remembering the hard look between the two at the pier, I sorted my bundle. I decided to carry the food and spirits, the blankets and clothes. Cousin Albert would surely need all that, and if he didn't—if I didn't find him—other prisoners could make good use of those things. Once I found him I'd pull out Emily's gifts.

Mrs. Maynard sent me off early next morning with a hearty breakfast and a hot apple pie for Captain Ames.

He grinned ear to ear when I set it in his hands. "A good woman, that Ida Maynard!"

No matter that it was nearly June, the cold river wind ripped through my jacket and trouser legs. It was all I could do to clutch my bundle for Cousin Albert, to keep it dry. That boat rocked and tossed, then dipped through every swell just to make me mind my belly. Each time I thought it might settle, it slapped me awake with an icy spray to start the torment all over again.

"Not one for open water?" Captain Ames chided. I gripped the side rail, slippery from the spray, shaking my head. "Ever been inside the fort?"

"No, sir." That was all Captain Ames needed to shout a first-rate history lesson into the wind while I heaved my breakfast over the side. "She wasn't built as a prison at all, but the war changed that. Filthy, overcrowded, a haven for smallpox and dysentery . . . and just wait till the hot weather steps in—mosquitoes and a whole new breed of the ague . . ." I tried to listen, but only wanted off that boat. "Officers' quarters for prisoners stand above the sally port."

"Sally port?"

"The fort's entrance. Enlisted prisoners are kept in those long barracks outside the fort. You can see them from here. Makes escape a little easier than the Federals would like." My eyes followed his finger to the long yellow buildings.

"Ah! Here we are, then! Land ho!" The captain gave me a friendly slap ashore, chuckling over my weak stomach and probably my green face. It was a relief to set my feet on Pea Patch's marshy ground—ground that didn't move. "Boy!"

"Yes, sir?" I stumbled, trying to get my land legs under me.

"God bless you for being merciful to them as can't repay your kindness." He eyed the fort, then shook his head. "Poor wretches." He secured the ropes. "I'll wait for you when I'm done unloading."

"Thank you, sir." I hadn't expected that much.

I'd never seen a real fort before. I'd pictured it like the wilderness forts out west sketched in the dime novels—hundreds of tree trunks standing tight, side by side. But these were massive, thick gray stone walls, parapets and ramparts, and windows spouting cannon—a solid, monstrous thing and enough to put the fear of God into anybody. I squinted into the morning sun to see the top of it, and couldn't imagine how such a thing could be built, let alone stand on a marsh island in the middle of a river. Did they cart every stone across by boat?

What looked like a still creek bed ran around the fort. It called to mind tall tales of knights and castles and drawbridges.

But the guards standing duty against the stone walls were real enough.

"Visitor?" The private stood near my height, not much older.

"Yes, sir." I pulled Emily's letter from my jacket.

"Close kin? We only allow close kin visitors."

"I'm the closest that could come. I'm looking for Col. Albert Mitchell, 26th North Carolina."

The boy private raised his eyebrows but ignored the letter. "No officer here by that name."

I swallowed. "You mean he's dead?"

"I mean I never heard of him. There's no officer here goes by that name. I know every one of them." The private gloated, then looked me up and down. "Sure you got the right prison, Johnny Reb?"

I felt my heat rise. "I'm Union, same as you."

"You're here to see a secesh, and you ain't in uniform. But you're old enough to be in uniform, ain't you, boy?"

"I'm seventeen." I didn't want to answer him.

"We got us a Johnny Reb in here twelve years old, and we can't get you Union boys to sign up when you're near growed." I wanted to knock the smirk off his face.

"Is there trouble here?" A captain, quick and brusque, stepped through the sally port.

"I'm here to see a prisoner, Col. Albert Mitchell, 26th North Carolina. I have a letter from his daughter, my cousin, asking me to come see about her father. He was captured last summer, at Gettysburg, sir." I rushed it all out in a breath, glad to sidestep the boy private.

"I told him there ain't nobody here by—" but the officer cut him off.

"Albert Mitchell? Colonel?" The captain raised his eyebrows, read Emily's letter. He smiled, as though I'd just explained something he knew all along. "Follow me. General Schoepf might wish to see you."

The boy private glared but stood smartly aside. I stepped light to keep stride with the captain, who was already halfway through the stone entrance tunnel. "Do you know him, sir? Albert Mitchell?" He didn't answer. I could only trail him across the parade grounds, jumping the night's rain puddles and black mud churned up by the soldiers' morning drill.

"Wait here," the captain barked. Any friendliness I'd fancied disappeared as fast as the heavy wooden door slammed behind him. "Here" was a stone step. But the fort kept me out of the wind, and I leaned against the sun-baked wall. Minutes dragged on. A half hour passed. I wondered if the captain'd forgotten me. I piled my bundle against the wall and sat down, determined to wait.

I tried to bring Cousin Albert to mind. He was taller than Pa. I shifted my seat. I'd never liked the way Ma looked up into his face, or how the lights in their blue eyes caught. His manners were polished fine, and he doted on Ma, stood closer than a first cousin ought, in my mind. I pushed away those memories, knowing that some of that was how they did things in the South, not wanting to think on if it was more.

I'd learned a lot from Cousin Albert. Besides the tutoring, he taught me how to shoot and care for a gun. I had admired the way he ran Mitchell House, his plantation next to Grandfather's Ashland, and the better way he treated his slaves—until the night I begged him to stop Jed Slocum, Grandfather's overseer, from beating Jeremiah for running away. But Cousin Albert refused to step in, no matter that Slocum had just axed the foot off an older slave for running. He said those slaves were

Grandfather's property to do with as he wished.

I realized then that it didn't matter how well you treated someone, that power of one human being over another is evil looking for a home. And I'd never believe God gave him the right to own another person. That night our paths forked.

If I found Cousin Albert alive, what could I say to him now, five years later? Besides my stand for abolition, besides the fact that my own ma lived next door to him instead of home with Pa and me, we were at war. As a Confederate officer Cousin Albert would be bound to shoot Pa as a spy—or me on the battlefield once I enlisted for the Union. But I'd also be bound to shoot him. I wondered if I could do such a thing. I prayed I'd never need to know.

I must have leaned back and closed my eyes. The door jerked open, and I fell onto the captain's boots.

"Up, boy!" he fairly shouted. I scrambled to my feet, pulling my bundle together. "General Schoepf's given permission to escort you through the prison barracks. We want you to identify your cousin."

My hopes stood up. "Thank you, sir." But something about that didn't ring right. "You mean he's not listed?"

The captain eyed me sharply, then stared across the parade ground. "Some of our prisoners are wounded and can't speak. A few have forgotten who they are—shocked from battle. We don't have a Col. Albert Mitchell on the roll, but you may help us find him among the enlisted men. If he is an officer he is entitled to better quarters, better fare. You'd be doing him a favor by identifying him."

That sounded fair, good for Cousin Albert. I shifted my load. Maybe that caught the captain's eye.

"What do you have there?"

"Food, clothing, blankets, spirits for my cousin."

"All gifts to prisoners must be searched."

"Yes, sir." That seemed natural enough, and I'd nothing to hide, save Emily's bundle sorted into small packets beneath my jacket. We trekked back through the parade grounds and entered the sally port. The same surly boy private stood on duty.

"Jenkins," the captain barked. "Search this prisoner bundle."

"Yes, sir!" It was the first time I'd seen a spark to Jenkins. He jerked the bundle from my arms and dumped the contents on the ground before him. The captain marched toward the fort's entrance.

"Wait! What about my load?"

He stopped, not turning to face me. "It will be searched. What is permissible will be passed to the prisoner. If you'd like to find your kinsman I suggest you follow me." I looked back and saw Jenkins had made two piles—one of a solitary blanket and some of the food. The second pile was everything else. From the grin on Jenkins's face I knew which one Cousin Albert would see. It was a mercy I hadn't pulled out Emily's gifts.

The captain marched fifteen steps ahead. I hustled after him, across the moat and out to a field covered in a couple dozen long plank buildings. Most were yellow washed, with six windows on a side, none on the end. They didn't look like houses—no regular chimneys—but didn't look like barns either—no silos.

The captain signaled two guards, then led me through the door. He pulled the guards aside to speak. I couldn't hear what he said. I'd never seen such a crowd of men swarming in one place.

There must have been more than two hundred scarecrow men packed into that building, bone-thin men in every sort of filthy, torn, and patched uniform and rags of uniform you could conjure. The smell ran powerful rank, like a twelve-hole outhouse. I pulled my sleeve over my nose and mouth, tried to get hold. Three plank rows, floor to ceiling, ran front to back along both sides of the eighty-foot walls. Men packed row after row, wedged tight, laid like spoons. It made me think of the hold in slave ships I'd heard tell of, only spread out in broad daylight.

"Look into every face and see if you recognize your man." The captain pushed me along the rows. But I could hardly look at the men, and I couldn't keep from looking at them. Their eyes were sunken, their faces thin, some yellowed. Those that took notice scratched vermin from their bellies and armpits. None of these men looked anything like I remembered Cousin Albert. And if he was here, how would I know him? "Can you identify him?" The captain kept talking.

"No. No, sir."

"You realize he might have changed some. These men were in dire shape when captured."

I didn't believe they were all in this bad shape when they came here. Even if I found Cousin Albert, I knew he wouldn't be getting the food and blankets, the clothes Mr. Heath sent. These men didn't have a solid, warm blanket between them. "He's not here."

"We'll try the next barracks." The captain led me through three more buildings just like the first one. I'd looked into so many hopeless faces I didn't think I could look into one more. I didn't even want to find Cousin Albert there. I didn't want to imagine he'd ever lived in such a place. Dying on a field of battle would be one thing; rotting in Fort Delaware was another thing, a vile thing. "Look carefully, son."

"He's not here. He wouldn't be here. He'd never be here."

And that is when I saw him on the top row of plank bunks. I saw him, and he saw me. Ma's deep blue eyes blinked in a man's hollow face. I started to speak. He looked away, dipped his head, and pulled back. I walked on.

"Did you see someone you know, son?" The captain kept steady, but I sensed his urgency. Why would Cousin Albert pretend not to know me? Why would he turn away? "Well?" the captain snapped.

"What?"

"Did you see someone you know?" Why would this officer care so if I found him? If he'd wanted to help him, he wouldn't have ordered that boy private to help himself to the bundle I'd brought Cousin Albert.

"Look again."

"What?"

"Look again," he growled. "Walk down this row a second time. There are a number of prisoners in this barracks from the 26th. Look carefully." I had no choice, and I couldn't help glancing up at him, though I dipped my head and tried not to show it. He was so changed—not only thin and unshaven, but unkempt and bent in ways that Cousin Albert would never be, could never be. I looked away, but was drawn back. And that was telling. "Michaels," ordered the captain, "stand down." Nobody moved. "Michaels! Stand down."

Half a minute passed before Cousin Albert uncurled himself from his place on the top row of plank bunks. Everything in the room stood still. Not a man spoke. Not a man moved, and yet the air crackled like they'd all jumped up and screamed. He took his time climbing down, row beneath row. At last he stood before the captain and stared him in the face. He never once looked at me.

"Is this your cousin?" The captain kept his eyes level with Cousin Albert's. "Look carefully." I couldn't catch my voice. I didn't understand why Cousin Albert wouldn't look at me. "Col. Albert Mitchell, didn't you say? Speak up, boy!"

"Yes, sir. I mean it looks like him, but—"

"How about it, Col. Mitchell? Do you recognize this boy? Says he's your cousin, come to visit you. How sociable." Cousin Albert didn't blink. He raised his chin and glared in the captain's face. The captain pulled a piece of paper from his coat and waited. Nobody breathed. "He carries a letter from a young lady, a young lady with a fine hand." The captain unfolded the letter and flaunted its signature in Cousin Albert's face. "Your daughter, I believe, Michaels. Do you have a daughter at home, all alone? Emily Michaels. Or is it Mitchell?" The captain smiled, taunting him. "Miss Emily Mitchell?" That is when Cousin Albert broke.

"Put this man in irons." The captain smirked. The order wasn't out of his mouth before the barracks exploded.

"Leave him! He ain't done nothing!"

"Get out! Get out, you filthy Yankee—!"

"You got no call—" The men who'd looked too weak to stir swarmed from the bunks to the floor, angry and cursing, shouting threats at the officer and his men. Two prisoners pushed between Cousin Albert and the guard, a living shield. A shot rang out, then another. Prisoners fell back. The two who'd shielded him lay dead on the floor.

Cousin Albert raised his hand. The room fell silent, as if they all, Northern and Southern, answered his command. He dropped beside the dead men on the floor, but the captain jerked him to his feet.

"Get back to your bunks!" the captain barked again. Two

prisoners stepped up to flank Cousin Albert. "Confine those men!" the captain shouted, but he was shaken. "Get Mitchell out of here!" The guards shoved Cousin Albert forward with the barrels of their guns, and me behind them.

"Traitor! Yellow belly! Spy!" Men from the bunks hurled their hate on me.

"You'd best move now if you value your neck," the captain warned.

I spun on the captain. "You said he'd be treated better! You said—"

"And he will . . . once he's out of solitary." He pushed past me.

"Solitary? For what? How long?"

"That's up to Gen. Schoepf, who, by the way, will see you now."

Three

I'd no idea where they were taking Cousin Albert, but I trailed, close on. We passed Jenkins, the boy private, through the sally port, smirking like he'd just told the best joke behind the barn, then cornered sharp left. Cousin Albert's eyes found mine, just as a door marked "Quarter Master" slammed between us. I saw in that second anger, sadness, blame, resignation, and more I couldn't lay a name to.

"Follow me." The captain, smug, still barked orders.

"You lied. You used me," I nearly shouted.

"General Schoepf will tell you what you need to know." He stopped short. "I might remind you this is the army. In case you'd not noticed, we are at war. I don't know if you're a spy or a godsend, but you've served your purpose as far as I can see." His eyes smiled coldly. "And apparently you've found your cousin."

This time I stayed on his heels. When he pushed through the heavy wooden door, I pushed too into what looked like a mail room. Soldiers sorted letters and packages; two more sat reading from the stack of letters, blacking through lines. Before

I got my bearings the captain had crossed the room and barred another door between us. "Wait here!"

He was back in less than a minute. "General Schoepf has been detained. His orders are that you be escorted from the fort. You may return to visit your kinsman in thirty days."

"Thirty days! I don't have thirty days!" Soldiers sorting mail looked up, astounded that I'd dared to challenge the officer. "What are you going to do to him?"

"He is in solitary confinement for those thirty days."

"But why? You said he'd be treated better if I found him—because he's an officer!"

The captain glanced at the mail sorters, who busied themselves at their work, then gripped my elbow and shoved me through the door. "I'll tell you more than General Schoepf would bother to tell you. There is every reason to believe Col. Mitchell organized a number of recent attempted prisoner escapes—and that he was planning to lead a grand-scale escape himself within the next forty-eight hours.

"We knew there was an officer among those enlisted men, organizing, planning. We just didn't know who until you showed up with your letter and identified our man. Col. Mitchell has successfully played the simpleminded Tar Heel private—Private Amos Michaels—to the hilt.

"Because he is an officer he will be spared a lashing, or worse. But he will serve thirty days solitary—little enough for the trouble he's caused. Then he will be imprisoned with other officers, where he will, consequently—and not to my liking—receive better food and clothing, better housing. He will no longer be allowed to communicate with his men.

"You have saved us a great deal of trouble and embarrassment, young man, and have served the Union well." He as good as sneered. "General Schoepf has offered that should you desire to be assigned to Fort Delaware when you enlist he will put in a request for you."

That was it. He ordered two guards to march me to the dock and see that I boarded the next boat back to shore. I barely remember the march, but I remember feeling like a prisoner.

I'd found Cousin Albert alive, but my finding him had made things worse for him. What would thirty days of solitary do? Would they starve him during that time, more than they had already? What word could I send to Emily?

And what about Ma and Emily? I couldn't wait thirty days before going south to them! I worried those questions over and over, across the river, not caring that Captain Ames kept a watchful eye on me.

In my anger and humiliation, in my fear for Cousin Albert and frustration about it all, I poured my whole long story to the Maynards over supper that night. "I thought we treated prisoners better than that. I know we're at war, but those prisoners were nearly starved and half-naked. I don't know what the officers looked like—I didn't see them. I don't trust those Union soldiers worth a dime." I spat out every word.

"It's disgraceful!" Mrs. Maynard was nearly beside herself.

But Mr. Maynard shook his head. "They're victims of the war too. I'm sure they're not all bad—good and bad everywhere. It's human nature. I hear those prison guards don't live much better than the men they're guarding—except for the officers."

"I can't stay here thirty days! I've got to get South to my Ma and my cousin. Emily said they need me—Ma needs me!" I worried the back of my neck. "But I don't see how I can take off the way things stand."

The Maynards exchanged their peculiar look, that language

37

I didn't understand. Mr. Maynard cleared his throat. "There may be something we can do, a way we can find out about your cousin."

"How?" I sat up. "They won't let anybody near him."

Mrs. Maynard poured hot chicory into our cups. Mr. Maynard cleared his throat again. "We know a person or two who works at the fort. We'll ask them to learn what they can. In the meantime you stay here with us."

"We won't take another penny from you, Robert," Mrs. Maynard soothed.

"I can't do that, and that's not the problem."

She reached for my hand. "You must understand. You'll need your money for your trip south. And helping you and your cousin will be the next best thing to helping our boy." She sat back. "I only hope some Southern woman is as kind to him."

Five days passed. We didn't hear a word, though Mr. Maynard went out each day to question I don't know who. I helped with chores and ran errands for them, cleaned stalls, and chopped kindling. I brushed Mr. Heath's horse until his coat shone like silk, walked him round the yard, but didn't ride him through the streets. No sense calling more attention to us. I could feel the neighbors peering out their windows every time I passed. I guessed boarding with Southern sympathizers looked nearly as bad as carrying the stars and bars through their streets. But I didn't see as I had much choice, and the Maynards were more than kind to me.

When a week passed I wrote Mr. Heath, telling him all that had happened, that I felt I had to wait to see what became of Cousin Albert, and as soon as I knew I'd be on my way to Ashland.

But the waiting was hard. That night I lay, staring into the ceiling, trying to remember Ma and Grandfather, Emily and Nanny Sara. As I tried to recall their faces, I was left wondering how four years of war had changed them, aged them. I wondered what welcome they'd give me. I wondered if Emily'd told Ma that she wrote, and, if she did, what Ma'd said.

I rolled over. I dreaded falling asleep. Sometimes I dreamed Ma was dead. Then I'd wake up, remember the truth of why she'd left, and the pain would flood me, nearly drown me all over again. If Ma'd died, sick and full of years like Miz Laura Heath, I could've understood. If she'd been killed, snatched out of her time like William Henry, I would have ached, like I ached for the loss of him, but I'd have known she had no choice going.

But she'd left Pa and me of her own accord, saying she was going to Ashland for a visit. Only the visit never ended, and she never came home. She'd written that without Miz Laura life was just too harsh at Laurelea and that Grandfather needed her in North Carolina. She "trusted" we'd "understand." I didn't understand, and I wondered that she didn't love Pa or me anymore.

Pa urged me to write her, to love her, to think well of her, to be glad she'd stayed at Laurelea as long as she had, as long as she could. I did write, and God knew I loved Ma, but thinking well of her didn't come easy.

On the tenth day I sat in the parlor when Mr. Maynard hurried through the kitchen door, breathless, and full of whispered news for his wife. They both took on new energy, and I heard the words "Pea Patch" and "officer." I thought it might have something to do with Cousin Albert. But when they saw me standing in the doorway they glanced up, stopped quickly, and eyed me hard. "You listen at our door?" Mr. Maynard's tone turned me cold.

"No, sir." I was taken aback. "I thought you might have word of Col. Mitchell." I could see Mr. Maynard trying to get hold of himself. Mrs. Maynard pressed her hand on his arm. He gentled like a skittish colt, but his tone kept its bite.

"Of course." He hung his hat on the peg by the door. "As a matter of fact I've just had word. Your cousin's not well."

I stepped inside the kitchen, steadying my hand on the doorpost. "Not well? What do you mean? Did they beat him?" It was the thing I'd feared.

"He's out of solitary—the good news." He turned to face me. "But he's gravely ill. He's in hospital—the hospital at the fort. I don't think they expect him to pull through."

I must have paled or dizzied. Mr. Maynard changed of a sudden and pulled a chair out for me. "Sit down, son. I'm sorry to bring you bad news. But you'll be able to see him now. They'll let kin visit the hospital."

"I'll send him some broth." Mrs. Maynard took charge.

Once again I sorted Emily's small parcels, separated the bits and pieces. I wouldn't risk a bulge in my jacket or Private Jenkins pilfering the things she'd intended for her pa. They were little gifts, tokens of comfort Emily'd collected or made. There was a soldier's housewife made of needles and thread in an embroidered case. I ran my fingers over the stitching and imagined Emily, her head bent to her needlework. I wondered if her forehead still wrinkled, if she still bit her lower lip when she concentrated. I felt the heat begin to creep up my neck again and pushed those thoughts away. She'd also sent a tin of shelled pecans, another that was now full of now-rancid and broken sweetmeats—that last I threw out for the birds— a half pound of real coffee, a hand-knit muffler, a small tin of lucifer matches, some fine writing paper, a pen and inkwell, two pencils, and a Testament, with a thick, sealed letter tucked inside.

I fingered the thick muffler, knowing Emily'd probably knitted it herself. "I'll be lucky to get any of this past that guard if he looks close," I said out loud. But inside a voice whispered, "We just got to be smarter than him. That can't be too hard, now, can it?" It was the voice of William Henry, plain as I'd heard it that last day we tried to outsmart Jake Tulley. I knew what I needed to do.

The next morning I wound the muffler around my neck and under my shirt, no matter that the weather had turned and the June heat was early rising. I tucked the Testament with Emily's letter inside my vest, tacked the lucifers inside the housewife and the housewife inside my pants leg. I strapped a flask of brandy around my calf. The pecans I wrapped in a handkerchief and stuffed in my pocket. The writing paper and inkwell were hardest to hide. But I figured they'd be the least likely to matter, even if they were taken away, so I carried them in hand, like I'd nothing to hide.

Mrs. Maynard sent me off, after a good breakfast, with another pie for Capt. Ames and a crock of broth for Cousin Albert. The wind was down and the water no worse than a river current could demand. We made Pea Patch with breakfast still in my belly.

Jenkins was not on duty this time. The private standing at attention outside the fort took my name and the name of the prisoner I wanted to see without a blink. He directed me to a guard sitting at a table inside the sally port, a ledger spread open before him.

"Col. Mitchell's on the hospital list."

"May I see him?"

The private nodded. "I'll get a private to take you over." He glanced at the small parcel in my hand and the crock of broth. "All packages for prisoners must be searched here."

I pulled back. "That's fine. But I want whatever is not allowed held till I come out; then I'm taking it home."

The private looked up, surprised. "Of course." He opened the crock and sniffed appreciatively. "The soup is not a problem." He unwrapped the package and weighed the paper and inkwell in his hand. "I don't know if this prisoner is allowed writing paper . . . though if he's in hospital I doubt he's up to writing." He hesitated, then leaned forward. "I'm going to let this go through—only because he might want you to write letters home for him. There aren't enough able to do that. You do write, don't you?"

I nodded, not wanting to get in a fuss then and there.

"When you leave here today the writing paper, pen, and inkwell must all come out with you. Do you understand?"

"Yes, sir." I didn't understand why he was allowing them at all.

The hospital ran a long, single-story room, high ceiling, with two long rows of cots, side by side, along the outer walls. High windows kept the light low, even though it neared noon. Soft moans, hacking chest coughs, and the running chatter of a man who didn't seem to know where he was kept a steady hum through the ward. I searched faces from the doorway, looking again for Ma's blue eyes, hoping Cousin Albert would agree to see me.

The standing guard listened to the private who'd walked me over, then led me to a bed at the far end of the room. The patient faced the wall, his eyes closed. The body under the sheets scarcely made a man's form—nothing like the tall, strong man

I'd known four years ago. I shook my head, wanting to say there must be some mistake, that he'd picked the wrong man. But the guard looked away, like he'd seen that question a hundred times. He spoke low, "Take all the time you need," then walked away.

"Cousin Albert?" I whispered, almost hoping he wouldn't answer. The form didn't move. I coughed, sat on the edge of the bed, and tried again, a little louder. "Cousin Albert?" His eyes opened, and there they stood, Ma's blue. He turned enough to see me. But the effort seemed to cost more strength than he had, and he looked away. "It's Robert." He blinked. "I've brought you some broth, and something from Emily." His eyes found mine, and I knew I held a lifeline in her name.

"Emily wrote that you were here. A soldier, an exchanged prisoner, found her and told her you'd been wounded, captured at Gettysburg. She'd heard you had the smallpox. She asked me to come find you." He looked as if he didn't want to believe me.

I looked over my shoulder, to make sure we weren't watched, then pulled out Emily's gifts, one by one. "She sent some things for you—this housewife—I think she embroidered it herself. See? Those are your initials, and these are hers." His eyes gained a spark of life. "She sent a tin of pecans." I pulled the handkerchief from my pocket and untied it, tried to place a pecan between his lips, but it fell away. I unwound the muffler from inside my shirt and rested it on his chest. "I'll bet she knitted this muffler herself. It was Christmas when she sent the package, but it came just a couple days before I found you. I don't know how it got through—who delivered it." I set the paper and inkwell on the small table by his bed. His eyes followed my every move.

"I'd have come sooner, but they wouldn't let me see you, not while you were in solitary." That sparked anger in his eyes and made me sorry I'd mentioned it. He turned away. "I'm sorry if my coming caused you more trouble, Cousin Albert. I never meant that to happen."

He stared at the wall, and a long minute passed. "If you ..." He tried to speak, but I couldn't hear him.

"Sir?" I put my ear close to his mouth.

"If you hadn't come I would be on my way home to Emily." The pendulum ticked off the minutes on the heavy wall clock at the end of the room. "I'm sorry," I said at last. I was sorry. But how could I be sorry that his prison break turned sour? Wouldn't that be disloyal to the Union, to Pa? Then I remembered Emily's Testament and letter, and pulled them from my vest pocket. "There's something else—the best yet. Emily sent this Testament too ... and I think there's a letter inside."

It was the most life I'd seen in him. "Help me sit," he whispered. I doubled up his pillow under his head, then rolled the blanket and stuffed it beneath that. I pulled him up by the armpits. He winced, but didn't cry out.

"Do you want me to read it to you?"

"Give it to me." His voice took on a breathless authority.

"Yes, sir," I said, glad he wanted something—anything.

He tugged at the seal and finally broke it. A heavier paper, a photograph, fell from the folds of Emily's letter to the floor, turning over and over, two faces coming and going. I picked it up, glad he'd have a picture of Emily and Alex, anxious myself to see what Emily looked like these four years later. But it wasn't Emily and Alex. It was Emily and Ma. I hadn't seen Ma in more than four years, and there she was, posed with Emily like a mother and daughter. Their faces, the faces I'd been racking my brain for, and all the memory of the two women, so alike, so different, so important to me, rushed over me till I could scarce breathe.

44

Cousin Albert held out his hand for the photograph. I swallowed and gave it to him. There were two letters in the envelope; one I knew to be Emily's writing. I looked away. If the other was from Ma I couldn't bear it. I'd prayed for a letter from her for nearly a year. That Cousin Albert should have both a letter and a photograph, when I had neither, made me hate him. And then I hated myself. What was I thinking, grudging a dying man the only air he wanted?

He took a long time to read both letters. I could tell from his face that it was food and drink. I tried not to seem too eager. I hoped he would offer to let me read them, at least the one from Ma, or let me hold the picture. But he folded both letters and lay there, drinking in the picture.

Twenty minutes passed. I felt a fool for sitting there, ashamed to ask for what I wanted from him. I had a mind to go, then remembered the flask hidden beneath my trouser leg. I lifted his head. He drank greedily, but ended in a fit of coughing, turning his head away. Still, the brandy seemed to bolster him. He lay back on the pillow and took up the picture again.

From where I stood I could see Ma's face. She looked older, thinner, but still beautiful. Her hair had streaked gray, something I never thought to see on Ma. The photographer must have caught her at an odd moment, the way she looked off in the distance, distracted. Emily was an hourglass, younger, a darker version of Ma, and I couldn't help that my breath caught. Cousin Albert pulled the photograph away, turning it so I couldn't see. I bit my lip and hated him for it. I couldn't stay. I couldn't speak to him, not anymore that day.

"I'll be back tomorrow." When he didn't answer I turned my back. "Is there anything you want me to bring you?" He didn't answer. I walked out, not caring two bits if I saw him again. He was holding the thing I wanted most in life and wouldn't let me look, no matter that I'd brought it to him!

I left the fort and never checked out with the guard, but made tracks for the dock.

I was grateful Captain Ames wasn't on deck. I was done talking.

Four

The Maynards waited, curious about my day, but I was not of a mind to talk. They didn't pry. I thought well of them for that.

At breakfast next morning Mrs. Maynard asked me if I'd be going over to the fort. I didn't want to go. I wanted to leave for Ashland and never look back. But I nodded. I owed Emily that.

"Perhaps your cousin would benefit from more broth. If he's not been eating, a good strong broth and bread could do him a world of good. I'd like to send some along if you are willing." Mrs. Maynard's kindness shamed me.

"Yes, ma'am. Thank you."

By the time I boarded the supply boat I toted a crock of soup and two loaves of fresh bread for Cousin Albert. The Maynards convinced me to ask the guards if I could carry fresh bread to other prisoners. I'd had good luck getting Emily's things to Cousin Albert, and what harm could asking do?

Cousin Albert needed help to eat the soup, to tear and soak the bread. But he seemed to gain a little strength with each mouthful. When he'd finished half the broth he turned his head away. "No more. No more." I hinged the crock for later. He closed his eyes and lay back against his pillow and blanket roll.

I watched him breathe. I couldn't hate him. I couldn't touch him in kindness and hate him at the same time, no matter that I struggled against it. And I wondered if it was like that for soldiers thrown together, left on the field. I wondered if they helped the men they'd shot, after a battle, or if they left them wounded or dying, and how a man would choose.

"Thank you, Robert." It was the first kind word he'd given. We sat in the stillness, listening as the pendulum of the ticking clock counted off the minutes. "Thank you for coming," he said, his eyes still closed. "I know you didn't mean me harm. War and starvation make a man—made me—behave in ways I never would have done before. I'm sorry." It was a long speech for a sickly man.

"I never meant you anything but good, Cousin Albert. And I'd do anything in the world that Emily asked me."

His face relaxed. "I'm too weak to talk on, Robert. But stay a while; talk to me."

I wanted to ask him for the picture, just to see the picture, to run my finger over Ma's face, to touch Emily's hair. But I couldn't ask him and keep my voice steady. Not yet.

I thought of when Miz Laura was sick, before she'd died, how she wanted folks to sit with her and talk, when it was just too much of a strain to keep her eyes open. So I talked about Laurelea, about the fields we'd turned, what we'd planted and hoped to plant. I talked about the fine tobacco at Ashland and Mitchell House, wondered how it was doing, wondered if Noah was still his driver. It was all small talk, safe talk, talk about home and the lands and people we both felt akin to. I was careful not to mention Pa, or the work that he was doing.

After a time Cousin Albert grew restless. I wasn't sure if he was in pain or dreaming. "Cousin Albert? Cousin Albert?" He

48

settled down. "Where is your Testament, Cousin Albert? I could read to you."

"No!" His eyes shot open, and he spoke sharply, then caught himself. "No, thank you. I read yesterday. I don't want it now. I'm tired, Robert."

"Maybe I should go now."

"Yes," he said, quickly.

I stood to go, then remembered the pen and inkwell. "Cousin Albert? Cousin Albert?" He opened his eyes. "Yesterday I left a pen and inkwell here on your stand. Emily sent them. The guard at the sally port ordered me to take them out when I left, but I forgot. I can bring them back tomorrow if you want me to write letters for you. Do you know where they are?"

While I talked his muscles tensed, but his eyes grew heavy. He mumbled, "Guard must have taken them away." And then he seemed to be sleeping.

I regretted that. Emily had sent those things especially for her pa. I picked up my jacket and found my cap, which had fallen to the floor. That's when I spotted the dark ink splotch on the floorboard by the bed, and another on the bed quilt just above it, as though someone had dropped a pen. It could have happened anytime, by anyone. But the ink stain on Cousin Albert's third finger was recent.

All the way to the boat I asked, "Why would he lie about such a thing?" Why would he think I'd care if he'd tried to write a letter? And then I wondered, why would the guard care if he wrote anything? He was stuck in the hospital, far from his men, too weak to escape or help anyone else escape. But the idea of him writing didn't ring true. He seemed too weak to sit up for such a thing.

By the third day I'd either smuggled or openly carried in

everything I had to take to Cousin Albert and was determined this would be my last visit. I needed to head South. Mrs. Maynard had piled my arms with sacks of bread for the prisoners that day, and sent a crock of vegetable soup and one of elderberry jam for Cousin Albert. She must have baked half the night.

"Make certain you give these loaves directly to the prisoners," she'd said. "If they go through the guards those suffering men won't get a bite!"

I got past the first set of guards.

"I brought this bread for the men of the 26th North Carolina. I want to deliver it myself." Helping his starving men would please Cousin Albert, and maybe that would help him set his sights to getting well.

"Shame to waste good bread." The guard spat a stream of tobacco juice across my shoes. "Five minutes I'll give you. If you last that long." He chuckled, and swung open the barracks door.

In the time it took my eyes to adjust to the low light two dozen ragged men swarmed off the bunks. "A lady in town made this bread for you, for all of you." The bread was ripped from my arms by more hands than I could count, then torn in pieces, shared in as many directions as it could stretch.

In the rush my arm was twisted high behind my back, till tears sprang to my eyes. A voice hissed near my ear. "Where is the colonel? Where is Col. Mitchell?"

"In hospital. He's in the hospital," I gasped.

"You lie. They took him away!"

"To solitary—but he's out now—in the hospital!" I never saw the face of the man who'd nearly broken my arm. As quickly as he'd grabbed me he was gone, melted into the swarm of men. I cradled my arm, blinked my eyes. The men lay back on their bunks, as if they'd never left them, chewing the remnants of Mrs. Maynard's bread.

Trying to steady my breath, I backed out of the room, quickly as I dared, keeping my eyes on the bunks. A hand tugged on my trouser leg. I jerked away, almost missing the voice near my feet. "Tell the lady thank you. Thank you for the bread." It was a boy, about my age, but gaunt, skin over bones, sitting on the lowest bunk platform near the door. His left trouser leg hung empty, pinned to his hip. "You'll tell her?"

"Yes." I blinked again. "I'll tell her."

I nearly ran up the path to the sally port, glad to get away from those men, hating that I'd turned my back on the one-legged boy. Is this what war does—turn men into beasts and boys into cripples, cripples I'm afraid to be near? What was the matter with me?

I passed the guards, laughing, playing gambling cards inside the sally port.

When I enlisted, would I become like these guards—hard, not seeing the sorry state of men in front of me, even if they were the enemy? Would I turn greedy, like Jenkins, a cruel streak running near my surface? Cousin Albert said that war and starvation make a man do things he never would've before. Then I remembered the guard who'd let me take Emily's gifts to Cousin Albert, and the one-legged prisoner boy I'd just seen, thanking me for bread. Good and bad everywhere, like Mr. Maynard said.

Cousin Albert looked stronger, seemed glad to see me, gladder still when I told him about the bread for the 26th. I didn't tell him about the man who nearly broke my arm. "There's never enough food. We eat rats when we can catch them. Fish from the river—when someone is allowed to fish—we divide fifty ways. Did you know five fish can be divided fifty ways?" I didn't. "I fed my slaves fifty times better than that."

"Why did you stay with them? Why did you stay in those barracks when you could have been housed with the officers?"

"It's an officer's duty to stand by his men, to lead. What kind of leader would I be if I'd deserted them?" His voice gained strength, authority. For the first time I saw something of the man I'd known four years ago.

I leaned forward. "The Union officer said you organized escapes, that you were planning to escape yourself soon."

Cousin Albert leveled my stare. "You saw those barracks. You saw the guards, the prisoners. Those prisoners are men who followed orders, did their duty in battle, defended their homes and country. Now they're starving—treated like animals. I never once treated my slaves in such a fashion. They deserve their freedom, Robert." He looked away.

"You, of all people, should understand that." He closed his eyes, exhausted from the talk. "It's the work you and Charles do with your abolition movement and your Underground Railroad."

His words gouged my belly. He'd spoken true. It was why I ran with Jeremiah, why I ran slaves north, against the law, time and time again.

I pulled on my jacket and hat. Slavery was war too. And slavery had to end. It seemed that wouldn't happen in the South except by war and bloodshed. But did that make it all right to treat prisoners of war like slaves or worse?

"What will happen to those men?"

"Men who rot in prison? They die, day by day. Unless they have the good fortune to fend off disease long enough to live out this war." He stopped to rest, and I thought he'd fallen asleep. But his eyes opened of a sudden. "They'll go home with broken health to live broken lives on decimated land. Their homes have been foraged and pilfered, if they're lucky. If they're not lucky their homes and barns have been burned. Their wives and daughters may have starved or been violated or had to relocate, God only knows where. Their families may be in hiding or dead. Win or lose the war, they've already lost what can't be restored to them."

I'd never thought of the secesh in that way. Why hadn't I? I'd seen those men as the enemy, men who might shoot my pa, who plotted to destroy the Union, who killed other men to hang on to slavery. They were men I was bound to kill when my time came. But they were men, just the same. And most of the war was fought on their homeland, not mine, not the Union's.

I thought of Ma and Emily living there, and my throat tightened. "What did Emily say in the letter? How bad is it for them?"

"She did not say. It is what she did not say that concerns me most."

We both fell quiet after that, both worrying our own worries.

I walked the grounds for an hour or so while Cousin Albert slept. Mid afternoon I asked him something I'd long wanted to ask a Union soldier. "What was it like? At Gettysburg?"

He stared into the light, remembering. "Hot. So hot you could see the heat quiver, ripple along the line." He licked his lips, motioned for water. "That third day. The order came about two in the afternoon." He cleared his throat, closed his eyes. "A braver set of men you never saw. We moved forward with the 47th and the 11th, North Carolina men all. Our lines—perfect, steady, slow—a river, a Yadkin River in late summer. Flags unfurled against blue—the sky. A southerly breeze cleared smoke from the field. Our regiments advanced on Cemetery Ridge."

He paused, opened his eyes, and stared ahead. "An appropriate name for the death ground of so many. Federals occupied the high ground, entrenched behind a stone wall. One of the finest positions I've ever seen. Nearly a mile we marched across that open field—with farmers' fences to cross. They never fired until we were within close range. Then they mowed us down, like summer grass before the scythe, shouting 'Fredericksburg! Remember Fredericksburg!'" Cousin Albert lay back, trying to catch his breath.

"Rest now." But he hadn't heard me.

"Elliott fell; his chest exploded. Elliott—my friend . . . and I dared not stop." Pools built behind his eyes; he didn't wipe them away. "The man on my right's head was shelled, cut clean from his neck. His blood blasted across my face so I couldn't see. The grass ran slippery with it . . . the blood of hundreds and hundreds of men. Color guard after color guard stumbled, fell. Private Cozort carried our colors almost to the wall before he died. Captain Brewer raised the flag. They shot him dead—an officer before the wall, and they shot him dead." He stopped, waited for his voice to steady.

"The last I saw, the last I knew, a Federal shouted to the man who lifted our colors, 'Come over to this side of the Lord!' He reached his hand across the stone wall. And I thought—" A fit of coughing came on him, but he caught his breath and pressed on, "And I thought—in that last moment—a sign of brotherhood in the midst of barbarism. Hope. But before our man could take that hand his life was blown away."

Cousin Albert closed his eyes, spent from the talk. I

thought he'd fallen asleep. I wanted him to stop, for his sake. "A hailstorm of open fire . . . a searing pain in my shoulder. The man in front of me flew two feet into the air. The butt of his Enfield must have smashed my skull when he fell." Cousin Albert frowned, remembering, and a minute passed.

"When I came to it was nearly dark. The private lay, cold, across my chest. His body shielded mine, saved my life." Cousin Albert gave out then and slept for the next half hour.

When he woke it was as though he'd never stopped his story. "The dead and dying lay across the field, like pebbles on the river bottom. Stretcher bearers and grave diggers couldn't walk for stepping on them, for slipping on that grass." His eyes glazed, then dried on their own.

"They took you prisoner?"

"The next afternoon. I'd changed uniforms in the dark with the private on the ground beside me—that took most of the night, getting my shoulder out of my uniform, getting it onto him. I knew they'd separate me from my men if I didn't."

Fury flamed his eyes. "The 26th was one of the first volunteer brigades. We marched over nine hundred men into Gettysburg, men who were already worn and half-starved, some in bare feet for want of shoes. After that third day there weren't enough men to bury our dead." He faced the wall. His voice took on an edge. "We'd have taken the hill if our cannon hadn't overshot their mark, if we'd been properly supported, if we'd not hesitated . . .

"We wanted only to be left alone, to continue ruling our state as we'd always done. We asked for nothing from the Federal government. We needed nothing!" A fit of coughing took hold, then a spasm. He sat nearly upright, fought for breath, heaved and heaved, then turned toward the wall, wiping his mouth. I called for the doctor, but there was none to be had. Finally Cousin Albert calmed and fell back on his pillow.

"You've got to rest now, Cousin Albert. Get your strength up."

"I'll die here," he panted.

"You won't die. I'll come back tomorrow and bring more soup, more bread. I swear it." And I would, though I wanted with everything in me to run south toward Ma and Emily, to think about living.

He grasped my hand. "Do something."

"Anything," I said.

"I will die here."

"Don't say—"

"My men," he wheezed. "They've got to know there is more than death."

"What?"

He reached behind his pillow and pulled out his Testament. "Go to the 26th. Ask for McCain. Give him this. Tell him it is life."

"But that's the Testament Emily sent you. She meant for you to have it."

"I won't need it longer. Do this for me, Robert." The coughing started up again. I pulled my handkerchief out and held it over his mouth, hoping he could spit the phlegm building inside his lungs. When he finally settled I pulled it away. It was stained dark red. His eyes found mine.

"I don't have long, Robert. I need to know my men have this Testament."

I couldn't speak for a time. "I'll take it to them on my way out tomorrow—if the guard will let me."

"Go today. Take it to them like you brought it to me. Do you have another handkerchief?" I pulled it out, thinking he needed to cough again. "Here." He wrapped my handkerchief around the book, and knotted it, fingers trembling. "Give McCain this—only McCain. Tell him what I said. Promise me."

"I promise. I swear it." He nodded, as if relieved of a burden, and fell back on the pillow.

"Cousin Albert?" He looked at me. "What about the picture? Is it still in the Bible?" I felt my face flame.

He stared at me, trying to take in my words. At last he shook his head and pulled it from beneath his nightshirt. He'd cradled it against his chest. "Never let that go."

"Please," I asked, "can I see it?" His eyes clouded. "I won't take it. I promise. I just have to see it." He stared at me a long moment. I didn't look away. He held the photograph out to me. I sat down, drank in every line, every shade and shadow. A long time passed before I asked my question. "Why? Why'd Emily send you a picture of Ma?"

Cousin Albert seemed to see me new. "She loves you, Robert. Caroline loves you."

"Then why'd she leave? Why is she there with—Emily?" I wanted to say, *Why was she there with you? Why did she choose you and Grandfather over Pa and me?* But I couldn't make my mouth form the words.

"You must ask her, Robert. I think she can tell you now. She couldn't before."

"What do you mean? What do you mean she couldn't tell me before?"

"I mean that I don't think she knew herself."

"Do you love her?"

His eyes grew, like I'd hit an open wound, then relaxed. "I've always loved Caroline, since we were children." He looked away.

"But she fell in love with Charles, Charles in his West Point uniform. And then she fell in love with you, her son."

"Then why did she leave us?" I wanted to shake him.

"Because what she loved no longer—" He stopped short, trying to catch his breath. "I can't answer for Caroline. You must ask her yourself."

"I'm asking you." My nails dug into my palms.

He shook his head.

"You mean you won't say." I pushed my chair away. "Then I'll find out for myself." I stood. "I'm going to Ma and bringing her home."

Cousin Albert's eyes shot wide. "You can't do that. She can't leave Ashland. And there's a war, Robert. You'd never get her safely through enemy lines—not ours or yours. And there's Emily."

"Why can't she leave? What's keeping Ma there?"

He looked so old. "Her world. Her world is there, Robert."

"You want her to stay there for yourself. That's the truth, isn't it?"

He looked away. "Emily understands Caroline." He reached for the photograph, holding out his hand until it trembled from weakness. I set it in his palm. "When you come tomorrow, bring your address." He wheezed. "Bring a stamp. I'll leave word that when I'm gone the photograph is to be mailed to you." His breathing came heavy. "Do you not have a photograph of your mother, Robert?"

"I've never had one—not a photograph, not even a tintype —never in my life." I walked away, past the guards and to the dock. I swiped again and again at the hot dam that built behind my eyes—a dam of fury, jealousy, and love, all mixed up and spit into the wind.

Five

I wanted to leave that night for Ashland. I wanted to leave and never look back. But I wanted that picture. I wanted it for Pa and for me. My only hope to ever get it was to take the envelope and stamp to Cousin Albert. And I'd vowed to take his Testament to the men of the 26th North Carolina. I'd sworn to do it yesterday, on my way out. But I hadn't. What difference could a day make?

Mrs. Maynard gave me a stamp, and paper, and glue. I fashioned an envelope large enough to hold the photograph, then addressed it to myself at Laurelea. I never told her why I wanted it. She didn't ask.

Mrs. Maynard baked cakes and bread and made up two crocks of oyster stew for me to cart to the fort next morning. I told her it was my last trip. I'd set out for North Carolina and Ashland the day after that. I'd already waited too long to go to Ma. I wouldn't wait another day.

And that's what I wrote to Mr. Heath, that I'd get back with Ma and whoever would come with me just as soon as I could. I hoped that meant Emily, but I didn't write that. But I told him not to worry. I didn't know what I'd find at Ashland. I told him to let Pa know where I'd gone if there was any chance he came home first, or if he got in touch some way. We'd all be together soon. I was sure of it.

A slow drizzle started as I stepped onto the boat. Captain Ames let me stow my load below, keeping the bread dry. I didn't step up to my end of the talk that morning. Captain Ames kept his eye on me, curious, I knew. But I wanted to keep my purpose up and feared talk might whittle that away.

I saw Cousin Albert first, gave him the envelope, and said my good-byes. I wanted to make it clean and short.

"You gave McCain my Testament?"

"Today. I'm taking it in today."

Cousin Albert frowned. "And then you leave for Ashland?" I nodded. He seemed to be thinking of something, distracted. It was a time before he spoke again. "God go with you, Robert. Thank you for coming. Thank you for everything." Cousin Albert's pillowslip was spattered red from his coughing. It was hard to talk and not be drawn to the blood. "I'll leave word that the photograph be mailed to you." He reached for my hand. I took it, thin as it was—thinner than at the first of the week, and it trembled more. "Give my love to Emily, all my love, and to Caroline. I made arrangements for them through Alex and his solicitor in England before I left Mitchell House. I hadn't planned against the blockades. I don't know what will be left after this war, what is left now. Take care of them, Robert—you and Charles. Tell them I . . ." He didn't finish, and he didn't brush the tears away.

I nodded, but my throat burned, and my head ached, a fierce pounding. "I wish—" I tried again. "I wish it was different. I wish you could walk out of here and go home. I wish I could take you home to them." I meant that. Though I despised his hold on Ma I meant what I said.

He smiled, but feebly. "I know, Ro—." A coughing spell took hold of him. The blood gush this time made me turn away, even while I held his head to keep him from drowning. The private on duty rushed over and pushed me away.

"You'd best leave now." A doctor appeared, pushing past me, taking over.

I stepped back, wiped my hands on a towel near the wash basin by the door. But the blood stained them, stained my clothes, reminding me of something . . . William Henry. The night we lifted his broken body from the train tracks . . . the night Joseph Henry carried his only son home to Aunt Sassy. I'd trailed, clutching, cradling my best friend's shoes . . . I didn't want to leave Cousin Albert like this. But I couldn't stay. I picked up the soup crocks and sack of bread and made myself walk out.

I stood outside the hospital ward, my back against the wall, struggling to get hold of myself. "Why?" It was all the prayer I could make. I don't know how long I stood there.

The drizzle turned to spit, then picked up and pitted my face, my vest, my boots. I hoisted my load and walked out toward the prison barracks, trying to swallow the live coal stuck in my throat. The rain swelled into a storm, grew fierce of a sudden, and a river wind, cold and sharp, slapped at my face, poured down my neck. It felt cool and right against the heat of my aching head.

I wrapped my arms tight around my chest, trying to keep the bread dry. Not that it mattered. Starving men would rather have rain-soaked bread than no bread. And I'd promised Cousin Albert I'd get that Testament to McCain. I'd no idea how to find the man McCain, or slip the book to him unseen. But I was relieved for something else to think about, something to do for Cousin Albert that mattered.

Thunder had rumbled and boomed the last hour. Lightning crackled the sky and struck ground near the sally port just as I reached the barracks.

"Whew! Would you listen to Gabriel's band play those drums!" The guard whistled, spraying tobacco juice. I wiped it from my sleeve.

"Bread. I have bread for the 26th."

"Come on in. They'd as soon eat you, boy!"

And I thought they might. Hungry men swarmed toward me again. I pulled out the bread. "Bread and soup—from the lady in town!" Before I could pull out the second loaf I was surrounded by men, more men than I could count.

"Fire! Fire!" The panicked cry sprang from outside the barracks. Lightning flashed, and rain pounded the roof, the windows, the walls in sudden torrents. "Fire! Fire!" The call erupted from the men inside the barracks, and they rushed toward the door. But there was no fire. Guards ran to block the door. In that moment, in all the screaming and pushing, a hundred faces came between me and the guards at the end of the barracks. A searing pain shot up my back and down my neck. A dozen arms and hands pulled me down into the dark.

Six

I dreamed that my body moved, crawled in flames. But I had no arms to slap the fire, no legs to run. I forced my eyes open to nothing, then realized a rag bound them. I tried to cry out, but another rag, dry and stiff, filled my mouth. I lay awake. Still my skin crawled, squirmed alive. And yet I felt no heat, smelled no smoke. I tried to roll over. But my hands and feet were roped taut, behind me. My head pounded. I couldn't place where I was, where I'd been. The smell of body odor and urine and something I couldn't name filled my nostrils. The clothes I wore weren't my own.

"He's awake!" hissed a voice at my ear.

"Quiet!" a deeper voice said. I heard, or felt, bodies moving beside me.

"Want me to hit him again?"

"It's too near time. He'd be dead weight." The deeper voice pushed against my ear. "There's not a man here has any qualms about killing you, Yank. The only reason you're not dead now is that we found that book on you from the colonel. He's the one saved your spyin' skin, no matter that you took his."

"Five minutes 'fore the watch changes," a third voice said.

"Untie his feet," the deeper voice ordered. Hands pulled at my ankles. "We're walking out of here. Don't slow us down. To the guards you'll be one more prisoner on the run. They'll shoot you dead or take you alive. They'll find the Bible from Col. Mitchell under your coat—escape route and all. The code's easy to break. You'll be shot or hanged as a spy and a traitor. Understand?"

I had to be dreaming but couldn't get out of the nightmare. The voice jerked the ropes tighter behind my back, cutting into my wrists. "Do you understand?"

I nodded, understanding too well. Cousin Albert had used me—tricked me with his dying breath into carrying escape plans to his men.

"Now!" a whisper shot from farther away. I was shoved along the wooden floor. Strong arms lifted me like a sack of wheat. The floor gave way. Down we climbed.

"Stand up," the man with the strong arms spoke. I stumbled but found my feet on solid flooring. "We'd best rip off that blindfold or he'll slow us down, stumblin' around out there."

"Remember what I said." The one with the deep voice jerked on my ropes again. I'd have cried out but for the gag. Other hands yanked the blindfold from my head. I could make out human shapes in the dark and the plank platform bunks lining the walls of the prison barracks.

"Steady. Steady." More shapes climbed down the bunks— too dark to count how many. "When the lantern passes through the door." In the waiting I heard rain, still steady, strong. "Now."

This time the strong arms pushed me toward a wall that smelled of rain. Men disappeared into a dark hole in front of me. Arms lifted me again, pushed me through behind them. I fell on my back, rolled in mud, twisting my wrists behind me.

"Get up! Get up!" the deep voice ordered, jerking me upright. Then we were running, slipping, sliding through mud and slick grass, through the black night and the pelting rain. Deep voice jerked my ropes again and again, the devil biting my back. My head still pounded. My heart nearly beat from my chest.

Lightning flashed across the marsh. In that moment I saw ten or a dozen men running toward the water, one a hunchback or carrying a load. A guard's lantern swept the marsh ahead, and the deep voice jerked me down into the mud. "Flat! Face down! Keep your face down." How long we lay there I don't know. It was the first relief I'd felt from the itching, the crawling in my armpits, along my legs.

"Now!" a voice called back to us. We were up and running again. The deep voice shoved at my back, jerked my ropes.

"Can you swim?" the voice shouted in my ear. I nodded, best I could. He tugged at the ropes behind me. I fell to my knees.

"This is only so you'll make it to the boat. But I'm roping your wrist to mine. If you run off, I'll jerk you back and drown you. Understand?"

Lightning flashed again. Men all around us plunged into the swamp grass. A light blinked across the water. Up and running yet again, still sliding, falling, scrambling through the high grass and mud. We hit the frigid river, running, swimming— pulling at the water. The crack of a rifle sped past our heads, then another. A cry. I kept swimming, pulled back every few feet for being tied to the deep voice. My limbs numbed in the cold. Breath came in gasps. And then we reached a boat, groped its sides. Strong arms pulled us over, shoved us to the floor, threw a tarpaulin over our bodies.

"How many?" A new voice.

"Ten."

"We lost one," the deep voice gasped. Then louder, "Pull!"

Oars slapped the water. The boat pulled away, fighting the blustering wind and rain. Two more shots rang from the shore, then a third.

I tried to count the minutes, tried to figure which direction we were headed—to the New Jersey shore, or the closer Delaware shore, maybe downriver. I couldn't tell.

The boat rolled and tossed. The stink of vomit overpowered the odor of the men around me. I tried to think of something, anything else. If I vomited into the gag, I'd drown. I tried to pull it loose, but the deep voice jerked my hands away, nearly breaking my fingers. I didn't try again.

It seemed an age before the oarsmen shook us. "Out with you! Our man's waiting on the shore with yours. Run toward the house lanterns. They'll find you. Keep low. No noise."

We scrambled from the boat then, a pack running through shallow water toward shore lights. The deep voice and I fell behind, trying to keep in step, keep from stumbling, falling.

"This way!" a new voice called from the shore. "Quiet! Stick close." Where had I heard that voice before?

"Good lads! You made it!" A second voice, an Irish brogue, pulled us ashore. "Grab hold this rope and follow along. No noise. We can't risk a light. Stick to the shadows."

The rain had not let up, and the lightning flashed. That's when I realized we were all dressed alike, all in Confederate uniforms. We tripped on stones along the shore before we reached mud, then grass. At last my shoes, the only thing on me that hadn't been stolen or swapped, slapped the cobblestone street.

"Quiet!" The word came down the line. "You've got to walk quiet!" Every man obeyed. I thought to make noise, try to rouse someone, bring the sheriff, or maybe some Federal troops on shore. What were my chances to get away? In a Confederate uniform? In the pounding storm? I'd be shot. I groaned inside. And I despised Cousin Albert, dying or not.

We wound through street after street, back alley after back alley. It seemed we walked in circles. Finally we stopped, bumping into one another. I heard a door open. "There's steps," the voice whispered, the voice I couldn't place. "Follow down." We stood in the cold and dank of what smelled like a cellar before the last man closed the door above us. The wind and the rain stopped, but so did the air. I wanted to yank that rag from my mouth. I put my hands out and touched stone walls—cold, and slick, slimed on either side, some kind of tunnel.

"Keep your hands down, or I'll knot them up again!" the deep voice growled in my ear. I took up the rope, just as it pulled ahead. One whack on the head and I kept low. The tunnel cut a sharp right. We climbed a short ladder. This time the walls opened up, and, cold as it was, breathing came easier.

"We're here, lads," the Irish brogue took up again. "Everybody strip."

"What?" the cry went down the line.

"We've got new clothes for you," the familiar voice soothed, "and a hot meal and a warm bed. But you've got to get out of those wet and lousy clothes. We've got to burn those uniforms straightaway. Federals will be combing the shore by morning. We don't want them finding a thing. And you've got to scrub the vermin away before my wife will let you set foot in her house. I'll take you two at a time to the stable. She's got razors and hot baths for you there." And then I knew. I knew where I'd heard the voice before.

A match struck stone and touched a lantern wick on the wall. The face of Mr. Maynard sprang to life.

$\mathscr{S}$even

$\mathscr{Y}$ou men help yourselves to apples in the bins while waiting your turn." Mr. Maynard didn't see me, didn't know I was there, among the men.

The deep voice ordered the other men to move ahead. "I'll tend our insurance policy," he whispered and pushed me down against a cellar wall, roping my feet and tying my hands behind my back again. I saw the outline of his face for the first time. He was about Cousin Albert's height, a similar build. I might be able to take him on if I could get loose—if we were alone, now, before good food and sleep got his strength back.

"This way, men." Two men followed Mr. Maynard up a cellar ladder. "Oh." Mr. Maynard turned back. "Which of you is McCain?"

"I'm McCain." The deep voice stood, grew suddenly respectful. This was the man Cousin Albert meant for me to give his Testament.

Two of the prisoners moved to stand between McCain and me. I couldn't see Mr. Maynard's face.

"There's a boy I sent with bread for the prisoners—bread with money and our address baked inside. He's not returned.

Do you know what happened to him?"

"We'll have to talk about that," McCain said. "Why do you ask me?"

"Your man that came for us was wearing the boy's clothes. He said I'd have to ask you what became of him. Said the boy loaned him his clothes so he could come out disguised as a visitor. He said the boy stayed on Pea Patch for the night, as a favor to Col. Mitchell's men. I don't know as I believe that." Mr. Maynard's footsteps started down the ladder. "He's a good boy, McCain. You wouldn't be here but for him. There'd best be no harm come to him."

"No harm's come to him, sir." McCain stepped toward him. "We'll have a talk later, in private."

Mr. Maynard hesitated. "All right, then." Footsteps disappeared up the ladder. The door closed behind him.

McCain's foul breath spat against my face. "Leaving you on Pea Patch was my first choice. Killing you now would be my second. For some reason you've got good friends, and that makes you very, very lucky. But if it wasn't for you, Col. Mitchell would be alive and here with us now. So your skin doesn't mean very much to me. You remember that. Anytime you think of making a commotion or slowing us down, you remember that." He pulled back. "Keep this Yank out of my sight."

I turned my head and closed my eyes. Cousin Albert was dead. I leaned my throbbing head against the wall, trying to take that in, to make sense of all that had happened. The cold and damp crept into my bones, made my muscles ache. Voices roused me again.

"We can't take him with us! We'll have to watch him every second. That, by itself, will give us away."

"Well, we can't very well leave him behind, now, can we?"

the Irish brogue pitched in. "He'll get past this soft old couple in no time, and the Federals will be on us as well as them!"

"I'd like to lynch the lit—"

"You know you can't do that, Sarge. His safety was the colonel's dying wish. You saw it in his own writing. He's his flesh and blood. You can't get past that! Not a man here would stand for it. We'll have to split up."

"We'd have to split up anyway. Ten men can't travel together without rousing suspicion," a new voice said.

"Let him go with me," a younger voice spoke up.

"With you? How far would the two of you get?"

"I think we'd do all right. Two boys—alone. Nobody'd know I'm a Reb." It was the one-legged boy with his trouser leg pinned to his hip, the prison boy who'd asked me to thank the lady for the bread.

"He might have something there, Sarge."

"If he squeals you'll never see your home or mother again, Gibbons. You know that, don't you? That boy didn't help us out of the goodness of his heart. He'll be madder than a hornet, out for revenge. The rest of you men split up and go first. Gibbons and I'll wait a day and go together."

"He won't squeal."

McCain laughed. "And what makes you think that? What makes you think he won't leave you in some ditch to rot, crippled and alone, while he runs off and calls the law on all of us?"

"He wouldn't have brought us bread." I could barely hear the boy's answer.

"What?"

He spoke up. "He wouldn't have brought us bread if he had no mercy, sir. He didn't have to do that." No one answered. "I trust him. Col. Mitchell trusted him. And who would believe I'm a dangerous, escaped prisoner?"

"Forget it, Gibbons. I—"

The door at the top of the ladder opened. "Next!" Mr. Maynard's voice called down.

"Wilson—take Gibbons up," McCain ordered.

"Right! Climb up, my friend."

"You go on, sir. I'd just as soon wait a bit," the boy answered.

"I'll not have you letting him go, Gibbons," McCain threatened.

"I won't, sir. I swear it. I'll just wait beside him and see what I think about us traveling together."

McCain seemed satisfied. "Well, I'm going. I'm ready to pitch these rags."

The door closed. That left the Irish brogue, who was wearing my clothes, and Gibbons, the one-legged boy who trusted me. I feigned sleep.

"And what will you do if he leaves you for dead somewhere, me boy-o?"

"I'll pray that God will make a way of escape, just like this time."

"You're too trustin' for your own good. It'll be the undoin' of you."

"Hello?" Mrs. Maynard's voice came from the top of the ladder. "Anyone still down there?"

"A couple of us, ma'am," the brogue answered.

"Can one of you give me a hand?"

"Right away!" He was on his feet in a second and up the stairs.

"Are you awake?" Gibbons whispered.

I opened my eyes.

"Lean forward." He pulled the rags loose from my mouth. I let out a heave that made my chest ache.

"Thanks. Thanks." I choked. "Can you get this package out of my coat? It's weighing hard on me."

Gibbons pulled the pouch from my jacket. "I'm sorry for what's happened to you. But I'm grateful for all you did to get us out."

"I didn't get you out. I was tricked." He didn't answer. "Is Cousin Albert—Col. Mitchell—really dead?"

Gibbons nodded. "Word came through the barracks during mess. He died this afternoon—yesterday, now. The guards told us. I'm sorry."

I couldn't say anything. I couldn't settle how I felt about any of it.

"It wasn't your fault, no matter what Sgt. McCain says. Colonel had consumption, had it long already."

Still I couldn't answer.

"I'll do all I can to help you out of this fix. But I've got to be able to trust you. My name is Wooster Gibbons—Pvt. Gibbons." I stared at him a time, not sure I should trust him.

"Robert Glover." The words came out of my mouth, and he nodded. "Did you mean what you said about us running together?" I'd have agreed to anything to get away from McCain.

Wooster nodded, then half grinned. "But I'm not likely to do much running. We'd have to travel south like you're my brother, or something—helping me out." He dipped his head. "But I'll have to get Sgt. McCain to agree. He might. He's not likely to want me slowing him down."

"Untie me?" I'd find a way to run once I was loose.

Wooster hedged. "If I do that Sgt. McCain won't trust us together. I'll do my best to talk him into untying you. If he doesn't, I'll make sure the man and lady upstairs knows you're down here—soon as I can get time alone with either one of them. I swear it."

The upstairs door opened.

"Duck your head. Pretend you're sleeping," Wooster whispered.

"Right, Gibbons. It's your turn. How's our prisoner?" the brogue called down the stairs.

"Still sleeping," Wooster answered, knotting my gag in place, but looser this time.

"Good. We'll leave him till later." The brogue reached the bottom of the ladder. "Climb up, then. You're going to love this hot bath, me boy-o. 'Tis a bit o' heaven." There was some shuffling. The brogue leaned down, and Wooster leaned into his back. He hoisted Wooster and disappeared up the ladder, as if he carried nothing. The door closed behind them.

"A way of escape. A way of escape," I prayed. They were Wooster's words, but I needed them now. "I don't know what else to pray for. I can't believe Cousin Albert did this—or that he's dead." And then I thought of Emily, and Ma. How would I get to them?

What about Mr. Heath? He didn't even know where I was. I wished I'd told him where I was, who I was stopping with. And then I could have kicked myself. I'd told him I was leaving straight for Ashland, not to worry if I was gone long. He'd have no reason to send someone looking for me, not now. By the time he did it might be too late. I'd be gone south with these prisoners or, if McCain had his way, left for dead somewhere. I had to trust that the Maynards would find me, help me.

I don't know how many hours passed. I heard footsteps above me, doors opened and closed. The chill and damp of the

73

cellar set deeper in my bones. I twisted and pulled, trying to pry the ropes from my wrists, but it was no use. I just pulled the knots tighter, dug the ropes deeper into raw skin.

My mind drifted to Granny Struthers, and her salve for rope burns, the salve I couldn't imagine needing because I'd never had rope burns. I'd give anything to be sitting in Granny's cabin now, watching her strip leaves from herbs or mix remedies or sing the old chants she'd learned from her Cherokee husband. And then I was there, floating over her cabin, staring into her fire, sleeping in her loft, breathing her cures, listening to William Henry urge, "Hold on. Hold on, now," all the while crows picked at my eyes, my arms, my feet.

I woke with a start, tried to steady my heart, my breath, but couldn't stop the shakes. I didn't remember ever being so cold, sweating so hard.

The lantern burned itself out, the dark complete. Faintly, a rooster crowed. Daylight must have come, but I couldn't see it in the cellar. Thirst set in, then hunger.

I figured Wooster had lied to me, or they wouldn't let him come. I called into the rag, hoping the Maynards would come. But no sound came out. My throat was swollen, nearly shut, and raw sore. I inched my way across the floor, rocked side to side till I knocked a crock off the barrel, sent it crashing to the floor, prayed they'd hear it. But nobody came.

Hours passed. Sleep pulled at me again. I fought it, but it pulled, and pulled, and then I wanted only to sink into it, to slide away, to dream of something else. But all my dreams flared into nightmares—running, chasing, guns blasting past my head, bayonets flashing in the sun, and more crows pecking at my eyes. The horrors kept on and on, spaced only by dark, slime-covered tunnels that ran on without end.

"Robert! Robert!" a woman's worried voice pulled me up, up. "Can you hear me, son?" It was Mrs. Maynard.

"I'm not your son," I mumbled.

She started to laugh, then cry. "No, you're not. But thank God you're awake." I couldn't pry my eyes open. "Wooster! Wooster, he's awake!" she shouted.

I heard the thump, thump of Wooster's crutch on the floor. A body bumped mine. I fell through air when the bed ropes sagged. "Hallelujah! We figured you were a goner!" It was Wooster's voice but stronger than I'd heard before. "You've been out two weeks! It's about time we got a look at your ugly face!"

I forced my eyes open. It was like a homecoming. "Where am I?"

"You're in Wooster's room at our boarding house, Robert." Mrs. Maynard pulled a quilt to my neck. "You've been down with a fever. Wooster's not left your side these two weeks."

And then I remembered. I forced my eyes open. "McCain?"

"Don't you worry. That horrid man is gone, and none too soon! Only I'm sorry to say he stole your Mr. Heath's horse. We had no idea what a scoundrel he was!

"Thank the Lord Wooster begged us to check the cellar, just to make sure Sgt. McCain hadn't lied about you running off. We just couldn't believe you'd have run off without your horse. It made no sense—but we never knew you'd been locked in that cellar.

"We're so very sorry we got you into this, Robert. I hope you can believe that. I hope you will believe it."

I closed my eyes. I didn't want to remember, didn't want to think about it.

"That's it. You sleep on. It's just what you need. We'll talk later."

But we didn't. My dreams came and went, light and shadow. Voices flew in and out of my head. Fevers raged and died and raged again. The only thing that stayed the same was Wooster's voice and the far-off sound of a bird I couldn't name, inside and outside my dreams. There were days I'd wake, and the air around me seemed still, the height and heat of summer. Then nights would pass, and I'd hear William Henry calling my name, sometimes a deep-down sadness in his voice, sometimes urging me to stand up and take hold. I'd hear Granny Struthers, "Go on, now. Work's not done."

And Emily, "Robert? Robert, are you coming?"

Sometimes the sun baked and pricked my face, but I couldn't open my eyes, couldn't turn my head, even when I felt the flies land on my cheek, walk against my nose.

Later I stared up into branches, all the russets and golds and scarlets of autumn flitting past in patches. I knew I rode flat, laid out in a wagon bed. I heard the cracking of whips, shouting of orders, and the honking and braying of mules, hundreds of mules, the smell beyond reckoning. Something in my mind recalled the mule training camp at Perryville. I figured I was not five miles from home, from Laurelea. I imagined Aunt Sassy's worried face looking down on me, her bronze hand cooling my brow, a cool vinegar rag mopping my face. Content, knowing I was going home, I slept.

But it was another trick, or a dream. Home never came. Sometimes I felt myself tugged, lifted, or knew water was forced down my throat till I choked. Once I smelled water, felt the rocking sides of a small boat, heard the ragged whispers of two men.

"We've got to get across 'fore daylight."

"Why didn't you just take them across on the ferry by wagon?"

"The boy's beginnin' to stir. Who knows what he'll say in his state? We can't risk it."

"Hush! I hear horses."

I heard them, too, and orders shouted, but through a fog. And then a familiar voice in my ear.

"Don't worry, Robert. I'm still here. I'll get you home. We're crossin' the Potomac now." But it wasn't William Henry, and it wasn't a dream. Because I knew William Henry was dead, and the voice in my ear was Wooster's.

When I woke next I forced my eyes wide and stared up at a gray sky and bare, black, rain-wet branches. Even flat on my back, behind a buckboard, a raw wind cut through my jacket. I tried to roll over, but my body still carried a lead weight. Voices came from over my head; the first one I didn't recognize.

"There's a good hospital in Richmond. We'll leave him there. It's the best we can do."

"I can't leave him. I promised. I wouldn't be alive if it weren't for him." It was Wooster's voice.

"You'll not be welcome anywhere. Nobody wants the typhus brought to their door."

"He's getting better. His fever's broke a week now. He just needs to muster his strength."

"You're joshin' yourself, boy. His fever comes and goes. The two of you need food and rest, help. Folks'll be more likely to give it to you than to him. But it's up to you, son. Richmond's as far as I go. I've a family to get back to."

"Yes, sir. Thanks for helping us. I'm beholden. We both are—my brother and me."

"You're a stubborn cuss. If you're a mind to go south, stay as far from Petersburg as you can. They've dug in—under siege—long already. Rebs and town people can't get out; Yanks can't get in . . . I still say leave him in Richmond and go on home before snow comes. We're deep in October already; it won't be long. Your ma'll be glad to have one son—better than none."

Wooster didn't answer.

"Suit yourself." The driver clucked the reins. We rattled on, and the rattling set me adrift again.

In and out, in and out. I couldn't tell dreaming from daylight, couldn't tell if the long stretches were passing days or passing weeks. I only knew that each time I woke the wind cut rawer, colder than the last.

Eight

"Well, well, well, at last we see those bonnie brown eyes, soldier!" The voice sang too cheerful, too bright, and belonged to a girl—all off kilter. I must've been dreaming again, but the poking and prodding didn't feel like a dream.

"What are you doin' to me?" I pushed the wet rag away, surprised my hand worked, but the thing kept coming at my face.

"I'm cleaning the grime of a lifetime from your noggin, soldier, and grateful you should be. It's crusty work for any poor soul!"

I knew that voice, that Irish girl voice, whose every word sounded like she was laughing at me. "Get away!" But my swipes at her arm fell feeble, and she just laughed out loud, red curls tumbling, tickling my nose as she leaned into her work. Then it came to me, and all I could do was stare. Four years ago, when Jeremiah, Grandfather Ashton's slave son, and I ran North, this girl had helped us, hidden us, saved us. At least it could be the same girl. She laughed at me now just as she'd laughed at Jeremiah and me then. And I hoped I wasn't dreaming.

"By Jim, it is you!" She stopped scrubbing my face long enough to marvel. "I thought you looked a mite familiar, but I couldn't fathom it so." She peered closer. "Do you remember me, then?"

"Petersburg," my voice whispered.

"Aye, Petersburg." She smiled, a mite sad. "You and—and your friend."

"You and your family hid us in coffins."

"Shh. You mustn't say such here! But, yes. Before this ugly war. And now I'm worried sick for them—the city under siege and Gen. Grant and his blue bellies circling the town." She pushed the worry away and made her green eyes twinkle. She whispered. "We're in a Confederate field hospital, you know." I felt my eyes go wide. "Not to worry," she said. "I'm nursing here, and you're my patient—all very proper." She rolled her sleeves down.

"I'll not be telling on your illegal journey if you'll not be squealing on me." She smiled, then frowned just as quick. "It's good to see you again, though I don't know what you're doing here. I'd have imagined you blasting away at Confederates, not joining up with them."

"It's not what you're thinking. I'm not a—"

"So, this young man's awake at last. You had us all worried, soldier." A doctor appeared from somewhere and leaned over me. "Your brother said you'd been in and out with fever for weeks. I'd say you're coming out of a bad case of typhus, with a hefty relapse or two. But it looks like you'll make it." He thumped my chest, listening, then peered down my throat, into my eyes. "I'm Col. Monroe. Hmm. No sign of pox. That's good. We're not wanting that here."

"Where is—?" My voice still wouldn't stand up like I wanted.

"Your brother's in camp, gaining some strength of his own.

We don't have much in the way of rations, no supply wagon for some time. But we do what we can for our boys." He stood up. "Your job is to get well. We need our soldiers in the field, not lying around field hospitals. Your brother, weak as he is, refuses to go home without you. But I'm hoping we can get you back on your feet for duty. He said you boys were separated from your regiment when you came down with fever."

"I don't remember." I swallowed. "My head hurts."

"That will pass. We've kept you quarantined until we know what we're dealing with. But I'd say, if the fever doesn't return overnight, we can move you in with some other men. We need all the tents we can get." He turned to the red-haired girl. "Nurse." He laid a hand on her shoulder. "I need you for surgery."

"Right away, Col. Monroe." The red-haired girl smiled up at him, blushed, stood to follow. I feared to see her go. Once the doctor turned she leaned down and whispered near my ear, "I'll be back when I can. My name is Katie Frances."

I didn't sleep for hours after that. I kept watching for red hair every time the tent flap lifted. The only red hair that came through belonged to a one-eyed private.

Dark settled in, and the temperature dropped. I pulled my thin blanket tighter around me, surprised and glad that both my arms worked. A single candle burned atop a stand in the midst of the tent. I kept my eye on it, tried to stay awake, tried to guess the day, the month. When I'd last gone into Fort Delaware it was June. Unless I missed my guess, the temperature had dropped below freezing. I remembered that the tree branches were bare when last I'd seen the sky. It must be late October or November. My birthday must have come and gone—eighteen. I should be enlisted by now! How could so much time pass without me knowing?

"Robert!" a voice whispered. "You awake?"

"Wooster?" I watched him struggle beneath the tent and hoist himself up on one leg.

"Katie Frances said you was awake. I had to wait till the guard left so I could come. They played taps already."

"Where am I? What month is it? What did you do to me?" I demanded, breathless from my own questions.

But Wooster grinned. "I reckon you'll mend. You're mouthy as the first time I met you."

I'd have punched him if I'd been stronger. But the tent flap lifted then, and a dark, cloaked figure backed inside, quickly pulling the flap taut. Wooster hit the ground and rolled under my cot. I tried to rise up. The figure started at our noise and whirled to face us. The hood fell back, and relief poured over Katie Frances's face. She smiled, then touched her finger to her lips. I never saw such lips, even in the lone candle's light.

"You gave me a fright!" she whispered, moving slowly among the supply kegs. She peered under my cot. "You can come out now, Wooster. I'll not bite you!"

I heard Wooster roll out and struggle to his foot. He dimpled red as beetroot, even in the dim light. "I thought you was the guard," he whispered back.

She shook her head. "I stepped clear of them." She gave me a smile that warmed me through, shivering as I was. "And how are you faring, Robert Gibbons?"

"I'm not Rob—" I started, but Wooster cut me off.

"He's faring a mite better, ma'am, but still a little woozy in the head—doesn't hardly know his name." Wooster tapped his head and rushed the words out in a breath, but Katie Frances was not taken in.

"Is he, then?" She tilted her head, searched our faces, then ran her finger down my arm. "And suppose you tell me your real name." Her green eyes bored into mine. I couldn't look away if I'd a mind to.

"Robert. Robert G—" I started again, but Wooster jumped in.

"Robert Gibbons! Robert Gibbons—my brother. I already told you, Miss O'Leary."

"And I'm sister to the Queen of Spain, Wooster Gibbons. For brothers the two of you don't look a penny alike! You—" she pointed to Wooster— "cornflower eyes and scrawny, tow-headed as the day you were born. And you—" she pointed to me "—chestnut waves, all arms and legs, and eyes the color of me uncle's cow!" That shut us both up. We couldn't even look at each other. "So what is it? Truth, now."

I glanced at Wooster, then, and his cornflower eyes pleaded with my cow ones. But I'd trusted this girl once, and she'd saved me. I'd trust her again. "Robert—" She rolled her eyes, not believing me. "Robert Glover, from Maryland." She tilted her head again, considering.

"And you?" she queried Wooster.

"Wooster Gibbons—Salem, North Carolina." Wooster frowned. "You won't tell, will you? You won't tell we're not brothers?"

"Why would I tell? And why should a soul care?"

Wooster and I looked at each other, and I realized Wooster would never tell, never betray me. "Because he's a secesh soldier, and I'm not," I said.

"A Federal? Spy, are you?"

I looked away and felt the heat rise up my neck. "I'm not a soldier at all. And if I was I'd deserve to be shot. Thanks to Wooster and his friends and my lying cousin, I'm a traitor to my country!" The more I said, the angrier I grew. The angrier I grew, the louder I talked.

"Hush up!—or you'll get us both bucked and gagged!" Wooster ordered.

"There's a bit of a tale here, I do believe!" Katie Frances looked ready to settle down for the telling when we heard the changing of the guard. "They'll be walking through the tents. Wooster, you've got to get out of here, and so must I." She pulled her hood over her head. "I'll be wanting to hear more of this." She stopped before the tent flap and turned. "But not to worry, your secret is safe with me."

That quick, they were both gone. I was madder than I'd been since I'd first realized what Cousin Albert had pulled on me. It felt good and clean to be angry. Worn from my fury, I fell back, panting.

I thought through all that had happened since I'd rode off from Laurelea—at least as much as I knew and could remember. But my neck and head ached. My eyes grew heavy again. I never heard the orderlies walk their rounds.

The next two days I lay in the tent, lost amid the kegs and boxes of supplies. Col. Monroe decided it best to keep me away from the other men a few days more. In that time Wooster caught me up on all we'd been through these five months. Five months is a long time to miss from your life. One minute I'd hate Wooster for being part of McCain's and Cousin Albert's treachery and secesh regiment, and the next I'd be grateful beyond words that he hadn't left me for dead.

I just wanted to get my strength back enough to stand, to ride, to walk—if I had to—to Ma and Ashland.

Before reveille one morning, Wooster leaned into my face, shaking me. "We've got trouble. Wake up, Robert! Wake up!"

"How could there be more trouble?" That didn't seem possible, unless we were being attacked and shelled by Union artillery. For the first time I felt strong enough to roll over, turn my back on him. But he jerked me to face him again.

"Sgt. McCain rode in last night. He's been reassigned to this regiment. If he sees you you're as good as dead! If he sees you he'll find me!"

"What?" McCain's name was like rotten potatoes in my mind.

"Sgt. McCain! He'd love turning you over as a prisoner. You'd never make it in a Union prison, Robert!"

"I'm a civilian! I never even enlisted, thanks to you and McCain—"

"Listen to me!" Wooster shook me. "We've got to get out of here. We've got to run!"

"I'm not going anywhere with you, Wooster! Soon as I get my feet under me I'm going to find my cousin and Ma—where I should've been months ago!" And saying it slammed the urgency, the fear of God into me. What had become of Ma and Emily in all this time?

"Mrs. Maynard told me that. Why do you think I've been draggin' you along all this way? She said you're headed South, toward the Yadkin out Davie County way—not twenty miles from Salem. Salem's where I'm headed. We can help each other, but a fat lot o' help you been to me so far—sick and puny and slowing us down!"

"Well, pardon me, General Gibbons! It wasn't my idea to sit days on end in that wet cellar, trussed up like a pig to slaughter!"

"Stop it! The both of you!" It was Katie Frances at the tent flap. "You'll wake the dead and bring every sentry within a quarter mile!" She brushed past the kegs and insisted, "I don't know what's got into the two of you, but you'd best take hold!" She stabbed my chest with her finger. "It was better when you were raging with fever. At least you hadn't so much to say!"

I sat back, angry but stronger for the blood boil. Wooster looked like he wanted to knock my teeth out.

"Now I want the story. I want it straight, and I want it quick. Do you understand?" Katie Frances stood with her fists pressed into her hips. When we didn't answer she grabbed Wooster's ear with a vengeance. "I said, do you understand me?"

"Let off! Let off!" Wooster wailed, loud as he dared. And then he poured our story. Every time he got something wrong or left out a part I pitched in till we'd told the whole mess from every angle.

Katie Frances drew a deep breath. "You two are in a nastier cow pie than I thought possible. Did you know there's a major here from North Carolina? Maj. McCain. He boasts he was once a prisoner, escaped from Fort Delaware—a hero at Gettysburg for all he tells."

"That's a lie," Wooster spat. Katie Frances raised her eyebrows. Wooster and I looked at each other, and I knew he'd spoken true before. "McCain was at Gettysburg, and Fort Delaware—but a sergeant then, and not much of a hero, except to hear him tell it."

"Ah," Katie Frances said, "a 'field promotion.'"

Wooster glanced at me, then away again. "Maj. McCain was the one wanted to kill Robert back at Fort Delaware or leave him to be shot, and I'll bet he'd do it for sure now. He'd have nothing to lose and won't want the truth about our escape getting out. It won't look so good for him—not the way he acted, not leaving me while he ran South."

"I thought you wanted to stay!" I said, confused.

"I wanted to help you, you idiot! It was wrong for him to leave you there to die or be sick on the Maynards' hands. Col. Mitchell wrote that you were to be treated with every courtesy, and kept safe, that you were his blood kin. Sgt. McCain knew that. He disobeyed written orders—code or not. He disobeyed orders and deserted a soldier. None of that's gonna look good for him. He won't want you—or me—running around spouting the truth about him!" Wooster thundered, nearly beside himself. "And it would be our word against his—a major!" The bugle called reveille. "You can't afford to be recognized, Robert."

"I'd say it's a little late for that." The uniform slid through the tent flap. Wooster paled. Katie Frances barely caught him before he hit the floor.

Nine

everend Goforth? Andrew?" It couldn't be.

"Wooster! Wooster! Wake up, boy!" Katie Frances slapped Wooster's face. "It's only the chaplain! Don't die on us! Wake up, you sleepy strawfoot!" She pulled Wooster to the cot and made him sit.

"Are you all right, son?" Rev. Goforth leaned down, reached for Wooster's hand, helped him stand.

"Yes, sir. I just thought you were Maj—somebody else. I thought you were somebody else."

"Apparently."

"You know the chaplain?" Katie Frances, flustered, demanded of me, but Rev. Goforth answered before I could.

"Robert and I are old friends. It's been too long, Robert, and it's good beyond words to see you—a blessing I never expected—here, of all places!" He reached for my hand and shook it and my arm heartily. He frowned. "Or is it a blessing?"

"You're a chaplain? For the Confederacy?" It didn't fit, but then what else would he be? Katie Frances tilted her head and raised her eyebrows again. Chap. Goforth smiled, a little sheepish, it seemed to me.

"And you're wounded? A Confederate private?" He looked puzzled.

"Well . . ." I didn't know how much to say. But I didn't need to say anything. Col. Monroe walked in.

"I must say I never saw one patient gather so many visitors—especially in a quarantined tent." He didn't look pleased, maybe suspicious. But he studied and thumped me, then stood back. "All the attention seems to have done you some good, soldier. I'd say you're out of the woods and ready to be released from quarantine." He turned to Katie Frances. "Nurse O'Leary, I'd like you to accompany me on my rounds."

"Yes, Col. Monroe. As soon as I get this patient his breakfast."

"I believe this soldier has help enough. You're needed elsewhere, nurse." He spoke to Katie Frances but shot a challenge toward Chap. Goforth. The chaplain didn't seem to notice.

Katie nodded but did not look pleased. She tucked my arm beneath the blanket. "I'll check on you later, soldier." To Wooster she said, "Mind your brother eats, then." But she gave Chap. Goforth a smile to shame the sun.

"Yes, ma'am." Wooster acted the penitent.

At the tent flap Col. Monroe turned to Wooster. "Didn't you say you and your brother are from the 26th North Carolina? And you were wounded—where?"

"Yes, sir. Gettysburg. Wounded at Gettysburg."

He nodded. "A Maj. McCain rode in from North Carolina this morning. He's been reassigned to our regiment. I believe he said he'd been with the 26th—escaped Fort Delaware's prison early last summer. You must know him."

"Maj. McCain?" Wooster stumbled over the name. Col. Monroe's stare bored down on him, then through me.

"You did say you boys were with the 26th?"

89

"Yes, sir." Wooster sounded miserable.

"Maj. McCain's just gone out, leading a much-needed foraging party . . . should be back in three or four days. With any luck we'll enjoy improved rations as a result." He hesitated, frowned. "I'll have him stop by to see you." He waited.

"That would be good, sir. Thank you, sir." Wooster didn't convince anybody, least of all Col. Monroe.

"Nurse? Shall we?" Katie Frances followed, not looking back.

Chap. Goforth looked from me to Wooster, frowned, searched our faces. "Are you two in need of help?"

Wooster shook his head. "No, sir. I'm just glad my brother's getting well."

Chap. Goforth smiled and placed his hand on Wooster's shoulder. "The last I knew Robert didn't have a brother." Wooster colored like a russet apple. "Now, don't you boys think you could use a friend?"

Wooster looked like he was fixing to die. "It's all right, Wooster. I've known Rev. Go—Chap. Goforth a long time. He's a friend—mine and my family's. We can trust him." I hoped that last part was true. I never knew where I stood with Rev. Goforth after I ran North with Jeremiah, but I'd long hoped he'd understood.

And then I told Chap. Goforth about Emily's letter, about Cousin Albert, and Gettysburg, and the captured men of the 26th, about Fort Delaware and how I'd gone to see Cousin Albert, what I'd found. When I came to the part about the escape, Cousin Albert's deceit, and all the rest of it, Wooster seemed to shrink into himself. I told about the Maynards and McCain and the cellar and stealing Mr. Heath's horse. By then I was mad all over again. Wooster looked shamed into a pecan shell. Even in my heat I felt a mite sorry for him, but I didn't cut him any slack.

Chap. Goforth took the reins. "And Wooster's stood by you all this time you were sick? He's fed and clothed and nursed you, bringing you South toward your mother and Emily?"

"I wouldn't have needed that if they hadn't—"

"Life is full of 'ifs,' Robert. What is important is what we do with what is. It looks as though Wooster has proven himself every ounce your brother. It looks as if he's as good as laid his life down for yours." And with every word Wooster looked up, a slim light growing in his eyes, a light I hadn't seen since I'd met him. "Wooster," Chap. Goforth said, "can you get Robert something to eat? He needs to build up his strength."

"Yes, sir. I'll do it now."

"Thank you. I'm sure I'll see you later." Wooster fairly glowed from Chap. Goforth's good nature. I didn't. Chap. Goforth was my friend, or I thought he was. When Wooster'd hobbled out the chaplain gave me his full attention. "It's good you're on your way to Ashland, Robert. I know Emily needs help with your mother."

My ears pricked up. "Ma? She's all right, isn't she?"

He hesitated. "I thought you said Emily wrote you about her."

"She did. But all she said is that the war had been hard on her." Now I frowned. "What is it? What's wrong with Ma?"

Chap. Goforth raked long fingers through his hair. Shades of silver ran through the brown, and I marveled at the change these few years had brought. "The war's been hard on everyone. Some are better able to stand up to the hardships, to accept the deprivation." He walked to the far side of the tent and back, taking his time, weighing his words. I held my breath, fearful to interrupt. "Caroline, your mother, is—not strong. The last I knew, Marcus—I'm sorry, your grandfather—was quite ill. I've tried to stay in touch with Emily, but we've had no mail these last months."

"You and Emily write?" Why did I think that strange?

He colored a little. "We did. I've tried to help her with—with her family and the plantation, but our expectations have changed."

I waited, but he didn't keep on. "What does that mean—your expectations have changed?" I wanted to understand.

He colored deeper, more like Wooster had. "Emily is an extraordinary young woman. She'll make someone a splendid wife." He turned to face me, then stepped away. "It just won't be me."

"You courted Emily?"

"I asked for her hand."

"She turned you down?" That was hard to believe, but I was glad beyond words, and relieved—a thing I'd never own out loud. Still, it made me wonder what chance I had, if she'd said no to Rev. Goforth.

"She chose a different path . . . That's not important now." He turned to face me. "What is important is that we keep McCain from meeting you. Or better yet, we get you and Wooster on your way to Ashland."

"Are they alone? Are Ma and Emily both at Ashland?"

Chap. Goforth shook his head. "The last I knew Emily was dividing her time between Ashland and Mitchell House on weekends, trying to keep an eye on both. She'd been attending the Girls' Academy in Salem—the only reason Col. Mitchell would hear of her staying in the South once he enlisted. You know he sent Alex to England?"

I nodded, and my bile rose at the mention of Alex's name. "I'm sure he's safe and sound." My sarcasm wasn't lost on Chap. Goforth. His raised brow told me that we thought alike.

"When your grandfather became ill and your mother— once your mother needed more help—Emily left school for longer and longer periods to stay with them. That is the last I heard." He took my measure. "It's good that you'll be with them, Robert. They need someone."

"Cousin Albert seemed to think Ma couldn't come home." I waited, but he didn't answer. "What's wrong with her?" He still didn't answer. "Chap. Goforth, what's wrong with Ma?" I demanded.

He looked miserable. "She's—frail. She's just frail."

I shook my head, tried to take that in, tried to understand what he meant. "What about Nanny Sara? Is she still there?" Nanny Sara had cooked for Grandfather forever and nursed Ma as a baby.

"Yes. Nanny Sara, old as she is, might just outlive us all."

"And Jed Slocum?"

Chap. Goforth frowned. "I'm afraid he is, as far as I know. He should have been conscripted, but your grandfather paid a substitute, saying he needed his overseer. And that worries me. Without your grandfather to keep Mr. Slocum in line, I—" He worried the seam down his trouser leg. "I'm concerned for the women."

The tent flap lifted, and Wooster struggled in with a steaming tin cup. "It's not coffee, but it'll chase the early morning shakes away." He grinned and pulled a broken tag of hard cracker from his pocket, pushing it into my hand. "It's not much. There ain't much to be had. But it's eats."

93

"Thanks." I took the food but stared hard at Chap. Goforth. It wasn't talk I wanted to carry on in front of Wooster. But we weren't finished.

Ten

$\mathcal{I}$ was moved, just before dusk, to a ward tent.

A storm brewed through the night. Northeast wind heaved and blasted, slamming the rain in sheets against our tent's sides. Paths trod by orderlies walking in and out of the tent flap rivered. Water streamed under the sides, soaked our pallets and thin blankets till we all smelled like wet dog, rotting flesh, blood, and urine. Plank flooring had long ago been burned for firewood, so the sopping floor straw was raked up, half dried, spread, and soaked again.

I missed my cot and thought it wry how a body conscious enough to enjoy the pleasure of a dry bed lost it just as quick as he realized he had one.

The storm blasted through the next day and night. By the third day every man dreaded the misery of waking and wished mightily for August's drought. Wooster and I figured the storm would either slow McCain down, causing him to hole up somewhere and wait for its passing, or make him give up his foraging and backtrack, returning to camp early. We prayed for the first but did what we could to get my strength up. Only that ran as risky as lying sick, so far as Col. Monroe's plans were concerned.

"Keep this up, Gibbons, and we'll have you back in the field before Christmas." Col. Monroe seemed more than satisfied with my progress.

"Yes, sir."

"As soon as this storm breaks I want you outside. Walk up and down between the hospital tents, then through the camp; build your strength."

"Yes, sir." I looked away. That sounded better to me than he knew. I'd have tramped through the rain and mud if I could catch my breath and get the lead weight off my lungs.

By the fourth day the rain had fallen off to a drizzle, though the wind kept blasting.

It was three days since Katie Frances had stopped to talk. Col. Monroe kept her by his side nearly every minute. Despite her easy smile and the fact that every man in camp would have died twice to bring it to her lips, she looked done in.

Chap. Goforth stayed busy, too. More casualties poured in from skirmishes between the camp and Dinwiddie. He helped tend the wounded, nearly as good as most doctors and good as any nurse. He washed and bandaged and sewed men up. He said words over those that didn't make it. Their bodies stacked up, waiting for burial, waiting for the rain to stop. He prayed with wounded men scared of dying, men too scared to die, and men scared of living with just one arm, one leg, one eye—or none.

Three of the fifteen soldiers crammed into my hospital tent died during that storm; one died from gangrene in a shoulder wound, two from dysentery. Chap. Goforth sat with them, every minute he could spare, talking, praying them out of this world, preparing them for the next. He looked older, more beaten down each day, and I worried for the broken way he carried himself.

One night, late, while the other men slept, I woke. Chap. Goforth tended a man on the pallet next to mine, a man so near dying I don't think he knew the chaplain was there. I didn't worry that he'd hear me.

"Chap. Goforth?"

The chaplain turned to face me. "Robert." He smiled, sad and tired. "I thought you were sleeping."

"I was wondering."

"Yes?"

"Why you stayed in the South. Why you joined the secesh." I spoke as quietly as I could. He moved closer on the ground beside me.

"Because these men need comfort and salvation, Robert. Because they are members of the body of Christ—or might become. Never is a man more ready to accept the Lord than when he faces his own mortality. This is the vineyard the Lord has given me to tend."

His words didn't ring clear in my head. "I didn't think you'd stay—for the South, I mean." And then I decided to press the thing I'd wondered nearly five long years. "What you said to me that night on Grandfather's verandah—two nights before I ran North with Jeremiah—all that from Isaiah about loosing the bands of wickedness, letting the oppressed go free, breaking every yoke. That made a difference to me. I never thought you'd hold slavery up as something worth dying for." I wanted to know where he stood on those things. I needed to understand.

He gave me a look I'll not forget. "While you and Jeremiah ran North I was in High Point that Christmas Day, holding services, and then I transported a family of five slaves to a safe house. How do you think Nanny Sara knew where to send the two of you that Christmas Eve? Did you ever wonder who got word to the conductor in the church at Mount Pleasant?"

"You?" I couldn't believe it.

"How do you think I know where you hid? In the bell tower."

"Why didn't you tell me?" I could hardly take it in. "Why didn't you go with us? Why aren't you serving the Union?" I'd wondered and wondered where he stood, what he'd thought. It would have meant the world and all to know he stood with us.

"I was needed there, at that time. Now I'm needed here. I'm where the Lord has called me."

I pushed that away. "But the South—"

"I told you long ago that I'd surrendered my life to the Lord. He is my general. He is the One I take orders from."

"But God's not fighting for the Confederacy! You know He's not holding onto slavery or wanting to tear the country apart! What are you doing here? Why aren't you helping the men of the Union?"

"Every day I hear men claim that God is on their side. I hear our soldiers invoke God's protection and leading to victory over the evil invader of their lands and homes. I hear them beg God to crucify the tyrant, Abe Lincoln! And when I tend wounded Union prisoners I hear them pray that God will save and restore them to His kingdom made manifest in these United States, that He will punish Jefferson Davis, chief devil of all the devils!" Chap. Goforth spat a fierce whisper.

"What I know is that the Creator of Eternity is not a marionette, thrown this way or that by our arguments or by our blood baths. The question is not whose side is God on, but whose side are we on? Do we stand for God or against Him? Do we stand and serve where we are called or where it is convenient? Think about that, Robert. Where are you called? To what are you called? Then answer Him."

The dying man on the pallet beside me cried out. Chap. Goforth crawled to his side. I stared after him, saw how he cradled the dying man's head, heard how he prayed over him. He used every bit of strength his body possessed for these men, these men who were fighting and dying for the Confederacy. That reminded me of Cousin Albert, and how he'd said he and his men were fighting to protect their homes, their families.

Is it possible to do the right thing in the absolute wrong place? Why would you stay, if you knew the people you were helping were serving the wrong cause? How could he be laying down his life in the opposite place of Pa and still be right? But what he'd said sounded right. I lay back, more confused than ever.

A good while before day broke, while the rain still poured and thunder still rumbled across the heavens, sounding for all the world like cannon exploding in the distance, Katie Frances O'Leary stepped into our tent. She slipped out of her oilskin and hood, shaking the rain from her shawl, her dress, her hair.

Kneeling beside a man who'd lost both legs and too much blood, Chap. Goforth had dozed off, his head on his chest—or maybe he was praying. But he didn't seem to hear her, didn't turn at her coming.

Katie Frances peered into every face. Something made me feign sleep. Satisfied we all dozed, she knelt behind the chaplain and took his stooped shoulders in her hands. She massaged them back and forth, back and forth, gently at first, then deeper. Watching her in the lantern light, watching as the rain sparkled through her hair like a thousand points of dew in the morning sun, I held my breath. A man might give all he had for such a woman's touch. I might.

Chap. Goforth didn't start when she took hold of his shoulders. He just leaned back into her hands as they worked their medicine, and let out a long breath. The two of them worked a rhythm, a slow dance without music.

It went on so long I nearly fell to dreaming, imagining they were my shoulders she worked, my back she rubbed. Only, in my dreams, the face behind me, the hands on my shoulders belonged to Emily.

Chap. Goforth pulled Katie Frances's hands from his shoulders, and turned just enough to draw her around him. He traced the line of her jaw with his hand, the line of her mouth with his thumb. Even in the lantern's low flame I saw the question in his eyes. She must have answered. They found each other's mouths like they'd been born knowing. He kissed her, long, and with more desire than I'd imagined he carried. It was a kiss with all the love and heat and tenderness I'd ached to see between Ma and Pa, the kind of kiss I hoped to know someday. I wondered that I'd not seen the love light between these two before.

I caught my breath and turned over, wanting to watch them, knowing I'd watched too long already. A sharp pain welled inside me. I prayed that Ma and Pa would find that kind of love again. I prayed that I would know it in my life. But I thanked God that Chap. Goforth—Andrew—my friend, had found her now, when he needed her most. And then I closed my eyes.

Eleven

Quick as the pallets of the dead were emptied and shaken by the burial detail they were filled with new wounded, men from a Confederate cavalry shot while scouting Union troops.

With them came rumors of two Union brigades marching toward Petersburg to resupply Gen. Grant. Fifty miles of open fields, timber, and our hospital camp stood in their path as the crow flies—more miles if they traveled the roads. That gave us roughly three, maybe five days, if the storm slowed them down. Wooster and I were hard pressed to guess which might be worse for us—McCain or Union troops.

The rain stopped altogether on the fifth day, leaving the whole camp flooded. Still the wind blasted, still rumors flared from couriers anxious to talk after three sips of John Barleycorn, and still McCain's foraging party did not return.

Wooster sat next to me in the late afternoon, shoving down my throat hot broth that I could just as well have eaten myself, when we first heard McCain's roar. "I foraged twenty miles east and west and never saw so much as a blue streak across that land!"

"I understand that the last courier said three days more. But you'll want to speak with Col. Monroe, Maj. McCain. That's all I know." It was Chap. Goforth's voice. "I believe he's in his tent. He's expecting a high-ranking visit shortly. I'll show you the way." We could hear the chaplain steer McCain away from our tent and blessed him for taking a quick hand.

"We've got to get out of here!" Wooster whispered. "That Col. Monroe'll send him our way, sure as we're setting here."

Memories of McCain jerking my arm high behind my back, cutting rope burns into my raw wrists, his threats—all of it swelled in my brain. I was more scared of McCain than of Union or Confederate armies, more scared of him than of dying on the run. I grabbed my boots. Wooster pulled on one while I tugged on the other.

Katie Frances burst into the tent to the delight of every man there. "Miss O'Leary! Nurse O'Leary!" they called, reaching for the hem of her skirts. She smiled at each one, promising to see to them in a moment, as she made her way across the tent floor to Wooster and me. She knelt down as I forced my arm into a woolen butternut jacket. Her green eyes stood wide.

"Col. Monroe is meeting with Maj. McCain now," she whispered. "The major's returned a 'conquering hero'—foraged a bounty—though where he could have found it no one knows, or is asking." She glanced over her shoulder. "The colonel's sure to tell him about you. He's been asking me every day if you're strong enough for field duty, Robert, and why I've taken such an interest in the two of you. He thinks you're deserters. They shoot deserters! Though why they'd do it when there's such a need for soldiers, I don't know." Her forehead creased, and her eyes grew fearful.

She watched the tent flap one second and worried over us the next. "You must move to a different tent—bunk in with

102

Wooster, or Andrew—and pretend you're well. Lend a hand with the wounded; blend in. We're expecting those Union troops before day's end. And a Brigadier General Somebody-or-other is on his way to camp—passing through. They're all in a tizzy. The confusion of it all is the only chance you'll go un-noticed. But you can't be seen together. They'll call you out in no time! You really both must go now! They'll be here, sure and certain, any moment!"

"I can make it to Wooster's tent." I pulled myself up. "I don't know about tending wounded. I'm still shaky on my feet."

"We'll think of something. Now, go!"

Twelve

Daylight faded. The mud made walking slippery and hard, harder yet for Wooster on his crutch. The first lanterns sputtered aflame by the time we made the lane for Wooster's tent, only the tent was gone.

"Get a move on, soldier!" a sergeant called to Wooster. "Find yourself a supply wagon, son, and hop aboard. The tents in this lane was flooded through. We're moving these wounded into wagons. You can sleep on higher ground for a change."

"Yes, sir!" Wooster saluted. "Come on, Robert, we'll find us a place."

"They're not gonna let me up there—with two good legs—not knowing I been sick." It was all I could do to pant the words.

"Come on, before you fall down!" Wooster pulled my sleeve. "It ain't like I can carry you!"

We slipped through the lines of unhitched wagons, two abreast, then down another three wagons, toward the rear of the train. Drivers, finished with the move, and orderlies just off duty stood to one end, arguing or boasting—it was hard to tell which. Wooster and I slid into the back of a wagon loaded to the gills.

"Ain't this a wonder? This must be the stuff they foraged!" Wooster whispered gleefully. "Have some corn." He tossed me a dried ear. "We're gonna sleep in style, and we got the kitchen car to boot! McCain'll never think to look back here."

"Till we get the boot, you mean! You know that driver's gonna check this wagon. They'll drag us out and send us—!"

"They won't put me off," Wooster boasted.

"Thanks a lot!" I sputtered.

"Listen, you knucklehead, and you might learn something!" Wooster pulled a tarpaulin and three kegs from the inside wall of the wagon. "Climb back in there. I'll get you food and water when I can. Just stay hid. When it's dark or all clear, I'll come get you."

It was a tolerable plan, and put me in mind of Pa and Mr. Heath, of Joseph Henry and the false-bottom wagon we used at Laurelea to cart runaway slaves from one safe house to the next.

I was halfway under the tarpaulin when I stopped and turned to Wooster. "You could get past this mess with McCain on your own. Why are you doing this? Why do you care what becomes of me?"

Wooster scrunched his forehead, then said simply, "Like Chaplain said, we're brothers." And he dropped the tarpaulin in place.

The path was so simple for Wooster, so plain for Chap. Goforth. Their only puzzle was why I didn't see my path clear too. Why didn't I? I wedged tight behind the kegs, wondering. I'd prayed for that very thing—a clear path—back at William Henry's grave, before I'd ever started this crazy, dangerous journey. But here I was hiding behind kegs in a Confederate hospital supply wagon, eighteen if a day, not fighting for the Union, and hadn't even reached Emily, or Ma—who was "frail." I feared to think what that meant. And I feared what Goforth meant about Slocum and the women? That gripped me.

It was hours before the blasts of wind and the chopping of wood for breakfast fires woke me. Even the stir of early morning camp lulled me; I was that tired. I heard Wooster chatting like a blue jay to the driver of our wagon. I shook my head in the dark. I'd not given Wooster enough credit. He was bold as brass. I'd not thanked him, either.

Sleep had bolstered me, and for the first time I felt truly hungry. I reached into the keg nearest my arm and pulled out an apple. Its sweet juice ran down my chin, the best thing I'd eaten in—I didn't know when. I even swallowed the core.

I wished I could get out, stretch my legs, answer the call of nature. But I'd promised to wait for Wooster's signal.

"Mind them supplies, boy, while I get some breakfast." It was our sergeant. "No pilferin', and don't let nobody else sneak off with nothin'."

"Yes, sir, Sgt. Pete!" Wooster sang out. Then I heard Wooster's crutch bump backward, into the wagon. "Robert! Robert!" he whispered, "Come on out. They're about to build the cook fires. You don't want to be in here with the food then!" He lifted the tarpaulin and pulled the splintered kegs toward him. I climbed through, glad to sit upright.

"Thanks, Wooster." I'd not forget to thank him again.

"That's all right." He grinned. "The wagon masters are off getting breakfast. See if you can make it 'round the camp for a time. If you get too tired, we'll have to find you a pallet in one of the tent wards."

I nodded. "I'll be back."

The walk around camp did me good—real grass and little

mud. The sun shone bright, and the wind had swept the land clean and a little drier.

I stayed shy of the officers' tents, any place I might run into Col. Monroe or Maj. McCain.

My legs worked better the more I used them, but the wind nearly knocked me over. I looked down at my wrists, my hands. Except for their color, like sand at the bottom of the run, I barely recognized them. I wore my own clothes—the extra shirt and pants I'd taken to the Maynards. They nearly fell off me, I'd lightened so. I hitched my pants and tightened my suspenders. The smell of hot chicory and the sight of hardtack made my mouth water. It felt good to be hungry.

I didn't catch sight of Katie Frances or Chap. Goforth. I hoped that McCain or Col. Monroe hadn't given Katie Frances a bad time about Wooster or me, that she'd been able to sidestep his questions.

Once I caught sight of McCain, pushing from wagon to wagon, searching, ordering a passel of privates to search. I thought of Wooster perched on our wagon seat and my blood ran cold. I watched from a distance as McCain's men searched the supply wagon. Wooster was nowhere in sight.

I waited till the wagons were nearly reloaded with supplies, while men doused fires, formed ranks—every sort of commotion. Then I climbed into the back of the wagon. Wooster lay there, hunched beside my kegs, a little paler.

"Did you see McCain?" I whispered. He nodded.

"I hid while he searched our wagon. But I heard him, Robert. He's looking for us. He's put the word out. It's one thing for you to hide a time. But there's not many one-legged runts in the army, at least not in this wagon train." His cornflower eyes widened. The crease between his brows tightened. "It won't be

107

long till he finds me, till somebody reports me. He's calling me a deserter and you a spy."

"What about our wagon sergeant? Did he talk to him?"

"I don't know. Sam Pete—Sgt. Pete—is in charge of this whole line of supply wagons—not just ours. He wasn't around when Maj. McCain came through." Wooster shook his head. "But he's bound to hear soon."

"We'll slip out after dark. We'll slip out and set off on our own."

Wooster looked doubtful. "You're not strong enough, and I'm not fast enough. We won't make it."

"You're right about that." Our heads jerked up. Maj. McCain's frame filled the wagon flap, blocking our daylight.

Thirteen

rag those deserters out, soldier!" Maj. McCain shouted. "Show the vermin the light of day." His eyes flashed in triumph as the private jerked us from our hiding place. "I figured you two would turn up sooner or later. You just made it easier than I expected."

"I never deserted, and you know it, Sgt. McCain!" Wooster half cried as they thumped him to the ground, taking no mind of his stump. He struggled up on his one leg.

"It's Maj. McCain, Private!" McCain barked.

"You're the one who left us—disobeyed Col. Mitchell's orders!"

McCain slapped Wooster hard across the mouth, sending him reeling to the ground again. "Arrest those two!" McCain ordered. A small crowd of men formed as we were hauled away, Wooster screaming his head off the whole time about McCain deserting his men, attempting murder of a civilian, about him disobeying Col. Mitchell's orders.

"Shut up, Wooster!" I begged him. But there was no stopping him. Something had snapped in Wooster, and a dam broke. They dragged us off, hauled us to a guard wagon, then trussed us back to back.

It wasn't enough for Maj. McCain. "Sergeant, tie those two to the back of the wagon. Sitting in a mud hole should take some of the starch out of their mouths."

That's when Katie Frances appeared in all her glory. "You can't be serious, Major darlin'! You've a one-legged soldier, wounded at the battle of Gettysburg for all our sakes, and a patient barely pulled through the fever!" she fairly shouted.

"Fever?" The sergeant stood back.

"To be sure, he's no longer quarantined. At least we don't think he needs to be! But it would be murder, sure as you're born, to leave these boys in the wind and mud." She turned to McCain. "And that is not what you're about, now, are you, Maj. McCain?" Katie blinked up at McCain, innocent as a new colt. But he wasn't taken in. He ogled her up and down.

"Not that this is any of your affair, Miss Irish Tarter, but they should have thought of that sooner." He'd done wrong to insult the flame-haired angel nurse Katie Frances O'Leary in front of the soldiers in camp. To a man they'd stand for her.

Katie Frances blushed with a vengeance but kept on. "Surely you're not afraid of these boys, are you, Major darlin'?"

McCain stepped toward her. His eyes flashed just what he thought of Katie Frances.

"Leave them where they are, sergeant." I couldn't see Col. Monroe but heard his voice. "Keeping them under guard should be sufficient, Major."

I breathed, glad for the first time to know the pushy doctor wouldn't let Katie Frances out of his sight. McCain colored and his mouth tightened. Col. Monroe pressed. "These patients are under my jurisdiction, Major."

"Begging your pardon, sir, but they're deserters. They deserve to be shot." McCain refused to back down.

But so did Col. Monroe. "As I said, they are under my juris-diction. There is a brigadier general passing the night in camp. You're welcome to petition the general." He turned to go, then looked back at Maj. McCain. "Execution seems an extravagance with our shortage of men."

"I'll see to it, Col. Monroe," McCain fairly sneered.

I heard Katie Frances's voice fading in the distance, "It's a fine man you are, Col. Monroe, standing up for all that's decent."

I'd just drawn a breath when McCain pushed past the guard, leaned in the wagon, and hissed, "I'll see you shot now or hanged. I should have drowned you at Fort Delaware, boy." He grabbed Wooster by the shoulder. "One more word out of you, Gibbons, and you won't live for a firing squad." And then he was gone.

Neither Wooster nor I said anything for a long time. I could feel Wooster's shoulders shudder behind me, but I had no com-fort to offer. I didn't see a way out of this mess, and nothing but trouble and death by the end of the day. I'd never see Emily again, or Ma or Pa, or Mr. Heath or the Henrys. I knew McCain would waste no time getting his petition to the general.

"What are you doing, Robert?" It was Wooster.

"I'm setting here, same as you."

"I mean, are you praying? We both need to be praying. Now would be a good time for a way of escape."

I couldn't answer him. I wasn't praying, hadn't prayed reg-ular for a long while. I'd pretty much forgotten about praying until the other night, until I'd seen Chap. Goforth and Katie Frances together and knew I wanted what they had. That was as much as God had heard from me since I sat in that cellar in Delaware City. How did God feel about me coming to Him only when I needed something desperate?

111

Hours passed. The sun traveled across the sky and sank beyond the wagons and tents. I tried to close my mind, to sleep, to pass the time without fear or pain, but sleep wouldn't come.

Tents shot up on dryer ground, cooking fires started, sentries changed guard. Night came on. From our wagon we could see a dozen watchfires, blinking every time a man walked in front of one.

I strained my eyes, needing to keep sight of the flames, as if they held safety—lone lights in the dark. They put me in mind of Miz Howe's song, the one that all the Union papers ran, "The Battle Hymn of the Republic." It had been so easy to sing, to rally around with everybody back home, back when President Lincoln issued his Emancipation Proclamation. I thought of that line, "I have seen Him in the watchfires of a hundred circling camps."

Only I couldn't see God in this watchfire. None of this war's watchfires belonged to me, nor one of those hundred circling camps—not North, not South. And I wondered, if I could not see God in them, if I could no longer see God in this war, like I'd thought I could, like I'd meant to, did that mean God could not see me?

We were out of the wind, but the cold and damp set deeper. Wooster and I shivered against each other, longing to sit by one of those fires.

We were nearly frozen when the guard stationed outside our wagon allowed a private to pass. "Sgt. Sam Pete sent these vittles over for you boys. Said to eat hardy." He stopped short. How you're gonna do that all trussed up, I don't know." He turned to the guard. "Don't you reckon these hardened criminals could be untied long enough to eat something?"

The guard pulled back the wagon flap and peered in at us.

We must have looked a pitiful couple of wretches—skinny, shivering, tied up. It wasn't like either one of us could have run off. "Oh, I don't see what's the harm. They may as well eat their last meal."

"Last meal?" Wooster's voice sounded small.

"Shut up, Wilson!" The private with the pan of vittles looked ready to shoot the guard.

"Well, they ought to know!" the guard defended himself. "Maj. McCain's seeing the general now for the execution order. He wants you boys shot at sunrise." He shook his head. "I can't see how you two could get in so much horse—"

"Just eat what Sgt. Pete sent. Nobody knows nothing yet." The private with the vittles unknotted our ropes, dragged blankets from the front of the wagon, and tossed Wooster and me each one. "Don't pay him any mind." But the private's misery spoke loud.

"Is it true? Is McCain—"

The private nodded. "He's with the general now." Then he shook his head. "It ain't right. It can't be right. You boys came to the hospital camp of your own accord. It's not like you run off home, not like real deserters." And then he backed out of the wagon.

Even then, Wooster remembered. "Thank Sgt. Pete for us, will you?"

The private caught Wooster's eye and swallowed hard. "You bet I will."

The fire outside our wagon gave enough light to find our plates. But we weren't hungry, no matter that it was the best grub either of us had seen in weeks. Sam Pete must've given us the best of the foraging or that meant for officers. That would send McCain into a fit. Even that knowledge didn't raise our hunger. The food grew cold and us with it.

I thought of what it would be like to face a firing squad. Would they blindfold us, or would we stare into the soldiers' eyes? I thought of Wooster, standing there on his one leg, and how neither of us should be here. Then I thought of Pa and Ma, of Mr. Heath and the Henrys. I thought of Emily. They'd never know what became of me. I remembered my promise to Aunt Sassy to come home—before my birthday—long ago already. I wondered if they'd let me write a letter home, and who I should write it to.

Before the watch changed we heard Katie Frances approach the guard. "A fine night it is, after all the rain, wouldn't you say, Private?"

"Yes, ma'am. Good to see them stars again. Good to see you again, Miss O'Leary."

"I'm just here to give these lads their medicine." I heard the smile in Katie Frances's voice. "I'll see myself in."

But the guard blocked her. "I'm sorry, Miss O'Leary. I can't let you do that. These boys are prisoners."

Katie Frances wasn't to be outdone. "I realize that, Private darlin', but they're also Col. Monroe's patients, and as long as they are, he prescribes their medicine."

"I don't know, ma'am. I'm under strict orders to—"

"As am I, Private—the very strictest orders. Now, if you'd like me to go and wake Col. Monroe, have him rise and dress, though it's the first he's taken to his bed in three days, I'll do so—just so he can march down here and explain to you that I should step up into this wagon and spoon this medicine into these wretched boys' mouths." She waited.

"No, no, I don't think you need to bring Col. Monroe down

here." There was a shuffling of feet. "I can't see as it will do any harm, nor any good, neither. Go on, then, Miss O'Leary."

"Thank you, Private, sir." And Katie Frances O'Leary, the Irish angel nurse and love light of Chap. Goforth's eyes, stepped up into the wagon. She looked like an angel, lit from the back as she was by the watchfire. She pulled out a bottle and spoon. "No complaining about this, now," she said loudly. "Tip your head back and take the full drop. There you are, now. That's it." She leaned closer and whispered. "Andrew is with the general now."

"Why?" we both asked.

"Is everything all right in there, Miss O'Leary?" The private lifted the wagon flap.

"Right as rain, Private, darlin'. Thank you very much!" Katie Frances sang. "I'm just astonished these two have not eaten the fine meal that's been provided them. And you so kind as to do it. Eat up boys! It's better than you'll see tomorrow."

"I don't reckon we'll see a meal tomorrow." Wooster pushed the plate away.

"Now don't be saying such!" Katie Frances fussed loudly. "You never know what the good Lord intends." Then she whispered, "Eat up and sleep all you can. Andrew's doing his best with the general. If it isn't enough we'll be back for you before morning."

"A way of escape?" Wooster pressed closer.

"A way of escape," she whispered and stepped down.

Fourteen

It was still dark when the guards dragged us from the wagon. For all our worry we must have fallen asleep. I don't even remember them calling our names. Wooster and I stumbled sleepily to the ground. The first blast of cold wind brought me to. My first thought was, *This is it—this is the end.*

"General's orders to see you fellas. Step smart." It was Sgt. Sam Pete.

"Sgt. Pete!" Wooster's hopes rose.

"Step smart, boy. The chaplain's been in an hour, done all he can." Wooster's one leg went weak. Sgt. Pete caught him just in time. "Stand tall, Wooster boy. Face up. You're a soldier." It took no more for Wooster to buck up. He put me to shame, seeing him take hold like that.

The guard at the general's tent saluted Sgt. Pete, raised the tent flap, and stepped aside.

The general sat, writing, in the pool of lantern light at his table. We stood, waited, wondered if he had signed our execution orders. At last he looked up, took us in, frowned.

"Sergeant, you are dismissed."

"Yes, sir!" Sgt. Pete cut a sharp salute, turned on his heel, and was gone. Shadows from the lantern danced crazily against the tent walls, blasted by the wind. The general still sat in full uniform. He'd never been to bed.

"You two have caused quite a stir in camp." He sounded tired. He lifted his chin, and his tone turned severe. "Maj. McCain has charged you with desertion, Wooster Gibbons. And you," he said as he looked to me, "with spying for the enemy." He paused, taking our measure. "I must say, neither of you look quite what I was expecting . . . though Maj. McCain did caution that I not be taken in by you." He frowned again.

"Col. Monroe and Chap. Goforth have both been to see me, each with something of a different story on your behalf." The general leaned back in his chair. "Now, I'd like to hear your story—one at a time."

Wooster and I looked at each other, then both started talking at once, running over each other with our words. The general held up his hand. "Let's start with you, Pvt. Gibbons." He motioned Wooster forward.

I stood back while Wooster hobbled a step ahead and spilled his story, starting with the 26th North Carolina's charge on Little Round Top at Gettysburg, part of Pickett's Brigade. "Twenty feet before the wall they shot me down. Two days I laid there, my leg wound festering in the heat. The flies was—were —terrible. So many others needed tending worse—just laid there, dying."

Wooster told about the capture of the 26th, or what was left of it, about the grueling trip in the July heat to Fort Delaware, the first leg by train, then the march overland. He told how Col. Albert Mitchell disguised himself as a private, stayed with his men, bolstered them, planned escapes, kept the men going while they watched their friends and brothers die, first from wounds, then from disease, and finally from lack of hope.

Wooster struggled to keep his voice steady. Even the general looked away. Wooster told about the day I identified Col. Mitchell as my cousin, how the Union guards dragged him off—they didn't know where—how the men of the 26th wanted to kill me for such a thing. I swallowed, better understanding what they'd lost that day.

The general seemed about to step in, but Wooster rushed on. "It was Robert brought us bread and soup from Mrs. Maynard —a rebel lady living in Delaware City. She baked money into the loaves, and slips of paper with her address. Only Robert didn't know about that."

What else hadn't I known?

"We used the money to bribe the guards the night of the escape. Sgt. McCain had it all planned out. He figured to take Robert down in a commotion and switch Robert's clothes with one of our men and him walk out like he was Robert. Those guards never looked too close to see who was coming and going. It all happened fast. We knocked Robert out to keep him quiet." Wooster glanced at me, uneasy.

"But that's when Sgt. McCain found Col. Mitchell's orders in the Testament Robert carried—escape plans coded between the lines of the Bible. Only we'd already sent our man out.

"Sgt. McCain wanted Robert dead. He blamed Robert for Col. Mitchell's dying and would have let him drown during the escape if the rest would've stood for it." Wooster shifted on his crutch. "But we wouldn't. Col. Mitchell's orders was clear in that Testament. He said Robert was his blood kin and that the men of the 26th were to extend him every courtesy, to see to his safety and guard him with their life if need be.

"Col Mitchell had the consumption, sir. He had it long already, and any man from the 26th can vouch for that. His death wasn't Robert's doing." Wooster shifted on his crutch.

"Sgt. McCain told us he'd gone back to the cellar but that Robert was gone—escaped. He said we couldn't trust him, that he might bring the Federals to the Maynards' door. He told us to move out, and fast." Wooster looked at me. "We believed him."

Wooster drew a breath. "But Sgt. McCain had left Robert tied and gagged in the cellar. He kept Mr. Maynard from going down there by going himself for any little thing the Maynards needed—acting helpful and grateful. The Maynards are old. They appreciated the help. It was a cellar they don't use much anymore."

I didn't remember any of it.

"Where were the other men during this time?" The general kept his eyes pinned on Wooster.

"They took off late that first night. Sgt. McCain said we dared not wait, that we should all split up in groups of two or three, make our way south, toward home, hook up with a new regiment soon as we could. Sgt. McCain and I were to be the last, to follow a couple days later."

"You didn't go with McCain?"

Wooster's face flamed, despite the cold. "He said I'd slow him down, make it too easy for us to be spotted and picked up as escaped prisoners. But he said not to worry—he'd find a way, and we'd work it out together. He left three days later, took Robert's horse before daylight, before we knew."

"Still you waited. Why?" The general was patient. I wished he'd let Wooster sit down.

Wooster colored again. "There wasn't much choice at first, sir. The Maynards were willing to hide me as long as they could, and help me find a way home. But when Mr. Maynard found

119

Robert, near dead and boiling with typhus, I had to stay. It was Col. Mitchell's orders."

The general waited, considering Wooster. "And how did you get to this field hospital?"

"People helped us, moved us from one house to another, always a little south." It sounded for all the world like a sort of reverse Underground Railroad, and I remembered the rumbling wagon, the talk of the driver. "Robert was still pretty sick, but I knew from Mrs. Maynard that he wanted to get South, not far from where I live in North Carolina, to find his ma. So I figured to tell folks we're brothers—the same as I'd planned with Sgt. McCain back in the cellar, when I thought we'd be taking Robert with us. Only now I'd say we were both wounded from Gettysburg, going home. And it worked. Folks helped us. But we needed medicine. So we stopped here, because of the doctors. I never figured I'd see Sgt.—Major McCain again."

The general sat back in his chair. After a time he motioned Wooster to a camp stool. "Sit down, Private."

"Yes, sir. Thank you, sir."

"And you—" he looked at his papers, then looked back at me. "Robert Glover—are you enlisted in either the Confederate or Union armies, or have you ever been?"

"No, sir."

"Have you ever borne arms against the Confederacy or tried to harm a Confederate soldier?"

"No, sir."

"How old are you, young man?"

"Eighteen in July, sir."

"Do you have anything to add to this man's statement?"

I thought hard. I didn't want to die, but I needed to live with myself. "I didn't mean to help those men escape. I wouldn't have done it if I'd known. I only went to Fort Delaware because my cousin wrote, asking me to see about her father, Col. Mitchell," I said. Wooster shot me a pleading look.

"I see. And you think that statement will help your case?" The general raised his eyebrows.

"No, sir. But it's the truth."

The general nodded. "I knew Col. Mitchell. He was a gentleman, even among officers." He sighed. "Fortunately for you, Glover, you are not bearing arms for the Union. Otherwise I'd have little choice. Unfortunately for you both, you have no proof of your story, other than Col. Monroe's report that you arrived here in a state of semiconsciousness and that this private has lost a leg." He looked at Wooster and back to me.

"Chap. Goforth tells me he has known you and your family for some time, Glover. He believes your story." The general stood up. "Unfortunately, it is your word against the word of a decorated Confederate officer." He shook his head. "If you had a witness, the letter you mentioned from Col. Mitchell's daughter, this Testament—anything that might corroborate your story . . . as it is—"

"The Testament?" Wooster's head shot up. "I have the Testament, sir—with Col. Mitchell's orders. They're in code. It got a little wet, but I have it."

"You have it?" I was surprised.

"Explain yourself, Private." The general didn't believe it.

"I kept it. Sgt. McCain stuffed the Testament with the plans inside Robert's shirt back at the fort before we escaped. He said it was our insurance policy that he'd cooperate—if the plans were found on him he'd be hanged—as a traitor to the Union. He wrapped the Testament in an oilskin he got off the guard we bribed, so it wouldn't get wet, so it could be read."

I remembered the weight of a package on my chest. Wooster looked to the general, then back to me.

"Remember when I took your gag off in the cellar that night? I took the oilskin out of your shirt. You said it weighed heavy on you. I didn't want to leave it on the floor. It didn't seem right to leave a Bible sitting on the cellar floor like that." He looked back to the general.

"And you still have it, Pvt. Gibbons?" The general waited.

"Yes, sir." Wooster stood. "It's in my bedroll, sir."

"And where is your bedroll, Private?"

Wooster thought a minute. "In Sgt. Sam Pete's supply wagon, sir. In the front corner, near the barrel of apples."

The general raised his eyebrows. "I hope to God you're right, Private."

$\mathcal{F}$ifteen

$\mathcal{W}$e heard that when the guard roused Sgt. Pete from a sound sleep to rummage through his supply wagon for Wooster's bedroll he was fit to be tied and let it be known in language that would've put a waterman to shame. But once he realized the oilskin bundle inside might somehow help Wooster, even save him, Sgt. Pete couldn't tear the wagon bed apart fast enough.

The general took his time reading the code penned between the lines of the Testament. I marveled that Cousin Albert had been strong enough to write at all.

At last the general looked up. He sat and stared. We waited, not knowing what his silence meant. Finally, he spoke. "Do you know the Scriptures, Glover?" It was a question I didn't expect.

"Yes, sir. Some, sir."

"And how is that? You go to church?" The general waited.

"Yes, sir. And, my family—we kept an evening read, sir."

The general nodded. He laid the Testament down, open to the pages Cousin Albert had encoded. He spoke quietly, without looking up, and I wasn't sure but that he spoke to himself. "Do you know the Scripture, 'There is no greater gift . . .'"

Wooster's head shot up, and he finished, "Than a man lay down his life for his friends."

The general looked at Wooster and half smiled, a tired smile. "Yes. You understand that, Pvt. Gibbons. Col. Mitchell understood it very well, very well indeed."

Then, just as day broke, the brigadier general scratched his pen across paper, signing our pardons and Wooster's discharge.

"As soon as the hospital is in a position to do so, I'll have Col. Monroe see that you boys are on your way to Salem." He drummed his fingers across his table, then looked up. "If the camp is, indeed, visited by Union troops, as Col. Monroe expects, all of this may change. In the meantime I believe you could both do with some breakfast, and I, some sleep."

"Thank you, sir. Thank you." Wooster and I could barely look at each other inside the general's tent, and once outside, couldn't stop looking at each other—wondering if we were real, if the day was real, slapping each other's backs for the relief of it all.

Word spread through the camp like smallpox. In no time Maj. McCain was on the rampage, demanding to see the general. We could hear the lieutenant stationed outside the general's quarters ordering McCain away. We heard Sgt. Pete explaining that the general had just gone to bed, half soothing Maj. McCain, half smirking, suggesting that Maj. McCain might like to rest himself, that the general was certain to be speaking with him sooner—and longer—than the major might like.

Wooster and I'd gone looking for Chap. Goforth and Katie Frances when McCain found us. We didn't hear him coming. He pushed from behind, jerked Wooster off the ground, slamming both of us into a supply wagon. "I don't know how you weaseled out of that, you lying little scoundrel. But enjoy your reprieve. You won't always have the general, or Col. Monroe, or that chaplain to hide behind." He spat in my face. "Either of you."

"Maj. McCain." It was Chap. Goforth, standing in the lane. "The general will see you now." McCain dropped Wooster. I steadied him with my shoulder. I'd have gone after McCain then, but Chap. Goforth pushed me back. "You have other battles to fight. Leave this one to the general."

"I thought the general was sleeping."

"He is." The chaplain smiled. "I'm sure Maj. McCain will learn that soon enough. It just looked as though you needed a little time." Then he turned serious. "You have your papers?" I nodded.

"Pardon and discharge!" Wooster straightened his collar, adjusted his crutch. "I'm going home just as soon as there's a way —free and clear."

Chap. Goforth smiled. "Thank God. There is a way. Or there will be, as soon as the colonel authorizes it. Follow me." He wouldn't tell us where he was going, but there was a spring in his step—one I hadn't seen since we'd met in camp. We passed the supply wagons, the hospital tents, even the latrine ditches.

"Where are we going?" I panted, trying to keep up with him.

"Just follow me!" Chaplain's voice nearly sang. "There's an old friend of yours here, Robert." He led us past the makeshift pen for mules and to the line of horses, all taking their feed, then stopped abruptly. We nearly bumped into him. "Do you remember when you and Jeremiah ran North that Christmas Eve?"

Nearly five years ago. I nodded. "I'm not likely to forget."

"Do you remember I told you that I'd arranged for the

conductor at Mount Pleasant to find you, that I knew you two had hidden in the bell tower?"

"Yes, but—"

Chap. Goforth shook his head. "Just listen. I ran slaves from safe house to safe house. My network covered three counties. I knew all the conductors in the area."

"You stole slaves?" Wooster's mouth nearly fell open, hearing such for the first time. Then he turned to me. "And you stole slaves?"

Chap. Goforth reached for Wooster's arm. "We're trusting you, Wooster. Don't let us down."

"No, sir. I won't, sir." But he looked confused.

"There was a boy there—a boy who helped you after his father was injured," Chaplain kept on.

I remembered that boy. He did find us, did help us. But he tricked me. Just before he left Jeremiah and me near a Quaker farm Christmas night he told me to say good-bye to Stargazer. I had no choice. The pattyrollers were already out looking for runaways. "He took my horse." I'd never forgiven him, never understood how somebody who risked his life helping people could take such advantage. Stargazer was the best horse I'd ever known or imagined, the first and only horse that was ever mine, my friend.

"That's right. And what he did was wrong. But he didn't know what else to do at the time."

"He could have left him with the Quaker family—he was the one told us how to get there. He knew where they lived! He went there himself! He as good as stole him from me."

"He brought Stargazer to me."

"To you?" Could I be hearing right?

Chap. Goforth took my arm. "When I enlisted as chaplain.

126

Every chaplain had to provide his own horse—if we were to have one at all. When Timothy knew I was joining up, he brought Stargazer to me."

I couldn't take it in. I never knew his name. I turned away, but Chap. Goforth still had hold of my arm.

Chaplain watched me, and all I could do was stare stupidly back.

"You've had Stargazer all this time?" A wall, thick, like stone, grew up between us.

"I swear to you, Robert, I never knew I had him until then. I'd have done all in my power to get him to you if I'd known. By that time the war had started. There was no way."

And then it came to me. "You mean—Stargazer's here? Now?"

The smile on Chap. Goforth's face shone broad. "I've been waiting for you to get well enough to bring you to him."

And then I saw him. Black, like a raven's wing. Milk-white blaze on his forehead, the cause of his name. He wasn't as tall as I'd remembered, but I was taller now. His coat needed brushing; his mane and tail needed combing. He'd been through a war, grown skittish, danced along the line. But still the most beautiful horse I'd ever seen, ever known.

I walked to him slowly, whispering his name, as I'd done all those years ago, when I'd first sat on my grandfather's gate and spoke gentling words, getting to know him. Andrew and Wooster stood back, giving me time. Stargazer whinnied and shied, then stood, his head slightly off center, staring back. I could tell that he had some recollection, made some connection to the past, maybe didn't know what. Well, there was time now, all the time in the world. And I would take it. I buried my face in his neck.

Chap. Goforth gave Wooster and me a corner in his tent. If men needed to come for prayer or counsel we ducked out, giving them time and space. But it was safer, far from McCain.

We heard that McCain was under disciplinary action. He might have been investigated more thoroughly or dishonorably discharged in another time. But there was a war on, and every man was needed. We steered clear of him for as long as possible.

Whatever route those Union troops took to Petersburg, they missed us. After two more days the entire hospital breathed easier, and the general and his officers pulled out.

Wooster wanted to ride for Salem right away. I needed to get to Ma and Emily. But Col. Monroe couldn't see letting a horse go, not with the army's shortages. And in truth I wasn't up to the ride yet. Spending time with Stargazer was like a spring tonic in the building winter. Somehow I knew that when the time came we'd all be ready.

To get reacquainted with Stargazer I repeated everything I'd done when Grandfather had first given him to me. The second day I groomed him, brushed his coat till it shone, his mane and tail till they felt like feathers in my hands. I fed and watered and mucked after him, did everything but help him breathe. The sergeant in charge of horses didn't mind. He was pressed to keep up with all he had, and they were chores he didn't have to tend to.

The third day I saddled and walked him around the camp. He shied at every little noise. I couldn't imagine what he'd seen during his years of war, what he'd gone through. I knew Chap. Goforth had not mistreated him. It wasn't in his nature. But he'd probably been ridden by any number of men since he'd been mine—either while he was with Timothy or here, in the army. I didn't want to own him. I'd never wanted us to be master and slave, but best friends. By the end of the week we exercised—trotting, then galloping. There were limits, limits I hated to keep. But they were posted for the safety of the field hospital. I kept to the rules. I didn't want to come up before the colonel again, didn't want to meet McCain outside of camp somewhere.

Life became almost comfortable. While I worked with Stargazer, Wooster repaired harnesses and mended bridles, polished saddles. He said he loved the smell of leather, that it put him in mind of Salem and the harness shop. "I might get work there when I get home, or with one of the cobblers. I could live in the single brothers' house—for now. Leather'd be a good trade for me," he said. I marveled that Wooster always seemed to know what he was about, what he would be about, and how he'd get there.

Because of the siege outside Petersburg, not so many wounded poured into the field hospital. Chap. Goforth got more sleep and Katie Frances's smile sprang easier, but for the worry for her family back in Petersburg. Even Col. Monroe, now that the truth was out, stopped giving Wooster and me such a hard time, though he still kept Katie Frances trailing him nearly every minute of every day.

One night I asked Chap. Goforth why he didn't marry Katie Frances. The question took him by surprise, and then he grinned. "It shows?"

"Like a watchfire!" I said. "On both of you." I couldn't understand it. "You're wasting time. You could be sharing a tent with her instead of Wooster and me."

He groaned. "When you put it that way . . ." He turned his back and busied himself with papers. "In time. After the war

... perhaps."

"You know Col. Monroe is after her. She's fending him off, but ..."

"Now isn't a good time to get married. Not with the war."

"This war could go on a long time, Andrew—Chap. Goforth. I see what you two have. Why don't you—"

"It's not your affair, Robert. Stay out of it." Never had he spoken so sharply.

"But—"

"No more!" And he walked out. It was the first I'd ever thought Chap. Andrew Goforth a foolish man.

I carried water buckets for the hospital tents as I grew stronger, even helped the burial detail after the third week. Sometimes that meant burying stacks of sawed-off arms and legs, fingers and toes, instead of whole men. Gruesome work.

My path crossed Katie Frances's many times each day. We talked and joked. Sometimes we talked about her family back in Petersburg. I could feel her fear for them. She never failed to give me a smile that made me want to dance a jig. Still, they were nothing compared to the smiles she shone on Chap. Goforth. She laughed and gave a wink when I asked her one evening why she didn't push him to the altar. But when I came behind her, unexpected, not ten minutes later, she was wiping away tears. I backed off, quietly as I could. It was the first time I wanted to punch Chap. Andrew Goforth.

Still, I was glad to be with Stargazer, glad that he and I both felt stronger, more sure of ourselves each day. I knew that growing strength was my ticket to Emily and Ma. I sometimes forgot about Andrew and Katie Frances and their foolish dance, nearly forgot about McCain, and the war. I didn't care about the rumors flying that more enemy troops had been spotted, headed our way. I didn't care about any of those things—until it was almost too late.

Sixteen

"f anything should happen," Chap. Goforth said, "now—in the next few days—anytime . . . I want you to take Wooster and Stargazer and go."

"What do you mean—'if anything happens'?"

"If Union troops invade—take over. Take Stargazer. You and Wooster ride to Salem, and Ashland." Then he walked outside the tent, into the night. It took a while for what he'd said to sink in. When it did, I followed him.

"I can't leave you, Andrew. I can't take Stargazer and leave you with Union troops! He's your only way out of here."

He shook his head. "They won't hurt the wounded or those tending them. They'll likely capture the hospital and add their wounded to ours—commandeer our doctors and nurses. They may take our medicine. But they're not likely to hurt us or move us. We're noncombatants." He pressed my shoulder. "But you and Wooster are no longer patients. Just because the general gave you and Wooster papers of pardon doesn't mean Union soldiers won't send you both to prison."

"What about you—and Katie Frances?"

"Katie Frances and I have talked. This is what we both want.

My place is here, with these men. I won't leave them, and she re-fuses to leave . . . she refuses to leave."

"You mean she refuses to leave you." Why wouldn't he say it?

"I've tried to make her leave, help her find a way back into Petersburg to her family, or to go with you. But she won't."

"She won't go because she loves you, because she'll stand by you even if you won't stand by her."

"I would protect Katie Frances with my life!" I'd raised the ire in Chap. Goforth.

"Oh, you'd die for her all right," I said sarcastically. "You just won't marry her!" He didn't answer. "What is it, Chap. Goforth? Are you ashamed that she's Irish? Is she just an Irish tarter to you, like McCain said?"

Andrew Goforth, Confederate chaplain, reddened nearly purple. He clenched his fists to a knuckled white, took two steps toward me, planting his face inches from mine. He spoke low, but there was no mistaking his growing rage. "Don't you ever, ever insult Katie Frances!"

"I could never insult her like you have!" I shot back, too loud. "She's given you what every man in this camp would give his right arm for! And you've thrown it in her face, like you're just too good for her!"

"You don't know what you're talking about." He shuddered, trying to get hold of himself.

"I saw you, Andrew! That night in the tent—I saw you kiss her! And it's not what I think that matters!" He turned to walk away. "It's what Katie Frances thinks! You don't deserve her!"

He stopped then. When he turned to face me I saw the color drain as fast as it had flamed. All the weariness of the war lay in his eyes. "She's much too good for me. She will always be too good for me."

"Then why?" I wanted to shake him. "Why don't you marry her?"

"Because I'm a chaplain," he pleaded, as if that explained everything. "In case you hadn't noticed, there is a war going on—a war we are losing!" He ran his hands through his hair, spread them out before me.

"Look around you, Robert! Look at the men I serve! They're wounded men—broken in body and spirit. If the surgeons are able to patch them up, we send them back into battle—to be shot again! Once they're beyond patching we send them home to their wives and mothers—to do what? Burden and drain their families for the rest of their lives? Be pitied by the women who love them—loved them when they were whole men?" He looked away, and when he spoke again, I doubted he spoke to me.

"Sometimes I think it's the lucky ones, the blessed ones, who are released from their bodies now, who die on the battlefield. At least they don't have to stare into their women's eyes of pity the rest of their days!"

"It's your pride!" I couldn't grasp it.

He threw up his hands in anguish. "I could end up like them—wounded and maimed. Then how would I provide for her? I wouldn't be the man she loves now. I'd be able to give her nothing!"

"Is that what you tell these men—you, their 'spiritual guide'?" He looked away again, passing his hands over his eyes. "And what if you're not wounded? What if you let this time go by? Or what if neither of you make it out of this war? What if it's all the time either of you have?"

"She'll make it. She'll live. And then she'll be free to marry someone whole." He choked on the words. He didn't see Katie

Frances step from the night into the firelight. He didn't see Wooster, leaning into his crutch, step in front of her, shielding her from the man who wrenched her heart in his hands. But we all heard what Wooster said next, soft as it was.

"Didn't the Lord say it is better to enter into life maimed than not to enter into life at all?"

Chap. Goforth spun. "Wooster—"

"Seems to me you're not entering into life at all, Chaplain. Seems to me you're letting the death you see around you make decisions for you."

"Wooster—" Chap. Goforth stepped forward, started again, but Wooster cut him off.

"If I get home—when I get home—I'll work a trade. It's a different trade than the one I'd planned before the war. But it's one I can do. I can make a living—a good living. It seems to me preaching is a good trade for a man—wounded or not, one leg or two, one eye or two. I can't see as it matters. But I aim to find a woman to love me—not from pity for my missing leg but for love of me. Because I can make her happy—happy in some way every day. And I'll provide for her. I'll be more whole than you are now, Chap. Goforth."

It was a long speech, the longest I'd ever heard from Wooster outside of our defense before the colonel.

Katie Frances gazed at Wooster as though he'd grown ten feet tall. "That is the most eloquent sermon I've heard in all these years of war, Wooster Gibbons. This woman you will marry, she will be the happiest woman, the proudest woman this country is likely to know." She reached out, pressed Wooster's arm, planted a kiss on his cheek, and walked away, never looking at Chap. Goforth.

The chaplain stood, stricken. "Wooster, please . . . " he

mumbled and then tried again. "Wooster, can you forgive me?"

Wooster stared hard at him, considered, waited. "You mean forgive your pride and arrogance, Chaplain? Your doubting spirit?"

Chap. Goforth's color burned. "Yes. That's what I'm asking. Forgive my pride and arrogance." He waited.

"Your lack of faith." Wooster pressed his ground.

Andrew swallowed. "My lack of faith," he confessed, meaning it.

Wooster shifted his crutch, blinked, waited longer, considered. "I will, Chap. Goforth . . . if—" and he waited another long minute—"if you'll stop acting the fool and go after her."

Now Chap. Goforth blinked, and waited. Seconds ticked by. A string of emotions passed over his face, one chasing the other. His first couple of steps were short, uncertain. The next landed him in Wooster's arms. He wrung Wooster's hands. And though he didn't speak, he took off in the direction of Katie Frances.

"In case you're interested, I forgive you, too, Chap. Goforth!" I called, only half sarcastically.

Wooster hobbled over, punched my arm, and grinned. "Looks like we might need a new place to bunk."

Col. Monroe bit his pride and married Chap. Andrew Goforth and Miss Katie Frances O'Leary the next afternoon. Every man in camp fumed with jealousy. Every man in camp cheered them on—except Col. Monroe and of course Maj. McCain, who hadn't returned with the scouting party.

Wooster and I bunked with Sgt. Pete. The conversation slacked off, but the food improved. Seeing Andrew and Katie Frances together made me pine for Ma and Pa, made me want to get along to Ashland, to find Ma and Emily. It worked a kind of homesickness on Wooster too.

"I'll walk," said Wooster. "I'll be walking on this leg the rest of my life. I may as well go now. And I've a mind to be in Salem by Christmas."

"Is some girl waiting for you there?" I teased him but was curious all the same.

Wooster colored. "Not yet. But the sooner I get home, the sooner there will be." He stared into the fire, and the light of memory came over him.

"I want to be in Salem for the Christmas Eve service. I want to be there for our Moravian lovefeast—our candles, the coffee and buns, the hymns." And then he laughed. "As if there'd be coffee now—or sugar, either—but maybe there will be candles.

"The old organ plays—it's a rare beauty, that organ—and each of those pipes sings. When I was a kid I pumped the bellows for it—up and down, up and down. It was an honor to hold that job . . . Every man, woman, and child holds a lighted candle while we sing." Wooster sang, every note perfect, "'Morning Star, O cheering sight. When Thou camest how dark earth's night. Morning Star, O cheering sight.' . . . We raise them high, and call to mind that the Christ Child came as the light into a dark world . . . It's my favorite service of the year—all cold outside—all light inside." Wooster looked at me. "A lot like us—if we have Christ living inside us."

I looked at my hands. I wasn't sure I knew what that felt like.

"I aim to be home for that," Wooster said. "We've got a month."

I didn't know as we'd make Salem in a month on foot—even if we left that minute—and I didn't want to leave without Stargazer. But Wooster meant to do it. We tried talking it over with Chaplain and Mrs. Goforth—which didn't do a lot of good.

It seemed they'd forgotten a war was on. Wooster said we should pray about it. And I guess he did, and maybe God answered, because neither of us could have planned what happened next.

We'd nearly forgotten the Union troops until, just about dusk the next day, a man with dispatches rode in hard, the fear of God sprung between his eyes. Sentries pulled him from the saddle. He'd strapped himself in, determined to ride till he reached us. He wasn't inside the colonel's tent ten minutes, but the drum rolled and orders to circle supply wagons, post double lanterns and double sentries flew through the camp.

The Union brigade had moved on, but their hundred-man foraging party on horseback flanked their sides, wandering far afield. Sgt. Pete said our men hadn't seen theirs until too late. "Sharpshooters got our foraging party—every man—all but the man who tied himself in." Sgt. Pete looked away, grim. "They'll likely reach us before the watch changes."

Seventeen

Chap. Goforth commandeered Stargazer and led him alongside the medical supply wagon, where I helped Katie Frances sort the last of the powders into packets. I turned my back as she hid the packets in pockets sewn beneath her skirts, while she fussed, "Pray the scoundrels don't search women! No sense handing them the medicines our dying men need!"

Chap. Goforth grabbed my shirt sleeve and ordered, "Find Wooster. Have him ride with you. Don't let him out of your sight. Drift out of our lantern light as the watch changes. I'll distract the sentry. Ride hard for the river. Where it's shallow—swim across, follow it south, and then southwest. We can't be far from the North Carolina line—maybe even below it. There's a bedroll and kit—keep them dry."

"They could turn aside, still miss us," I said.

Chap. Goforth jerked me from the wagon, shoved a jacket into my arms, and clamped my hands over Stargazer's reins. "They're coming, Robert. Don't you feel it?"

"Feel wh—?" Then I did—a pounding of the earth in the distance, a sort of rumbling, like thunder, growing steadily under my feet, coming from the earth instead of above it. I couldn't hear anything for the cracking of whips, the creaking of wagons, the braying of mules, and the ugly epithets thrown to whoever listened—all our own. But I felt it. It traveled through my boots and up my two legs.

"Go! Now!" The chaplain shook me.

"I can't leave you! I can't leave you and Katie Frances."

"If you don't take this horse the Union will—unless they shoot him first. They'll send you and Wooster to prison—where neither of you are likely to survive! Find Wooster."

Chap. Goforth pushed me toward the saddle, but I shook my head. "No! No! Col. Monroe will blame you for our taking Stargazer."

Katie Frances Goforth must have been listening. She rose from her tucking and pinning, leaned out the wagon, and kissed me firmly on the mouth. "We'll be seeing you after this war, Robert Glover. You're not to worry—they'd not dare to take a woman prisoner, nasty though they be. And Andrew's never borne arms. But you and Wooster are another matter. Your encoded Testament will do you no good with the Yankees, and Wooster'd not survive a prison camp. You know that. For all that is good and holy, go, and look after your mam and that girl whose name you can't speak without blushing; finish the work you've been given to do. Let us finish ours."

It was good I stood outside the lantern light. I didn't want anyone to see my face. I couldn't speak. I didn't know how to move, couldn't leave them.

"Go! You owe that to Wooster," Chap. Goforth urged, pushing Stargazer from the wagon's edge. "And God go with you." Stargazer reared and shied. It was all I could do to steady him. He was ready to run. All the days of gentling him couldn't erase his memories of war, the instinct this pounding in the earth brought him.

I rode back along the column of wagons, searching faces in the lantern light, looking for Sgt. Pete and Wooster. They were near the rear, one of the last commissary wagons.

"Wooster," I called, "ride with me."

"I'm staying with Sgt. Pete—he needs me. We're circling the camp with wagons."

I hadn't figured on Wooster turning me down. "Chap. Goforth needs you. He sent me for you—said to bring your bedroll—too many sick to watch. He needs us both." I was surprised how smooth and easy the lie came.

"Go on, Wooster boy. It's a good thing. I don't want you outside the circle with those bluebellies comin', anyhow. Better to be up with the wounded."

"But—"

"Go on now! Chaplain's called you." Sgt. Pete sounded gruff, but it was plain he hated to see Wooster go.

I rode up alongside the wagon. Wooster reached for my arm and threw his leg over Stargazer, then pulled hard to right himself. Sgt. Pete tossed Wooster his bedroll, and I felt the oilskin lump of the Testament through the thin blanket, the thing Wooster never let out of his sight.

"Hold tight!" I called over my shoulder, doing my best to steady Stargazer, doing my best to steady the pounding in my chest, my head. We walked ahead, edging the light. Wooster asked nothing as we faded into darkness. He didn't speak when we felt our way through the night, skirting trees that loomed black and gnarled over the river's edge. He braced his bedroll as Stargazer stepped into the frigid water, and held tight to my waist as we swam across, a long ripple in the cold moonlight.

We held our feet as high as we could, as long as we could, trying to keep them from the icy water, swimming, begging God in the night, and finally climbed up the opposite bank.

In a little copse of trees we clung to Stargazer, shivering. I pulled Andrew's jacket, the Confederate jacket he'd pushed into my arms, tight around me, and we listened and listened, straining against the stillness.

We saw the sudden flash from the Union repeating rifles even before we heard the crack of gunfire. Stargazer reared time and again, and would have bolted had I not reined him in sharp. Too far away to separate one voice from another, the din of horses and mules, the screams of men too ill to defend themselves—the turmoil shredded our souls.

I steadied Stargazer again—I don't know how. Helpless, we watched the stray flashes of rifle fire—sharp and quick, the sudden flares made by lanterns extinguished or overturned. Sometimes a flame would shoot high—something afire—maybe a blanket. It would flare for a minute, then go out. It never lasted long, and maybe that was good. We prayed that was good—surrender and not slaughter.

"Let it be! Oh, God, let it be surrender!" I wanted to soothe Wooster, but it was me crying, praying out loud in a way I hadn't prayed for—for so long I had no memory. I don't know when Stargazer finally settled, how long we stood there, or when I dropped the reins. But long into the quiet he led us away.

I came to when I heard Wooster urge in my ear, "Steady, boy! Steady." I thought he was talking to me before I woke up enough to realize Stargazer was slipping, stepping, sliding down a steep bank. I picked up the reins and helped best I could, till we reached more gently rolling ground, flatter, along a stream bank. The moon had crossed the sky. I'd no idea how long I'd slept. I couldn't believe I'd slept—not when Andrew and Katie Frances might be—

"Robert! Robert! Wake up!" Wooster was surely talking to me now, but I wanted to shut him out. "Robert!" He jabbed me in the sides, shook my shoulder. And he wouldn't stop. But I didn't answer him.

Next I knew Wooster stood on the ground. I didn't know how he got there. He'd taken Stargazer's reins, was doing something with them. Wooster pulled his crutch out of the saddlebag, and I laughed. We'd just been in battle—almost—and we had a crutch in our saddlebag. No rifle, but a crutch. It was perfect. I sat on a horse meant for a Confederate chaplain, who might or might not be dead. And I was whole—able bodied, but no soldier—after a battle I didn't fight in, or a surrender I didn't surrender—with a crutch.

Once I started laughing I couldn't stop. Pretty soon I couldn't remember why I was laughing or what was funny, but I kept on laughing just the same. Wooster shook me, harder and harder. I laughed, louder and louder, clean off the edge of reason, till he pulled me to the ground and slapped me. Still I laughed. I laughed so hard I might have split in two if Wooster hadn't socked me in my jaw.

I stopped laughing and rubbed my jaw. That's when I remembered Katie Frances's kiss. I stopped laughing and started shaking—from cold, from fear for Andrew and Katie Frances, from I don't know what. And then I cried. And Wooster cried with me. We sat in a heap on the ground, crying, shaking, like there was no end to it all.

It was near daybreak when, finally spent, we fell quiet—so spent and so cold we couldn't move, even if we'd had a mind to. We might have frozen to death if it was just one of us. Stargazer nuzzled my ear, my cheek, bit my hair. I looked at Wooster. He slept now, a tangle over his stump and leg, sprawled across the frozen ground, looking more dead than alive.

I pulled my legs out, rubbed life into them, felt my toes. Beyond Stargazer stood a building, tall and dark against the breaking sky, and a waterwheel, edging the stream.

I shook Wooster. He didn't move. I shook him harder. "Wooster! Wooster, wake up!" Still he didn't move, and his limpness scared me. I took hold of the stirrup on Stargazer's saddle and pulled myself up, stomped my feet, rubbed my arms, then went to work on Wooster.

It wasn't clear if Wooster was dead tired and sleeping—or if he'd lost consciousness. "Stargazer," I soothed, pulling Wooster to his leg, pushing him up. "We've got to get Wooster across your back—get him into that mill—warm him up. Help me, Stargazer." Somehow, we managed it.

I led Stargazer inside, Wooster hanging over his back.

The mill stood empty, except for a woodstove in a corner boxed off from the rest. It looked like the owner had built himself a storage room with the comforts of home—a coffee pot, a pallet on the floor, a tin cup and plate. I led Stargazer to the door of the small room, pulled Wooster off, and dragged him to the pallet, wrapping both our blankets tight around him.

There was no way of knowing if anyone would come to the mill that day, if the miller lived there, if he'd gone home, or if he'd moved on. Lots of mills had been destroyed, shut down by the Federals. I'd heard that, even in Maryland. With all the foraging from both armies few farmers in the South had wheat left to mill, and mills didn't run for customers that never came. Starting a fire in the stove seemed risky. It might draw attention. But one look at Wooster's pale and chalky skin told me there was no choice.

I blessed whoever'd left the small stash of firewood, split to size, on the floor. I checked the stove and pipe, pulled out a bird's nest, glad for it; the mill had been abandoned a while.

Once the fire sputtered, caught, and blazed inside the stove, the little room warmed quickly. I pulled off Wooster's boot, rubbed his foot and calf, hoping to rub some life into him. The wood couldn't last long, but I didn't want to leave him to go hunt for more. He didn't move, not a twitch, and I began to worry. I wished I'd thought to bring food, but there was no time. I hardly knew I moaned.

Stargazer whinnied. I looked up, fearful somebody might be coming. I checked the mill, looked through cracks between the boards, but there was no sign of anyone. "It's all right, Stargazer. He'll come around. He's got to." When I knelt once more by Wooster, Stargazer whinnied again, tossing his head in the doorway.

And that is what made me see. His saddlebag—both saddlebags bulged against the doorframe. Why hadn't I realized it before? "Good boy, Stargazer! Good boy!" I could barely pull up the flap in my eagerness. Oats. Oats in one. I cried out for joy— knowing Andrew had thought of that, provided for Stargazer even before he brought him to me. The other bag was stuffed with food, rations and things he must have pilfered from the commissary—or Sgt. Pete. I looked at Wooster and knew Sgt. Pete would have given anything he had to help Wooster. In the bottom was a little pouch of tea, tied with a hair ribbon—a gift from Katie Frances.

I nearly choked in my thankfulness. "Thank You, Lord," I prayed out loud. And the sound startled me. It came strange

145

and foreign to my ears. I swallowed. It was just so good, so unexpected.

I grabbed the coffee pot from the floor and ran outside, washed it in the stream, dipped it into the icy water, and carried it back to the stove. I'd use some for tea and some to wash Wooster's face. Maybe it would bring him around.

I wondered where Andrew and Katie Frances and Sgt. Pete were now—if they were prisoners, if they were still alive. What happened to all those wounded men? Surely the Union wouldn't murder surgeons and wounded soldiers in a field hospital. Surely they could see it was a hospital. We'd posted double lanterns. Even in the dark they should have been able to see the red flags posted everywhere with all that light. But it was war, and I'd already learned that bad things happen in war, things that should never happen. The skirmish hadn't lasted long. I needed to hope, to believe they were alive and safe.

All morning Wooster lay without opening his eyes, without moving, his chest rising and falling just a little. The firewood was gone before noon. After feeding Stargazer and leading him to the creek to drink his fill, I took him along to comb the nearby woods, searching for fallen limbs. I had no axe, not even a hatchet. I swung longer limbs against stone outcroppings till I got a crack big enough to step on, then wrenched the limb in two, two again, and two more.

When we returned Wooster lay as still as ever. I kept the fire going through the night and slept on the floor, using Stargazer's saddle for a headrest. It was the warmest I'd been in a while—till the fire died near morning. Even then we were out of the wind, and the floor was drier than the tarps in the hospital tents had been. There was enough food to last four more days—eight if we divided them in half, or if Wooster didn't wake up.

146

But I pushed that thought away, determined to pour more of Katie Frances's slippery elm tea down Wooster's throat, determined that he would get well and we'd ride on to Salem. I wasn't sure of the day, but I guessed it to be early December. If there was any way to get Wooster home in time for his Christmas Eve, I'd do it. "Please, God," I prayed, "let Wooster make it home." I didn't even pray for me, for Ma or Emily. I was afraid to ask too much.

Late that second day Wooster's color perked up. Near morning he opened his eyes, saw me filling the wood stove. "Heat feels good," he said.

"Hey! It's good to see your ugly face!" I nearly shouted for the gladness of it. "Here, have some tea." I helped him sit enough not to slosh the tea down his front. He sipped the hot liquid on his own, and I thought my heart would burst out of my chest. "You're gonna be all right, Wooster. You're gonna be all right."

He looked at me like I'd gone mad. "'Course I am. I'm on my way home—in time for Christmas Eve."

"In time for Christmas Eve." I laughed. "If there's a way, we'll make it. I swear it."

It took more doing—more rest for Wooster, more firewood trips for Stargazer and me. I set some rabbit snares and speared a fish in the stream, then roasted them on a little spit I built in the woodstove. I didn't mention the rations Andrew had stored in the saddlebag. We might need those later, and we weren't likely to find a room with a woodstove between here and Salem. On the fourth day Wooster sat up. That night he hobbled outside, testing his leg and the strength in his arms.

"A couple more days and I'll be ready to ride," he said.

"Me too. Time's getting on."

Wooster sat quiet on his pallet through the evening, his back against the wall. I figured the trip outside had tuckered him. But at length he said, "Should we go back?"

I looked up at him, sharp. I stood, poked the fire in the stove, then settled down again. "I been wondering that, too."

"I guess whatever's happened has happened. There's no undoing it," Wooster said. "But I can't help but wonder . . ."

"I'm not sure which way we came that night, are you?" I snapped a twig in two. "I'm sorry I fell asleep. I can't believe I fell asleep for all of that."

Wooster shook his head. "I was too numb to know you were sleeping till we'd almost stopped." We sat for long minutes in silence.

I told him what Chap. Goforth had said to me, about the kiss from Katie Frances and her instructions. "They must have planned it long. They'd filled the saddlebags already—everything was ready, waiting."

"You don't think it was provisions they'd meant to take themselves?" he asked.

I considered that. "No, I don't. It seemed like they had it worked out in their minds—what they'd do and what they wanted us to do. Katie Frances said for us to finish the work we'd been given to do, and let them stay and finish theirs."

"We'd best pray about it," Wooster said.

And we did. Wooster prayed out loud, as we sat together there by the woodstove. I prayed again when I'd bedded down for the night.

But praying raised something inside me, something I couldn't name that gave me no peace. And in the end I thought again of Cousin Albert and his deceit. I understood from Wooster why he'd done it; I just couldn't forgive him—not for that, and not for Ma. And now my fear for Andrew and Katie Frances had been added to the long list of struggles in my brain. Were they lying dead now because we'd taken Stargazer? Would Andrew have tried to run with Katie Frances if not for me? Could I lay that at Cousin Albert's door too? I wanted to. I wanted to blame somebody, blame him.

Blaming him had become a well-worn path in my brain. No matter what the colonel or Wooster thought of him. Of course they'd think he'd done right. He hadn't lied to them. He hadn't conjured a hold over their mothers or kept them from getting to them. He was a hero in their eyes. And what of Emily? She nearly worshiped her pa. I turned over, angry again. How did one man do all that? I thought again of Ma looking up at him, smiling, like all was well when she stood beside him. Cousin Albert's pull on her must have been stronger than I'd guessed all these years. Knowing that raised a bitter gall.

Eighteen

The next morning, as I fed and brushed Stargazer, Wooster surprised me by getting up, rolling and stowing his bedroll, heating the water. He carried his load of chores, such as they were, all morning. "I'll be ready to ride tomorrow," he announced at noon.

I nodded. "I'll check my snares. We can cook up whatever's caught to take along."

Just before dusk we wrapped the last of the roasted rabbit in leaves and stowed it in Stargazer's saddlebags. I hid the bags upstairs, where they'd keep cold, where no animals could get them. We meant to get an early start. I was tempted to turn in before moonrise.

We'd used most of our firewood to cook. I didn't want to go out in the cold again, but Wooster kept nagging me, edgier than a cat. It wasn't like him, and that made me edgy besides. Neither of us hankered after a cold night. So I saddled Stargazer, wrapped my bedroll tight around me, and set out to collect a final load.

I'd wandered about a half mile from the mill when I first felt the pounding in my feet. It rose up from the earth, lighter but the same sort of pounding I'd felt before the Federals invaded the field hospital. My tongue crusted dry. My heart skipped its beat and shot to my throat. "Wooster!" It was a prayer. I shoved the wood from Stargazer's saddle, swung up, and dug my heels into his sides. He needed no urging. We flew through the woods and over the hill. We'd reached the last wooded ridge, just before the steep bank to the mill, when I saw the riders. Stargazer reared as I reined him in. There were seven or eight. I couldn't count for sure in the waning light, but it looked like too many to take on. Where was Wooster? Had he heard them coming? Was he still inside? I slid off Stargazer and led him back into the stand of trees. I couldn't risk him being seen.

That's when a shot blasted from inside the mill. My stomach lurched and my fingers fumbled as I tied Stargazer's reins to a low branch. "Please, God, no. No! Not Wooster. Don't let it be Wooster!" Loud, drunken laughter rolled up the hill. I hit the ground and crawled over the ridge, down the bank, along the stream. Crouched low, covered by the spreading darkness, I circled the mill. There was a window just over the waterwheel. I prayed they'd strike a light, so I could see something—anything.

That's when I saw him. Teetering on the slats of the waterwheel, climbing over the top and down the front, about to jump or fall, inched Wooster on his one leg. He threw his crutches and bedroll across the frozen stream. I stole to the bottom of the wheel and hoot-owled softly.

"Robert?" he whispered into the dark. A light sprang in the window behind him. Two men stood, arguing in the lantern light. They'd have seen Wooster, sure, if they'd only turned a little and if they weren't so caught up with their own fire.

"Jump!" I called in a whisper, loud as I dared. And I marveled

151

that Wooster did it, that he trusted a voice in the dark when he couldn't see what was below him. He fell, on top of me, and we both fell against the frozen stream, heard it crack with our weight. But we rolled over again and again onto the bank, just as a head thrust out the window above us. We scrambled into the shadow of the waterwheel, grateful for the darkness.

"I tell you I heard something," said a voice from above us. "Something's out there!"

"Bill, you take the light and go see."

"Why me? What does it matter what's out there? Probably some wild animal, looking for supper. I don't want to be it!"

"We can't risk anybody spying after us. Now, go on. Then you take the first watch."

We didn't stay to hear the argument. "My crutch!" Wooster begged—the first begging I'd ever heard in his voice. "I threw it over there!" I left him to grab the crutch. We heard the mill door close out front. Our time was gone.

"Climb on!" I whispered, crouching in front of him. We'd do just what the Irishman had done the night he carried Wooster out of the Maynards' cellar. Wooster grabbed his bedroll and crutches in one arm and tightened the other around my collar bone. I gripped his legs. Together we climbed the hill.

"Somebody out there?" a voice behind us called. "Show your face—now!" We didn't wait to know if he'd really seen us. A shot fired above us. I slipped, tumbling us both onto the ridge.

"Wooster! Wooster! Are you all right?" He didn't answer right away and all the fear of God swept over me. "Wooster!"

"Shut up!" he hissed. "You'll bring the whole passel of them down on our heads!"

I breathed for the first time. "Thank God. Thank God." The man below swept his lantern back and forth over the hillside, looking for us. I was pretty sure he'd heard us by now, but he didn't seem sure which direction our noise had come from. Then he turned and headed straight toward us.

"What you shooting at, Bill?" A new voice came from outside the mill.

"There's something out here, or somebody. Get the boys!"

"Climb up again!" I whispered, and Wooster leaned over my back. I stumbled, running as fast as I could, before I stumbled some more, toward Stargazer. We reached him, breathless, and Wooster scrambled from my back to Stargazer's, shoving his crutches in the saddle without missing a beat.

I was about to swing up behind him. "Your bedroll! Grab your bedroll!" Wooster pushed me toward it. I just wanted to go. I didn't want to think about anything else. How could he be thinking about all this stuff at a time like this? But I grabbed it and shoved it in his arms, grabbed Stargazer's reins, and led him through the trees, quiet as we could.

"There he is! I told you I heard something!" Another shot rang out.

This time the shot found its mark. Wooster cried out.

"Wooster!" I swung up behind him. "Wooster!"

"Ride, Robert!"

I dug my heels into Stargazer, only once. He took off as if he'd been shot, and raced up to the second ridge. We hit the road flying. Two more shots fired somewhere behind us, but they flew wide. Not knowing if they'd follow, we raced on and on, maybe an hour, until we couldn't breathe, until Wooster slumped against me.

I reined in Stargazer and pulled off the road, toward a stand of evergreens. The moon rode high, bright white above us, but the trees' heavy branches swept the ground, shielding us from passersby. "Wooster? Wooster? Can you hear me?" I shook him gently. He moaned, but didn't answer. I laid out my bedroll, then pulled him from the saddle to the ground.

"Take it easy!"

"Where'd they get you?"

"My arm. I think it's just a graze. I'm just so tired."

"We'd best take a look. Let me pull your arm out of your jacket." It took some time, but we got the arm out. The moon was full enough to see that it wasn't too bad. It looked like the ball had passed clean through, and near the surface. The bone seemed all right. It needed cleaning, but had stopped bleeding fresh on its own. "Thank You, God," I whispered.

"Thank You, Father," Wooster echoed.

I ripped off the tail of my shirt and tied it in a bandage around Wooster's arm. "We can rest here a while, till you're stronger."

"No. If you can hold me up, let's ride. They might follow—especially as it gets daylight."

"They seemed bound on going the other way. They came up this road, pounding dirt hard."

"Sounds like deserters," Wooster guessed.

"Maybe. Which side?"

"Rebels. Didn't you hear them talking? They sounded like South Carolina men to me, low country. We'd best stay clear of them. Deserters got nothing to lose. Bands like that think the law doesn't mean them—think they're above the law, that the countryside owes them. All they fear is being caught."

"Maybe that old mill's their hideout."

Wooster shrugged. "Doesn't matter. We just need to make tracks. South."

"I think we are. Look at the stars." The night sky was ablaze with white lights, pinpricks through a dark blanket. We found the North Star. I could have stayed lost in their patterns. I didn't want to breathe or blink for fear they'd move.

Wooster lay back, breathing hard, tuckered through. "How can a soul look at that sky and not believe in God?" Wooster whispered.

How could it be done? I wondered. But I looked away, feeling my own restless pricks.

Wooster tried to stand, and it brought me around. "Help me up, Robert."

"You don't want to rest longer?"

"No, I want to go home. I want to get to Salem."

"You're an ornery cuss."

"Yes, I am. Now, help me up." I whistled for Stargazer, who'd wandered off to graze in a hidden patch of old grass.

"Did you get enough, boy?" I patted Stargazer's rump and leaned my head against his shoulder. "Hold steady, now." I could tell Wooster's climb over Stargazer's back pained him. I swung up behind, and we were off again, slower this time. The moon, traveling across the sky, made good company as we picked our way south.

Nineteen

$\mathcal{D}$ays and nights rode into one another. We followed the road slowly by dark and slept by day—the same as I'd often done traveling North on the Underground Railroad, before the war. Sometimes we'd find a stream and follow it a while, always making sure we headed south or southwest. That way we could fish a little, let Stargazer graze.

We came across a deserted farmhouse once. We stayed there two nights—slept easier and warmer with a roof and a door. I tried snaring small game. But the land had been picked clean by more than three and a half years of war and foragers. Luring the scrawniest rabbit or squirrel turned out next to impossible. My luck was out, and our spines gnawed at our bellies. We rested most of that second day, then saddled up at dusk to avoid travelers and followed the road.

The sun hadn't colored the east when we edged into a town, the first we'd ridden through. Even in the dusky light something about it tickled the edge of memory. I don't think I'd have remembered but for a sign nailed to a lamppost, "Jamestown." Ma and I had ridden through Jamestown on the train years ago, on our way to Ashland. That was less than a day's ride to Salem!

It was almost five years since Jeremiah and I had stolen through Jamestown on our way North, Christmas night 1859. We'd hidden in a tight cave behind a Quaker family's farmhouse. The next day we'd ridden in their false-bottom wagon north, toward Petersburg.

Jamestown was where the boy Timothy had done me out of Stargazer, just before we reached the Quaker farm. The memory knotted my stomach, and I was anxious to ride, to get beyond this town. But it would soon be daylight. We needed a place to hide, to rest, needed food and something solid for Stargazer. I remembered the strips of rabbit meat, roasted and wrapped in leaves, sitting in our bags upstairs back at the mill. For the hundredth time my mouth watered, and I groaned.

I wondered if I could find the Quaker farm where Jeremiah and I had hidden. I wondered if they would take us in, or at least let me feed and water Stargazer. The sound of an early morning wagon rumbled toward us. I pulled Stargazer off the road and into the woods until the wagon passed.

"We'd best do something, boy." Wooster'd slumped forward, asleep for the last hour or so. Back on the road I picked up the pace, hunting for the farm. I remembered it sat back, along a main road, that the barn was built into the slope of a hill. We'd nearly passed it when I recognized the barn. No lights burned.

Down the road we came to more woods. I walked Stargazer down the hill, through the trees, then backtracked along the riverbank, just as Jeremiah and I had done. When we reached the back of the Quaker family's barn, the ground floor where they'd kept livestock, I pulled open the door, praying it wouldn't squeak on its hinges. It never did, and I thought how careful these Quaker abolitionists were about everything. I wondered if they still hid the false-bottom wagon on the second floor of their barn, where they could pull it out onto the top of the slope, near the main road. I wondered if the cave was still behind the tanning table, or if it had been blocked up. Maybe we could sleep there.

The barn and its smells, the lowing of the cattle, even the way my feet trod the path all brought a rush of memory. I held Stargazer's neck so tight he whinnied. "Shh. I'm sorry, boy. I'm sorry. You have to be quiet." He snorted like he understood.

I made a temporary bed on the hay for Wooster and set to feeding and watering Stargazer. I meant to brush him, to check his hooves, but never even pulled off his saddle before I fell asleep on the hay beside Wooster.

I felt the prod of the pitchfork against my shoe before I heard the boy's voice. Blinding daylight shone through the cracks in the barn walls, and I covered my eyes with my arm.

"Thee is alive."

"What?" I tried to wake up.

"Is thee a deserter?" The voice came from a boy, curious, wide-eyed, not more than eight or nine.

"No. No, I'm not."

"Then why did thee steal our hay?"

"I'm sorry. I should have asked, but there was no light burning. I didn't want to wake anybody." It was a half truth, and the boy stood waiting. "I stopped here some years ago. I hoped your family wouldn't mind if I fed and watered my horse, if—if—my brother and I rested before heading on home."

"I must tell Father."

"Sure. Tell him I'll work for the hay, and if your family could spare a little food, I'll work for that too. Tell him, please."

"Father does not allow deserters. He does not want trouble."

158

The boy stared at me, then turned to run for the house. A name crept on the edge of my memory.

"Wait! Wait—Jedediah?"

The boy stopped in his tracks and turned to stare again, his eyes wider yet. "How does thee know my name?"

I grinned, trying to put him at ease. "Tell your pa that I was here the Christmas of '59, and that his two packages made it to the promised land."

"But what about me? How does thee know my—"

"You and your brothers and sisters played in the snow that Christmas night. One of your older brothers swooped you up and called your name. You were the littlest. Five years back. I figured it must be you."

Jedediah puffed his chest and lifted his chin. "I am the littlest no more. Hannah Grace is the littlest now!"

"That's good to hear, Jedediah. Will you tell your pa what I said?"

"I will!" And he turned, running full speed for the house.

"Robert?" Wooster mumbled. "Robert, who's there?"

"A boy, Jedediah." It felt good to know his name, to know him, sort of, from before. "He's gone to tell his pa that we're here. I'm hoping they'll have food for us, maybe let me work it off."

"We need to get home. We need to get home to Salem."

"We will. I swear it." Wooster looked paler, thinner in the morning light. Two bright red spots stained his cheeks. Dark circles spread under his eyes, darker than the day before, despite his sleep. "How you doing, Wooster?" I tried to keep my voice steady, not to sound as alarmed as I felt.

"I don't know. Not too good, I think." Wooster sat up, held his head with his good arm, and looked like he was having trouble focusing.

"We're not too far from Salem. Hang on till we can get to your family."

"How do you know we're not far? Did that boy tell you?"

"No, but I saw a signpost. We're in Jamestown. Not more than a day's ride to Salem."

"A day! A day—I can hang on another day."

The Quaker family did better by us than I'd imagined. They took us into their barn loft, fed us, bathed and dressed Wooster's wound, gave him tea for his fever, and let Stargazer eat his fill. Food and sleep work wonders—at least they did for me. But Wooster didn't rally, and that night the Quaker lady drew me aside.

"Thy brother needs a doctor. There is no more I know to do."

"I'm taking him to his ma in Salem."

She frowned. "There are good doctors in Salem, or there were before the war drew so many away. But I don't know if he can withstand the ride." She'd said the very thing I worried over.

"I've got to try. He's got it in his head to be there for Christmas Eve."

"But tomorrow is Christmas Eve! He is not fit to travel so soon."

"Tomorrow?" I looked at Wooster, then back at her. I'd lost track of the days. I sat down. "I promised him. I promised him I'd get him home for his Moravian lovefeast on Christmas Eve." I ran my hand through my hair. "It's the thing he wants most in all the world."

"And thee does not?"

"What? I mean, ma'am?"

"It is what thy brother wants, but thee, a Moravian also, does not?"

160

I felt the heat rise up my neck, the way it always did when I was caught in a lie. "Wooster's my friend. He's not my real brother, and I don't know too much about the Moravian religion."

"Thee was not truthful with us." It was a statement. Then more kindly, "Why?"

I looked at her. She waited patiently for my explanation, and I wanted to give it. I wanted to pour out the whole long story about Ma having left and Pa being gone, about Cousin Albert's deceit and death, of Wooster helping me, and Rev. Goforth and Katie Frances saving us, of wondering if they'd been killed, and how Wooster was shot at by deserters. I wanted to tell her how scared and worn I was, how this had all grown too big, and now Wooster'd better not die on me. He just plain better not die!

But how could I say any of that? I was all of eighteen, supposed to be a man, and should have been a Union private. I was in the South helping an escaped rebel prisoner get home, looking for my ma, hoping against hope that Emily cared what became of me. Even if I enlisted now, how could I kill rebels when my mother and my new best friend, and the girl I—the girl I cared about—were all rebels? I nearly laughed. How could you shoot at the idea of war without shooting at real people? And where did that thought come from now? My head went light. I steadied myself against a hay bale.

"Thee must sit." She steadied me, guided me to stretch out on the hay. Then she sat beside me, still waiting.

"When my friend—another friend—and I stayed here all those years ago, when you and your family helped us North, you didn't want to see us, so you could honestly say you hadn't seen any runaways staying in your barn." She nodded. "It's like that now. It might be safer if you didn't know the whole story."

She weighed that. "Does thee put my family in danger?"

"No, ma'am. No one will ever know we were here. I swear it. And my brother—my friend—will honor that promise. I know he will. We're grateful, ma'am, for all you've done for us."

"Deserters." She sighed.

"No, ma'am. We're not. Wooster has discharge papers, because of losing his leg. And I never joined at all." I colored, ashamed and relieved all at once, that I could tell that truth.

"Thee art a Friend?"

"I'm Wooster's friend." I meant it. "But nobody'd believe I'm not enlisted with one side or the other. They might take me for a deserter or a spy, and neither of those things would be good for you or your family."

"This war makes fools of everyone, North and South, men and boys, even women. It is a thing I do not understand."

"Neither do I, ma'am." I meant that too. I looked back at Wooster. "But I promised him I'd get him home for Christmas Eve—if there was any way to do it. And it would be better for you if we didn't stay."

She nodded, smiled sadly, and pressed my arm. "Rest now, and we shall get thy friend ready to ride."

"Ma'am?"

"Rest, and let me talk with my husband."

She didn't have to tell me twice. I figured Wooster and I would set out at first light, keep to the woods and back roads. But I didn't think on it long. For all I fared better thanks to their food and care, I was tired clean through and slept beside Wooster. I believe I'd have slept through the night and all the next day, but Jedediah woke me again. This time a stream of lantern light probed my eyes. It was pitch dark outside.

"Father says to come. Come, and bring thy friend downstairs. I will help thee with him."

I tried to rouse Wooster. He moaned but would not be roused. I felt his forehead. The fever nearly blistered my hand. "Oh, no, God. Please, no. Please let him get home for his service —home to his ma."

"Yes, Father in Heaven, let it be so," Jedediah echoed my prayer.

It took the two of us to carry Wooster down from the loft. There, in the light of another lantern, stood Jedediah's ma with a quilt, and Jedediah's pa, holding up the plank to the false-bottom wagon. Inside the wagon hidey-hole they'd laid a tick mattress. The Quaker man motioned Jedediah and me to lay Wooster inside. He pushed Stargazer's saddle in behind him.

The lady pushed her quilt into my arms and laid her hand on my cheek. "My husband will drive you both as close to Salem as the night will permit. At first light he will help raise thy friend to the saddle. Thou will be on thine own then. We do not believe he could ride horseback all the way in his condition."

I tried to speak, to thank them. I realized they were going against everything they'd been so careful to protect for years and years, risking that we could be trusted, risking that we'd not be stopped by patrols or caught or questioned. "Thank you. All of you. Thank you." The Quaker man nodded and guided my elbow to the wagon. I climbed in. "Thank you!" I said again.

"It is best if traveling packages do not speak." The Quaker man set the plank in place.

"It is a thing I hope is true," answered the Quaker woman.

I laughed and cried—all in silence. They were the very words my journey with Jeremiah had started off with in this very wagon five years ago. Good, good people. And that made me think of home and Aunt Sassy saying, "Good and bad people everywhere, Robert."

"Oh, Lord God," I prayed, "bless this family."

The wagon rumbled on and on. It was cold, but we were out of the wind. I wrapped the quilt around Wooster and me. I knew Stargazer was tied to the back of the wagon. I heard him, smelled him, and found that a comfort. I didn't worry that the Quaker man would try to keep him or steal him.

Wooster slept like the dead. Every once in a while I'd feel his forehead, hoping the fever had crept away. But it continued to grow. I didn't know if it was because of his arm or something else. I prayed he'd make it home to his ma, that she'd know what to do. I wanted to know Wooster would work in Salem, plying his leather trade. I wanted to wear shoes he'd make one day, visit the children he'd have with that lucky woman Katie Frances talked about. I wanted to see them play round ball in the streets—using a leather ball their father'd made.

There was only dark through the wagon cracks. At last we rumbled and bumped across a tangle of roots, then smoothed to a stop. When the Quaker man lifted the plank I saw we were hidden from the road by a thick stand of trees. Silently, he pulled out the saddle and threw it over Stargazer's back. I climbed out and tightened the girth.

"There is food in this sack, just in case thee does not find the family thee expects."

"Not find them?"

"Remember," he said, "thy friend has not been home for several years. Many families have had to relocate to provide what is needful." I'd never thought of that, never even considered it. "Help me pull him out."

"Wooster. Wooster, can you wake up?" I pulled Wooster and

shook him at the same time. But it was like shaking a sack of feed.

"Let us steady him in the saddle. I will hold him while thee climbs up behind."

Once we were settled into the saddle, the Quaker man tied on our bedrolls and the sack of food and stowed Wooster's crutches. I reached for his hand. "I don't know how to thank you, sir. For everything you and your family have done for me—twice over now."

He grasped my hand and nodded. "Thee would do the same."

"Yes, sir. I would. I will." I meant that true.

"Take the road straight ahead. At the crossroad is a sign for Salem, near the edge of town. Even riding slowly thee should reach Salem within the hour, before dawn, before too many stir."

"Thank you. Thank you!" He slapped Stargazer's rump and we set off.

It was a job to hold Wooster steady. But in the cold he came to a bit. "Where are we?"

"We're on our way to Salem! And we'll be there any minute. You're going to have to tell me how to get to your house."

"Is it true?" He couldn't believe it. I held him tight.

"I told you we'd make it. Here it is Christmas Eve, so you haven't got a minute to spare if you want to get there for your lovefeast!" I tried to laugh.

He nearly cried but shuddered, then slumped, limp. "Get me home."

I felt the heat from his head against my chin. "I swear it."

Twenty

 $\mathscr{I}$ rode as steadily as we could, as fast as I dared. There weren't
many out so early. Most of the faces I passed along the streets
shone only in lantern light. They were dark and solemn, and
kept their eyes from mine. North Carolina, outside Quaker
farms and Confederate field hospitals, beyond the walls of
Union occupation, was still very much the land of slavery. I
wondered for the first time if Wooster's family owned slaves. It
hadn't even crossed my mind to ask him.

But the bigger question now was where to go. Where did
Wooster live? "Wooster! Wooster!" I shook him, but he was out,
burning with fever.

I wandered down what looked like the main street of town.
A few lamps and candles burned in windows and cellars, probably kitchens. A stooped colored man, his hair nearly white,
stood near a stable, lantern in hand, watching us. He drew a
younger, dark woman to him and pointed our way. Stargazer
snorted and sidestepped. "Whoa, boy. I don't know what they
want." It was all I could do to keep him steady, to keep Wooster
in the saddle.

We'd reached the town square. I'd a mind to water Stargazer

from the town square pump when a young colored boy ran up to me. "What your name, Mista?"

"Why do you want to know my name?" I took in the street, up and down, to see who might be watching.

"Don't want to know. My mama want to know. You sure got a pretty horse."

"Thank you. Look, maybe you can help me."

"Help you what?" He stepped back, suspicious.

"Gibbons. Do you know where the Gibbons family lives?"

"Gibbons! The Widow Gibbons? Miz Eulalia Gibbons?"

"I don't know. Is she the only Gibbons in town?"

He nodded. "She live over by the ladies' school."

"Then she must be the one. Can you show me where she lives? I have her son, Wooster, here."

The boy stepped back again, wide-eyed, afraid. "Wooster done died in a Yankee prison."

"No, he's here. He's not dead, but he's sick. See? Tell me where the Widow Gibbons lives."

But the boy kept stepping back, shaking his head, too frightened to speak, too shaken to run. That's when his mother called to him from across the street. "Samuel! Samuel!" The boy turned and ran in her direction.

"Ma'am!" I called to her. "Can you please tell me where I can find the Widow Gibbons?"

The woman drew her shawl tight around her head but pointed beyond the square. "Church Street!" she called, then clutched her young son's hand and hurried away.

I headed Stargazer in the direction she'd pointed. I couldn't understand why the few people on the street stared at us so. I guessed we made a sorry sight. I found Church Street, just a block over. But which way to go? That's when I saw the shingle for the Salem Female Academy. The boy had said the Widow Gibbons lived next to the ladies' school.

A little house sat to the right of the school, a house I could imagine Wooster growing up in. A single candle burned in the window and a brighter light beyond that. I slid down and pulled Wooster gently from the saddle. He'd lightened over the weeks, but I'd weakened some, and it was all I could do to get him to the front door. I kicked the door with my shoe, balancing Wooster against me as best I could.

When the door opened a small but wiry silver-haired woman in a white cap took one look at us and gasped. Once her blue eyes fixed on Wooster her hands flew to her face, then to his, and she cried, "Wooster! Wooster!" She pulled us in without me saying a word. "My boy! My boy!"

"He's burning up with fever, ma'am."

"Bring him here." She led the way toward a small room near the back of the house, turned down the bed quilt, and helped me settle him in. "Wooster. Wooster!" She kept repeating his name, running her hands over his face, his shoulders, his arms, trying to take in that he was really there. Tears filled her eyes and spilled down her wrinkled cheeks as she ran her hand over his stump. I knew they needed time alone.

"I'll bring in his crutches and such." I was glad to get out of the room. Seeing her worry so over Wooster made me want Ma in the worst way. And it scared me that Wooster's fever raged.

I don't know what made me do it, but I pulled off my butternut jacket before I went back outside, even though the cold December morning ate through my clothes. I closed the front door behind me. That's when I looked up and saw the stooped figure of the white-haired colored man beside Stargazer, running a dark hand over the blaze on his forehead, stroking his chest. Surprisingly, Stargazer didn't shy. "Something you want, Mister?" I didn't like strangers getting so near Stargazer.

"I seen this horse before. I'd recognize him anywheres," the man said.

"I doubt that. I just rode in." But something in the old man's voice sounded familiar, not challenging.

And then he turned. "Masta Robert, it is you. Rebecca thought it was you riding this horse, but I didn't believe it."

"Old George?" I couldn't believe my eyes. "Old George?" I wanted to laugh, or maybe cry. "What are you doing here?" But the last was lost in the bear hug he gave me.

"Oh, it's good to see you, Masta Robert. I thought never to see you this side of Jordan!" He laughed and hugged me again, then stood back. "I told Rebecca it couldn't be you, not riding tall in that Confederate uniform." He looked truly confused.

"It's only a coat. I needed a coat and somebody gave me one. I'm not a Confederate."

He nodded but warned, "Well, you sure looked like one, and that all the home guard gonna care about if they catch sight of you. They's hard on deserters. Only able-bodied young men about be deserters." He shook his head. "What you doin' here? I'da thought you'd be off fightin' with the Yankees, no matter what your mama said."

"Ma! How is she? Are you on your way out to Ashland? What are you doing in town so early?" I had a million questions for him, but there would be time. We could ride out to Ashland together, and Old George could fill me in on the last five years.

"Whoa, now. I don't slave for Masta Marcus no more. I don't even know if he still be alive."

"What?" Old George had been Grandfather's horse trainer and stable keeper since he was bought as a young man. He was as much a part of Ashland as my mother, had lived there longer, by far.

"You don't know, do you?" Old George looked concerned for me, and that sent a chill up my spine.

"What—"

"Sam!" the widow called from behind me. The small, dark boy who'd been so frightened of Wooster appeared from behind a lamppost, skittered past me, and ran straight to the widow's skirts. I heard her urge, "Dr. Macey! Run, Sam!" The boy took off like slick shavings down the cobblestone street.

"Old George—what about Ma? Is Ma all right?" I couldn't breathe.

"Far as I know, she's with Miz Emily. Miz Emily take good care of her. Take good care of all of them." Old George looked over his shoulder. The town was beginning to stir, and a man stopped across the square, staring in our direction. "Best get off the street. This fine horse causing too much stir. Not many good horses left by the Confederacy. They'll be wantin' this one, and what they want, they take. Folks'll be asking."

"I just rode in. I don't know where to stable him."

"You let Old George see to that. I take care of this fine boy. Yes, sir, I'll take good care of him."

"Where will I find you?" I had every reason to trust Old George and every reason to trust nobody when it came to Stargazer.

He nodded across the square and down the street. "Over yonder, beyond the tavern. I'll feed and water him inside the stables. If folks come asking about him, I'll move him, hide him." He smiled. "There's always friends among us. Don't you worry.

"I saw you brought the Gibbons boy home. That's good. The widow set great store by her boy—thought he be dead. She a fine woman." He picked up Stargazer's reins and handed me Wooster's crutches and the bedroll. "Don't you worry none. I'll take good care of this boy, and I'll send Rebecca over with news if I can't come."

The man across the square started toward us. I wanted to ask Old George more questions, get some answers, but his eyes took in the stranger and motioned me toward the widow's house. "You'd best get inside." He walked off with Stargazer like he'd done it every day. I swallowed, uncertain if this was right, fearful I'd regret this action, fearful I'd lose Stargazer again, but I turned and walked back into the house just the same. I stood with my back pressed against the door, my knuckles white around Wooster's crutches. Old George had helped Jeremiah and me escape all those years ago. I couldn't imagine he'd betray me now. Footsteps walked right up to the door, hesitated, waited, then walked away. I breathed, finally, wondering what he wanted, wondering why my heart beat so fast.

"There you are!" I jumped. It was the Widow Gibbons. "Are you all right, young man? You're not feverish, too?"

"No, ma'am. Just tired."

She felt my head, then nodded. "Are those my Wooster's things?"

"Yes, ma'am." I handed her his crutches, his bedroll. "Wooster won't want these out of his sight. How is he?"

She shook her head. "I've sent for Dr. Macey. It's a high fever. How long since it took?"

"Yesterday. He's been in and out, and weak. I don't know if it's from infection or something else. His arm was dressed last night but might need looking at. Been running as fast as we could. Wooster had it in his head to get home for the Christmas Eve lovefeast you all hold."

171

She smiled and nodded, but the smile faded quickly. "I was told my son had likely died in a prison escape. I don't know what miracle brought you here, but I thank you, with all of my heart."

There was a tapping on the side door. The widow and I looked at each other. She stepped to open it and a tall, slim black woman and the little boy that I'd met near the pump nearly fell inside. "It's you! It really is you, Masta Robert!"

"Rebecca, you know this young man?"

"Rebecca?" I wouldn't have believed it, but I remembered Old George saying he'd send Rebecca if he couldn't come. I hadn't imagined it would be Rebecca from Ashland.

"There's no time. I heard the home guard talking over their breakfast at the tavern where I carry Miz Adelia's pies. One of the men spotted you riding in. Everybody's mighty skittish, what with all the talk about that Gen. Sherman burning his way through Georgia, tearing up every rail line and telegraph pole, doing the Lord knows what to folks in his path. It's all anybody talks about for fear he'll come on up here. That Maj. McCain warned that some of those bummers might come our way. They's coming to see if you are one of them or maybe a deserter."

"I'm none of those things!"

"You best have proof, or they haul you off, take your horse, and slap you in the jailhouse."

"I'm not even enlisted!"

Widow Gibbons looked near horrified. "But you rode in here in a—"

"A rebel soldier's jacket, but it was given to me in a field hospital—in a field hospital where Wooster saved my life." She frowned, confused. "It's a long story, ma'am, but I swear to you that I'm a friend of Wooster. I wasn't in the beginning, but I am now."

"You're a Yankee?" She could barely say the word.

"I've never enlisted. I'm here to find my mother."

"You come for Miz Caroline?" Now Rebecca seemed horrified.

"Caroline Ashton? You're Caroline's son—Emily Mitchell's cousin?" the widow asked.

I nodded, surprised the widow knew Emily, or Ma. But I turned sharp on Rebecca. "Emily wrote me that Ma needs help." Rebecca looked away, but I pulled her to me. "What's wrong? What's wrong with Ma?"

Rebecca looked afraid. She looked at me, Widow Gibbons, and back to me. "Let go. You hurting my arm."

"I'm sorry, Rebecca. I didn't mean to, but—Ma—how is Ma?"

"Rebecca?" the widow asked.

Rebecca licked her lips and looked away. "She be poorly. Real poorly, last I saw her."

"What—"

"She be feeble." Rebecca stepped back. "She be feebleminded."

That's when I heard the knock on the door. But I couldn't take it in. "What do you mean, 'feebleminded'?" I teetered on the edge.

"Masta Robert, you best hide. You hide now, or they gonna drag you off!"

"But I haven't done anything!"

Now the widow took hand. "I'll not let them take you, for Wooster's sake, for the fact you brought my boy home to me. Come in here." I followed her into her bedchamber. The knocking grew to a pounding. "Climb between the mattress and the ropes, face down, so you can breathe. Help him, Rebecca, while I answer the door."

I felt a fool, letting two women hide me in a lady's bedchamber. But in the last few months I'd been shot at, nearly drowned, half starved, sick near to death, arrested, and nearly shot for being a spy. I sure didn't want to be hauled off by the home guard, especially now that I was so close to Ashland and Ma. So I climbed between the ticking and the ropes, staring straight at the floorboards, while Rebecca made the bed above me. When everything was to her liking I heard the window lift, a swish of skirts, then the window sliding into place.

Voices rose from the next room. Footsteps pounded the halls, searched the very room in which I hid. "You're certain he didn't come in here?"

"Mr. Hubner, the boy left my son's bedroll and crutch, then took off. I've no idea where he's gone, and I don't expect him to return. I'm only grateful he helped my Wooster home."

"Maj. McCain wrote for us to be on the lookout for a boy answering his description, said he might try to bring Wooster home. He said Wooster got mixed up after Gettysburg. Thinks his enemies are his friends now. Said that boy is a Federal spy, might be using Wooster to get information, and if we can we ought to catch him and take care of him."

"I don't know anything about all of that. And as you can see, Wooster isn't fit to tell you anything. Now, I must ask that you leave here so I can prepare my boy for Dr. Macey—before it is too late."

The bedchamber door closed. Voices argued, rose and fell. I heard the front door open, footsteps fade down the walk, the door close, and a bar slide into place.

174

Twenty-One

Minutes passed before the window creaked open. It sounded as though someone climbed over the sill. Soft footfalls padded across the room, came near the bed—and I knew they were not Rebecca's footsteps. I tried not to breathe. There was a swooshing sound on the floor beneath the bed. Suddenly a small, dark face peered through the bed ropes into mine, our noses not five inches apart.

"My name's Hezekiah. Mama calls me Hez." It was the same small boy that had asked my name in the town square that morning, the child whose mother had swept him down the street.

"I'm Robert."

"That's right. That's what Mama said."

"You were in the town square this morning."

"Nope. That was my brother, Sam."

"You sure about that?" He looked like the very same boy. Hezekiah giggled.

"Sam and me's twins. Can't nobody tell us apart but our mama. She named Sam for a prophet and me for a king—said it suits us." He nodded, solemn.

Then it hit me. These were Rebecca's twins—the mulatto twins born in the slave quarters at Grandfather's Ashland the first time I visited there. He'd be about the right age. "Is Rebecca your mother?" Hezekiah nodded. "Where is your mama now?" I felt ridiculous talking to him through bed ropes.

"She working down to the tavern. She tell me come see you. She said for me to tell you stay right where you are this day. Those mens is combing the streets, searching every house for you."

"Does Mrs. Gibbons know you're here?"

"No. But that's fine. Sam and me runs errands for the widow all the time. She won't mind. Mama said the widow's got to tend her boy and don't have time to be minding you too. She say I can keep you company."

"I can't stay here. I've got to be on my way."

"Mama say you stay here till dark. She said Old George'll take care of everything." Hezekiah stopped, considering things. "You sure got a pretty horse."

I swallowed. Where was Stargazer now? "Do you know where my horse is?"

Hezekiah shook his head. "But Old George know. He's the best with horses anybody ever was." Then Hezekiah patted my arm through the rope squares. "Don't you worry. Old George takes care of everything. Everything be all right." I wanted to believe that. "I got to go now. I'll bring you something to eat later."

Hezekiah's lips turned up into a smile before he scooted away. I heard him climb over the window ledge. Later the front door opened, and I heard the voices of the Widow Gibbons and a man, maybe Dr. Macey. The door to the widow's bedchamber never opened, but I could hear their muffled voices through

176

the wall. I never heard Wooster. I wondered if he woke up, and if the doctor could bring down his fever. I wished the widow would come tell me something—anything—but I knew she had more important things on her mind.

Light passed slowly across the floor. I dared not move, and I could barely breathe. I tried to sleep, but the ropes cut into my face—first one way, then the other. Finally my throat was crusted and the call of nature strong. It called to mind days Jeremiah and I'd spent riding in the false bottom of the Quaker family's wagon. We learned mighty quickly to plan our eating and drinking and the times we'd be able to get out. I surely hadn't planned for this.

When I thought I couldn't stand it a minute longer, I heard the window raised. In half a minute Hezekiah—or Sam, I couldn't tell which—slid under the bed and stared into my face. He pressed his finger to his lips and whispered, "As soon as Mama come see the widow and they start talking loud you can slip out and do your business. Mama said she sure you got some by now. Said to use the widow's chamber pot. She send some vittles for you, but says to be real quiet so the doctor don't hear you in the next room."

"How's Wooster? Did he wake up?" I whispered.

Hezekiah shrugged. "Maybe Mama know after she see the widow."

A moment later I heard a knock and a door open in the far reaches of the house. Rebecca called, "Miz Gibbons? It Rebecca. I brought you some broth for Wooster. I made it fresh this morning over to the tavern. Is your boy awake yet?"

"Oh, Rebecca, how thoughtful of you. It will be just the thing when Wooster wakes up! I haven't wanted to leave his side, so I haven't prepared a thing. Come in, come in." There was some scuffling in the hallway. "There's no change yet, but the fever's just beginning to break."

"Thank the Lord. That a mercy."

"Yes. Yes, it is . . ." The widow and Rebecca kept a chatter running.

Hezekiah lifted one corner of the mattress ticking, and I wriggled out. After I took care of everything needful, Hezekiah passed me a crock of stew and a slab of warm cornbread. I nearly choked it down, knowing there was not much time.

Conversation in the next room slowed with the doctor's plea. "Ladies! You must contain yourselves! This commotion will not help my patient." Both ladies apologized at once. Their words came hushed, back and forth, still trying to cover for me.

I slipped under the mattress ticking again as Hezekiah adjusted the covers above me. He slipped under the bed once more and whispered, "I near forgot. Mama said tell you when it gets dark she'll send me to get you. Everybody goes to the love-feast early tonight. That be the time for you to sneak out."

"What about Stargazer—my horse?" I whispered.

"Old George fix you up." Hezekiah's lips turned up as he pressed his finger to them again, then—just as fast—he slipped out and through the window.

Maybe I did sleep after all, for it was nearly dusk when I heard Wooster moan through the wall, and the voice of his mother, "Wooster! Wooster!"

There were murmurs and thanksgivings, and I knew Wooster must have woken up. Maybe he'd get his lovefeast, after all—or maybe they could bring it to him. I smiled, glad for him. But it made me itch to get on my way to Ma and Emily. I was so near—on Christmas Eve—half a day's ride—and here I was, hiding under a mattress. Not for long. Surely Hezekiah would come soon. It was almost dark, near as I could tell.

What had Rebecca meant about Ma being feebleminded? Was that what Andrew had been trying to tell me? I wanted to think on that and I didn't. I tried to stretch. My muscles and joints had grown stiff in the cold room.

A few minutes later I heard Dr. Macey in the hallway. "It won't do him a bit of good to go out in the cold. He can attend next year's lovefeast!"

"But it may do his spirit a great deal of good, Doctor. His heart is set on it."

"I can see that, Widow Gibbons, but I must object. His fever's just broken, and he's weak as a kitten. There's no buns, you know—the war . . . it's only candles this year for the children."

"The Christmas Eve lovefeast is never 'only candles,' Doctor," the widow chided. "And his mind seems made up—don't you think so?"

Dr. Macey sighed. "If you can't dissuade him, make certain he is wrapped up warm and sits nearest the stovepipe in the church. I don't believe he's taken anything catching—just exhausted and undernourished. Fatten the boy up a bit!"

"You know I will, Daniel!" The widow's voice was smiling now.

"More hot broth before he moves an inch and something solid tomorrow. I'll check on him the day after. Call me if the fever returns."

"Thank you, Doctor. Thank you so very much for coming."

There were footsteps and then, "The Lord has seen fit to spare this boy to you, Widow Gibbons. I'm grateful."

"And I, Dr. Macey. And I." The widow's voice trembled.

The door closed. The bar slid into place. The widow's light footsteps hurried back to Wooster's room. I slipped from the ticking, and, careful to crouch below the window ledge, rubbed life back into my arms and legs. A crack of light spread from beneath the door. I knew the widow was lighting her evening lamps.

"Robert," she whispered, stepping inside the door and closing it against the light just as quickly. "Wooster's awake and asking for you."

"That's good news!"

"But you must be quick. Now that the doctor's gone, my neighbors will all be stopping by to see how Wooster is and bringing their greetings and broths. There will be much coming and going. You won't be able to hide here."

"Robert?" Wooster's call was weak, but the sound of his voice blessed my ears.

"Wooster!" I whispered back, creeping toward the door.

"Stay low," warned the widow. "We want no shadows before the windows."

I crawled to Wooster's room while the widow busied herself in the parlor, lighting lamps to attract attention from the street.

Wooster's eyes stood wide in his pale face. He looked small and scrawny and lost in the mountain of pillows and quilts piled around him. It was all I could do not to laugh—mostly for the joy of knowing he was safe and finally home. But what I said was, "You lazybones."

He grinned. "Go home," he said. "Go home to your ma and that girl."

I felt the heat creep up my neck, and I aimed to go and do just what he said. But I didn't know if I'd see Wooster again, or when. I couldn't think of anything fitting to say. I crawled across the floor, beside his bed, and reached up for his hand. His grip was weak, but he held on, and that was enough.

180

His blue eyes bored through mine. "God go with you, Robert."

I nodded, tried to speak, but gave it up.

"Robert," the widow whispered, passing the doorway. "You must go now."

"Hezekiah said he'd come at dusk—that Old George would help me—"

"They'll be true to their word. Take this muffler." She scooted it across the floor with her foot. "Wrap tight, and—"

A knock came at the door.

"Ach!" she blustered. "It's started already." She adjusted her cap and whispered, "You'd best slip outside the window as I answer the door. Crouch behind the shrubbery there and wait for him." She turned to go. "If I don't see you again, Robert—thank you. Thank you with all of my heart for bringing my son home." She squeezed my arms as I crawled past. I swallowed hard. "Hurry now."

And that was it. I crawled back to the widow's room and was out the window and crouched behind the shrubbery before I knew it, before I spoke again to Wooster. I wanted to tap a good-bye on his window, but I heard the widow and another lady talking, exclaiming over Wooster's being alive. I knew I dared not risk it, for Wooster or for me. And then a tug came at my elbow. I nearly jumped out of my skin.

"You ready?" It was Hezekiah.

"I never heard you coming."

"That right." He tucked his hand in mine. "Old George say keep low and make our way to the north end of town, up by God's Acre. He say put on this jacket and pull this hat low. If somebody come near, walk like you old—like you him."

I pulled on the coat and hat. Hezekiah grabbed my hand

again. I followed him, amazed by how small he was, how he took it all in stride. He put me in mind of William Henry, when we were young boys, and the way he had of taking charge in everything we did, no matter that he was only six months older.

We kept to the shadows along the bricked walks and sometimes cut through yards or wintered gardens. Wherever Hezekiah led, I followed. We reached the back of the churchyard as the town square lamps were lit. Hezekiah pulled my hand into the shadows. "We late. We got to wait now till they close the church doors. Too easy for somebody to see us cut up through the cemetery with those street lamps."

As if they'd heard, a group of men, shouldering muskets, marched down the path near the front of the church. "They's home guard," Hezekiah whispered and pushed against me, crowding us both into the church's shadow. "They been lookin' for you all day. I heard 'em talkin' down to the tavern. They say you a spy—that Maj. McCain want you took, no matter what." Hezekiah waited till they'd passed. "Is you a spy?"

"No," I whispered. "I'm not a spy. I'm just trying to get to my family."

Hezekiah nodded. "That right. That what Mama said."

"Your Mama is a fine lady, Hezekiah."

"You can call me 'Hez.'"

"Thanks, Hez—King Hez." I smiled and squeezed his hand. "And thanks for helping me."

"That all right. I like to do it. It better'n sweepin' round that tavern all day, all night." He peeked around the church corner. "Let's go."

We'd started up the path again when we heard a long, shrill whistle—a man's blast on two fingers. "Stop! You, there! Stop!"

"Home guard!" Hezekiah cried. "Run! Run now!" He

pushed me away from him and ran back down the hill, straight for the home guard, his arms outstretched. "Help! Help me!" he cried.

I was too startled to run, didn't know where to run.

"Robert!" It was Old George, hidden behind a stone pillar. I dived into the shadows. "A block over and up this street— there be a coffeepot—on a post—climb inside—up from the bottom! I'll lead them off this way. Stay put!" He pressed a penknife into my hand and took off through the graveyard.

Hide in a coffeepot? Old George must have gone off his noggin. And what was the penknife for? I couldn't protect myself with that!

But I ran the direction he'd pointed. I kept to the shadows when I could, but gaining time was the thing needed now. Behind me I heard Old George cry out, "Help me! Help me! He here! He come by here!"

I ran as fast, as hard as I could. Most of the town filled the church, so the streets were bare. I ran till my side hurt, till I could barely breathe. I took a side street and ran the two blocks, having no idea where I was going, wondering if I was already running in circles, still wondering what Old George could mean—hide in a coffeepot on a post. How would I find a little pot in the dark? How would I hide inside?

And that is when I saw it. A twelve-foot coffeepot stood, like a sign, an advertisement, on top of a wooden post outside a darkened tinsmith shop. The pot was gigantic—so big it stuck out into the street. It had to be the thing Old George intended. I could try running on, but I didn't know where I was or which way to go, let alone how to find Stargazer. If I stayed I'd be a sitting duck—but a hidden sitting duck. "I trust you, Old George," I whispered and headed for the pot.

The street was empty, the windows of houses and shops darkened. How was I supposed to get inside? Old George had said to climb up through the bottom. I reached up, ran my hands around the outside, across the bottom, and found the latch for a door, a trapdoor. It wasn't easy to pull it open, harder still to hoist myself up and pull the door to behind me. I had to straddle the trapdoor and try to catch the latch. That's where Old George's penknife came in handy. I shook my head. He'd thought of everything.

There was room inside for three or more of me, but I had to keep my feet off the trapdoor. I was out of the night air, but in no time the cold from the tin seeped through my bones. There was no way I could stay there long without freezing. I prayed Old George had another plan.

Twenty-Two

$\mathscr{T}$wenty minutes passed before I heard horses' hooves pound the road in front of the tinsmith's shop, and voices shouting directions for a search of the area. My heart beat a pounding rhythm right along with them, and I prayed the riders would not see, would not think of the coffeepot standing in plain view. It seemed an unlikely place to hide. I wondered how Old George had conjured it.

I wondered, too, what had become of him, if the home guardsmen had roughed him or believed whatever yarn he'd spun. They were still searching—that was certain—and knew for a fact I was somewhere in the town.

An hour passed, and I shivered so I wondered that the coffeepot didn't shake. I couldn't stay in the pot until morning. I was tempted to slip out and make a run on my own, when I heard voices coming up the street—Christmas hymn singers; hushed, happy conversations; and the skipping sounds of children's feet. Church must have let out.

I wondered if Wooster'd gotten to his lovefeast after all. I prayed so. Christmas greetings were called from neighbor to neighbor, some in English, some in what I took for broken

German. More feet shuffled past—the heads of the church-goers inches from my feet. Doors opened and closed against the cold. Finally, a strange quiet settled over everything.

I'd just decided to climb down when the steady clop clop of more horses sounded in the distance. It sounded like eight, maybe ten horses headed my way. They might have been the riders—my posse, returning to Salem—or they might have been late-night travelers come home for Christmas Day. It set me more fearful about climbing out. Ten minutes later I was still arguing inside my head.

A gentle tapping came against the post of the coffeepot. "You in there?" The voice was small, and I could picture its anxious owner.

"Hez?"

"Yes, sir! It's me. You can come on out now," he whispered.

I slipped the pen knife through the trap door's latch and it dropped open. Stiff and cold, I jumped to the ground, quiet as I could, then closed and latched the door.

Hezekiah grabbed my sleeve and pulled me along. I shook my feet, made them walk, one in front of the other, though I could barely feel them from the cold. We made our way back the route I'd come, kept to shadows, avoided windows, ran from tree to tree and corner to pillar whenever we could. We'd almost reached the cemetery again, but Hezekiah kept going south, avoiding the street this time.

"Aren't we meeting Old George in God's Acre?"

"No. Changed his mind after that home guard came along. Said to meet him back of the slave church. We go the long way. No home guard comes through these woods."

We walked, up hill and down, until I'd warmed through. Clouds covered the moon, in and out. Hezekiah, sure of himself,

186

never slowed, and I wondered if he'd done this before. He surely seemed older than his years.

We climbed one more hill, then stopped at the edge of the woods. Hezekiah gave a low bird call. A lantern shutter far away flipped open once and closed.

"That the signal. It safe to go now." Hezekiah tugged my sleeve again and took off on the run. I stayed close on his heels, grateful for the bit of moonlight that helped me find my footing. I was nearly breathless when I heard a familiar snort.

"Stargazer!" I whispered. And it was. Old George stepped from the shadow of a building and held out Stargazer's reins to me.

"You got to take this horse down the west side of town and head due west. You remember your way to Ashland?"

"If you can start me from Main Street I do."

He led me around the corner of the building and pointed. "A block and a half that way. Keep clear of the tavern. Some of them home guard fellas live over that way."

"Thank you, Old George. I won't forget this."

"You best forget, for all our sakes." He gave me a push up. "Masta Robert, you best brace yourself for whatever you find at Ashland."

"What do you mean? What's happened out there, Old George?"

"I can't say, and it ain't that I won't. I don't know. Two years ago, when things got bad with the money, Masta Marcus sold most of us off. Miz Caroline took it hard. Miz Emily used to go to the ladies' school here in town, after Mister Albert joined the army. She always good to us, whenever she see us. These Moravians been good to us, too—better'n Masta Marcus or that Slocum fella. But it still slavery. We just biding our time. Freedom's coming."

"There's a torchlight comin' down Church Street!" Hezekiah whispered.

"You go on now, and God go wid you!" Old George slapped Stargazer's rump, grabbed Hezekiah's hand, and slipped away.

Stargazer kept a better head than I did and steered straight for the shadows. We slipped around the building, which I realized must have been the slave church, then headed for Main Street, keeping as far south of the tavern as we could, walking on grass whenever we dared so as not to draw attention to Stargazer's hoofbeats. We travelled south until I found the road west, then picked up speed and rode hard.

The clouds were clearing, and the moon spent more time out than in. Light enough to ride by, and I never met another horse and rider on the road to Ashland. I guessed, by the moon, that it was somewhere between ten o'clock and midnight. If I rode steadily I should reach Ashland by two or three in the morning.

With every mile that passed my spirits stood up, till I thought they might fly right out of my body. I hadn't seen Ma since the spring of 1860—close to five years now. Despite all I'd been through these last weeks I laughed out loud, so glad to think I'd finally see her, hold her close, and Emily too. I admitted that to myself at last. I wanted to see Emily and hoped she'd be as glad to see me.

If Maj. McCain sent word to the Salem home guard about me, he'd likely written Emily, warning her against me, too. He'd probably given his version of Cousin Albert's death. I was thankful I wouldn't have to break the news of his death to her, but feared what lies McCain might have told her, what she might believe. I set my face grim. There was nothing I could do about that. I'd have to trust Emily's good sense, and her heart.

The miles peeled away, and as they did, so did the seven months of trying to reach Ashland. I wondered how Grandfather would react to my coming, if he'd allow me to stay, if I could trust him, if he'd agree to come North with Ma and me, and if he was well enough to travel.

I wondered about Jed Slocum, Grandfather's overseer, if he was still there or if the Confederacy had been desperate enough to force his conscription. We'd stood on opposite sides of every fence in the months I'd spent at Ashland. When I stole away that Christmas Eve I took the slave he hated most—the slave he was determined to sell or kill. That must have galled him in the worst way. I knew Jed Slocum was a rattlesnake of a man, and a man of long memory. For the hundredth time I prayed that he hadn't taken it out on Nanny Sara, Jeremiah's grandmother, or any of the other slaves. I wished I'd had more time to talk with Old George or Rebecca, time to learn the particulars of so many things.

Old George had taken good care of Stargazer, fed and watered and groomed him. He seemed in livelier spirits than he had in weeks. Maybe he sensed we were going back to where we'd started. I rubbed his neck and leaned down to throw my arm around him. I was cold and tired and hungry, but happier than I'd been in months—maybe happier than I'd been in years.

The last few miles, as excited as I was, I could barely keep my eyes open. When we reached Ashland's boundaries I slowed Stargazer to a walk. I still didn't know the time. It wouldn't do to wake Ma or Grandfather in the dead of night. I surely didn't want to rouse Slocum and give him an excuse to shoot me for an intruder.

I walked Stargazer in the grass, up the side of the lane leading to the house. Not a lamp burned anywhere. I circled the house and kitchen garden, as far out as I dared, and made our way to the stable. I'd settle Stargazer and bunk there for the night, then see Ma first thing in the morning. I'd clean up before visiting Emily at Mitchell House.

I pulled the stable door open, quiet as I could, wondering who the new stable boy might be. It still seemed impossible that Old George wouldn't strike a lamp and welcome me there.

But there was no sound. I reached for the lantern that had always hung from the hook by the door, then changed my mind. I didn't want to wake anyone, didn't want to startle the animals. But there was nothing. No animals snorting. No pawing the hay, not a whinny, not even the heavy, quiet breathing of the carriage horses. And then I understood. There were no horses. The South's horses had been sold, donated, or confiscated by the Confederacy. The stable stood empty.

"We've got to keep you out of sight, boy," I whispered to Stargazer. "You'd make a prime catch for foragers." Stargazer stepped closer, as though he understood.

I led him to the stall that had been his when we'd both lived here all those years ago. "I don't think we can do much tonight, boy, but I'll find some water and see about some oats." I pulled off his saddle and bridle, then stole out to the well. The rope had broken. I knotted it and sent the bucket down, then hefted it back to Stargazer. While he drank I searched all the places I knew for oats but didn't find anything. They had probably been cleaned out when the horses were sold or taken. In the morning I'd let him graze.

And then I wondered about the slaves. Who had Grandfather sold off besides Old George and Rebecca and her twins? My heart lurched. Not Nanny Sara! She'd been with the family since before Ma was born. But no, I couldn't imagine it. Ma would never stand for that, and Nanny Sara must be near ancient now.

There was nothing to do but bed down for the night. I pulled out my bedroll and spread it on the ground, blessing Old George for having tied it on. I wrapped the blanket tight around me and fell asleep before I finished thanking God for my journey's end.

Bright morning light shone through an open knot in the stable wall. It was a full minute before I realized where I was, remembered that it was Christmas Day. Christmas morning— and I'd see Ma in no time. I jumped up and set my clothes to rights as best I could. I lifted my armpit and smelled, then turned my own face away. Ma wouldn't know me.

"How you doing, Stargazer?" He snorted and rubbed his nose against my arm. I rubbed him down with a brush I found against the ledge, getting up my nerve to walk across the lawn and knock on the door of the Big House. Finally I set the brush down. "That's it, boy. I won't know if I don't go over there." I patted his flank and rubbed his forehead. "I'll be back before you know it. Then I'll lead you out to graze."

I pushed open the stable door and took in the Big House. It seemed late enough that somebody should be about. But I didn't see a soul. I decided to knock at the back of the winter kitchen. Even if Nanny Sara was no longer cooking, she'd surely be supervising whoever was there. Today being Christmas Day I'd be bound to find something tasty in her bake oven. But there was no answer. I waited a spell and knocked again.

I pushed the door open to a cold kitchen, an empty fireplace. That made no sense. "Nanny Sara?" I called. There was no answer. The kitchen had been emptied and the chairs overturned. Foragers? At Ashland? That didn't seem possible.

Where was Ma? I pushed through the kitchen door, into

191

the saving room, through to the dining room. Empty. Some of the furniture was still there—the heavy old sideboard and the dining room table. The carved wooden table, the one Ma'd always been so proud of, showed a deep gash down its middle. The chairs were all missing, and no silver tea service sat on the sideboard.

"Ma?" I called, running through to the hallway. "Grandfather?" I pushed open the door of his study. The room had been ransacked, most of the volumes pulled from their cases, then thrown across the floor. Grandfather's gun cabinet stood empty, its glass smashed. My breath came in starts, and my heart beat so hard against my chest I couldn't call out.

I ran to the front parlor, the back parlor, but it was all the same. I steadied myself against the mahogany staircase and peered up. All the draperies had been ripped from the windows. The grandfather clock on the staircase, the one with the maddening pendulum that ticked off every second, was gone.

I gripped the banister and climbed the staircase, dreading what I might find in the upstairs bedrooms. "Ma? Grandfather? Emily?" Where was everybody? I searched each room. The house had been stripped of everything worth anything—even the heavy four-poster bed in Grandfather's room.

And then a sickening thought came to me. Emily had written that Grandfather wasn't well, that she didn't expect him to see the spring. That letter was written last Christmas. And Rebecca said that Ma was poorly. That information was months old.

"Please, God," I prayed. "Not Ma. Not before we make things right between us." I ran down the staircase, through the front door, and out to the family plot on the hill, not far from the Big House.

The gate had rusted shut, and I pushed and pulled to get it to swing open on its hinges. I didn't want to look but had to know. Brambles and weeds had died down after frost but left their winter tangles across the graves. There was one marker new since my last trip to Ashland. I swallowed hard and made myself step close enough to read the name on the stone: Marcus Ashton, b. 1802 d. 1864, beloved husband and father.

I pulled off my cap and sat back on my heels. "Thank You, Lord, that it isn't Ma." That seemed cold toward Grandfather, but I could only think of Ma. And though I'm ashamed to say it, there was something of relief in not having to confront Grandfather, in wondering if Ma could be her own self now that he was gone. But where was Ma?

Rebecca and Old George had both said that Emily was good to Ma. I remembered Emily's promise in her letter to look out for Ma. "Mitchell House," I whispered. "They'll be at Mitchell House." I stood to go. I swept the leaves from Grandfather's stone and prayed that he would rest in peace. I didn't know what else to pray about my grandfather. I hoped he hadn't suffered long. I hoped he was kind to Ma. But he was a cold man, selfish, and sometimes cruel. I didn't think that another fifty years would have set things easy between us, no matter how much Ma or I wanted it. I couldn't imagine Grandfather being anything other than what he was.

I pulled the rusted gate to and headed for the stable. I didn't even check the quarters. Slocum and the slaves would surely be gone. And no matter, I didn't want to run into Slocum.

I turned Stargazer into the side yard and let him graze for half an hour. Then I saddled him and rode the mile to Mitchell House. "Please, God," I begged, "let them be all right. Let them be well and safe."

Twenty-Three

Every step of that mile to Mitchell House brought memories —memories of Cousin Albert tutoring me, teaching me to handle and shoot a gun, coaxing Ma to loosen her rein on me; memories of Emily and the walks, the talks we'd shared—the time her hand brushed mine and mine came away smelling of peaches just ripened. I thought of Ma, all excited, getting ready for her Christmas ball. And then came a bitter flood of memories of Slocum, Grandfather's overseer, and his brutal treatment of slaves—the cutting off of Jacob's foot and the beating of Jeremiah—both because they dared to run toward freedom. And Alex, Cousin Albert's only son, with his selfish, cruel streak, his fear that I'd inherit Ashland, and his threats to me and my family if I didn't cut Emily out of my life.

Those memories felt like a heavy cloak that settled over my spirit. A cold drizzle began just before we reached Mitchell House. It seeped through my coat till I shivered, wet, a small misery on the outside to match my inside. I tried to push back the growing fear of what I'd find when I did see Ma.

This time I took the lane from the road, looping Stargazer's reins over his saddle so he could stand under the verandah's overhang. I took the steps, two at a time, to the front door.

No lights burned in the front windows, but I told myself that might not be unusual. They might all be keeping to the back of the house, near the winter kitchen. With wood in shorter supply they'd be bound to light fewer fireplaces. I pounded the door, waited a spell, then pounded again. When no one came I pushed open the heavy front door. "Emily? Ma? It's Robert!" But there was no glad cry, no sound at all.

The front hall was cold, and a sudden draft from behind whipped through the door. I pushed it closed. The dark was complete. I called again, but no answer. Where could they be? I opened Cousin Albert's study door. Except that there was no fire and fewer books, everything seemed in order, as if Cousin Albert might have just stepped out and planned to return shortly. The parlor across the hallway was the same—sparse, but clean. The furniture gleamed as though it had been polished within the week.

I raced up the staircase to the bedchambers and knocked on the doors, one by one, then opened them. Nothing. No one. Everything looked done up, as if the house slaves had just finished making the beds and putting all the rooms to rights.

I checked the wardrobes and remembered which room had been Cousin Albert's, which one was Alex's. I was glad that Alex's stood nearly empty, glad that he was probably still in England. When I walked into Emily's room my heart lightened. The room itself was brighter, and there was fresh holly in vases on her table. She must be here!

"Emily! Emily?" I called and called, but there was no answer.

The guest room must be used by Ma. The secretary was open, and I recognized a letter opener that Pa had once given Ma for her birthday. I picked it up and held it near, my closest link to either of them. When I checked Ma's wardrobe I realized there was no cloak hanging there, and only a couple of older dresses.

Maybe they went visiting for the Christmas season. But where?

That is when I heard the first small shuffle. Downstairs. My breath caught. I hadn't made any secret of my presence. Why had no one answered if they were here?

I crept down the stairs, kept close to the wall. There was no more shuffling or scuffling. It could have been a squirrel or a bat, but I couldn't risk that.

I pulled off my boots and inched toward the dining room at the back of the house. The door from the hallway stood open, same as always, and the table was set for half a dozen. They must be expecting to come back—today.

I was just wondering what day it was, if maybe it was Sunday and could they be at church, or if there was a special service for Christmas Day—when I heard the sound of iron on iron, coming from behind the saving room door.

"Who's there?" I kept my voice steady, like I wasn't afraid, like nothing in the world scared me.

There was new shuffling, feet moving, a rush of whispers, then silence. This time I didn't call out. I crept toward the door, even though it seemed every floorboard creaked.

I stood against the wall, hoping whoever was on the other side would step through the door if I waited long enough, if they thought I'd gone to another room. My heart pounded hard and stood in my throat.

At last the door began a slow swing, just a crack. I swallowed and jerked it toward me, just as it pushed wide. Out charged six feet of coal-black man, brandishing a fire poker.

I jumped back, but too late. The big man grabbed me as he hit the air running. We both sprawled over the floor in a tangle of arms and legs and poker. Breath knocked from my chest. The weight of his muscled arms and legs nearly crushed me. I crab-scrambled backward, quick as I caught my footing. He grabbed my foot. I kicked the poker across the room with my free foot.

I didn't reckon on the short, wiry colored woman shooting through the door to grab it up, to shake it, threatening, at my head. "Back off! Back off, you thievin' scoundrel! You'll not be stealin' Miz Emily's belongings! Not one more thing, you won't, you poor white trash!"

The colored man was on his feet now, ready to strangle me. "Let me have that, Mamee. Let me have that poker, you hear?"

"Noah?" The man's head shot up. "Noah?" I recognized Cousin Albert's black driver. "It's me, Robert—Robert Glover—Emily's cousin."

"Mista Robert?" He looked like he didn't believe me.

The little woman wasn't buying it either and crept closer, ready to swing the poker at my head.

"Tell her to put that down, Noah! Tell her who I am!"

"Mamee, give me that thing before you kill us all!" Noah lifted the poker from behind her. "This be Mista Robert, Miz Caroline's boy. You remember him?"

"What? Miz Caroline?" she scolded, miffed over losing the poker.

"Miz Caroline's grown-up boy," Noah repeated. "I never expected to see you here, Mista Robert."

"Emily wrote me to come." I caught my breath, wanted to be sure the poker stayed put. "Where is Emily? Is Ma here?" Noah pulled me to my feet.

"Don't you say nothin', Noah! Don't you tell nobody nothin'!" Mamee screeched.

"Mamee, ease yourself. This is Miz Caroline's boy. He's got a right to know where his mama be." Noah soothed the little woman, but she sputtered just the same and rocked on her heels, shaking her head. "Mamee, you go on and fix us up some of your soup. We be needing some of your good cooking—right away."

"Soup . . . soup . . ." Mamee repeated absently. All the while Noah guided her to the door.

"I apologize about the poker, Mista Robert. I thought you be some army forager or deserter fixin' to rob us or do us harm."

"Well, I didn't know what to think, you coming at me like that."

"We all lost our senses. This war's made us all skittish. Crazy." He turned the poker over in his hands. "If I'd killed you with this I'd be swingin' from a tree before sundown."

"It's all right, Noah. Nothing happened." He looked so distracted, distraught.

Then I remembered Mamee. "What's the matter with Mamee?"

Noah nodded. "The war been hard on her, that's all. We been foraged by the Union Army and Confederate Army. They took the harvest, the animals, most of the food. Miz Emily'd already sold off some of the furniture and what all she could. There ain't much left, but what they is Mamee vowed to protect for Miz Emily." He set the poker against the wall.

"Where is Emily? Where's Ma?"

"Why, they gone."

"Gone? Gone where?" I felt my insides falling through.

"They gone south near four months now. Gone to Miz

Emily's great-aunt Charlotte. Them and Nanny Sara, from over at Ashland."

"Aunt Charlotte?" I felt dizzy.

"You best set yourself down, Mista Robert, 'fore you fall down."

I steadied myself against the table. Noah pulled out a chair for me and settled me into it.

I'd come all this way, and they'd gone off. I couldn't take that in. "Where?"

"South Carolina. Down along the Edisto River. Miz Emily say it be a hundred fifty miles or so."

"Why?" It was all I could ask. "Why'd they go?" Noah looked away. "Noah?" I wanted to shake him.

He wouldn't meet my eyes. "You got to ask Miz Emily that."

Twenty-Four

꧁

$\mathcal{D}$usk had fallen when I opened my eyes. I barely remembered wolfing down Mamee's hot soup and cornbread. I remembered they'd led me to the parlor, the sun still bright in the sky, and laid a rug on the floor for me to rest. Noah had pulled off my boots. And then it was dark.

A single candle burned on the parlor table, reflecting its light against the window glass. Someone had covered me with two quilts, and even though the room was cold, I'd slept as warm and comfortable as I'd been in a long while.

I lay there, glad to be warm, pushing against the worries that nagged my brain. The parlor door squeaked open on its hinges. A face peered in. I forced my eyes wide, to focus.

"Mista Robert? You awake?" Noah's deep voice nudged me.

"Yes, Noah. Come on in." I pushed myself up and rubbed the sleep from my brain. "I guess I fell asleep."

"That good. You looked done in."

"We need to talk, Noah."

"Yes, sir. That we do."

"Why did Ma and Emily leave? Emily wrote me to come. Now she's gone." Noah didn't answer. "Did they go alone? What's happened here? And what happened at Ashland? The place is near emptied."

"Yankee soldiers—cavalry foragers. And Confederate soldiers—they foraging, too. Only I don't know they all regular soldiers. Some of them be grayback deserters taking what they think they got a right to." Noah shook his head. "Ashland got the worst—thievin' and tearin' up the place. It a mercy they didn't burn the Big House." Noah eyed me steadily.

"Things hard enough what with shortages of everything. No seed to plant, too many mouths to feed. Masta Marcus sold off most his slaves these last two years, trying to keep food on the table."

I nodded. "I saw Old George and Rebecca and her boys in Salem."

Noah's eyes lit up. "They be all right, then?"

"They're looking for the war to end, but they're doing all right. If it wasn't for them and the Widow Gibbons I wouldn't be here."

Noah nodded. "They good people." He hesitated. "You know if that Rebecca got a man?"

"I don't know. But she didn't make mention." Noah didn't answer. "You and Rebecca keeping company?"

Noah's mouth turned grim. "After this war, maybe. After this war if we all be free. I won't marry a slave woman. Like to be sold away, and our children." I understood that. "I know what you did for Jeremiah—helping him run North. We all grateful for that."

"You know?" That surprised me. "Well, Jeremiah helped me as much as I helped him. He's in Canada now."

Noah nodded again. "Good. That good." His forehead creased. "When those soldiers come and help themselves to

Ashland's furniture and draperies and animals and such, it scared Miz Caroline so bad she just screamed and screamed. Couldn't nobody stop her. Nobody at Ashland and nobody here. Never was a bloodcurdling rebel yell like Miz Caroline's screaming that day." Noah shook his head. "After that she just wasn't right in the head."

I hated taking that in, hated to imagine Ma at the hands of deserters—men with nothing to lose. "Did they hurt her?"

Noah looked away. "Not them. Not that I know about."

"Old George said she was feebleminded. Is that when it started?"

Noah's voice gentled. "Miz Caroline be what you call 'delicate' ever since she come back to Ashland, Masta Robert. She have her spells—sometimes be real normal, sometimes like she in some far-off place."

"But after those soldiers came, she was worse?"

Noah licked his lips. "Soon after. She never stepped out of that far-off place after that. We sent for Miz Emily, and she come right away."

"Is that when my grandfather died? When the soldiers came? I saw his grave."

Noah shifted in his seat. It seemed to me he avoided my eyes. "Masta Marcus died about the time they come."

I tried to understand that. "So, Ma was alone there at Ashland when the soldiers came? Was Jed Slocum there?"

Noah hesitated, and it seemed to me he measured his words more carefully than was his wont. "Mr. Slocum ran off about that time."

"Ran off?" I couldn't imagine Jed Slocum running off from Ashland. He'd pretty much thought he owned Ashland and all its slaves. "Why would he run off? What about the slaves?"

Noah stood up, began pacing, just a little. "Like I say, Masta Marcus sold off most of his slaves. Some run off. Run North. We hear Yankee soldiers take slaves in—contraband of war. They follow the soldiers, and then they be free. Some folks get jobs digging their ditches, cooking their food, washing their clothes. Some just follow from camp to camp."

"But where would Slocum go? Ashland was all the home he had. Right?"

"He run off." Noah stumbled over his words. "I reckon he afraid the home guard gonna come take him—conscript him. They takin' near every man can walk, now." Noah stared me down. "That all I know."

But I sensed that wasn't all he knew. There was more—something he was not telling.

"Was Emily here when the soldiers came?" I didn't want to think it.

"She in Salem, at the Ladies' School there! She not here." Noah spoke too quickly. "Masta Albert insist she go there when he went off to war if she wouldn't go with Masta Alex to England. He didn't want her home here, alone. But she did come home here most every weekend, and she'd visit Miz Caroline over to Ashland. That when she went over and found Miz Caroline in such a state—after Masta Marcus died and Mr. Slocum run off." Noah looked for all the world like he dared me not to believe him. Something about it all didn't ring true. But why would Noah lie to me?

"Have you heard anything from Alex?"

"No, sir. Miz Emily was expectin' him to send her money, but she say what with the blockade he couldn't do it even if he remembered." Noah sat down again. "I hope he remember sometime, or Miz Emily not be able to keep Mitchell House."

"What about the slaves here? How many are left?"

Noah stared at me a long time before he answered. "I tell you something because I trust you, Masta Robert. I trust you for what you done for Jeremiah, because I know what your daddy do for runaways. Mostly I trust you because Miz Emily trusts you."

I waited. He waited. "You can trust me, Noah."

"Miz Emily done give all her slaves they freedom. She sign papers for every one of us." He stood and pulled from inside his shirt a folded paper, creased and handled so many times it nearly fell apart in his hands. He took my measure again, then passed it to me.

There, in Emily's fine hand, was her manumission of one Noah, known as the driver for Mitchell House. I was amazed, and proud of Emily in a way I'd never imagined. "You say she freed all the slaves here?"

Noah nodded. "She told us right out that she didn't have the legal right. She say that her papa was the one hold that right. Even before she got word Mr. Albert was took prisoner, Miz Emily say she don't know if he make it home again, and that Masta Alex be set to inherit Mitchell House when Mr. Albert die. She say they might take these papers from us if the North don't win this war, but she do her best to make us free."

"But you stayed?"

"I stay for Miz Emily. I drive her and Miz Caroline and Nanny Sara to South Carolina, then I come back, all this way. A Yankee soldier stop me on the road, took my horse—Miz Emily's last horse—and wagon. I felt real bad about that. But I promised Miz Emily I take care of Mitchell House best I can, and take care of Mamee, till she come back."

"But why stay here? What if the North doesn't win this war, Noah? What if you lose your chance?"

Noah stared at me, patient, like I was too young to understand. "Mitchell House my home since I was brung into this world. It be my home after this war, whoever hold that bill of sale." He walked across the room, stared into the dark window.

"Something else Miz Emily done." He turned to face me. "She taught every one of us to read."

"She did?" I knew Cousin Albert would have forbidden it, that it was against the law.

"In this very room. Learning to read was the price for our freedom. She say we need that no matter where we go. She didn't have no money to give us, she say, but she give us that, and it be something we keep forever, something no man can take from us. Soon as a slave learn to read she write out their paper and let them go off if they want—free and clear. Most did. She plan to stay till every last slave learn to read—all except them too little or too old to make the change." He looked away again. "She just had to go sooner than she expect." He ran his dark fingers across his chin. "She free all the rest just before she leave South. Just Mamee and me now."

There was still something missing from all he said, but I couldn't place what. And my head spun, groggy. "I just don't understand why she left Mitchell House."

"They nothing left here. Not enough food, no money. Miz Caroline doing poorly. Nanny Sara so old she not likely to last. Miz Emily say her Grandma Grace always told her she had a sister loved her mightily—Miz Charlotte, in South Carolina. That all I know."

"But you drove them there."

"Yes, sir."

"Are they better off there? Is there food?"

"Not much, as I can tell. Knowing Miz Emily she be feeding anybody comes beggin' by her door."

"Aunt Charlotte must be as old as my grandfather was. Was she still living there?"

Noah sighed. "She there, but near the end of her days."

"Then why didn't they come back with you?"

Noah would not meet my eyes. "You see Miz Emily. Whatever she tell you, you know is the truth."

"Did Emily tell you she wrote to me? Asked me to come?"

"She say you might come. She didn't know you got her letter or not. But that be long ago."

Now I sighed. "I left home as soon as her letter came. A lot's happened these months." I waited. Should I tell Noah about Cousin Albert? It seemed only fair. But it did no good for him to think ill of Cousin Albert now. "Emily asked me to go see her father in the prison before I came." Noah nodded. "I did see him . . . He died there."

"Miz Emily had a visit from Maj. McCain this summer just passed. He told her Masta Albert dead. Say you kill him."

"He told Emily I killed her father?" Heat traveled up my neck, and my head pounded.

"Miz Emily say she don't believe that. She say no way you do such a thing, and she wonder just how it was Maj. McCain knew so much about her papa's death and done so little to prevent it. Maj. McCain got mad, real mad. Called Miz Emily 'naive in military ways and the ways of this world.'"

"Did he touch her?" I would kill McCain if he'd hurt Emily.

"Didn't lay a hand on her. But she call for me. I waiting in the hallway—see if she need me. I'm thinking if I wasn't here, maybe he might of tried something. He trash of a man. But he

206

rode on then. Ain't been back since. Miz Emily say she think he came here to set her against you, but she don't know why."

"He's in the field again, but not too far from here."

"You seen him?"

I nodded. "Wish I hadn't. He's got it in for me. But I did not kill Cousin Albert. He was planning an escape, pretending to be a regular soldier—not an officer. My visit and Emily's letter spoiled that for him. But he died of consumption, there in the prison hospital. I gave him Emily's letter and picture before he died. If anything happens to me, tell Emily that. Tell her it meant the world and all to him."

"What you mean, 'if anything happen' to you? What you fixin' to do?"

I stood up. I'd waited long enough. "I'm going after them. I just need you to tell me the way."

Noah nodded, relieved. "Miz Emily left a map in case you come. She hopin' you come."

That warmed me through. That told me full and clear that Emily didn't think I'd hurt her pa, that she trusted me.

Noah walked to the bookcase and pulled down a heavy, black Bible. "Miz Emily say give this only to you—nobody else does she want to know where she and Miz Caroline be."

"What do you tell people that come looking for her?"

"Say she off tending her sick relatives two counties away, but I don't know which county. Say she loaned her slaves out to her kin there since we got no crop our own to harvest. That what Miz Emily told me to say." Noah pulled a folded paper from the pages of the Bible and passed it to me. "Some doubt me, but don't know what to make of it all. If it come to it we got our freedom papers. But I hope to stay on for Miz Emily's sake. She do right by me if she able. She promised."

207

I wondered over Emily, prouder than I could say for all she'd done for all of them. And I wondered over Noah. They seemed as sure of each other as Aunt Sassy and Joseph Henry were of Mr. Heath.

The map was detailed, and I knew enough of the roads leading out of the county to believe I could follow the directions. I recognized a couple of the towns, and remembered some things from the maps I'd seen Pa draw. I wondered if he had any idea about this South Carolina relative. I'd never heard Ma or Grandfather speak of her.

"Thank you, Noah."

"You going tomorrow?"

"Now." I stood up and folded the map into my pocket. "It'll be best I travel by dark and lay low as I can in the day."

"Anybody see that fine horse they be taking it from you."

"I know. And he'll need to graze whenever I can find a good spot."

"I pack some bags of oats to take along. They still some out back I kept hidden from them foragers. Mamee get you a sack of food and a skin of water. You be careful, Masta Robert, and you give our best to Miz Emily. Tell her we takin' good care as we can of things here."

I reached for Noah's hand. "I'll tell her, Noah."

"I saddle your horse. You come on back to the kitchen, get you somethin' more to eat before you ride out."

"Thanks. I'll do that."

After Noah left I took a long look around the room. I wondered if I'd ever get back to see it. Suddenly the burden seemed too heavy, the route on the map too far, too hard. The dizzy feeling swam over me again, took my breath, and forced me to sit down. Once I caught my breath, I sank to my knees beside the settee.

"Lord," I prayed, "it's a long time since I came to You for anything besides a quick beg for help. And it seems every time I come to You I'm asking something bigger, more impossible. But I'm here again. Thank You for taking care of Emily and of Ma through all they've been through.

"Keep them in Your care. Keep me as I ride to find them. If there's something I should know, something I should do, please show me in a way I can understand.

"Thank You for Emily, for her strength for Ma's sake, for teaching the slaves to read, for signing over their freedom to them, for all the signs of Emily's love in this house."

The dam behind my eyes built for love of Ma and Emily, for not knowing what had become of Pa, and for the goodness of Noah and Mamee, of Old George and Rebecca. I choked it back. I prayed God's blessing on Noah and Mamee, His strength to see them through. When I finally got to my feet I felt deep in my need, and grateful, and a small flicker of hope.

Twenty-Five

In the kitchen Mamee ladled a bowl of stew and set a bag with ham slabs and cornbread beside my chair. "I won't take all your food."

"And I not givin' it." She pressed her small fists into her hips. "I know how to ration my house and hide what's left from those thievin' soldiers—both sides—makes no difference. They all thievin', and they all hungry. Me and Noah talked it over. We givin' you what we can, and we still get along. Come spring we all do better."

"I pray that's so, Mamee."

She softened. "We all prayin'." Then she stiffened up. "But the thing is, Masta Robert, you riper than a peach past its prime! They put some old hound dog on your trail today, they track you from here to Kingdom come! We got to do somethin' 'bout that."

For the first time I minded the big washtub at the other end of the kitchen. It already held a couple inches of water, and Mamee simmered big kettles over the fire. "Is that bathwater?" I asked.

"See there! It done been so long since you cleaned up you

don't recognize a washtub no more! It's high time you scraped some of that road off you."

"But I'm leaving now. Noah's saddling Stargazer."

"That horse can wait. He don't stink half as bad as you. Now, soon as you done eatin' you pour this kettle in that tub and strip off your clothes. I'll wash them with a stick, see if they hold together."

I looked at Mamee, then at the hot water. I surely could use a wash, but I hated to wait. It might take hours for my clothes to dry. The night was moving on. I sniffed my armpits and pulled away. "I guess it won't do much good to argue with you."

Mamee grinned from ear to ear. "None a'tall."

The hot bathwater soothed my kinks and sores, even if I did stir a mud pool. I scrubbed my hair, which had grown long and scraggly these months. I howled when Mamee crept up behind me and poured a pitcher of cold water over my head to rinse out the soap.

"That get rid of that caked-on mud in your scalp. Scrub it again, and I pour clear rinse water."

"That's clean enough!" I sputtered, shivering.

"Not till I say so!" Mamee harped for all the world like Aunt Sassy. There was nothing to do but follow her orders, especially as I was sitting in a tub in my birthday suit.

I'd not given much thought to what I looked like these past months. Men everywhere marched grimy, gritty, and fighting graybacks. I was lucky not to have the varmints for company! I rubbed my hand over my jaw and realized a beard had grown. It wasn't all dirt. Before I left home I'd been working on stubble —"peach fuzz" as Aunt Sassy called it.

Like she could read my mind, Mamee pulled out a straight razor and soap cup.

"Soon as you done there you shave, and I cut your hair. It best if you don't look like a runaway, you travelin' South. They shoot deserters, or they cart them back to the army. You look like a prime runaway."

She was right, and I'd never thought on it. "Thanks, Mamee. I'm beholden."

She nodded, showing an easy, open smile—the first one I'd seen. It seemed right that Mamee stood in charge of something, even if it was only me and only for an hour. She left the room. I stood up and wrapped the bed sheet around me. She'd set it on a chair and hung my pants and shirt and jacket on a line by the fire. They were half dry. It wouldn't take long.

Mamee marched in with an armload of clothes. "These be Masta Albert's. He won't be needing them no more, and I believe with a little adjustin' they fit you fine."

I bristled. "I can't take Cousin Albert's clothes." I didn't want to take them. I didn't want anything of his. "Mine'll be dry in a while."

"They be dry, but they soldier boy clothes. You be treated better you look like a gentleman." I hated that she was right. I hated that I hadn't just ridden off already. "Now you put these on, and I'll get that shavin' water ready."

The clothes hung loose, but the length was like they'd been made for me. I hadn't realized how I'd shot up these last months. I caught sight of me in the looking glass. I ran next to scrawny, like all my meat'd shot straight up, stretched thin over bones.

Mamee helped me with the straight razor. The face that stared back at me looked thinner, older than the boy who'd left home.

I'd just finished buttoning the shirt and trousers Mamee'd adjusted for me when there came a pounding from the front of the house. Not a second later Noah burst through the back door, eyes wide, out of breath. "Home guard!"

"Stargazer!" I cursed myself for not having ridden earlier.

But Noah shook his head. "Safe. He safe—in the quarters. They won't go there—not this time—not if you pretend to be Masta Alex back from across the water."

"What?"

"That it!" Mamee cried. "You be the Masta since yo' daddy died."

"Come home to look in on things. It the only way," Noah pleaded. "Otherwise we all be taken." The pounding came again, louder, more determined. "I answer the door. You go upstairs, like you gone off to your room for the night. Mamee, clear away those soldier clothes."

We all rushed to our places, Mamee passing me a candle in a cup. As Noah passed me in the hallway he whispered, "Do somethin' with that Yankee accent."

I raced up the dark stairs, doing my best to save the flame. I found Alex's bedroom, lit the lamp, pulled the quilt down from the bed, rumpled it like I'd slept, and pulled an old coat from the closet, tossed it across the chair. Then I stood near the door, half listening, half rehearsing my memory of Alex's voice. Mimicking voices and playing parts was not new to me. We'd done it a dozen times or more when we'd disguised ourselves or slaves running North. I heard Noah speaking below.

"Please, sir. Can't it wait till morning? Masta Alex done retired for the night."

"We heard Col. Mitchell's son had gone to England."

"He was, sir. He did go there. He only just got back, this week. But he retired for the night, and he won't like to be disturbed." I heard a shuffle of feet, as though a half-dozen men pushed their way into the hallway.

"I don't believe your Master Alex is here. How'd he get through the blockades? I believe we'll just take a look for ourselves and satisfy—"

"Noah! What is the meaning of this? Who's down there?" I'd stepped to the top of the stairs and, with all the superior authority I could muster, barked down at Noah. The men stood back.

"Mr. Mitchell? Alex Mitchell?" The leader let go of Noah's collar.

"And precisely who is asking?" I sneered. It set the man off guard.

"Zach—Zachary Lincoln, home guard. We heard they wasn't nothin' but colored runnin' around here. All the family run off."

"As you can see, Mr. Lincoln, that is not so."

"We'd heard you was over in England." He eyed me suspiciously.

"Apparently, no longer." I stepped down a couple more stairs, leveled the man's stare, then made to look like I took pity on him. "I realize, Mr. Lincoln, that you are doing your job to keep our countryside safe. In that, you are no doubt to be commended. But I might suggest you stop terrorizing loyal citizens and our people, and get on to something more crucial to the war effort."

He looked at me like he didn't know what I was talking about.

"How do I know you're Mr. Alex?"

"And who else would I be?" He looked a mite uncertain. "I must say 'Lincoln' is an unusual name for a loyal man of the

214

Confederacy." I narrowed my eyes. "Just who are your people, Mr. Lincoln?" Zach Lincoln's color mounted.

I held up my hand. "There is no need to explain yourself, Mr. Lincoln. I trust our offices investigated your affiliations thoroughly before assigning your position. Now, if there is nothing further you require, and if you have discharged your duties, I suggest you leave my home in peace this Christmas-tide."

"We're just doing our job, Mr. Mitchell. We'd heard—"

"Noah, you may show these gentlemen the door. I trust, Mr. Lincoln, that in this new year you will not trust in rumors as much as your own valuable sense. Good night."

Noah walked to the door and held it open. I turned and made to go upstairs, but Lincoln's voice called me back.

"Confederacy needs every able-bodied man, Mr. Mitchell." The challenge was called in bluff.

I turned. "Of course, Mr. Lincoln. Just as soon as my affairs are settled here. After all," I said with a smile, "I wouldn't want rumors regarding the mismanagement of my family's affairs to cause you further alarm." I turned to go, then stopped, and turned again. "Is that sufficient?"

"Yes, sir. I reckon it is."

"Good night then."

Noah shut the door behind them but pressed his finger to his lips. We heard the men arguing, their horses sidestepping one another, but couldn't make out the words.

Mamee appeared in the doorway of the dining room and whispered. "They splittin' up. Some circling the house, some ridin' toward the quarters."

"The quarters? Stargazer!" I flew down the stairs, two at a time. Noah grabbed me before I reached the door.

"He all right! He be all right!"

"They'll hear him! They'll take him!" I was no longer the rich, spoiled young slaver I'd played. I was scared to death of losing my best friend.

"No! They never hear him," Noah vowed. "I muzzled him after I fed him—just in case. You got to get your bearings, Masta Robert, or you'll set them to searchin'!"

"Muzzled Stargazer?" I stopped, dead in my tracks, hating that he'd been muzzled, thankful beyond words that Noah'd done it. We waited, and waited. At last we heard the riders circle, then thunder down the lane.

"Do you think they've all gone?"

"I 'spect," Mamee said. "Those men not happy bein' called out for nothin'. I heard them tellin' that Mr. Lincoln so."

That's when Noah turned to me. "You like one of them actors from the theater up in Raleigh, Masta Robert! I never knew you such a fine talker!"

"I've put on some before, when I had to, but never so much. You think they bought it?"

"Like men beggin' whiskey!" Mamee declared.

"You saved me, Noah."

"The Lord saved us all. Without you here they'd take the run of the place."

"Well," Mamee said as she pressed her fists into her hips, "'nough of this. Just goes to show how you needed that bath. You ready to ride now?"

"I am," I vowed and pecked her cheek.

It was after midnight. I cut through the back acres of Mitchell House and Ashland, then took the road south, along the river. Noah had packed oats for three days and water for two. Mamee'd packed all the ham slabs and cornbread they could spare. I rode in Cousin Albert's clothes and his long coat and toted a change of clothes besides. It was the warmest and cleanest, the best fed I'd been since summer. I prayed that God would bless them for it.

I rode hard, by the light of a three-quarters moon, until the sky streaked red in the east. Along the way we passed a few houses, some abandoned. We stopped for the day by the burned ruin of a barn. An old trough filled with rainwater held plenty for Stargazer to drink. We feasted on the bounty of Noah and Mamee. I slept most of the day away. By the time the shadows lengthened we were both antsy, ready to ride.

We rode five nights straight like that—sometimes finding day shelter, sometimes sleeping in the woods—without once running across another man, woman, or child. I thanked God for the night's safety each time I laid my head down and thanked Him again each time I woke with only Stargazer nuzzling my hair.

The land flattened, stretched endlessly. Pine needles grew inches longer, making the trees easier to hide behind.

By day I slept and studied the map, tried to estimate how far we'd come. We steered clear of towns. That made our traveling less risky, but it also made the miles hard to figure. Still, by the sixth night I believed we were less than a day's ride from Aunt Charlotte's. I wanted to get there soon, but I was glad for those nighttime rides with Stargazer.

Riding by the light of the moon is a sacred thing. Thoughts don't wander the same as they do in daylight. Every hoofbeat is focused. Every sense sharp. A hole in the road might mean a broken leg and the end of everything we'd labored toward.

We rode not like horse and rider but like one creature, glad to be alive, glad to be together, glad to run against the wind.

Twenty-Six

We crept into town hours before first light. Noah had said that Grandaunt Charlotte lived near the edge of town, in the finest house on the block. Three out of five of the biggest houses were deserted. One was stripped clean, as if the owners had long planned a move—lock, stock, and barrel. The other two looked like their owners had fled but traveled light. Family portraits lined the hallways, and books stood in rows across shelves. Pianofortes, sideboards, and settees kept their place, half-draped, but not a piece of silver or clothing, not a scrap of food remained.

Twice through the night Stargazer and I'd hidden in the shadows of weeping willows as wagons loaded with every sort of household goods rumbled down the dirt road. They didn't straggle out of town, half-starved. They nearly ran against the moonlight, loaded down. Thinking of the food they carted off started my backbone gnawing on my belly. I searched every abandoned pantry, every storehouse—even the stables. Food was one thing nobody forgot. Still, the empty stables made a safe place for us to bed down for the night and a safe hideaway for Stargazer while I searched.

Dawn showed the houses off. Their high, white columns and wide front verandahs, lined both sides of the street. The homes stood side by side, close enough to bow, but far enough apart to ward off talking over the hedge. Brown lawns grew weed wild, and I wondered if all the slaves and servants had run off, and where they'd run to this far South. The town didn't show the beat-up, burned-out look that an invading army leaves, but it didn't have the storm-ripped, picked-clean look of foragers, either.

I tried to look at the houses through Noah's eyes, but they all looked fine to me. I dared not search by day. But I peered through the stable cracks and window for any sign of Ma or Emily. I never saw a soul. By nightfall I began to fear that one of those deserted houses belonged to Grandaunt Charlotte. How would I know if they'd moved on, or where they'd gone?

That night I searched three more deserted houses. I was a full block into town and tried to keep the panic inside my chest, to think through how I could ask somebody about them without raking up too many questions. At least I'd found two eggs in a henhouse and ate them raw, licking the broken yolks from my fingers.

We'd spent the second day in a deserted carriage house that backed up to a wooded lot. During the day the high-pitched squeals of young children woke me. It sounded like a game of chase and later Blind Man's Bluff in a nearby yard. If I could catch one of them alone I could ask about Emily. It was late afternoon when a woman called the children in. They all disappeared together. I'd have to think of something else.

When dusk finally fell I led Stargazer into the yard between the woods and the carriage house to graze while I searched the outbuildings for food. I thought about going back to the henhouse where I'd pilfered eggs. I considered stealing a chicken but wondered if I dared light a fire to cook it in one of the empty houses. The thought of taking such a chance, the worry of somebody seeing the smoke, of catching me, of losing Stargazer, stoked my fear and gave me pause. But I'd have to do something. Stargazer's grass was beginning to look good.

I'd just drawn well water and shut Stargazer back inside the carriage house with the bucket when I heard a scrape, scrape coming from the yard next door. A high hedge separated the two yards. I pulled the shrubbery back, enough to peer through. Dark as it was, I saw the back of a woman, tall and slim, bent to a shovel, digging. I couldn't tell what she was digging—a garden, a hole. I leaned forward to see. That is when the rifle cocked near my ear.

"Cry out or move, and I shall blow your head off." The steely voice of a cultured Southern woman vowed low. "Lace your fingers and place them behind your head." I did. "You are the thief who stole our eggs yesterday morning." It was not a question. The muzzle of the gun stabbed my back.

"Yes, ma'am. I apologize . . . I was hungry."

"We're all hungry. It doesn't give us call to steal the food out of our neighbors' mouths." She spoke low.

I started to turn. "Turn your head and I'll shoot."

"And I'll help her." It was the shovel-digging woman, come to bolster the rifle-toting lady.

"How many are with you?"

"Just me."

"Don't you lie to her!" the shovel-toting woman demanded,

poking the blade of the shovel into my side. I turned, just enough to see, and was surprised that she was brown and bold as brass. "We saw you come out of the carriage house, talking."

"To myself. I was talking to myself," I stammered, fearful that they'd seen me. Had they seen Stargazer? Had anyone else?

"Then you won't mind if I shoot holes through my neighbor's carriage house window?"

"No! No! Please!"

"How many?" the brown shovel woman spat.

I didn't answer right away, and the rifle woman, the one I'd still not seen, stabbed my back with the barrel. "Hold that shovel over his head while I take some target practice."

"No!" I swayed, unsteady. "It's my horse. It's my horse. Don't shoot . . . please."

"A horse?" The rifle woman brightened. I couldn't answer. "Does he pull carriage? Wagon?" I groaned inside myself, knowing I'd stepped in the biggest cow pie yet.

A window from the house on the other side of the hedge shot up, and a woman's shrill voice cried, "Ruby? Ruby! Where are you? There's a chill in the air, and you forgot to light my fire, you silly girl!"

"Don't answer her!" the rifle lady hissed. "We don't want her coming out here."

"She'll come looking if I don't—you know she will!" the shovel woman warned.

"Ruby! Answer me! Don't make me take a strap to you!" The voice rankled at the edge of my memory.

"Ma?" I whispered. "Ma?" I lunged toward her voice, turning just in time to see the shovel swing over my head and slam into my face.

Twenty-Seven

I was moving—dragged, jerked, bumped across grass, but that might have been a dream. The next pain, besides the one throbbing my head, was the jerk of a rope across my wrists, tight behind my back. For a moment I was back inside Fort Delaware, sure that McCain had bedeviled himself into a woman's body and that the misery and his unholy tricks would go on forever.

Next I was sitting in a rocker, trussed up like a pig with my feet bound to the rockers and my hands tied behind the spindle back. I heard women fussing, whispering, arguing, and a candle flame danced before my face. My hair had fallen over my forehead. A cool hand pushed it back.

"Charles! I declare, Papa will have your hide for sneaking about like this!" And then the same voice took on a different tone. "But it is mighty flattering, you couldn't wait till morning. Now, Ruby, you mustn't tell Papa. You know it would not bode well for either of us." The voice giggled. I had to be dreaming. It was the sound of Ma, only young and girlish, and she'd called me by Pa's name. I couldn't bring her face to focus.

"It's not Charles, Miss Caroline, you know that. Mr. Charles gone off to war . . ."

"Oh, I hate all this talk of war! He's playing games—look at him! They're all playing games in their West Point uniforms. But don't they look dashing? The blues and the grays and the butternuts—every one of them. I wonder that they don't all keep the same color, as they used to—or take better care!" And then the hand came again. "But, Charles . . . where is your uniform? You can't be skulking through the neighborhood like a common criminal! Why, you haven't even shaved!" She tsked. "What would Papa say if he saw you now? It wouldn't do your suit any good, my dear—not any good at all!"

"Miss Caroline, it's long past your bedtime. Let me help you up to bed. You leave this young man to us. We'll take good care of him." The shovel lady spoke from behind me, and I winced, ready for another blow.

"I suppose you're right, Ruby. I do need my rest. Now, Charles, you come tomorrow, like a proper suitor—through the front door! No more of this skulking through the yard like a robber. I'm still hoping Papa will hear you out and consent." She scolded. She lifted my chin, pushed back my hair. Her lips brushed my forehead. "Good night, my love. Until tomorrow."

"Ma!" I pleaded, or meant to. My throat was so parched I don't know if the word came out, and I couldn't open my smashed eye.

"Come now, Miss Caroline. Come along," the shovel woman said. She whispered to the other woman, "If he gives you any trouble, shoot him." The two women swept past my chair. I listened until their footsteps faded away, and wondered again if I was dreaming. I couldn't open my eyes. Somewhere a clock ticked off seconds and minutes.

"Thank you for not correcting her." It was the rifle woman, not so steely now. "She thought you were her husband." I didn't

223

answer. I couldn't sort the dreaming from the throbbing in the back of my head or the pain above my eyes. "I'm sorry Ruby hit you so hard. She thought you were going to attack me."

That's when I laughed. It started in as a grunt, a snort, a low chuckle, and built till I was coughing, past reason. Then the icy water slammed my face, and I was choking. But it opened my eyes, and at last I could see the shape of a fuming, dark-haired beauty before me, pitcher in one hand, the other firmly planted on her hip.

"Just what do you think is so funny?"

"You're the one with the gun, Emily!" I couldn't stop laughing —more for the joy of finding her than anything.

She gasped, "How do you know my na—Cousin Charles? Can it—? No! It can't be . . . Robert? Robert? Is it you?"

"Emily," I whispered. I tried to squint up at her. She was still fuzzy in the swimming candlelight but more striking than I remembered. I swallowed hard. The pain in my head, the worry of losing Stargazer to a crazy woman's gunshot, the months of little food, little sleep, of battling every way I knew to reach them—all swam together until I was falling, drowning.

The next I knew she was untying my feet, my hands, helping me to a settee in the parlor, pushing me down. Then she was bathing my face, my eyes, till I howled from pain. "Oh, Robert, I'm so sorry! I didn't know it was you! Why didn't you tell me who you were?"

"I didn't know who you were till just now." But something at the edge of my memory didn't sit right. "She thought I was Pa. Ma thought I was Pa."

Emily sighed. "She's not herself, Robert. She's not been herself for a long time." I closed my eyes. "You must rest now. We'll talk in the morning. There's so much to talk about. I've no idea how you found us. I'm so thankful you did." She laid a cold vinegar cloth across my head and covered me with a blanket. "Rest now."

"Noah. Noah told me how to find you."

"You were at Mitchell House? Is he well? And Mamee?"

"They're holding their own." The room began to spin. "I saw Grandfather's grave. I came as soon as I could. But things happened. I tried to . . ." My voice trailed as my mind wandered.

"I'm so sorry Ruby hit you," Emily soothed. "You really must rest now. We'll talk in the morning."

If she said any more I didn't hear it. I'd found Ma. I'd found Emily. Stargazer was safe. And my head hurt like mad. It was enough. It was enough for now.

Twenty-Eight

I slept through the night and long into the morning. Sun streamed across the parlor floor by the time I opened my eyes. My head still ached, and my right eye bloomed nearly shut, but I could see out the left one and counted myself lucky for it. If the shovel woman had swung two inches lower I wouldn't be seeing anything.

Somewhere in the house I heard the shuffle and running of small, light feet, giggles, and scolding. I wondered if I was dreaming. I closed my eyes against the light.

A soft sniffle and softer fingers trailed the length of my arm, stirred me. I dreamed, in that moment, that Emily stood over me, her dark hair tumbling across my cheek. But when I opened my eyes there sat the shovel woman, her brown forehead worry creased, her cheek streaked with tears. I jerked back, sharp enough to make my head pound.

My jerking startled her. She jumped, too, and I thought she meant to slug me again. But she reached her hands toward me, and every line in her face spoke sorrow.

"No, no. Settle yourself, Mista Robert. Settle yourself. I won't hurt you. I swear I won't hurt you. I'm ever so sorry I hit

you with that shovel last night. I thought you were fixin' to
pester Emily—Miz Emily."

Still, I held my breath.

"Do you know who I am?" she asked, resting her hands on
my arm.

I tried to pull back. "You're the shovel woman," I croaked,
half sputtering, knowing my mouth wasn't working right, not
able to make it do better.

She looked sorry all over again. "Yes, I can see why you'd
call me that—think of me in that way. But I have another name.
It's Ruby. I've known your mama a long, long time."

I didn't believe her. Ma only just came to South Carolina.
Surely my face showed that.

"You don't believe me. And you have every right. But it's
true."

I didn't answer, didn't want anything to do with this crazy
woman. But something nagged at the edge of my memory,
something I couldn't place.

"Your mama, Miz Caroline, and I grew up together—at
Ashland." "Ashland" seemed to catch in her throat. "Almost like
sisters, we were. Only I was her slave." She pulled back and
breathed deeply. "Nanny Sara is my mother."

"Nanny Sara?" I repeated. "Ruby?" My mind tried to connect what I knew, but it was slow. I tried to sit up. She braced
my back.

"I helped your mama and daddy elope. It was the thing Miz
Caroline wanted most in the whole world then, and I was her
friend. I'da done anything for her—both because she was my
friend and because I was her slave. And I paid the price."

"Jeremiah's mother?" I couldn't believe it.

Tears sprang to her eyes, and she nodded. "I haven't seen

my baby since the day they pulled me off and sent me South to Miz Charlotte."

Now I did sit up, searched her face. My head pounded, but my mind remembered things Jeremiah had said about his mother—how my grandfather had been so angry when he learned that Ruby had helped Ma run off to marry Pa that he'd locked her in the attic at Ashland. He'd taken her over and over, ten nights straight . . . no matter that she'd never been with a man . . . then sent her to the quarters. When it was clear she was pregnant he called her a whore, till the baby came out near as white as him. I remembered Jeremiah's walk, the odd little ways he reminded me of Grandfather.

"Jeremiah?" I said again.

"Jeremiah," she answered. "I named him for that sad, old prophet in the Bible. 'Cause I knew he'd have a hard life. And if he lived, he'd have hard truth to live by."

"He did. He did have a hard life. But he's free now. He's living in Canada. He's helping other freed slaves get their lives started. He's looking for you." I tried to pour that understanding into her.

She looked like she could hardly believe it, like she wanted to believe it. "Mama told me you and he ran off together. She say she believes he got to the promised land, for nobody ever brought him back." She leaned closer, needing more. "Is it true? Do you know for a fact it's true?"

"It's true. For a fact, it's true. He's safe, and well, last I knew. He's learned to read and write. He wrote me a letter—more than one." And I stared at her, unable to believe she was kneeling here before me. I tried to piece together my questions, but my head still pounded, and then I swayed.

"You best lie down again, Mista Robert. I swung that shovel

with all my might. You gonna nurse a headache for a week, I expect."

I lay back on the settee. "You'd be proud of him, Ruby. You'd be proud of Jeremiah Henry." And then, though I didn't want to, didn't mean to, I fell asleep. I felt Ruby's cool hand, smooth against my forehead, as I drifted off. And I wasn't afraid.

The next I woke, late afternoon shadows stretched across the room. Voices came from the back of the house, rising and falling—some childish and some older—shrill, then soft, then shrill again. Another voice broke in, soothing, comforting. I knew that last voice was Ruby's. So I hadn't dreamed her. Her words came back to me. "Jeremiah's mother." How she came here, I couldn't guess. Grandfather'd vowed he didn't know where she was sold. Somehow, I'd have to let Jeremiah know.

And then the irony hit me. Jeremiah and I had both been searching for our mothers these last four years—mourning their loss, wondering where and how and even who they were now. But Jeremiah's mother had been taken away long ago by force; mine left willingly, and now didn't seem to know me.

I knew that I'd soon learn the truth about Ma, about why she left Pa and me, about why she'd stayed away. I'd been yearning to understand all these years, and trying every way I knew to get to her these last months, sure that everything would work out the way I wanted. But now that she was just through the doorway and down the hall, now that I could ask her face to face, I feared. Whatever she said could not be unsaid. I no longer nursed hopes about what might happen when we talked, and last night didn't make me feel better about that.

There was a knock at the door.

"Robert? May I come in?"

I pushed my hair from my eyes and took a deep breath.

"Come in, Emily." This time I saw her clearly. It was like looking at a younger, darker version of Ma—younger than the Ma I remembered from my childhood.

"How is your head?" She knelt beside me, and her nearness confused me, threw me off kilter.

"Fine. It's fine," I stammered. "It hurts, but it's fine."

She smiled. "I imagine it will do better once you get a bite of food in your stomach. You must be famished." My stomach rumbled, on cue. I felt the heat creep up my neck, and we both laughed. "Ruby's cooked up the best of our ham and grits. There's cornbread and the last of our potatoes, fried with onions—the way you like them, if I remember."

"You remembered I like fried potatoes?" It was a dumb thing to say.

Now it was her turn to blush. "I remember a great many things, Robert." She helped me sit up. "We've much to discuss, and there may not be much time. But first you must eat. The children have eaten already and gone to bed."

"The children?" Had Emily already married, borne children?

"You'll meet them tomorrow. Orphans, mostly. Children left alone by the war. Some are truly orphaned; some the parents or older siblings can no longer feed. There are children everywhere, begging now."

"You opened an orphanage?"

"Well, not intentionally!" She laughed. "Aunt Charlotte and Ruby and I. There's Henry, the oldest—maybe five or six—and little Lizzie, and Jubal. Then twin girls—so young we don't know their names. We call them Mildred and Martha, and a toddler we call Jacob. We couldn't turn them away." She looked like that was the only sensible answer. But then she frowned. "Any-

way, we'll all eat—the adults—and that . . . might be difficult."
She helped me to my feet. "Cousin Caroline . . . is confused. She
might not know who you are." I waited, watching Emily's face.
"She thinks time has turned back on itself."

"What do you mean, 'turned back on itself'?"

Emily drew a deep breath, and I could tell she didn't want
to go on. "She thinks she is a young girl again. She believes you
are your father—Cousin Charles—come to court her."

I leaned back. Last night's scolding from Ma rushed back.

"We've tried to bring her into the present, but she becomes
anxious—shrill. I'm frightened for her, Robert." Emily sat down
beside me, took my hand, but I pulled away. This was not what
I'd worked all these months to come and find. "I'm afraid that if
we force her, insist on her understanding the truth, that it will
destroy her." I couldn't answer. Emily waited. Finally, gently, she
said, "Do you understand? Do you understand what I'm trying
to say?"

Now I did look at Emily. She was concerned for me, but
strong. This was not new to her. She'd been caring for Ma a long
time now—time Ma should have been helping her. But I
looked away. "How long has Ma been like this?"

"Since the war broke out, most particularly. Since the day
Papa left—in his uniform." Emily stood up and walked toward
the window, pulled back the drape, and gazed out on the lawn.
"There were signs before that. I thought for a long time that she
was just happy being home—back at Ashland. I thought she
was making the most of every minute of her visit, that she was
being brave, pretending not to miss—" Emily's back straightened, and she stopped.

"Not to miss Pa, or me," I finished for her.

She dropped the drape and turned to face me, anxiety

231

written in her forehead. "Yes. And I couldn't understand that. At first I admired her, certain that she was just there to help Uncle Marcus, but that she'd be going back to you soon. I wanted to get to know her so well, Robert. I even wanted to be like her—so full of life and gaiety. Sometimes I even pretended that she was my mother. I scarcely remember my mother." Emily studied her hands. "It was like she and Papa and Alex and I were a family—the first whole family I could remember." She dropped her hands, helpless. "But, of course, we weren't. It wasn't right. And I saw how she and Papa—"

"Loved each other?" I finished again, trying to keep a grip on the heat of my anger, knowing my voice fell cold.

"I would have said, 'cared for each other.' But, yes, I believe they did." Emily looked me in the eye. I turned away, unable to face the young woman who looked so much like Ma that it confused my feelings toward her, who'd pretended my mother was hers while Pa and I did without. "It was wrong, Robert. It was wrong of them both. I don't think either of them intended it to happen, but—"

"But it did! They let it happen, and they didn't do anything to stop it!" I wanted to shame someone for the shame I'd long felt, the shame everyone in our families had pretended to sweep under the rug.

She lifted her chin and spoke quietly, "That isn't true. Papa did something. He left. He never touched Cousin Caroline, and he went away. He went to war."

"He'd have gone to war anyway, Emily!" I wouldn't let her idealize Cousin Albert, not in this. "His beloved 'country' was at war. His South—his way of life—the threat of losing his precious power over other people—his slavery!" I poured every ounce of venom into my words. "You can't justify what they did! You can't make a saint out of him!"

Tears welled in Emily's eyes. "I don't make a saint of him. I don't justify his love for her. But I've forgiven my father—my father, who is dead!" She took several deep, shuddering breaths. "And your mother. I've forgiven your mother for coming back to us, for putting them both in temptation's way, whether or not she knew what she was doing." Emily looked up. "I've prayed for you and Cousin Charles, every day."

"And that should make everything all right." I sneered, hating myself, but set on hurting someone. Emily would do.

"I had no idea if your parents had a falling out or came to some arrangement or what. But I couldn't imagine you losing your mother. I knew it would be like me losing Papa."

I turned away. I didn't want her sympathy. It made it too hard to hate her, and in that moment I needed to hate her—as if her telling the truth laid the fault at her door—at someone's door—someone I could see and yell at. Someone alive and sane I could blame, could hurt for all the hurt and craziness—if only for a minute. I wanted to shake her. I wanted to pull out my own hair. Crazily, I also wanted to hold her. I wanted her to run into my arms and comfort me. But I did none of those things. The room had shadowed, and I could no longer see her face clearly. "Well," I whispered sarcastically, "it seems we've lost both of them."

"You'll need to forgive her, Robert," Emily whispered back.

"Forgive her? You've just told me that my mother is crazy and before that she—"

"If you don't forgive her it will eat you alive. I know. Forgive her, for yourself."

"Is she sorry? Has she ever been sorry?"

"Your father forgave her."

"He doesn't even know!" How could Emily lie to me like that?

"He knows."

I'd had enough. I began to wonder if Emily's mind was as warped as Ma's. I reached for my jacket, ready to head out the door. It didn't matter where I went, but I wouldn't stay in that dark room. I needed air.

Emily blocked the door.

"Out of my way, Emily. Get out of my way." I didn't touch her, and I measured my words.

"He came to Ashland. Cousin Charles came to Ashland."

I stopped cold. "What?"

"He came to Ashland to convince Cousin Caroline to go home, to Maryland."

"When?" I didn't believe her.

"Two winters past. Late January—maybe early February."

I stopped. The time would fit with Pa's leaving. "What happened?" I challenged.

Emily braced herself. "She wouldn't go. She refused. She told him she'd chosen—differently." I looked away, my fists clenching, unclenching, clenching.

"She doesn't know her mind, Robert. She's fickle as a child is fickle, from one day to the next. Realities change for her. Sometimes she plays a role so convincingly for weeks that we all begin to believe that is her true self. Then one day, it is all suddenly different, and she cannot understand why we don't see as she sees, why we can't conjure the very memories she has created in her fancy." Emily moved closer. "It is as though a war rages inside her—one we can't see, but one she is losing . . . a little more each day."

A bold little knock came at the door. Emily opened it to a saucer-eyed, gap-toothed colored boy in a nightshirt trailing the floor, five times too big for him. "Henry? What are you doing out of bed?"

"I heard you talking, Miz Emily. I want you to tell me a story."

"I've already told you a story, Henry, and you are supposed to be asleep, aren't you?"

Henry nodded but reached his hand up to Emily, giving her a smile only a crusted heart could resist. Emily pressed her hands to her hips and feigned impatience but broke into a tired smile. He giggled as she shook her head, swooped him into a bear hug, then hoisted him in her arms.

"Henry, this is Robert." She turned to face me. "Robert, this is Henry. You'll both get better acquainted tomorrow." Henry gave me a shy wave, and I nodded back, not wanting to be interrupted but taken with the little boy. "I'll be right back, Robert," Emily said over her shoulder, and they were gone, whispering, giggling, up the stairs.

I shook my head to think Emily'd taken in war orphans on top of Ma and everything else. And then I thought again of what Emily'd said about Ma's inner war. I knew about that. She'd waged that war for as long as I could remember. I'd never understood it, only knew it kept her apart from Pa and me—even when we lived under the same roof.

When Emily came back I'd gotten hold of myself, spoke quietly, knew she meant to help. I asked, "What did Pa say?"

Emily pushed stray wisps of hair back and stepped away from the door. "He tried to reason with her, at first. But she was certain he was trying to steal her away. She fought him, like a tigress." She crossed to a chair near the settee and sat, looking suddenly weary. "She was cruel to him, Robert. She'd conjured a demon in her brain that did not exist, and she believed he embodied it. The things she said to him . . ." She shook her head at the memory. "How I pitied him."

I remembered the spring before Ma'd left us, the angry things she'd said to Pa, even then. Things that made no sense to me. I'd sometimes wondered if Pa had hurt her in some way, if he'd carved some breach between them. I'd even blamed him for her leaving for a time. But it wasn't Pa. I knew that even then. Yet it was all beyond my ken. How could there not be a reason—anyone to blame?

"Early in the war, she caught the fever for the 'Glorious Cause,'" Emily continued. "For a time it seemed like true patriotism. But when Papa left, she pined unreasonably, inconsolably for him. She believed herself a seventeen-year-old belle who'd given her colors to a gallant knight of the Confederacy." Emily shook her head. "Papa did not encourage that, Robert. Cousin Caroline created her own world. Her world, her kingdom, was Ashland—until Papa left. She was so distraught I dared not tell her when word came that Papa had died. And then Uncle Marcus died. She could no longer pretend. There was nothing left, no gentleman to play her roles before."

"Is that why you left Mitchell House, why you brought Ma here?"

A bell rang from the kitchen. Emily didn't answer but stood, and smoothed her skirt. "That's Ruby—calling us to supper." She searched my face. "Are you ready? Are you ready to see your mother?"

Twenty-Nine

I'm so glad you've come, Lt. Glover." Ma flashed a smile across the table, for all the world the smile of a young girl. "It's become entirely too predictable, all these women at the table. It is high time we enjoyed the company of a gentleman caller."

Emily nudged me but spoke up, giving me time. "I'm sure our guest is tired from his journey, Cousin Caroline—and famished. Are you not?" She turned to me.

"Yes. I am—hungry—and tired, I mean."

"Well, you eat up, Mista Rrr—you eat all you can hold," Ruby broke in.

"Ruby! Our guest's name is Lt. Glover," Ma scolded. "You must remember that!"

"Yes, Miz Caroline." Ruby nodded, looking at me, waiting.

How could I play this part? How could it be good for Ma to have us all kowtow to such crazy notions? Starved as I was, I nearly lost my appetite and choked on what I forced into my mouth. I couldn't take my eyes off Ma. I'd waited four years to see her, be with her. And now she sat across the table, flashing smiles I might have hoped for from Emily. Emily didn't smile. She looked tired, as if she'd long carried the weight of the world on her shoulders. And I guessed she had. When I looked at Ma I feared for Pa. What had this done to him? Emily'd said that he forgave Ma—that he forgave Cousin Albert. I couldn't believe it. I didn't believe it.

"And what are your plans during your stay in our fair city, Lt. Glover?" Ma asked brightly.

"My plans? Oh, I . . ." And then I realized this might be my chance with Ma, to persuade her. "I came to offer my services to you—to all of you ladies. I was hoping you'd allow me to escort you to—to escort you North."

"North?" Ma paled. "Surely you don't suggest we abandon our home!" I could see Ma's tenor creep toward a fearful edge. I could see Emily tense across the table.

"It's just a suggestion, Cousin Caroline," Emily soothed. "And most gracious." She nodded to me. "But travel is far too dangerous just now. We're safer here, I believe . . . for the moment."

"Besides," Ma admonished, "we're expecting guests any day now."

"Guests?" Emily said with surprise.

"Of course! Oh, I heard you and Ruby talking, Emily. You thought I didn't, but I listened at the door," Ma quipped. "As a matter of fact, he's a friend of yours, Charles—Will Sherman. You remember him from West Point, surely. He was a few years ahead of you, I believe. It's delightful you're here. He'll be so pleased!"

"Gen. Sherman's coming here?" I looked to Emily, but Ma cut in.

"Oh, is he a general already? My! My!" And then she flashed her coquettish smile. "Do you remember our dance last summer in Washington City?" Ma blushed. "Albert intended that Will overwhelm me just enough that I run, trembling, back into his arms and Mitchell House!" Ma laughed. "But, of course, all that backfired the moment he introduced me to you. You swept me away in your arms, and I never spoke again to Will the entire evening—or Albert, for that matter." She tilted her head. "Do you remember?"

"It's been a long time." It was all I could think to say. Ma bristled, but smiled.

"I declare, Charles, this late unpleasantness has done strange things to us all. We women have continued to age—just a little, mind you, but you—you look even younger and more handsome, if that is possible, than that night we first danced." Her smile faded, and her brow creased. She glanced around the table, as if seeing us all for the first time.

"Ruby," she said, "you've positively aged. You look as old as Nanny Sara." The crease deepened, and she picked at the brooch at her neck. She looked to Emily for reassurance. "It's uncanny. We're like twin sisters, Emily."

Emily smiled. "Everything but the color of our eyes, Cousin."

Ma relaxed, but the hair on the back of my neck prickled. "Where is Nanny Sara?" I wondered out loud.

"Why, in the kitchen, where she belongs!" Ma returned. I looked at Ruby, confused. Why would Ruby sit at the table while her mother cooked, especially at Nanny Sara's age?

"Mama's been feeling a little poorly. She's resting just now," Ruby answered, but she looked away.

Ma ignored her. "Aunt Charlotte should have joined us. She would have found your company refreshing, Charles."

I looked at Emily, wondering for the first time where Grandaunt Charlotte was, why I hadn't seen her. But Emily gave me a warning shake of her head, and I knew there was more I didn't know.

239

"Has she retired already?" Ma asked. "She should be mindful of her guests. I hope you will forgive Aunt Charlotte's negligence, Lt. Glover. She's usually a gracious hostess." Ma dabbed the edge of her napkin to the corner of her mouth. "Though she does hold some rather queer notions regarding our peculiar institution—a thing that has always rankled Papa." She glanced meaningfully at Ruby. Then Ma whispered, but loud enough for all to hear, "It is why Papa forbids her name at home. She's rather the family's black sheep, you know."

Ruby rose, as if on cue. "I believe it's time for us to retire, Miz Caroline. We'll all feel more rested in the morning."

"Oh, must we?" Ma sighed. "This has been delightful." She smiled, more contented than I'd ever seen her. "You will come again tomorrow, won't you, Lt. Glover?"

I felt the heat creep up my neck. I stood to bow as Ma rose to leave the table. But when her dress brushed my sleeve I reached out to her. "Ma," I whispered, begged. She froze, and her face blanched. Ruby guided her elbow toward the doorway. Emily touched my arm, urging me not to talk. I wouldn't look at Emily but swallowed hard.

At the doorway Ma turned, a little off kilter, picking again at the brooch at her neck. "There is something about you I can't quite place, Lt. Glover. Something . . ." She sighed. "Perhaps it will come to me." Ruby pulled her through the doorway.

I wanted in the worst way to reach out to her, to hold her, to beg, "Ma, don't you recognize me? Don't you know who I am?" But Emily stood beside me, pulling me back. My throat tightened. My chest hurt.

"Don't, Robert. She can't help who she is. She can't change what she has become," Emily whispered. I couldn't answer her, didn't want her to touch me. I pulled away. "Robert—" she began.

"No. No, Emily. I can't do this. I won't accept this!" I stepped back.

"It is the way things are," she insisted. "Sometimes we have to surrender to what is, to accept things we cannot change."

But I shook my head, and once I started shaking it I couldn't stop. "Maybe you've accepted it. Maybe you've given up—surrendered—but I haven't. I didn't come all this way to play courtship to my mother! I can fix this. I know I can. I just need some time. She'll remember me. She nearly did remember me. You saw her!"

Emily shook her head sadly. "You don't understand."

I shook mine harder.

"Robert, Grandaunt Charlotte died six weeks ago. We all attended her burial, even Cousin Caroline. You saw her tonight. She has completely blocked Aunt Charlotte's death, the funeral, the burial—everything—from her memory, no matter that it just happened. She's convinced herself that Aunt Charlotte is playing petulant and rude, not joining us at meals, convinced that she keeps to her room all hours of the day and night. There is no reasoning with her. Her reality is whatever she tells herself. You must come to grips with that!"

"But I'm her son, Emily! How can a mother forget that?"

"She wants to pretend that you are her suitor, Robert. She pretends that things are as they were when she was young. As far as she is concerned she never married, never bore a child, never witnessed a war, never saw her father die, never was attacked by—" Emily froze.

"Attacked? What do you mean?" Emily turned away, but I grabbed her shoulders and spun her back to face me. Anguish plagued her face. Fear shot through me. She tried to look away, but I shook her. I shook her, and I was not gentle. "What do you

241

mean she wants to pretend that she was never attacked? Tell me. Tell me now!"

Emily fairly slumped beneath my hands. "I'm sorry, Emily—I'm sorry. I didn't mean to—but what do you mean? What do you mean Ma was attacked?"

Emily groped for a chair. She leaned forward on the table, her head against her hands. I waited, but it was all I could do not to shake her again.

"After Uncle Marcus died. Jed Slocum—"

"Slocum attacked Ma?" I shouted.

My shout raised the ire in Emily. She sat up, swiped her eyes, and hissed. "Be quiet, Robert! I have not held this household together for four years so you can come and destroy it through your brutishness in one day." She waited till I sat in the chair across from her.

"Tell me." I kept my voice level.

"Uncle Marcus was sick a long time. As he declined—even before—especially after Papa left, Cousin Caroline retreated into her fantasy world. None of us realized how far she had retreated."

"But you saw," I said.

"I noticed the changes because I was not with her all the time. Papa had insisted I enroll in the female academy in Salem while he was away. He felt I would be safer, and he didn't want me to feel the burden of the plantation."

I nodded. I knew that.

"I came home only some weekends and holidays. No one ever expected the war to drag on so, or that Papa—" Emily searched my eyes. "With Papa gone, and Uncle Marcus so ill, and Cousin Caroline—well, Mr. Slocum seemed to forget that he was only an overseer of field slaves. He took more and more

242

upon himself—so much that he even seemed to believe Ashland belonged to him."

I tensed, but Emily shook her head, warning me not to interrupt.

"There was no one to stop him. He'd seen Cousin Charles come and go and Cousin Caroline remain. I don't know what he heard or saw, but it was not hard to assume that their marriage had ended."

I studied my hands. "Slocum was frightful in his sense of ownership and power. He grew ever more brutal to Ashland's slaves, and of course he drank without caution, without consequences." Emily locked her fingers, unlocked them, and locked them again.

"The evening Uncle Marcus died Nanny Sara sent a slave child running to Mitchell House. She begged Noah to ride to Salem for me. She was terribly frightened for Cousin Caroline. She had every reason to be frightened. We left straightaway and drove to Ashland that very night." Emily hesitated.

"Go on."

"When I arrived at Ashland the house was dark and empty, except for the parlor, where Nanny Sara and some of the slaves had washed and laid out Uncle Marcus. No one kept vigil—not even a slave, which seemed so odd. Then I remembered that Cousin Caroline had said Mr. Slocum ordered all the house slaves to sleep in the quarters. She'd not had the courage to oppose him, and Uncle Marcus was too sick." Emily drew a deep breath. "Upstairs, I heard a muffled weeping. I took a candle from the parlor and made my way to Cousin Caroline's room, believing she must be awake and upset."

Emily stood, walked the length of the room, agitated. She

sat down again, heaved a sigh. "She wasn't alone, Robert. Jed Slocum—"

I groaned and looked away, felt my heat rise, thought I'd be sick, but forced myself to listen.

"I set the candle on the table. That is when I saw the pistol in your mother's hand, and the blood from Jed Slocum's chest spread across the coverlet." Emily waited while her words sank into my brain, while the bile rose in my throat.

"She killed him. Ma killed him?" I whispered in wonder.

"If she hadn't killed him, I would have done it for her." Emily stated it as fact, as simple as weather or news of ground just turned.

I tried to take that in too. I started shaking, stuck on the image of Jed Slocum and his dirty hands, his filthy, thieving hands on Ma.

I began to cry, deep inside, without any sound. For all the war that ran inside Ma these many years, this would break her —must have broken her—beyond repair. Once my hands started shaking I couldn't stop them. I knocked over Ma's wine-glass. I saw the red wine spread over the white linen like newly spilled blood, then fall to the floor. I tried to pull the linen, stained by the wine, from the table, meant to wipe the floor, to stop the spread of blood or wine, but the floor seemed far away and I'd forgotten the china was still there, on the table. It clattered, shattered to the floor.

"That is the real reason we left Mitchell House." Emily was still talking, taking no notice that I'd broken our dead aunt's good china. "That is the reason I never returned to Salem, to school. I simply sent word that there was a family death, that I was needed at home. No one thinks twice of such things in these times." Emily stood up and walked to the window, pulled back the drapery, gazed into her reflection.

"Noah dug Uncle Marcus's grave in the family cemetery by lantern light. We planted Jed Slocum's unwashed body, wrapped only in the bloody coverlet, beneath Uncle Marcus's coffin, before dawn." She dropped the drapery into place. Time slowed down.

I sat on the floor, absently mopping the wine that looked like blood, the broken china, with the linen. Emily kept on. "We told the neighbors there would be no funeral, that Uncle Marcus's body was so diseased that it could not be viewed, that the grief upon his only daughter was too great to bear callers. We closed the doors and pulled the drapes, and waited."

She turned to face me, seeing me there on the floor for the first time. "We told people, the few who asked, that Jed Slocum stormed off once he realized Uncle Marcus was dead and he would no longer be paid. Ashland would have to be sold to make good Uncle Marcus's debts. That might not be true, but—" She shrugged and spread her hands. "I don't know if they believed me, but there it is . . ."

Emily sat in the chair nearest me. "And that is why you can't force your mother to remember, Robert. Because once she starts to remember, she'd have to remember everything. Even if she doesn't collapse under the weight of so great a burden, she'd talk, could not keep herself from talking. We'd be hanged for murder, for complicity, or conspiracy—your mother, Noah, Nanny Sara, me."

I stopped mopping and stood, holding broken pieces of china, still shaking, still stuck on the image of Jed Slocum forcing Ma, of Ma shivering, trembling on her own bed with a gun in her hand—Ma, who'd always been so afraid of guns of any kind.

I dropped the china, heard the last shards splinter across the polished floorboards, then shot out the back door.

I found Stargazer in the stables, leaned my head into his shoulder, and heaved shudder after shudder. Even then I felt that his coat had been brushed sleek, his mane and tail brushed fine as feathers. I didn't wait to saddle or bridle him, but climbed on his back, leaned down into his mane, and dug my heels, with a vengeance, into his sides. We charged through the stable doors and into the darkened street. I knew it was foolish. I'd been careful so long. But now, what mattered?

Thirty

We pounded the road until the town gave way to country-side. We ran and ran until we both were spent, until hot tears dried on my face. When we finally slowed to a trot it was just the two of us, the stars, and the moon—not a tree or house or light or campfire as far as my eyes could see.

And that is when I raised my fist and screamed at God. "Why? Why Ma? Why didn't You stop him?" Stargazer snorted and reared. Skittish, he danced, side-stepped. I slid off him and stomped apart. I didn't mean to scare Stargazer, but I meant to hurt something, someone. I wanted to pound something, kick something, make somebody pay. But even Slocum was dead and beyond my reckoning. I picked up speed, broke into a run, ran until my sides ached, till sweat streamed, and swore, and cursed every vile word I knew. I stumbled at last, panting, to the ground.

"Why didn't she hold on? Why didn't she try harder?" Tears that I thought were gone came new, and I pounded the earth. I pounded until I felt blood, warm and sticky, between my fingers. At last I rolled to my back and stared, spent and dry-eyed, at the stars, bright in their constellations. My chest trembled.

The world revolved. Days and nights would keep turning over on themselves, even though Ma was broken, crazy. That she still walked around in her body was scant comfort, harder almost than if she'd died.

When Ma left us I'd grieved, but I'd clung to the belief that she'd come back—come back and be Ma again. Even after four years, when Emily's letter came, I'd hoped. I'd hoped while getting my strength back in that field hospital and while riding toward her. I knew I'd find her, and that once I did things would work out, be all right. But things were not all right, and they could never be all right again—not for Ma . . .

I grieved for what was broken in Ma, but also for what never was between us and for what could never be. Even if Ma lived another twenty, thirty years she was lost to me. I couldn't call her back to a world so filled with pain and nightmares. But I couldn't have her looking at me like I was Pa, like I was her lover. I couldn't do it.

"What do You want from me, Lord?" But I knew the answer—had known it long: *surrender.*

I remembered Chap. Goforth, and all he'd said about surrendering his life to the Lord. But that wasn't me.

"I've given everything," I spat defensively. "I've heeded Your callings, ever since William Henry died, since I first ran North with Jeremiah. I ran the railroad when I was afraid. I even stayed at Laurelea like I promised—when I didn't want to, when I should have come down here and dragged Ma home, no matter what Pa or Cousin Albert or Ma or Emily or any of them said! She'd have been better off than this!

"But You've taken everything away—Miz Laura, William Henry, Pa, Ma—everyone I loved. There's nothing left to give!"

But I knew there was: *myself.* I'd never given myself. I knew that was what Andrew had meant, but I'd fought him, not wanting to understand. And now I fought God.

"Myself is all I am!" I stood up, shouted at the sky. "I won't quit! I won't lay down and break apart, like Ma! Do You hear? I'm not quitting! I have to—"

Surrender. The thought, the image stood clear in my brain. But that made me angrier still.

"I can't fight if I surrender! Look at them! They need me!"

But I knew the answer to that too: *They are Mine.* I had always known it.

I also knew that I knew what was best for them—best for all of us. I knew better than God. So I laughed out loud. "Yours? Look what's happened to them! Is that how You take care of Your own?" Still the words stood clear in my mind, rang with the truth of Scripture. I kicked at the dirt, kicked at the images in my brain, and trudged down the road, determined to shut out, to drown the voice in my head.

Finally I stopped in the middle of the road and demanded, "I want to love Ma, even though she's what she is. But I can't. I can't love her like this. I want her to love me!"

Love Me first. The idea was not new.

It was the thing I'd never done. I'd loved God, but never first. I'd begged His help, His protection, even His direction. I'd followed His dictates from the Bible the best I knew them, but only when it helped my feet walk the path I'd already set. I'd asked Him to guide me, help me out of tight and sorry spots—like those runs for the Underground Railroad. But part of me had wanted the thrill of all that anyway, and I'd come to think of God's will and care as a clap on my back, a hand on my shoulder, helping me do whatever I thought best, whatever I'd set out to do.

None of this was going according to my plans.

A Scripture pestered my mind, one I'd learned long ago: "Trust in the Lord with all thine heart, and lean not on thine own understanding. In all thy ways acknowledge him, and he shall direct thy paths."

"It's too hard to trust You now!" I screamed. "I don't want to lose anyone else! I want You to do it my way!"

My shout jarred me. Even I recognized that same shrill, demanding, bound-up plea I'd heard in Ma when she ordered Ruby, treated her like a slave, no matter that Ruby was busy doing what was best for Ma. That knowledge slammed me with the force of Ruby's shovel.

In my bent to have my way I was just as crazed as Ma—just as demanding. I'd ordered God like He was my slave, there to wait on my wants and whims, hand and foot—no matter if those orders were the worst thing for all of us. That thinking unsettled me.

Could God know something I didn't? What if I did trust Him, surrender to Him? Would that make me His slave?

I remembered something Rev. Goforth had said, years ago, about being a slave for Christ. He'd said, "Slavery comes in many forms. Some people, like the Negroes here, are slaves to other people. Some of us are slaves to sin, or worldliness, or greed. I aim to live as a slave to Christ, because only then am I free. . . . We're all in some kind of bondage. . . . Most of us have the freedom to choose that slavery, whether we realize it or not."

I'd not understood what he meant. But maybe it had something to do with giving up control. What if I didn't have to plan it all, fix it all? Could I be free of the pain, the worry? If I stopped waging my own war inside, like Ma had done all these years, would He—could He—lead me into some path of peace?

I needed peace. Had Ma ever tried to surrender—to give her load over to God?

"Ma's forgotten me," I whispered.

Another Scripture filled my mind. "Though a mother forgets her suckling child, I will not forget thee."

And then the promises, learned over all the years of our evening read, the read I'd not kept for months, but that had been engraved in my mind, written on my heart since I was a toddle baby, came flooding back:

"I will never leave thee nor forsake thee."

"I will love thee with an everlasting love."

"I know the plans I have for you," declares the Lord, "plans to prosper and not to harm you, plans to give you hope and a future."

I needed hope. I needed a future. I needed to trust someone.

On that dirt road, in the middle of that dark night, I surrendered my life to the Lord—my broken plans, my purposes, and the longings I'd been so set to see through. And then, because I couldn't hold it any longer, I gave Him my hatred of Cousin Albert, my fear for Pa. I gave Him my love of Emily. I held nothing back, not Ma, not even my revenge toward Jed Slocum. I figured God had already taken care of that.

I emptied myself of me and asked Him to fill me with His Spirit. It was not the bargain most of my prayers had been. I could not hope that Ma would change, held no expectation that she would be anything different than what she was. I knew I could not keep going on that path in my own strength. It was not enough, would never be enough. So I asked Him to be strength in me. It didn't mean quitting. It meant beginning. It meant I no longer walked alone.

Thirty-One

$\mathcal{I}$ felt, but couldn't see Stargazer through the pea-soup fog as he nuzzled me awake by the side of the road. With my first conscious breath I sank again into the peace God had poured into me. I couldn't help but wonder if it would still be there when I stood up, took a step.

I reached up to stroke Stargazer's velvet nose, grateful for my friend. "You're right, boy. We should get back."

I shook the sleep and cold from my limbs, stamped my feet to get my blood moving. I could have climbed on Stargazer's back but wanted to walk with his nose at my shoulder, to share this time as long as we could. Gray fog swirled around our feet, our legs, and grew up, like clouds, around us. Except that I could feel the dirt road through my shoes, hear my own footsteps, I wouldn't have known if we walked the road or wandered off into a field.

If we could get back to town before the fog lifted, we might slip into Stargazer's stall unseen. I was cautious, straining my ears to hear the hoofbeats of other horses, the footsteps of other men, but I wasn't afraid. It wasn't all up to me.

I climbed on Stargazer's back. Even in the fog he seemed to have a homing sense, and we made good time.

I'd stabled, watered, fed, and brushed him before the fog began to lift. Outside the stable, near the garden, I heard the digging, scraping of a shovel. I knew the garden was no more than fifteen feet in front of me, but I wasn't about to get whaled by a shovel again. "Ruby?" I whispered across the yard. The digging stopped.

"Robert?" I'd startled her.

"It's me. What are you doing out here?"

"I'm fixing to hide Miz Charlotte's things, before those dirty Yankees run over the place, steal us blind." Her strained whisper scraped the edge of fear.

"You're really expecting Yankees here? I thought that was Ma's fancy." It seemed unlikely to me.

"Why you think folks pulling out of town day after day?"

"But we're so far from anywhere. There's no ports, no forts anywhere near here."

"There's railroads nearby. Near as I can tell, that Gen. Sherman is bent on tearing up every rail in the Confederacy. They say his soldiers rip them up, burns them hot in the fire, then twists those rails round trees—Uncle Billy's neckties, they call them."

"I heard about that," I said.

Ruby kept digging. "His bummers drink and burn and lynch till they don't know what all they done. Burn barns, houses, churches—makes no difference to them. After they eat or carry off all they want, they salt the land."

I remembered what I'd heard in Salem. But Ruby seemed sure of so much. I didn't know if it was truth or fear talking. "They say he burned his way from Atlanta to the sea," I said.

"We know that. What we don't know is whether or not we

standing in Gen. Sherman's path. Emily—Miz Emily—say she expects him to turn north and march up to Petersburg, Virginia, to help Gen. Grant take Richmond. Not much standing between but South Carolina and North Carolina, and nothing stands between Gen. Sherman and his bummers, lest it's hid so good they can't find it."

I didn't want to tell Ruby that her garden would be one of the first places they'd search, the first pie they'd poke their ramrods through. Men who'd been living off the land for years knew about hiding places, knew a garden with loose earth would be a likely place to dig. She stopped digging of a sudden.

"Let me do that for you, Ruby." I reached for the shovel.

"I know it's not much use. I know they'll look here. They'll tear up the garden and the attic and the cellar, and they'll likely throw Mama out of her deathbed." Ruby's voice caught. "And I've got to get this garden ready to plant. God only knows how we're gonna keep feeding all those children." She swiped at her forehead. "But I got to do something. I'll go crazy with the waiting."

I saw her outline through the lifting fog, reached for her arm. "We've got enough crazy people around here without you going down that road, Ruby. You've been strong a long time. You have to stay strong." I tried to make the smile come through my voice, but her words about Nanny Sara's deathbed scared me. I'd not even seen Nanny Sara yet. "You've got a son—your own son—to see to—a son who's willing to march against both armies to find you."

"Oh, Mista Robert, I pray it's true. I pray it won't be too late by the time he finds me."

"Keep faith, Ruby. You couldn't be Nanny Sara's daughter unless you carried more than a normal woman's share." And then I asked, "How is Nanny Sara? I haven't seen her yet, and you said she was feeling poorly."

"More than poorly. Mama be dying."

"Nanny Sara?" I didn't want to take that in.

Ruby shook her head and looked away. "She's old. She's so old and full of care. It's high time she laid that burden down. I think she's just waiting to know we'll all be all right." Ruby handed me the shovel. "Trouble is, I don't know that we're gonna be all right. I almost wish she could go to sleep believing."

"We are going to be all right, Ruby. I know it."

She laughed, a sad and hopeless laugh. "How can you ever know such a thing? Especially now, with that Satan nearly at our door?"

That's when we heard the high-pitched laughter from inside the house and the banging of the front door knocker.

"Oh, Lord. That's Miz Caroline. I thought she'd sleep through the morning." We both took off at a clip. I held the back door for Ruby.

Ma stood in her nightdress in the kitchen, pouring across the floor whatever had been cooking in the kettle on the stove.

"Miz Caroline! What are you doing?" Ruby nearly screamed. "That's all the food we've got for today!"

"Ruby! You expect me to eat this pig slop?" Ma screeched her high-pitched laugh. "I'd sooner eat the leavings of slaves." Her laughter changed to anger, each word bitten with spite. "You'll prepare me something decent to eat, or I'll tell Papa you've been stealing my food. He won't stand for it, you know! He'll have you whipped! I'll have you whipped!"

I couldn't move. I'd never heard such talk from Ma. I half expected Ruby to grab the shovel from my hand and use it on her. But Ruby, the woman who'd nearly broken a moment ago, calmed and soothed Ma out of her tantrum.

"Miz Caroline, let's get you cleaned up and ready for visitors today. We'll worry about breakfast in a bit."

"I want my breakfast now!" Ma spat, like a spoiled child.

The knocker at the front door pounded again.

"Do you hear that?" Ruby soothed. "There's visitors at the door already. We really must do your hair before you receive your callers, Miz Caroline."

"Callers? For me?" Ma fiddled with the ribbon at the neck of her nightdress. "Why, yes. I should wear my rose taffeta. Hurry along, Ruby. I mustn't keep my guests waiting."

Ruby ushered Ma from the room and up the stairs, never looking back at me. I knew this scene must have played a dozen times before, but I didn't know how Ruby could stand it.

I pulled the kettle up from its side, saving all the porridge I could, scraping it from the floor. I knew there was little food, and my coming had added one more mouth to feed. I stoked the stove and saw that the wood box was nearly empty.

From the front hall I heard Emily greet someone, heard heated whispers of "that Federal demon" and "Sherman's bummers" and "you shouldn't stay—you won't be safe, they'll—" I heard her invite the fearful speaker in, heard him say, "No, Miss Mitchell, we've got to be on our way. We just wanted to ask you—" And then Ma's singing from up the stairs cut them off.

I scrubbed the sticky porridge leavings from the floor and set the kettle back on the stove to warm, then walked out back to fill the kindling box and draw fresh well water. By the time I hefted the bucket onto the table the callers had gone. Emily, flushed and distracted, sat in the stairway, absently plaiting a little girl's hair.

"Emily?" I didn't want to startle her.

"Robert!" She turned to face me. "I didn't know you were back. I've been so worried about you. You were gone all ni—" She searched my face, dropped the little girl's braids. "Go out to play for a while, Lizzie. Find Henry and Jubal." Then she turned to me again. "What happened? What happened to you?" She stepped closer, searching my face.

I wanted to take her in my arms and tell her that I'd surrendered my life, my arrogance, my selfish bent to the Lord. Like Paul on the road to Damascus, God had shown me my need to trust Him, to wait for Him. I wanted to tell her that I didn't know where it would all lead, but that I was making the journey. But when she stepped closer still I saw, in the pools of her brown eyes, that she already knew, that she understood. And I realized that somewhere in this awful war she'd traveled her own Damascus Road. So I only breathed deeply and didn't look away.

She shook her head, just a little, and smiled up at me. I felt her hand touch my face, heard her whisper, "Welcome home, Robert." She nearly dropped her hand, but I pressed it back against my cheek and breathed again.

Now the color in her cheek deepened, and she pulled away. I let her hand go, but I couldn't take my eyes from her. That embarrassed us both. So I asked, "Who was at the door?" I was sorry I asked, because her agitation crept back.

"Aunt Charlotte's neighbor, Mr. Nealey. He and his family are pulling out, leaving this very morning." Emily locked and unlocked her fingers. "He said rumor has it that Gen. Sherman is no more than three weeks away, two if the weather holds."

I wanted to reach for her, to tell her it would be all right, that we'd be all right, but she turned and began pacing. "I don't know what we're going to do, Robert. More families are leaving.

Many have evacuated already. Some refuse to leave—say they'd rather die defending what's theirs. We should go—take the children—but we don't have a wagon. We've no place to go. And if we did—six children and Nanny Sara is sick and Cousin Caroline is—" Emily whirled to face me, frantic.

I knew in that moment that the Lord had emptied me, filled me, brought me here to do the thing I'd longed to do all along—help them—but not the way I'd planned and not because I could rescue them. Only He could do that. But, if I was willing, He could use me, be strength in me. If I'd enlisted, if I'd done the thing I was bound and determined to do in the way I'd intended, I could not have been here. The wonder of that, of how the Lord had gone ahead of me, of all of us, and prepared the way, awed me.

"Robert? Are you all right?" Emily stopped her pacing.

"What? Yes, I'm fine. We'll all be fine." I didn't draw Emily into my arms, much as I wanted to. "What else did Mr. Nealey say?"

"He said they'd be back after the scourge, to see what was left. He said they were taking their food, but if there was anything we could use we might better have it than let the Yankees steal it."

I nodded. "Maybe we'd best take a look. We'll need fuel, and food for sure. If they left wood I could split it for the stove."

"I'm glad you're here, Robert." Emily leaned against the doorjamb. "I don't know what we'll do if Gen. Sherman and his men are as brutal as they say. I don't know what will become of us."

"Will Sherman? Brutal?" Ma stood on the stairs and laughed at us both. "How little you young people know!" And then she hesitated, glanced back and forth between Emily and me, confused. "Charles, you of all people should know Will's a perfect gentleman! He's a West Point man."

But I was not Pa, and I wondered if we could count on that brotherhood making any difference.

Thirty-Two

$\mathcal{W}$e kept busy the next ten days. Ruby hid and buried Miz Charlotte's treasures in between coddling Ma and nursing Nanny Sara. Emily took over the cooking and met callers at the door. She taught reading lessons to the three oldest children, young as they were, while I played indoor games with the smallest ones. I chopped wood, fetched and carried, and emptied slop jars. By day I kept low. Nobody'd understand what an able-bodied young man was doing at home when all their men and boys were off fighting, dying for the Cause. At night I searched empty houses, chicken coops, stables, and carriage houses for food, fuel, feed—always hoping someone forgot a laying hen, a stash of oats, or the thing we needed most—a wagon.

Curious Henry, a night owl if there ever was one, followed me everywhere. I was his new best friend and older brother. I confess his company on those late-night raids was welcome, and put me in mind of the antics William Henry and I used to raise.

Neighbors that remained did the same. We scurried like squirrels headed for winter, sure there was fire at our tails. Most folks pulled together, sharing what we could, but as the days passed and fears of Gen. Sherman's army and rumors of burnings, raids, lynching, and all sorts of frenzy ran weed wild, we could feel the shades being drawn. One by one, we shut ourselves in and waited.

I spent long afternoons by Nanny Sara's bedside, telling her everything I could remember of my run North with Jeremiah, everything I knew of his life in Canada and the good he did other runaway slaves settled there. I recited every letter he'd written me and all I could remember of what he'd written William Still, our friend in Philadelphia. I told her how Jeremiah was determined to get back to her and that he vowed to find his mother, Ruby. It was tonic to her.

"Promise me you tell him something when this war be over."

"You'll tell him yourself, Nanny Sara," I insisted.

"You such a liar, Masta Robert. You know this old body can't last. You promise me you tell him. Promise me, Masta Robert."

"I'll tell him anything you want, Nanny Sara—only don't call me 'Master.' Your days of slavery are gone. President Abraham Lincoln emancipated all the slaves in the states of rebellion. You're free. You don't call anybody Master, never again."

Her small body shuddered beneath the pieced quilt. "Yes, Father Abraham. I'm free at last." She drew a ragged breath. "You tell my grandbaby that I be proud of him, of all he make of hisself. You tell him take good care of my Ruby." She choked out Ruby's name.

"I'll tell him. I swear I'll tell him, and I'll make sure Ruby gets to him."

"Don't promise what the good Lord might not let you live to."

Her words sounded like the dire predictions of Granny

Struthers, and a chill ran up my spine, though I wasn't cold.

"You take my bones to Ashland."

"Ashland?"

"Ashland my home . . . the only home I ever known." She clutched my sleeve. "Don't you let them bury me in this foreign land. Bury me in the slave cemetery at home."

"You deserve better."

"Promise me. You promise me." She groped for my hand.

"I promise." I held her hand in both of mine. "I promise, Nanny Sara." She relaxed in my arms. "Now you rest."

"You read to me." She motioned to the Book on the mantel. I took it down, opened it, wondered where to begin.

"Psalms. You read me that one about my shepherd—tell me about those green pastures. It be water over these dry roots."

When I started my nerves stretched tight—like a new skin sun-dried across the side of the barn. It had been a long time since I'd picked up the Word—longer still since I'd read it out loud. But the words of David, shepherd boy turned king, eased me.

"The Lord is my shepherd; I shall not want. He maketh me to lie down in green pastures: he leadeth me beside the still waters. He restoreth my soul: he leadeth me in the paths of righteousness. . . . Yea, though I walk through the valley of the shadow of death, I will fear no evil: for thou art with me. . . . Thou preparest a table before me in the presence of mine enemies. . . . Surely goodness and mercy shall follow me all the days of my life: and I will dwell in the house of the Lord for ever."

When I looked up Ruby stood in the doorway. Soon after, Ma pushed past her and sat on the bed beside Nanny Sara. One by one, the children, up from their naps, toddled in to stand round the bed, leaning their elbows across Nanny Sara's quilt, or to sit cross-legged on the floor. Emily, wondering where we'd all gone, came looking for us and took a post by Ruby.

I read Psalm 91 and then some of Matthew 5—the Sermon on the Mount—because right then I felt like we were all "poor in spirit," mightily in need of the Kingdom of Heaven.

The words toppled off my tongue like they'd birthed there—awkward and halting at first—a new colt on spindly legs. But as I read, as peace filled my aches and hollows, I knew those words were meant especially for me, especially for each of us. Then the reading ran sure and true.

The words sprang from a God who loved us so much that He'd given His Son to die for us, from a Brother who'd laid down His life for us. It was war for God, just as it was for us—only I figured God warred against sin and fought for our eternity while we butchered one another over land and slavery and our own peculiar notions.

"You don't read like Charles," Ma interrupted me, puzzled. She picked at the brooch at her neck.

"No," I said. "I don't." I knew what she meant. I remembered evenings, as a boy not much older than Henry, lying long on the parlor floor, my hands locked behind my head as Pa read from the Word.

The stories he read leapt into the night sky, casting shadows among the fire dancers, conjuring battles and bloody sacrifices. Long treacherous journeys, spoils of war, and riches beyond anything I could imagine in daylight played through the air while Pa read. I could see a story unfold as if all the characters loved or warred right there, standing in the middle of our parlor. I could never read like that.

Ma didn't answer but sat listening, and I think the words calmed her. Then Emily prayed for us all.

It became a pattern. We'd all meet in Nanny Sara's room once our chores and the children's naps were done. We'd read and pray, and after a couple of days Ruby took up hymn singing. Where we knew the words, the rest of us joined in. It became the best part of every day and the only time we all let our guard down—grateful to do it.

But after two weeks of watching wagons and neighbors roll out of town, after finding those that stayed too frightened to come out of their houses, our nerves frayed and splintered.

I'd hidden and moved and hidden Stargazer so many times in so many places that I was afraid I'd forget where I'd hidden him last. Emily'd sewn six gold coins into the hem of her cloak, then covered coins with padding and fabric to replace the buttons on her everyday dress, on Ma's dress, and on Ruby's. Ruby'd hidden, buried, dug up, and buried again food and jewelry and silver and metal boxes of papers in so many places I figured the Yankees would think they'd stumbled on a child's treasure hunt.

The night before Sherman's troops reached the town we saw the plantations along the river flame like watchfires, snaking toward us.

Only Ma and Nanny Sara and the children went to bed that night. Ruby, Emily, and I stood watch from the third-floor window, counting the burning houses, wondering why the burning stopped near town, wondering if they'd spare our house or give us time to get out before setting the torch. Would they let us keep the stable for the children and Nanny Sara's sake—a bed on the hay?

Come morning the flames died, and chimneys I'd never noticed stood stark, stone sentinels against an ash gray sky. A red dust cloud rose in the distance and mingled with the mist, two hours before we heard the tramp of boots or the creek of wagons.

Emily cooked breakfast. The toddlers and youngsters ate. Ruby took some up to Nanny Sara, who'd taken a turn for the worse and might not live to need a bed of any kind.

Emily and I waited for the pounding on the door, arguing over who should answer it and who should hide. I wanted the women and children to stay in Nanny Sara's room, while I talked to the soldiers. Emily was certain that would be the worst, believed they'd shoot a man first and ask questions later. "They'll not shoot a defenseless woman. They can't all be barbarians!"

I thought they could and meant to tell her so. We were still arguing in the kitchen when the front door opened and Ma's coquettish laughter rang across the lawn. "You tell that old devil Will Sherman that Caroline Ashton demands to see him. Tell him to come here right now! Tell him I owe him a dance!" She laughed again and slammed the door.

Ma ran up the stairs, skipping over two little girls playing "Which Hand Holds the Thimble" before Emily or I could leap from our chairs. Emily tore after Ma, tripping over the girls, starting a new uproar. I heard Ma's door slam, heard Emily plead with her, beg her to open the door.

I herded the whimpering girls to Nanny Sara's room, then peered through the draperies, hoping nobody'd heard Ma. But they'd heard her. A detail of soldiers marched away, looking like they were bent on a mission. I ran my hand through my hair. "What now, Lord? What do we do now? I know You've brought us safe to this time for a purpose. I don't know what that purpose is or what to do here." In less than an hour the door shook from a pounding.

Emily ran to the head of the stairs, but I blocked the doorway. I'd lifted the latch and barely opened the door to the Union corporal when Ma pushed past Emily and ran down the stairs, dressed for all the world like she was off to a summer ball. "Go upstairs, Caroline!" I shouted, hoping that just this once I sounded like Pa to her.

"Don't be silly, Charles! I've invited our friend Will Sherman to tea. This is likely him now!"

I tried to shut the door, but the officer shoved his foot inside, determined, wary, and pounded again.

"I hear the devil knocking at our door! Pray, let him in!" Ma flitted past me, nearly stumbled into the officer's arms. He removed his hat and bowed toward her. "Miss Ashton, I presume?"

"You presume correctly, gallant sir. Now, where is he? Where's Will?" Ma teased.

"The general will be here soon, ma'am. I'm afraid he does not remember you—your name."

"Not remember me? Oh, fiddle-faddle! He'll remember the moment he sees me—the moment he sees us!" And Ma inclined her head to me. "Will and Charles are old friends."

The captain frowned, bowed slightly, then stepped through the door, taking in the empty hallway, the parlor, the stairs. Emily stepped behind the upstairs drapery, but I think he saw the movement. He placed his hand on his revolver and his foot on the stair.

"It's just my cousin there."

"Show yourself!" he called.

Emily peeked from the drapery and stepped to the landing. The captain took her in, running his eyes long up and down her, seeming to like all he saw. I wanted to smash his face, but he was the one with the gun.

"Where is Gen. Sherman?" I asked, blustering confidence I

266

didn't feel. The captain looked back at me, surprised, I think, that I was there.

"The general will be here in good time." He took my measure. "Gen. Sherman is at no one's beck and call."

"Of course he isn't!" Ma broke in. "We do so want to make him welcome, that's all."

The captain eyed Ma suspiciously. He opened the door wide and motioned for a detail of soldiers to enter. "Search every floor. Confine inhabitants to one room."

I stepped forward, fearful for the women and children upstairs, but Ma pulled my arm toward the parlor. "Come with me, Charles. We'll need to receive our guest."

"But—" I began.

"No one will receive insult or injury unless they call it on themselves." The captain tossed his hat on the settee and poured himself a brandy. He sat down, crossed his legs, and toasted us. "The general will determine—"

"The general will determine, won't he, Captain?"

"General Sherman!" The captain stumbled all over himself, jumped to his feet, spilled his drink, grabbed his hat, and tried to salute all in one clumsy movement.

"You'll wait outside, Captain Gray." Gen. Sherman removed his hat. The captain was outside the parlor door before Gen. Sherman took Ma in. She hung back a moment, then reached her hand toward his.

"Dear Will Sherman. You do remember me, don't you?" Gen. Sherman nodded but looked like he did not. "We last danced at that lovely Washington City ball, all you handsome young men in your West Point uniforms!"

"West Point was a long time ago, madam." But a glimmer dawned in Gen. Sherman's eyes.

Ma's laughter rang like bells. "Caroline Ashton, if I must remind you. My cousin, Albert—Albert Mitchell—introduced us, and we enjoyed a lovely waltz, with the promise of a second. Until—" and now Ma's cheek colored, and she flashed her eyes toward me—"until he introduced me to Charles." I felt my face flame. "I'm afraid we rather forgot everyone else." Ma flipped her fan and adjusted her hoop, took her place on the settee, and smiled up at him. "So you see, Will, I really do owe you a dance."

Gen. Sherman looked as if he didn't know what to make of Ma's performance. He looked at me like I'd gone crazy, then looked again, more closely. "I remember Albert Mitchell. You can't be Charles Glover, but you look a good deal like him—like him twenty years ago."

I stepped forward, between them, and held out my hand, tried to whisper, "I'm Robert Glover, sir—Charles Glover's son." I tried to motion toward Ma, hoping he'd understand that she was not in her right mind. Either he didn't catch on or meant not to.

"Robert Glover! Charles told me about you, young man. You are the spitting image of your father." Then he frowned. "From all he said I would have expected to see you in blue uniform—" he looked at Ma and back to me—"rather than holed up in a secession mansion." He pulled a cigar from his pocket, lit it, and ground the lucifer into the carpet.

"That was my intention, sir." I looked back at Ma, who picked furiously at her brooch, a string of emotions, all of them confused and frightened, flitting across her face. "May we speak privately?"

Gen. Sherman nodded, watching Ma, maybe gaining some understanding. "Tonight, Glover. I've got some things to attend to now. We'll be setting our headquarters here for a couple of days. You'll cooperate, I trust."

"Yes, sir." I realized that as much as we feared him, Gen. Sherman's presence might mean protection from his men. "The ladies and children, sir?"

"They won't be troubled." He frowned. "Why you've collected that infernal passel of darkie babies I saw up the stairs, I don't know." He waited, but I didn't answer. He shouted, "Lieutenant!" The lieutenant must have been listening by the parlor door, quick and smart as he stepped in.

"General."

"See that a watch is set before the ladies' room. Every courtesy extended. That's all."

"Yes, sir!"

Now Gen. Sherman turned toward Ma. "Mrs. Glover, I thank you for your hospitality."

That helped Ma find her ground, though the "Mrs. Glover" seemed to throw her. "Our West Point men are always welcome, General. I hope you will join us for a little supper at six."

Sherman bowed, flicking cigar ash on the carpet. "My staff and I will be delighted."

Ma picked up a porcelain dish and handed it to Gen. Sherman. "For your cigar, sir." She lifted her chin, stretched to her full height. "You were a perfect gentleman when last we danced, Will Sherman. I trust you will behave every bit that gentleman now."

Sherman inclined his head, half-amused, but nodded in obedience. "Have no fear, madam."

Ma nodded slightly and glided from the room. Sherman looked at me, raised his eyebrows once, then turned his back. I was dismissed.

Thirty-Three

Supper was a nightmare. Ma and Gen. Sherman danced their words and memories across the table. Ma recollected every tidbit like it was yesterday, forever correcting the general's version.

Gen. Sherman talked about everything in the "long ago." But he indulged Ma, just the same. I think it flattered him, the way she teased. It was hard to watch. He couldn't help but see Ma as a beautiful woman. I guessed that had been true for Pa and Cousin Albert too.

In some odd way the evening seemed to help Ma. She'd let up looking at me like I was Pa ever since I'd started the evening read—at least until that morning when she'd introduced me as "Charles" to the general. But over supper Ma seemed to find a more real sense of time. It flattered her to have Gen. Sherman there, paying her heed—not acting as though she was a young Southern belle, but a belle just the same.

Ma talked on and on about Albert and Charles and how they both courted her shamelessly. I couldn't look at Emily.

"It's understandable, Mrs. Glover. Charles was obviously the more fortunate man. You've a son to prove it, the image of his father."

Ma blushed. She looked confused but seemed to loop one memory onto another, forming some sort of picture in her mind. I wondered if she took in that I was her son, that she was my mother, that Pa was not here. I wondered if she'd ever realized, despite Emily's care, that Cousin Albert was dead. If she did, or if she'd overheard our talk, I prayed she wouldn't remember now, hoped she wouldn't realize that Gen. Sherman was part of the army that imprisoned him, the head of the army that even now swept her South, blasting and burning everything she loved.

Ruby and Emily had cooked all afternoon. Sherman's men, who'd foraged the land liberally, brought more food to the kitchen door than any of us had seen for months. With Emily busy, I minded Ma and the children, who were quartered in Nanny Sara's room.

All six children, vexed and fractious from being stuck inside night and day, had quarreled and tussled through the afternoon. I'd tried to keep them busy with story after story but made the mistake of leaving to haul water. While I was gone one of the guards told young Lizzie that they were powerful hungry—so hungry, in fact, that he planned to roast her and the twins over an open spit and eat them alive. It set Lizzie to howling and screaming, and that started up a chain—one child after another screaming their heads off. Only Emily could convince her it was a lie and finally stay their tears. I wanted to strangle the soldier who'd teased her with that whopper.

Ruby served the meal. Emily, exhausted and the picture of distraction, sat beside Ma. I don't know what worried Emily most—Gen. Sherman and his men in her aunt's dining room with the children upstairs or the looming threat of Ma and what she might do, might remember and unleash.

After dinner the general shut himself in the parlor with his staff officers. The ladies retired to Nanny Sara's room. On the stairway Ma paused, looked down to me, and said, "Good night, Robert."

My heart caught. I steadied myself on the newel post. She'd already passed up the stairs when my voice croaked, "Good night, Ma."

I cleaned up the kitchen, glad to help Emily in some way, then wandered to the backyard, needing to see Stargazer, to tell him Ma knew me. But Gen. Sherman's men had searched the buildings and outbuildings right off. Most of Ruby's hiding places had been discovered, the garden poked through with ramrods. Stargazer was penned with the Union horses. My best chance, my only chance to get him back—and it was slim— was to plead with Gen. Sherman. He'd promised to see me later tonight. I wouldn't let him forget.

Already the light through Nanny Sara's window burned low. I didn't know if the ladies slept or wanted Gen. Sherman's men to think they did.

It was well past eleven when the officers left the parlor. As the guard changed I told the new corporal that the general was expecting me.

"Come in." Gen. Sherman stretched his legs long, still in his unbuttoned coat and muddied boots. He puffed a stubbed cigar, nursed a brandy.

"Gen. Sherman, may I see you now?" I waited by the door.

"Glover," he answered, swirling his brandy, "come in."

The fire burned low in the grate. "Would you like another log for the fire, sir?"

"Soon. Sit and tell me what in thunder is going on with your mother."

Gen. Sherman carried a reputation for not wasting time. So I sat and told him, as best I could, how Ma had left home before the war, how Pa had left to help the Union after President Lincoln's Emancipation Proclamation, about the letter from Emily and my long journey to find them, how I'd found that Ma had retreated into the past during the war, how tonight was the first time she seemed to remember that she had a son, and that I was not my father. I never mentioned Fort Delaware, or Cousin Albert, or Slocum, or any of that. All the time I spoke the general swirled his brandy, staring into the dying embers. Ash from his cigar dropped onto the carpet.

"War is hard," Gen. Sherman said, grinding his cigar stub into Ma's porcelain dish. "It needs to be so brutally, sickeningly hard that the civilian population cannot rise to fight another day. As long as they supply their soldiers this war will not end. When they stop supporting the war, when they can no longer support the war, the soldiers will be done, and we can all go home." The general's eyes flamed and ebbed.

That explained the burning of mansions and barns, of cabins and lean-tos, the ripping out of gardens, the destruction of crops, the wholesale slaughter of animals, and the salting of land they didn't need to forage. But I was sure the people of South Carolina and Georgia would never see this scourge as some lofty cause to end the war so everybody could go home. No wonder some called him crazy; some called him Satan; some called him the avenging angel.

"Your father's a good man . . . some radical notions to my thinking, to military thinking, but he came through for us. A great deal of the success of my campaign's been due to our fine cartographers. Your father is one of the best."

"You've seen Pa?"

273

He downed his brandy. "Two months ago. Before Savannah." He set the glass on the table beside him. "I don't believe he knows you're here—or your mother. He thought her fairly safe in North Carolina."

"He doesn't know. We've had no word from him since he left for the war—no way to get word to him. I knew from the beginning that his work is secret, that he couldn't let me know where he was. It's been hard not knowing if he was—"

"It's always hard." Sherman rubbed his hand across his eyes. "I think there must be more to this, more you've not told." His eyes roamed my face till I looked away. "For instance, how you all find yourselves in this hotbed of secession." I didn't answer. "Why it took you the better part of a year to find your mother. . . . Be that as it may, you need to get out of South Carolina immediately."

"We've no way to travel, sir—no wagon. Your men have confiscated my only horse."

He waved his hand. "Easily remedied. But you'll leave in the morning, under my escort, or I'll not be responsible for your safety or that of the women. My bummers, as they're so irreverently called, comb a fifty-mile swath on either side of our march, and though I don't sanction all their activities, I don't nursemaid them." He looked me over. "Do you understand?"

I nodded. "Yes, sir."

"I'll see that you have passes and a guard well into North Carolina. I'll have a map drawn up for you, which you will receive somewhere beyond the state line. If you decide to return to Maryland you'll need to go unescorted. But I'll provide you with passes through Union lines—and the safest routes to travel. Avoid Petersburg and Richmond at all costs. Do not deviate from the map, and do not share the map with any other eyes."

It was more than I could have hoped. "Thank you, sir. Thank you."

Gen. Sherman stood and loosened his collar, signifying the end of our discussion. "I owe your father this." He reached for my hand. "Good luck, young man."

"Thank you. Thank you, Gen. Sherman." Grateful, I shook his hand, wondering at the same time how much blood was on them. He turned his back. I was almost out the door when he called my name.

"Glover."

"Yes, sir?"

"As soon as you take care of your women I expect to see you in Federal uniform—if we're still fighting this war, which I hope to God we are not."

"Yes, sir!" I vowed. "Sir, if you see my father—"

"I'll tell him why you're not in uniform, and that your mother offered me the dance he stole."

"Thank you, sir. Thank you." I hoped he'd forget the part about the dance.

Thirty-Four

❧

We pulled out just after dawn the next day, no matter that a cold and steady drizzle began during the night.

We layered ticking and blankets for Nanny Sara across the back of the light wagon Gen. Sherman's men had confiscated for Stargazer to pull, then covered the bed with oilcloth to keep out the rain and damp. General Sherman sent along a mule, a wagon with supplies for the journey, and a kindly note to Ma, which flattered her to no end. The ladies wore double sets of clothes, careful to keep the gold from clanking in their buttons, their hems. Emily tucked the Bible and a packet of papers beside Nanny Sara, then loaded the children in the supply wagon. She and Ruby would take turns minding them.

The private, who'd hungry-eyed Stargazer from the moment he saw him, offered to swap Stargazer for a bigger horse, a farm horse born and bred for hauling wagon. I assured him we'd be fine and reminded him that Gen. Sherman's order gave me back my horse. I didn't tell him that Stargazer had spent most of the war in a Confederate field hospital, hauling wagons and ambulances and who knew what all. If the hills became steep, we'd walk. I'd do whatever Stargazer needed, and I wouldn't leave him behind.

Nanny Sara's breathing ran wispy and shallow. She drifted in and out of consciousness. This trip was the last thing she needed, but we made her as comfortable as we could. Each time her eyes opened she whispered, "I'm going home. My Ruby's going home."

Ma picked at her brooch every waking minute. Ruby soothed her, sang low, trying to ease the tension.

"Did Will say why we are being transported in such a fashion?" Ma leaned forward from the wagon bed, anxious, and gripped my arm as I drove.

"Gen. Sherman was worried about the soldiers coming. He wanted us to be safe, so he gave us this wagon."

"I see," she said and sat back. Then, not ten minutes later she leaned forward again. "Where are we going? Are we going home, Robert?"

"Yes, ma'am," I answered, thankful she still knew my name, wondering what *home* meant to her.

There were seven members in the escort—one drove the supply wagon, two rode in front, two beside, and two behind. We were as safe as Gen. Sherman could make us, and as imprisoned.

Early on the second day I whispered to Emily that we'd made a wide turn from the way I came. "We're avoiding Columbia," she whispered back. "Gen. Sherman must be planning on taking the city, the railroad."

Sherman's men eyed us suspiciously each time we whispered, so I pretended to brush Emily's ear, to tease her as I would a girl I courted. It was an act, but it felt good to sit so close to her, to feel her hair against my cheek, beneath my hand.

The children were played out with fussing and fear of the blue-coated soldiers. They kept us busy, and maybe that was good. We didn't have time or ease to worry. Henry's eyes searched out mine each time we stopped, begging me not to leave him. I reminded him I was in the wagon just in front of him. But I wondered what his young life had been that he was so fearful, and what would become of him with no ma or pa.

On the fifth day we figured we'd passed the state line. The soldiers didn't speak of leaving, and I have to admit I was glad of their help, glad of the extra wagon.

Nanny Sara weakened by the hour. Ruby lay next to her day and night as we rumbled along, singing spirituals, sweet and low, in her ear. Ma absently patted Nanny Sara's feet, soothed her legs, then patted her feet again until Ruby gently laid Ma down on the other side of her. At night she tucked all six children in and around Nanny Sara. They and all the women slept together in the one wagon. It was warmer that way.

I was always glad of the morning, glad to see Emily's smile, tired though she was. Whenever possible Emily rode on the wagon seat next to me. I was glad for her company.

We built a small fire the eighth night and sat around it, roasting old ears of corn and a few potatoes. Ruby tried to feed Nanny Sara a thin gruel, but she'd stopped eating.

"We'll be pulling out in the morning," the captain said to no one in particular. "You're a day or two from your county."

"Thank you for bringing us so far," Emily offered. The captain looked up, nodded to her, held her gaze, and looked back into the fire.

"You'll need to keep moving," he said.

"Gen. Sherman said you'd leave us a map." I hoped this man would carry out his orders.

"I'll give it to you in the morning."

"I'd like to look it over now. I want to be sure I've got my bearings before you leave us."

The captain smirked. "Don't know your own neck of the woods, do you, son?"

I held my temper. "I've got four women and six children to get home safely, sir—four women Gen. Sherman wanted escorted safely out of hostile territory. One of them may not see the new moon. I'd like to get her home to her own bed before that happens."

The captain straightened, threw the last of his brew in the dirt, and pulled a roll of paper from inside his shirt. He tossed it across the fire, barely missing the flame, and strode into the dark. I grabbed the roll from the dirt, smoothed it out, pocketed the passes, and studied the map against the low flames.

A private emptied the last of the chicory on the ground and swirled water round the pot. "Don't mind him. He's always edgy before a skirmish."

"Shut up, Fitzhue!" the sergeant barked. "You talk too much."

Insulted, the private mumbled, "How would I know how much is too much?"

"None at all would suit best!" the sergeant barked again, then threatened, "You're still in the army, Private."

Fitzhue stood grim, saluted, then disappeared into the night.

I recognized the Yadkin River and parts of North Carolina drawn across the roll of paper. The map had led us due north, then far west. It was not the fastest way, but after what I'd heard from Fitzhue, I wagered it had been the safest.

I'd have to trust the general. It sounded as though Pa had. I couldn't help but wonder if Pa'd known what Gen. Sherman would do with those maps once he'd drawn them. I wondered if Pa knew Sherman's plans to burn his way from Atlanta to

Savannah, if he'd understood Sherman's idea of making war brutal on a civilian population. None of that sounded like things Pa would support. But it was war, and he'd drawn those maps for a Union general. I knew from all Pa'd told me about the military that a soldier only knows what he's ordered, what is in front of him. That is what he answers to, and he must answer straight.

I sure would've liked to talk with Pa, to see him. I prayed he was all right, that he'd come home safe.

When we woke the next morning the escort detail was already saddling up. The captain never spoke but tipped his hat to Emily as he led the detail and nearly empty supply wagon away.

It was a relief to see them go. We took extra time before pulling out that morning. The children breathed easier, were less quarrelsome, and Henry begged to ride shotgun with me. Nanny Sara couldn't last long, and Ruby wanted to make her as comfortable as she could. We took the roads slow and easy, for Nanny Sara's sake, and because Emily and Ruby and the older children took turns walking to lighten the load, especially as we reached the foothills. Only Ma refused to walk.

Late that morning we knew Nanny Sara teetered near her end. We left the road and pulled beneath the bare branches of an old oak tree, sheltered from the wind by a stand of pines. It seemed a little like a church, and I hoped Nanny Sara thought so. I wondered if she'd ever set foot in a church. Grandfather Ashton had not seen to his slaves' spiritual needs any more than to their bodily needs or safety. I wondered how she'd come to the Lord, found such comfort in the Word, how she'd learned so many passages by heart.

"My daughter. My precious daughter," Nanny Sara's last words, last look, were for Ruby. Her eyes slipped closed. The labored rise and fall of her chest stopped. For all we'd known for days and days it was bound to happen, it seemed too quick, too sudden an end.

Ruby's tears gave way. She held Nanny Sara's hands as long as there was any warmth in them, and I heard her long, whispered prayer, talking to Jesus, who must have been her long-time best friend, too. "Thank You, Lord Jesus! Thank You for bringing my mama to me, for all the days and weeks we've had to get reacquainted, for all the love we've shared. Thank You, Lord Jesus, for keeping death away so long that she knows her wishes will be tended to, that . . ." Ruby went on and on, but I stepped away, knowing I was eavesdropping on a lovers' talk.

I sat near the edge of the small grove of trees, wiped the moisture from my eyes, thanked God for Nanny Sara's love and wisdom, for all she meant to this family all her life long.

"I never thought Nanny Sara would die." It was Ma, standing behind me. "She was there when I was born, there when Mama died, there all the days of my life till I married your father."

I turned to look up at her. Ma's face looked sad, but serene in a way I'd not seen. She spread her skirt and sat on the grass beside me. "Ma?" I said, afraid to break the spell.

She looked at me like that was a perfectly normal thing to say. "What is it, Son?"

I swallowed, not knowing what I wanted—just that I wanted her—wanted my mother to be my mother, stay my mother. "Nanny Sara said she wanted to be buried in the slave cemetery at Ashland." It was all I could think to say.

Ma nodded. "I know she made you promise that." Ma shook her head. "Though I suppose she has every right to be buried in the family plot."

"She was part of your family." I tried to agree with her, to understand Ma's unlikely generosity.

She snorted softly. "You mean Papa's, before he married Mama."

Now I didn't understand, and I guess Ma read that in my face.

"Oh, Robert. We all knew. Papa never said and Mama tried to keep it from me. But Ruby is my half sister as surely as her son was my half brother." Ma stared into the distance. What was she saying? "They thought I didn't know, but Ruby was too like me not to notice." Ma ripped up dead grass and tossed it absently. "Papa was a naughty thing in those days, but I guess it was his right."

I couldn't answer. What could I say—my dead grandfather was more despicable than I'd known? I was wrestling with that when Ma spoke again. "So you bury her in a nice spot. Make sure she has some shade." She waited for me to speak.

"Yes, ma'am," was all I could say. Ma nodded, as if that was taken care of, and stood.

"I'll tell Papa. I'll be the one to break the news to him. He will surely miss her biscuits." Ma turned to walk away, and I could only stare after her, too flummoxed to talk. Then Ma half turned, and I saw the tears on her cheek. "I'll miss her, too. Ashland won't be the same without Nanny Sara."

I waited another hour or so before going back to the wagon. Ruby had wrapped her mother in a soft quilt, the best we'd brought, and laid small pine swags around her. Emily stood by Ruby, just stood there, comforting her with her nearness. The children sat, tired from their walk, in a solemn ring. Ruby handed me the Book, asked me to read Psalm 23. I kept my voice as steady as I could, but I kept remembering that first time

Nanny Sara asked for this reading, while I forced Grandfather's face from my memory.

"Let's us go on, now." Ruby voiced the decision none of us could make. "We've got to get Mama home to her resting place. We promised her."

That helped. We all had something to do, something to do for Nanny Sara.

"I'll ride beside my son now," Ma said, just as though we'd been taking turns all along.

"Of course, Cousin Caroline," Emily said, pulling Henry back, just as surprised as I was.

Ma chattered for the next hour as though we'd been talking all along. "You will need to see to the planting, Robert. Your father will need your help." It was the first time she'd mentioned Pa, and I couldn't but hope there was some piercing to her darkness. Then she began to pick at her skirt. "I know I've not always been the best mother to you, Robert."

"Ma—"

"Let me finish," she ordered. "Life does not always turn out as we expect when we're young. Sometimes in youth, in passion, we make rash decisions. Sometimes we are unable to live with those decisions." Did she mean marrying Pa, bearing me? "But that is no reason not to live up to our responsibilities. I just want you to know that I see many things more clearly now." She smoothed her skirt. "I'll not have Nanny Sara, but we'll have Ruby, and we'll get by."

"Ma, Ruby might have other plans."

"Plans?"

"Plans to get to her son, to Jeremiah."

"Oh, that. Well, I'm sure Papa will let him come back if he'll behave himself."

My heart sank to my boots and my head swelled, pounded. I couldn't sort Ma's fancy from her facts. I wondered if anything she'd said to me that day was true—about Nanny Sara and Grandfather, about her being a better mother, about Pa.

We rode on, no longer needing Gen. Sherman's map for this leg of the trip. Emily recognized the road and knew her way. We passed houses, but if anybody lived in them they kept to themselves. Families on the road were a common sight. Nobody had food to share, and neighborliness was not what it was before the war. It was just as well. We needed to get Nanny Sara's body in the ground. Emily figured we'd reach Ashland and Mitchell House late the next day.

"I can't wait," Ma said. "I've had more than enough of this wagon, this dirt."

"I think we all have," Emily said, pulling the twins onto her lap.

"How are you doing, Ruby?" I asked. She'd not said much since she'd wrapped Nanny Sara tight in her quilt.

Ruby sighed. "We've got to get Mama in the ground. That's all."

It had to vex her that the children giggled, crawled, and kicked one another all around her ma's body. But we couldn't keep them still every minute.

That night we stopped by a stream, built a fire, roasted the last of our corn and potatoes. I let Stargazer drink his fill, brushed him till we'd both had enough, and set him to graze. Emily and Ruby bedded down the children, then sat again by the fire. I stirred the embers.

"Emily, what about the children?" I waited while she stared into the flames. "Our food is gone. I'm thinking we'll reach

284

Ashland and Mitchell House tomorrow, but I don't think Noah and Mamee have anything to spare."

"We'll manage," Emily snapped, then pushed her hair back and sighed. "When Henry first came knocking on Aunt Charlotte's door he was all alone and starving. It took days for him to tell me that his mother set him down by the road one day, that she never got up again. Even when he told us, it was a long time before we understood that she couldn't, that she'd died there." She sighed again. "I couldn't turn him away."

"Next we knew, children were left on our doorstep. We don't even know who their parents are—or who they were," Ruby said, turning a worried face to Emily.

Emily covered her face with her hands, then looked up, trying to blink the weariness away. "There are thousands of displaced families—starving women and children, old folks and freed slaves—all with no place to go and nothing to eat." Emily straightened, defending herself. "I couldn't leave them to Gen. Sherman and his men."

I covered her hand with mine. I needed, deserved no explanation. I hope I'd have done the same, and loved Emily that she did the thing that needed doing. Still, starvation painted an ugly picture, and I didn't know how to change the colors.

"There'll be catfish in the Yadkin. I remember that," offered Ruby.

"That's right." I remembered too. "There are seines at Ashland and Mitchell House both, or there were. I always caught a good string with a pole. We won't starve."

"There's the gold in our buttons," Emily reminded me. "If there's food to be had we can still buy some." Her eyes brightened. "Thank God Aunt Charlotte didn't put her money into Confederate bonds."

285

"She paid for that—for not doing that," vowed Ruby. "Her neighbors looked mighty hard on her for not putting her gold into the Cause."

"Then I'll not feel bad to have it," said Emily. "It was dearly bought."

"Water under the bridge, Miss Emily. Miss Charlotte would be proud—you taking these children." Ruby stood, and her voice turned sad. "It's the future that's so uncertain, for all of us ... I guess the past and the future get so balled up sometimes it's hard to keep one from the other."

"Ruby?" Emily looked up. "You know you'll always have a home with me—wherever that is."

Ruby didn't answer but brushed her skirt and walked off into the night. Emily frowned, concerned, but then Lizzie called for her.

I knew what ailed Ruby. Sometimes it ailed me too. It was hard to explain to anybody who'd not walked under Grandfather's power. I said goodnight to Emily, waited half a minute, then followed Ruby's trail.

"Ruby?" She stopped. "I just want you to know I'll do all I can to get you to Jeremiah. We'll go North soon as we can. It'll just take some time." And then I said the thing I most wanted her to understand. "I know going back to Ashland can't be easy for you."

She didn't answer, and since I'd said all I needed to say, I turned to go.

"Robert."

"Yes, Ruby?"

"I'm glad that old man is dead."

I nodded to the darkness, picturing Grandfather's face, his hands. "I'm glad, too, Ruby."

Thirty-Five

$\mathscr{I}$t was dusk when we pulled onto the road leading to Mitchell House and Ashland.

"Papa must be beside himself!" Ma clapped her hands like a child. "He'll wonder we've been gone so very long."

"I think we'll stop at Mitchell House tonight, Cousin Caroline," Emily cut in. "Mamee will have rooms ready, and we all need a good night's rest. You can help me get the children to bed."

"But I want to go home to Ashland! I want to go home now!" Ma pouted.

"We'll talk about it tomorrow, Ma." I rested my hand on hers.

"Tomorrow?" Ma acted as though I'd slapped her.

"We've got to bury Nanny Sara. That's the first thing we'll do in the morning." I tried to sound firm, like it was long decided.

"Who?" Ma puzzled.

"Nanny Sara," Emily insisted, losing patience.

"Oh," Ma said. "Yes, I suppose. But Papa will be vexed if we delay."

I sighed, turning Stargazer down the lane toward Mitchell

House. I couldn't conjure how the next few days would play out.

A lone lamp shone through the window of Cousin Albert's study. Emily reached for my arm. I knew she ached for her father, the father she'd known all her life before the war. I was thankful that was all she knew.

Noah and Mamee, surprised and glad and fearful as they were to see us, made each one welcome. They marveled over Ruby's homecoming and grieved over Nanny Sara's passing. They rejoiced that Emily was restored safe to them, then delighted and feared over the six hungry, dark, saucer-eyed children. They did all they could to distract and settle Ma, who seemed not to notice anything amiss from her world.

"There's something you should know about Ashland," Noah began. Ma's ear perked.

"Not now, Noah," Emily warned. "Whatever it is can wait till morning. We're all done in."

"But you should know—" Noah tried again.

"What about Ashland? Speak up!" Ma demanded.

Noah looked uncertain.

"Tomorrow, Noah," Emily insisted, guiding Ma, who fussed a mile a minute, firmly up the stairs. "Tell us everything tomorrow."

I retreated, like a coward, to the stable, where I brushed Stargazer till the house lights dimmed.

Thirty-Six

It was dark when I woke. Not even the birds were awake or singing their morning call. I reached for my boots and pants, then crept down the hall. I stopped at Ma's door, pushed it open just a crack, and pressed my ear close to listen. The fluttered whisper of her sleep came through. I breathed easier.

Down the stairs and out the door, I pulled on my boots and wrapped my jacket tight around me. A fierce March wind had blown up during the night.

I figured to go to Ashland's slave cemetery and dig Nanny Sara's grave before the others woke. Ruby'd told me about a pine tree that Nanny Sara'd loved, where to dig if there was room for a grave there. I meant to have it ready for whatever service she wanted. I also figured I'd best be handy when Ma roused. I didn't know how she'd manage once she realized all over again that Grandfather was dead. What other memories might that trigger? How could we contain her?

Digging helped, the pushing, pulling, hefting. My hands nearly froze, and I wished mightily for gloves. It was only March, the air carried a bite, and the Carolina clay gave way only because it had to. I was less than halfway down. The morning light filtered through the trees as Ruby showed up, shovel in tow.

"That's the way I met you." I smiled.

"Don't you worry. I won't be using this one on you, Mista Robert. I appreciate all you doin' for Mama."

"Nanny Sara was one of the best people I've ever known, Ruby. I'm proud to do whatever I can by her."

"That makes two of us. Let's dig this grave." And we did. Together we dug it deep, and the deeper we went the less the wind ripped at us. We'd finished by the time the sun, shooting in and out between clouds, rode high over our heads. We found a slate to set at its head till we could carve a proper marker. Noah'd said he wanted to do that for Nanny Sara.

Ruby pushed windblown tendrils of hair from her eyes and looked around at the other graves. She walked among the markers, reading the few pine-carved and slate-scratched names out loud, saying who she remembered, who she'd not known.

"You read real well." Not many slaves could read, and I wondered how she'd learned.

"Miss Charlotte taught me." Ruby sat on dried needles behind the shelter of Nanny Sara's pine. "Miss Charlotte was the best white woman I ever knew, besides Miss Lydia."

Miss Lydia was Grandmother Ashton. "I never knew her."

"You missed out. Miss Lydia a fine lady, a good heart, even though her husband's ways sometimes shamed her." Ruby turned away. "I apologize, Mista Robert. Sometimes I forget he was your grandfather. You're not much like him."

"I knew my Grandfather for what he was, Ruby. You don't need to apologize. And don't call me 'Mister'—please."

She smiled. "All right, then."

I wondered how such a fine woman got tangled in with

Grandfather. My wonders must have been written on my face.

"Masta Marcus was a weak man, a selfish man, but he didn't seem such a bad man till Miz Lydia died. When he lost her he lost everything that held him back from ugly." Ruby closed her eyes. "I guess I don't have to tell you. Mama said you know."

I sat across from her. "I know about you helping Ma and Pa elope. I know about Grandfather taking you—" I looked away, not wanting to finish, not able to look in her eyes. "I know about Jeremiah, and that Grandfather sent you away."

"I never saw my mama or my baby again." Ruby wrapped her arms tight around herself.

"How did you end up with Grandaunt Charlotte?"

Ruby looked up. "It was because of Miz Grace, Masta Marcus's older sister. Miz Grace was the mistress of Mitchell House, Miz Emily's grandmother. When Masta Marcus vowed to sell me off, Miz Grace said she knew just the buyer. Masta Marcus didn't care, didn't want the money. His only concern was that he never set eyes on me again. Miz Grace assured him I'd be sent so far South he'd never hear my name." Ruby looked away, shivered. "Miz Grace protected me, all she could. She sent me to her younger sister—her black sheep sister—Miz Charlotte, in South Carolina."

"Why did they call her the 'black sheep'?"

"Oh, she ran off with a French-speaking man—rich, and just off the boat. He was an abolitionist to boot—if you can dream there'd be such a thing. Mr. Marcus wouldn't have anything to do with his sister. Even though Miz Charlotte married the man, her brother never spoke her name again. It was like she was dead to him.

"Miz Charlotte treated me more like a hired servant, never like a slave. She taught me to read and write, to speak proper, though she couldn't tell nobody about any of that. She never had children of her own. I think she thought of me like her daughter sometimes." Ruby smiled. "But, oh, how I missed my mama."

"She never knew where you were."

Ruby shook her head. "As long as Miz Grace was alive she'd send news about Mama and Jeremiah along to Miz Charlotte, who'd let me read her letters. They couldn't risk letting Mama know where I was. If word ever got to Masta Marcus, there'd be the devil to pay, and his name was still on my bill of sale. Miz Charlotte couldn't bring herself to sign her name to it, and Miz Grace didn't dare."

"Aunt Grace died, when?"

"About the time Mista Albert's own wife died—when that baby boy born."

"Alex."

Ruby nodded. "Sixteen years ago. Miz Grace was so sick and grieved she followed Miz Rose to her grave. That was the last I heard of Mama or my boy, the last Miz Charlotte heard."

I thought about that, about all the secrets that pulled down Ruby's life, over and over. I wondered if even Ruby knew them all. I yanked the dead grass, angry for the many years she'd missed with those she loved most in this life, and how all of that heartache fittingly lay at Grandfather's door.

Ruby stood and clutched the pine tree, leaned her cheek against it. "I helped your mama run off with your daddy because of the way he looked at her. I'd never seen a man look at a woman like that. He looked at her—not like he owned her, but like he cherished her—treasured her—held her high in his thoughts. I never knew your mama to be so happy, not since before we laid Miz Lydia in the ground." Ruby shook her head sadly. "I thought, simple as it sounds, that if Miz Caroline could have that kind of love, that kind of happy, maybe someday it would find me too."

Ruby pulled the turban from her hair and wiped her eyes. "You know, after he take me I never wanted a man. Miz Charlotte offered to let some good colored man court me." She shook her head. "But I couldn't bring myself to think there'd be any love in that. There was no love in what Masta Marcus did to Mama. There was no love in what he done to me." She shuddered, and the tears fell like rain.

I waited, not knowing what to say.

"So all these years later I'm still asking, where is that happy? And I'm still asking . . . is there never any end to sadness?"

I turned away. It was a question I'd asked, even before the war. It was a heated, dark question that, at least for me and my family, had its roots all tangled and bound up in slavery. My fists clenched. I felt the fever rise inside me. I vowed again to do all I could to rip slavery from our family, from everywhere I could reach, to cast it forever into a pitching, burning fire.

I thought about what Gen. Sherman was doing and the reasons he did it—how it didn't seem to have much to do with ending slavery but how slavery would end if the North won the war. I thought about Pa and his part—aggressive, but without a gun. I thought about Mr. Heath, and the Henrys, and our years helping the Underground Railroad. I thought about Cousin Albert and how he thought the coloreds needed slavery, how he thought they'd be lost without it. I thought of his men, fighting and deceiving and dying to protect what was theirs, and what they believed was theirs. I thought about President Lincoln's Emancipation Proclamation, and how far that had to go to be more than words on paper.

My heart pounded and the heat behind my eyes built. I paced, away from Ruby, fearful that if I stood too close I might explode. I had to do something.

I pictured myself in Federal uniform, blowing holes in shackles and chains, blasting away at auction blocks with the Sharps my grandfather had given me as a boy. Then I conjured an image of Grandfather and Jed Slocum.

It was all I could do not to grab my shovel, leave Ruby standing there, and walk to Grandfather's grave, dig it up, rip the casket apart, and spit openly on his bones.

But what I did was walk up behind Ruby, behind my blood aunt, and wrap my arms around her while she cried.

Thirty-Seven

The warning bell from Mitchell House rang wildly, not stopping, not pausing for breath. Ruby and I started, tripped over our shovels, and ran the mile against the growing, biting wind, back through the fields, to find Mamee jumping, blindly yanking on the rope.

I grabbed it from her, sat her down even as she fought me, saw the fear and tears spring from her eyes, saw the children huddled, fearful, on the front steps. "What is it? What is it, Mamee?" But she couldn't speak, couldn't stop crying. "Mamee! What's wrong? Where is everybody?"

"She shot him!" Mamee sputtered. "She shot my Noah!"

"What? Who?" Ruby ran her hands up and down Mamee's arms, trying to calm her. "Where is he? Where's Noah?"

Mamee pointed to the house, weeping. Ruby stood to run inside, but I grabbed her arm and held her back. "Who shot Noah, Mamee? Where?"

Mamee nodded, weeping. "Noah—in the study. She shot him—run off crazy with the gun."

A sick sense grew in my stomach. I was halfway up the steps

when Mamee cried, "Miz Caroline! Miz Caroline got a gun—
she crazy! She shot him! She shot him!"

Cousin Albert's study door stood open. Noah lay sprawled,
his leg twisted beneath him, blood seeping across the carpet.
Emily had already ripped her petticoat, tied a tourniquet around
Noah's upper arm. When I fell into the room Emily's eyes
sprang wild.

"Robert—" she began.

"Should I go for a doctor?"

Emily shook her head. "There's no time. I can dig the ball
out. Mamee can help me if you get her calmed down. Help me
lift him to the desk."

It took the two of us plus Ruby and Mamee to half drag his
six-foot frame across the floor, to lift him. He'd lost a good
amount of blood, and maybe that's what made him pass out—
that and the pain from his splintered leg and arm. Ma'd shot
him twice. I couldn't figure why or where she'd found a gun.

Mamee ran to boil water, and Emily bade Ruby stand by
Noah while she ran for a knife, something to dig the bullets
out, bandages, whatever she needed. She pulled me to the hallway behind her.

"You've got to find your mother. You've got to get that gun
away from her!"

"What happened? Why did she shoot Noah?"

"She heard Noah telling me that Ashland burned to the
ground." I steadied myself on the doorpost. "We didn't know
she was there. She must have been listening at the door." I
trailed Emily to the kitchen while she searched for supplies.

"Ashland? Gone?" I couldn't take that in. "We were just
there."

"What?"

"No—I mean we were in the slave cemetery—not near the Big House."

Emily shook her head. "Nobody knows who started it—bummers or deserters—Noah said they've been all over the countryside the last month. It could even have been lightning from a storm. Cousin Caroline walked in just as Noah was saying there's a rumor that Ashland's slaves set the fire—but that couldn't be. Ashland's slaves are long gone. But that's all she took in, and she suddenly believed Noah was responsible! She demanded to know what he'd done with her father.

"Before I could stop him he reminded her that Uncle Marcus was dead and buried in the family plot." Emily pushed her hair back from her eyes and looked up into mine. "She tore from the room and came back with Papa's revolver—the one he kept locked in a secret drawer of his desk."

"How'd she—"

But that's when we saw six small heads crowding the doorway. Emily took charge again. "Henry, I want you to take the children upstairs and stay there till I come—no matter how long it is."

"But—" he began.

"You heard Miss Emily, Henry. I'm counting on you." I gave his shoulder a squeeze, and he squared up, then herded the others up the stairs.

Emily rummaged through the cupboard. "Before Papa left he taught us both how to shoot and showed us where he'd hidden the revolver, just in case we'd have trouble with slaves or Yankees. I never dreamed she'd remember that!" Emily pushed scissors, twine, a needle, a knife, and a whetting stone into my hands. "Carry these to the study. I'll see if Mamee's got water and bandages ready."

297

Noah moaned, semiconscious. His black face had grown darker in pain. Ruby sponged his forehead, crooning softly to him.

"I heard some of what Miss Emily said," Ruby whispered to me. "You know she's gone to Ashland, to see for herself, to find Masta Marcus."

"I'll go after her."

"Be careful," Ruby warned. "She might not know you now, and she's got that gun."

"She crazy! She'll kill you!" Mamee warned as she and Emily set the kettle of steaming water on the floor by Ruby.

"Ma won't hurt me. She knows me. She remembered me."

Ruby held my eyes. "That was yesterday. This is today."

Emily pulled back Noah's shirt, swabbed the bloody wound.

"Do you want me here?" I asked. "Do you need me?"

"No." Emily shook her head, slapping the knife across the whetting stone. "Go after Cousin Caroline. Get that gun away from her." She looked up, frightened. "But be careful, Robert. Oh, please be careful." I pulled her forehead to mine, held her face between my palms for only a moment, then took off at a run.

Thirty-Eight

I kept to the road this time, thinking that's what Ma would have done, sweeping my eyes over the wind-raked fields, searching for signs that she'd passed.

I'd check the family plot first. Maybe if Ma'd seen Grandfather's stone, the carved words, the date of his death, maybe reality would take hold of her. But if it did, what else would she remember? The night Grandfather died? Jed Slocum?

"Father," I prayed out loud, "help me find Ma before—" I couldn't finish. "Guide Emily's hands. Be with Noah. Please don't let Noah die, Lord. He's a good man. He doesn't deserve this. Mamee needs him. We all need him."

Fierce blasts tunneled the drive. I ducked my head, shielded my eyes, and elbowed my way through the flying grit and leaves. I dodged frenzied maples. Their limbs writhed like supple, black snakes fighting the sky, and grabbed at me from both sides.

The brewing storm rumbled and drummed, troops on the march. I had to find Ma before it broke, had to keep my mind set on that. She'd run from the house—likely without her cloak. I could feel the temperature dropping.

"Ma! Ma!" I screamed, desperate for her to hear me, fearful she might hear me, praying she'd dropped her revolver.

At last the maples gave way to long-needle pines. I stumbled from the wind tunnel onto the circular drive.

I stared into the stark, fire-blackened heap that was Ashland. Death—bigger, wider than I'd seen—stared back.

The white stucco was gone. Gray stumps replaced the tall, white columns that once stood sentinel across the front verandah. Stone chimneys—black monuments—framed the ruin. The roof—broken, bent, caved—created a giant lean-to against the sky. The solid oak front door was burned but stood open—open against open space. The grand staircase climbed into air, landing nowhere.

I swallowed, needed to scream, to laugh, to spit. But all I could think was, *fitting end*. And that shamed me, for the pain this would give Ma.

I circled the house, pushed against the blasting wind, searching. Parts of the first floor remained. Parts gave way to open cellar. "Ma? Ma!" I called, fearful she might have tried to walk into the house, might have fallen through to the cellar. I thought to climb down while it was yet daylight, to search through the burned and broken beams.

But it was as if God Himself pulled a dark veil across the day. A shaft of lightning split the sky, shattering one of the tallest pines in a burst of fire. Thunder boomed. Freezing rain, partnered with sleet, shot from the sky in a million tiny knives to pierce my face, my ears, my hands. "Ma! Ma!" I screamed. But even I couldn't hear me in the rushing wind and fire.

That's when the old dream, a dream from my childhood, flashed through my mind: I'd dreamed that William Henry and I and a sea of black bodies with no names and no faces hoed behind the Heaths' house in the heat of the day. A tiny speck of a funnel blew up from the south. The wind rose until it grew into a great black funnel that pulled the green corn from the ground, split the barn, and uprooted the entire Laurelea. The funnel swallowed William Henry and the black bodies with no names and no faces, pulling them upside down and backward through the sky. William Henry's skin split a seam down the middle, all in one piece, and came flying in my face. When I looked down I was wearing William Henry's sleek black skin, and it felt good and cool and right. But when I looked up, there stood Ma, six feet above me, weeping as the world's end came on. I reached up to comfort her, calling, "Ma! Ma!" But she narrowed her eyes in hate and glared on me with shame. She shoved me away, swearing by God Almighty, then whistled a shrill blast on two fingers and set the hounds on me. She turned and ran South, away from the storm and Laurelea and me.

I'd not dreamed that in years, not since I was thirteen. It had its end in William Henry's death—there could be no more to the nightmare. But it welled a fear inside me, a monstrous thing I couldn't quell, and I screamed over and over, "Ma! Ma! Ma!"

I couldn't breathe against the driving sleet, could not see into the cellar. Pelting rain slammed my face, my chest. But I couldn't leave. What if Ma was out there? What if she was picking her way through a part of the ruined house I couldn't see? She'd never stand up to a storm like that.

I searched and searched, called and called. No answer. I couldn't see, tripped on a beam, fell headlong down steps. I ripped my jacket on some long hook, clean through my shirt, right through my skin. I didn't have to see it to know the gash ran near my bone. I tasted blood from somewhere above my lip, but it seemed nothing compared to the pain shooting through my arm. I stumbled toward the barn, hoping, praying it stood, hoping, praying that Ma'd taken shelter in a corner—calm, without her gun.

The barn stood—the same barn Stargazer and I had found shelter in Christmas morning. But Ma was not there. Only rats scurried from empty stall to empty stall, corner cowards.

I slumped against the wall behind the door, shivering, shaking all over with cold, grateful to be hidden from the storm. My arm wouldn't bend right, wouldn't stop bleeding. The tiny piercing knives gradually left off their hunt beneath my skin. I no longer felt the gash in my arm—only numbness, and gradually a spreading warmth, seeping in my feet, up my legs, across my weighted arms and chest. Sleep sang inside my head, calling me down.

From somewhere far away I heard Granny Struther's warning screech, "Don't you never give way to sleep when you be freezing cold—it be the death of you! Get out of those clothes, boy! Out of those wet clothes!"

"Yes, ma'am," I mumbled, not sure if I was dreaming, or if Granny wagged her finger before my face. But in my dream, or in my motions, I pulled myself up, slung my arms tight around me and out again, forced my feet to jump up and down, punching myself to stay awake, even as the barn swayed. I jumped and jumped, tearing at my wet and bloodied clothes, until the swinging, swaying barn overtook me. Then nothing.

The old dream came in earnest. Only this time it was Ashland, not Laurelea. And the crops hoed were not green corn, but tobacco. There were no black bodies, nameless and faceless, working the fields as before—only a hundred hoes in midair pummeling the crops, beating, tearing at their roots before the tiny black funnel ever specked the horizon. But at last it blew down—from the north this time—a blue-black speck in a corner of the sky. It grew and grew till it ripped up everything—the barn, the house, the chickens, the tobacco plants—the ones with roots and the ones without—sending long, green, curled leaves with sticky spines spinning through the air upside down and backward.

William Henry was not there, fighting the wind funnel, as he'd been so many times before. Jeremiah was not there. But there stood Wooster, strong on his one leg. The storm ripped all around him, fierce, and dragging, pulling everything with it, near and far—all of Ashland—everything but him.

Just as I asked how he could hold against the storm, Ma appeared, standing six feet above me. I knew she'd whistle for the hounds, and I couldn't bear it. I lifted my arms, torn and bleeding, over my face, hoping to save my eyes. I waited and waited. But the whistle never came—only her shouts, on and on, from a long way off.

At last I dropped my arms, cracked my eyes against the light. There stood Ma, hate and shame claiming the corner creases of her eyes. I crunched my eyes, hoping the image would fade. But when I opened them, Ma stood with a Colt 44 leveled at my head. "Be a dream," I prayed, "be my fevered dream."

"Get up, you filthy Yankee pig," she ordered. "Get up before I shoot you dead."

"Ma." I tried to speak. My throat tightened, swollen, parched. I can't say if the word came from my mouth.

"Get up, or I'll shoot you here!" she screamed.

I tried to stand, stumbled, and caught myself against the wall.

"Ma," I tried again.

"What did you call me?" she shrieked.

"Ma." I heard the word.

"Don't call me that. How dare you call me that!" She swung the gun in my face. "What have you done with Papa?"

"It's me, Ma—Robert," I pleaded, but no words came out.

"I shot those thieving darkies dead—those Yankee bummers set them to it! I'll shoot you too, you Yankee cuss! Now, show me! Show me where you've tied him!" She threw open the barn door, shoved the gun in my ribs. It scraped my arm. I cried out, stumbled forward, slid, fell across slick ground, a thin sheet of ice.

"Get up! Get up!"

I willed myself stronger, able to stand, but my crooked arm weighed me down. What did she mean she shot the darkies? Who did she shoot besides Noah? The children? Where was Emily? Ruby? How long had I been out? Everything spun off kilter.

"Get up! Get up, or I'll shoot!"

I pushed to my knees, off the frozen ground. The storm had stopped—no more sleet shooting from the sky, no freezing rain. The wind, not so fierce now, had blown the storm and clouds out, leaving a three-quarters moon to glisten off the layer of ice covering all the world. Hours must have passed since I left Mitchell House. How strange, I thought, to die there, in the barnyard of burned Ashland, all the world a-shimmer.

The gun dug into my ribs, shoving me upward. I cried out, "God! Oh God, help!"

"He won't help you. He never helped me! He didn't save Mama!" She laughed hysterically. "He couldn't even save Ashland!" Ma's venom spewed off the edge of reason, but she kept on, swinging the revolver through the air.

"I'll never ask a living soul for help—not ever again. I trusted that fool Will Sherman—I trusted him to be a gentleman, a man of his word—and look what's happened! He freed those slaves, and just see what they've done!" Ma shook the revolver at my face. I prayed it was not loaded.

"The slaves didn't do this, Ma. It was a storm."

"Get up! Get up, I say!" Ma kicked at my leg. "My home was already burned to the ground before this demon storm ever started! I had that fool Yankee in my sights just before the sleet started, sifting through my ashes. You're all alike, snakes slithering through the spoils! Show me what you've done with Papa!"

I was her fool Yankee, sifting through the ashes, saved by the storm. What gave me the strength to stand I don't know. It was strength beyond me, but in me. There was nowhere to go, no way I could take her to Grandfather. I turned to explain. The gun exploded near my ear.

"I told you I'd shoot! I've got three shots, and I won't miss! Where is he?" Ma held the gun in two shaking hands, aimed at my face.

"This way." I stumbled again but started walking. Three shots meant she'd only used three—two on Noah, one just now. Emily and Ruby were safe—if Ma was telling the truth, if she knew the truth, if she'd loaded all six chambers. I could only think to take her to Grandfather's grave, to show her the marker, try to reason with her once we got there.

We both slipped and slid through the ice and ash, stumbling through the dark. I tried to take her the long way around the house, hoping she'd calm in the walking, hoping if all else failed that I could outrun her in the shadows, try again in the morning. "Father," I prayed, "I don't know what to do here. Help us."

"What did you say?" she demanded.

305

"Praying. I was praying."

"Stop it! I told you it doesn't work."

I nearly laughed. Crazy as that is, stumbling through the dark, hounded by my crazy mother with a loaded gun, yelling at me to quit praying, I nearly laughed. But I said, "How do you know it doesn't work?"

"I tried it, you fool. I asked God to bring my Albert back from the war, back to me. I heard what they said—that he died in some foul Yankee prison! Murdered by Yankees! Murdered by you!"

"No, Ma," I whispered.

"Shut up! All I want now is home and Papa, and look—look at my home!" Her anger turned shrill, but the gun did not leave my shoulder. "If God was real He'd blow you stupid Yankees to kingdom come!"

"I'm not a soldier. I swear I'm not a soldier."

"Take me to him! Take me to Papa!"

We groped our way to the family plot, to the iron fence covered in ice, a ghostly border in the moonlight.

"Why did you bring me here? Papa is not here!"

I pulled open the gate, praying for wisdom, for some understanding of how to get through to Ma. "This way."

She followed me through the gate. I counted the stones. I couldn't read the words in the dark. Grandfather's stone was rougher, newer than the others. I remembered that Jed Slocum lay there too, buried beneath Grandfather's casket. Did Ma know? Would she remember?

I could feel her step back. "You're trying to trick me."

"I'm not, I swear. The words on this stone tell where he is."

"Strike a light."

"I don't have a lantern." Surely she could see that.

"Strike a match—from your pocket."

"What?" Then I remembered. I did have a small tin of lucifers that I always carried in my pocket. Ma knew that. How could she know that and not know me? I pulled out the tin, thankful, fearful, and struck the lucifer. That tiny flame sprang between our faces in the dark. The woman that was Ma looked older, harder, fearsome. But in that moment she must have seen me.

"Robert?" The match burned low. "Robert?" Her face drew, puzzled. She pulled the gun from my side.

"It's me, Ma. It's me."

She seemed confused about her surroundings, anxious, but tried to connect a thread. "Where is Papa? What have you done with him?"

"Grandfather died in the winter, Ma. You and Emily buried him here." The match died out.

"No, no. That is not possible." Fear crept back in her voice. I struck another match, saw her grip on the revolver tighten.

"Look. Look at the words, Ma." I pulled her finger to Grandfather's stone, helped her trace the words. She shook her head.

"No. No." My chances were slipping.

"Hold. Hold, Ma."

She looked at me, seeing me, not seeing me, confused, frightened. "Why do you call me that?"

"Because you're my mother. I love you, Ma." I said it, meant it, with all my heart.

She sat back onto the frozen ground, limp. "Why? Why would you love me?" She held the revolver, but loose, in her lap.

"Because you're my mother," I said again. "Because I love you." What else could I say? My mind wouldn't hold anymore, and the night began to spin again.

"I didn't love Papa," she said as she touched the stone. "I

didn't." She pulled her hand away. "I was afraid of him." She almost laughed. "I needed him. I wanted him to love me. But I don't think I loved him." She sat quietly a moment. "How could I do that?"

I didn't know what to say, didn't know if I should speak.

She touched my arm. "Where did you learn such a thing—to love me?"

"Where?" I repeated. I wondered if I was dreaming—if I'd passed out and was dreaming this graveyard nightmare in the three-quarters moonlight. "It's the love God gave me. His love in me." They weren't my words. I didn't have any more words. I didn't understand it, but the words came, and even though I couldn't form them in my mind, I meant them. I said them. "Christ in me."

"I never knew that." Ma shook her head. "I heard Rev. Goforth —do you remember him? He used to talk to me about that—Christ in me—before the war. I never knew what he meant."

"I didn't know what he meant either, Ma—not then. But it's something that grows inside—all our life, I think." I felt her stare at me through the dark. "Ask Him, Ma. Ask Him to come, to live inside you."

I felt her shake her head again. "He wouldn't want to, not in me."

"He does, Ma. He loves you. He loves you—even more than I can—more than Pa or Emily or—anyone."

"Albert. You were going to say, 'more than Albert.'" I couldn't answer that, and silence stretched between us. "I loved him, you know. I loved Albert. And I loved Charles. I loved you, and Mama, and Miss Laura. Divided. My heart was always divided. Loving one betrayed the others. But I couldn't stop loving them—any of them. And I couldn't stop hating, though I don't know why." She pressed her fist against her forehead, rocked back and forth. "I don't know why." She sighed, "Oh, I'm tired, Robert. So very tired. I can't keep fighting like this."

"I know, Ma." I pulled her to me with my good arm. The effort made the gravestones tilt in my head. And then another thought came. It wasn't a thought I'd ever held, but my mouth formed the words. "Loving is who God is. It's a way we're like Him." And then I said the thing I never thought I'd say to her, never thought I'd link between her and Cousin Albert. "Don't begrudge the love you gave."

"Oh, God," Ma whimpered, her head turned into my chest. I couldn't hear what else she said, didn't know what sense, if any, formed in her head. The wind picked up again and the pounding of horses' hooves beat; the rattle of wagon wheels rumbled down the lane, onto the circular drive. We strained toward the sound. A lantern bobbed through magnolia and bare maple branches, a ghastly dancing in and out among the pines.

"Jed Slocum!" Ma whispered.

"No, Ma. It's not. He's gone. He can't hurt you."

But the flame, the sputtering light through the dark trees shot fear up my spine. Even though I knew Slocum was dead, it brought back the night he returned to Ashland by torchlight, dragging two runaway slaves behind his horse. He'd axed the foot off one—off Jacob, who'd died. He'd beaten the younger boy, Jeremiah, senseless, a nightmare in blood.

Ma whimpered again, "Jed Slocum," and shrank back.

"No, Ma, no. It can't be. He's dead." I wanted to say, "Stay here. Wait for me. I'll find out who it is." But she pushed me back, pushed for all she was worth against my torn arm. I cried out, still reaching for her. But she was up and running, stumbling full tilt toward the house. I groped for the revolver, praying she'd forgotten it. But it was nowhere on the ground. "Ma! Ma! Wait!" I scrambled after her, but she was gone.

"Robert? Robert! Where are you?" It was a man's voice, strong above the reining in of horses. I knew the voice but couldn't place it.

"Stay back!" Ma screamed. "Don't touch me, Jed Slocum! I'll kill you! I'll kill you, I will!"

"I'm not—I'm Wooster Gibbons, Ma'am. I'm from Sa—" He never finished because Ma's fourth shot rang out, the lantern shattered, and the horses reared, whinnied, cried, pawed the sky in their traces.

"Wooster! Wooster!" I cried, tripping over the iron gate, gouging my knee, stumbling across the lawn toward the horses. "Ma! Stop it! Put that gun down!" But whatever moments of sanity Ma'd cradled were gone. A fifth shot whizzed past my head. I flew to the ground, belly-crawled toward the wagon. "God, stop her! Stop her!" I begged.

"Whoa, whoa!" Wooster, half standing, reined in the horses, stopped them from bolting. Only the darkness kept him from Ma's sights.

"Wooster!" I'd reached the wagon.

"I'm all right. Who's shooting?"

"Ma—my mother. You've got to get out of here. Go—now! She won't stop!"

"Emily sent me to help you. I'm not going till it's settled."

"She'll kill you, Wooster. She's cra—she's not in her right mind. You've got to get out of here!"

"We've got to get that gun away from her. We can do it together." He ignored all I'd said.

"She'll shoot. She'll even shoot me. She doesn't know me now."

310

"How many shots has she fired?" he whispered.

"Five, I think."

"One left. If we can get her to fire that without hitting us, we can take the gun away from her."

"I don't know if she has more—if she can reload."

"She'd have to be good to reload in the dark."

"She's better than good," I said. "She's a better shot than I am. Better than you are."

He swore. "We'll just have to be careful. Here, take the reins." Wooster climbed down from the wagon, grabbed his crutches, slipped across the ice. I tried to catch him, but he brushed me away and righted himself.

I tethered the reins, shaken that I'd not been able to help Wooster, shaken more that he'd nearly been killed, thankful beyond knowing that he'd shown up and I was no longer alone. "Wooster, I don't know why you're here, but—" He pressed my arm, and I felt the strength from him—strength he'd never carried the months we'd traveled South.

"Where do you think she's gone?"

"I don't know. I'm guessing near the house—she thinks she's guarding the house."

"The house? Emily said it burned." Wooster squinted to see through the darkness.

"To the ground, but she thinks she has to protect it, guard it. Wooster, she's—" I didn't know how to finish.

"It's all right, Robert. We'll get her." He pressed my arm again, and I felt new strength seep into me. "We'd best round the house. You come in from one direction, and I'll come from the other. If we're quiet she's not likely to hear us, and we can close in till we find her."

"But she'll shoot—"

"She can't shoot two directions at once. If we're careful we'll see her first—at least see her move. Just wait—like you wait for a snare."

I shook my head, not knowing what else to do, worried sick that she'd shoot Wooster. He must have felt that.

"We've got to try," he said. "You don't want her saving that shot till daylight. Chances are good she'll miss in the dark."

The chances didn't seem so good to me, but I sure didn't want to face Ma with a gun at dawn. Cousin Albert taught her well. "Well, let's do it," I said, knowing I might be giving away Wooster's life—or mine. "Keep to the pines on this side. I'll come around by the barn."

"Done," he said. "I'll see you in the morning." I heard the forced smile in his voice.

I pressed Wooster's arm, prayed that morning would be only a few hours away.

We circled the house in wide arcs. I couldn't see Wooster as he moved among the pines and magnolias. I prayed Ma couldn't either. Once I heard a sharp intake of breath—maybe Ma's—but I wasn't sure. I waited and waited, crouched in the dirt.

It reminded me of times as a boy that I'd crouched in the dirt beneath the Heaths' front porch, waiting, straining to over-hear my parents and the Heaths and the Henrys talk, tell each other secrets and plans not meant for my ears. How I wished that was what I was doing now.

But I was waiting, again, for Ma to speak, to move, to show me somehow where she was—so I could do what? Overpower her? Push my mother to the ground and pry a gun from her hands, knowing one of us might end up dead? That's exactly what I needed to do, and the idea made me sick. How could I do this thing?

312

Because it needs doing. The answer seemed so plain. For her own sake and everyone's sake I needed to stop her, protect her from herself—from the horrors that some sick part of her was capable of. That didn't make it easy.

From somewhere to my far left I heard a whimpering, a whispering, a running prayer or pleading. I realized I'd circled too far out, too near the back of the house, almost on a path to the summer kitchen. Ma's voice was somewhere near the front of the house, so I circled closer, keeping low to the ground, almost crawling, keeping to the shadows, sliding over the ice. And then it cracked. The ice cracked, and the sound carried far on the soft wind.

Ma screamed. I saw her jump, stand, aim her gun in the moonlight. I froze, knowing it was the end. From the other side of the house Wooster let out a rebel yell, as loud and shrill and bloodcurdling as any dying rabbit I'd ever heard. Ma turned toward his scream, firing the revolver, screaming in return.

She stumbled backward, screaming, "No! No!" She slammed the front door standing open in open space, and rushed up the staircase. Ma's screams followed her up until she reached the landing that landed nowhere, then dropped down, down into the cellar, ending only with the crash of boards and the sharp thud of her body against the earthen floor.

"Ma! Ma!" I knew she could not have survived that fall. "Ma! Ma! Ma!" I yelled into the cellar at the top of my lungs. I was still screaming into the darkness when Wooster jerked me, dragged me, fighting, back from the edge, knowing she was beyond my reach, always and now forever beyond my reach.

Thirty-Nine

$\mathcal{M}$a's body was broken in three places. I still pray that the first break made it so she didn't feel the others.

Wooster and the Widow Gibbons stayed three weeks. They'd driven out from Salem to visit Mitchell House, arriving just before the storm, wanting to see how Emily was doing and if I'd found Ma. They hadn't known about Grandfather's death or the journey to South Carolina—none of it.

Only God knows how much it meant to have them there. Now Wooster was the strong one, the healthy one who took charge, who'd saved my life yet again.

It was beyond my ken. Ma couldn't really be gone, couldn't really be dead, could not be buried in the family plot beside Grandfather and Grandmother Ashton.

I could not understand how the children played, why they cried, forever hungry, how it was that Noah's leg and shoulder mended. Nothing in life had stopped—nothing but me and Ma.

I caught them laughing once; Emily and Ruby and Wooster stood in the kitchen, laughing at one of Henry's antics. I stared at them, not angry, not exactly—just not understanding. What could there be to laugh about—now—ever?

The morning Wooster and the widow were to leave, Wooster and I walked early the mile to Ashland, to Ma's grave. Old George had fashioned a false leg for Wooster back in Salem, and a shoe made to fit. With one crutch he stepped along at a good clip—faster than I felt up to—but we pushed on just the same. We didn't talk. It was a thing I liked about Wooster. When we reached her stone, I sat, just sat, tired beyond telling, on the rain-wet ground.

"You might like to plant some flowers here, Robert, before you go," Wooster said.

"Flowers?" I repeated. "Before I go?" The words stood fuzzy in my brain.

"Ones that will come up every year, whether you're here or not."

I thought, *Where else would I be?* but didn't say it. "Flowers," I said again, wondering what kind Ma would like.

"You've got to pick up, Robert, to go on."

I wanted to say, I *can't, and what do you know about it anyway? You've got your ma! And she's a real mother!* But I didn't say that, either. And what I couldn't bring myself to think clearly was that I wouldn't wish her back, not the way she was.

"As hard as it is, your life goes on," Wooster started.

"I don't want to hear this, Wooster—not now. I don't want to think about it."

"But you've got to think about it. There's a house full of hungry people back there, most of them children. They're looking to you for food, Robert, for answers."

"Answers? I'm fresh out of answers. Come back some other day—some other lifetime," I said. *When there's not so much death,* I thought. I stood and stomped away, sure I could outwalk him. But that was wrong, too.

"Do you remember what you told me Chap. Goforth said, about serving where you're called, about answering God's call on your life?" Wooster panted but kept up with me.

I wanted to stick my fingers in my ears, to shout at the top of my lungs, not listen to any of this. Wooster grabbed my arm.

"What do you want from me?" I shouted.

"It's not me that wants it, Robert!" he shouted back. "Why did you come here? Why did you fight your way all through the South, risk your life and mine to get here?"

"I did it to find Ma! Well, I sure found her! And look what happened!"

"Yes! Look what happened." He wouldn't let go of my arm. "You helped them get from South Carolina to North Carolina. They would have starved, the women would have been left alone—to the hands of deserters or foragers or Sherman's bummers—if you hadn't been there."

"They were doing fine before I showed up!"

"You saved those kids, found Stargazer, brought Ruby's mother back to her burial ground! For the sake of all that's holy, Robert, you found Ruby—Jeremiah's mother! Do you think Gen. Sherman would have provided a safe escort to two colored women, a passel of slave children, Emily, and your addled mother if you hadn't been there—if he didn't believe all you told him?"

"How did you know—"

"Emily told me. Ruby told me. Ruby told me you promised to get her to Jeremiah. Emily and those kids are counting on you to take care of them. You know they can't stay here. There's nothing for them! Emily won't complain, but there's not enough money to pay the taxes. They'll be turned out before next winter."

"Alex has money in England."

Wooster snorted. "From everything you told me about him, from what I know from Emily, he's probably already spent it. Even if he hasn't, he can't get it through the blockades, and after the war, who knows what will get through? Do you think he'll pay to raise slave children as his own? Do you think he'll provide for Emily once he learns she's freed all the slaves—didn't get a penny for them?" He shook my arm. "Think, Robert. Think!"

"I don't want to think!" I shoved him away. "I can't take responsibility for them. Look what happened to Ma when I tried to help her. She's dead, Wooster. She's dead! I killed her!" And then the dam broke—the dam I'd been holding back three weeks.

"You didn't kill her, Robert. You kept her from killing innocent people—me, Emily, Ruby, Noah—the children. She couldn't help herself, and she couldn't stop. You know that."

I did know that, but I needed to punish someone. I needed to punish myself for failing—failing Ma and Pa, failing to pull our family back together, failing to get Ma home. "I couldn't stop her." I swore. "I couldn't change her." I swiped at my eyes. "She could have lived a hundred more years, and I couldn't change her."

"That's the truth you have to remember. It wasn't your job to change her. It was your job to love her, and you did that. Now you need to forgive her, to let her go."

"I did forgive her! I knew she couldn't help it!"

"Knowing she couldn't help what she was is not the same as forgiving her. You know that. You know that because you know that not being able to help her is not the same as not loving her."

His words spun in my head. I didn't want to listen. I didn't want to heed. My temples throbbed. "I don't know how to go on, Wooster. I don't know how."

"One day at a time. One minute at a time. The strength doesn't come from you. You know that, Robert." I looked at him, wondering how he knew, if he really knew. "Emily told me you learned that, too. I'm glad, Robert."

Why would Emily tell him anything so personal about me? I hadn't even said it to her in that many words, and yet she knew—enough to tell Wooster. They were alike in many ways, and I was surprised I hadn't paid better heed. "You aren't courting Emily, are you?" It was the first time the idea had swept through my mind.

Wooster started, then snorted. He chuckled. The chuckle spread till he laughed out loud. "That's you! That's a lot more like you, Robert Glover! That's the grumbling, bumbling friend I ran South with!" He laughed till he clutched his sides. He laughed till tears stood in his eyes, but he hadn't answered my question.

"So what is it? Are you? Are you courting her?"

He stopped laughing—almost. "No, you fool. But if you don't wake up and do it yourself, I'm bound to!" I felt my dander rise, but he punched me in the chest. "Somebody's bound to —and soon. Just make sure it's you."

"I mean to."

"Then do it. You remember what you told Chap. Goforth about Katie Frances? Well, you're every bit as slow and stupid as he was."

"It's not the same! Katie Frances loved Andrew. She wanted to marry him, but he didn't see it. He was afraid of what the war would do to him—to her."

Wooster stared hard at me, like he was trying to read my

thoughts, trying to figure who I was. "And you're not?" He started to walk away, then turned back. "Emily has eyes for you and only you. You're a fool not to see it, and a bigger fool not to ask her to marry you." I stared after him, wondering if he could be telling the truth.

"But I'm eighteen. I don't have anything. I can't ask her. And there's a war on!"

"The war is nearly over. Gen. Sherman's already in North Carolina. Petersburg and Richmond are nearly broken through. We both know the South can't hold. It can't be news to the generals! When this war's done there won't be many men with a penny to rub between their fingers. That won't keep life from going on."

He started to walk away again, but turned back. "If you can't offer Emily anything now, court her. Promise her you'll make something of yourself—then go out and do it." Wooster raked his fingers through his hair, frustrated. "Because if you don't, you fool—I will." And he stomped off. He stomped off and left me standing in the road.

I couldn't take all that in, not yet.

I walked back toward Ashland, stopped in the circular drive. I saw the Big House's black ruin with its chimney monuments, saw the cemetery plot on the hillside—Ma's newly dug grave, and the lane to the run-down slave cabins beyond, broken and empty. I turned again and saw Wooster, my friend, clomping unevenly out the lane and down the road toward Mitchell House, toward Emily and Ruby, toward Noah and Mamee and the six small slave children in need of a home. I thought of Henry's brown eyes, imagined him growing up, learning to read, working at Laurelea with me and the Henrys.

I shook my head. I didn't feel equal to taking responsibility for Henry, for any of them. I didn't know how I could offer them protection or a home, or offer Emily a life when I owned nothing. But I didn't for a minute think that would stop Wooster from doing all of that.

Everything in front of me promised long years and hard work. Maybe I could make a different home, a different family. Maybe Emily would agree to be part of that. I shook my head. That seemed too good to be true, but I wondered.

Everything behind me, even the grieving, promised the laying down of struggle, an uneasy peace made of giving up. It seemed safer, an easier path, not so frightening. The going forward seemed too big, too hard, too uncertain.

Wooster had turned onto the road. I saw him between patches of new leaves as he thumped out of sight, determined, strong. He'd lain near death three months before. What made him so strong, so sure now? The love of his mother, the people in his church, his faith? The belief that his life could be different, new, that it could go on? What?

I remembered him back at the field hospital, when Andrew talked about war-maimed men and how they'd have nothing to offer a woman, no life worth claiming. Even then Wooster knew that was a lie, knew he was stronger than that.

But I knew, for my own part, that war maimed in ways a body couldn't see.

The old, easier path pulled hard at me. It would be so easy to give up, to quit fighting. Was that the decision Ma'd made? Did she have a choice—ever? Or did something broken inside keep her from having choices? I'd begged her to hold on. I knew she'd tried sometimes. She'd waged her inner war, long as I could remember. She'd run from one life to another, back and forth. But for some reason she couldn't hold on. She couldn't.

But I could. I could choose life and all that meant, or I could sit in my darkness.

"I can't do this alone, Lord."

I *will never leave you nor forsake you.* That Scripture promise came as clear in my mind as it had on that South Carolina road.

"But how can I do this?"

And I remembered: I *can do all things through Christ, who strengthens me.*

Christ in me. I sighed. Ma understood, I think—even if it was only for a few minutes, only at the end. I wondered what Ma had prayed for, what she'd thought in those last moments—before she thought Jed Slocum had returned, and after—when she thought I was her enemy.

I wished time could turn back, wished things could have been different for her, for Pa, for all of us. I guessed that is what everyone living through this war wished. I knew Andrew had wished it for him and Katie Frances. I prayed they'd made it, would make it through the war.

But what about after? Wooster was right—most of us wouldn't have a penny to rub between our fingers. Most of us lost loved ones, farms, everything that matters in this life. It would be hard to find our way, hard to find my way.

Trust in the Lord with all thine heart and lean not on thine own understanding. In all thy ways acknowledge him and he will direct your paths.

I breathed that Scripture in, let it take hold, let it settle. It was all right. I'd long known that you never reach a thing without setting your feet straight and walking toward it. I could do that. I could trust Him.

I breathed again. The air was new. That surprised me. I hadn't noticed when winter passed, when spring came on. The violets were blooming. It was time to plant. That surprised me too.

I looked again for Wooster but couldn't see him. He was beyond the line of trees and probably most of the way to Mitchell House.

I started down the lane. Maybe I could catch him, talk to him. Maybe I'd thank him, or just shake his hand.

It would be good, would be right to see Wooster and the Widow Gibbons off to Salem. They'd done so much for us all, in so many ways.

I picked up my pace. I thought of Emily standing in the morning sunshine, standing in the doorway of Mitchell House, waving good-bye to our friends, then waiting . . . waiting, maybe, for me to come home. I pondered that till the thought stole my breath. I smiled . . . all over . . . and began to run.

Epilogue

*T*he Salem newspaper reported rumors that Richmond and Petersburg were being evacuated that first week in April. Gen. Sherman, it was believed, was in Goldsboro, North Carolina. No one was certain which way he'd head next. A "terrible battle" had been waged at Dinwiddie, the roads strewn with the dead and dying. Dinwiddie was not far from the field hospital where Wooster and I'd left Chap. Goforth and Katie Frances.

Wooster rode from Salem the next week to tell us that Gen. Robert E. Lee had surrendered the Army of Northern Virginia to Gen. Grant outside a small Virginia village called Appomattox Court House the morning of April 9. Gen. Stoneman crossed the shallow fords into Forsyth County, North Carolina on the 10th. Union troops, under Col. Palmer, occupied Salem that same day.

We heard later that when President Lincoln celebrated the war's end at a White House reception he ordered the band to play "Dixie," saying it was one of the best tunes he'd ever heard. I thought well of him for it.

Folks wondered if the president really intended reconstruction "with malice toward none, with charity for all" like he'd talked about in his second inaugural speech.

But I think most, North and South, were relieved to lay down their guns. We all wanted to go home—those that fought on the battlefield with courage and rifles, and those that fought from home with courage and prayer.

We were sure there'd be lean times, and we worried for those we loved, but it seemed things might eventually straighten out. And then Wooster rode from Salem again, this time bearing news that President Lincoln had been shot in a theater house in Washington City on Good Friday, shot in the head, and killed. The world turned over on itself. Even the South knew it had lost its best hope for mercy. Nothing felt safe. Little felt sacred. And all of us who'd grieved through the war, grieved again.

Emily and I decided to wait two months to start our journey north—partly because the roads and railroads were a shambles and would surely be filled with starving soldiers making their way home, and partly because there were too many of us to travel together, too heavy a burden for Stargazer to pull. Wooster helped us find a second horse, Gus, old though he was, to team alongside Stargazer. Still, I feared the trip north would be too much with all of us. Noah changed that.

The day we learned that the war had ended, Noah disappeared for two days. Later we learned that he'd walked all the way to Salem, courted Rebecca, and gave her the first love poem he'd ever written. She couldn't read it. Noah promised to teach her—over a lifetime together. In less than a month they married. They took the twin girls, Mildred and Martha, thinking they might be a sweet and civilizing influence on Sam and Hez. Last I heard, all four children fight like roosters and play like whelp pups.

Mamee moved near Salem, where Rebecca and Widow Gibbons found her a job cooking for the tavern. Old George, white haired and stooped though he was, made a pretty sight toting field flowers in his stained leather apron to the tavern's back kitchen door.

Wooster and his cornflower eyes took to courting a Moravian girl who baked the best sugar cake in Salem and who didn't seem to notice or mind Wooster's false leg. Plying his leather trade, Wooster made Jubal and Henry each a round ball before we left and taught them some new game he'd learned in the army, called baseball.

The journey home to Laurelea was a long grind through a beaten backroads Virginia. The land lay wasted, houses and farms and even some whole towns in ashes. We passed hundreds of soldiers still trying to get home—mostly on foot. We saw desperate families led by penniless mothers or by youngsters no more than twelve, begging for food, searching for a place to lie down, to rest, if only for the night. Freed slaves, in groups of eight and ten and twelve with no place to go and no hope, roamed the roads, searching for somewhere, anywhere to call home.

We carried little food and took to hiding it under the children's legs in the wagon. It shamed me that we hoarded. There must have been a million times I wished for Jesus to come right down and do His miracle with the loaves and fishes, feeding the five thousand all over again. But I didn't see Him, and I wondered that I didn't have the courage or the faith to be His hands, His feet—but how could I do it without enough to feed our own?

Gen. Will Sherman's name and the signed passes he'd provided afforded us more movement and protection than I'd ever thought. Nobody would mess with those carrying the signature of "Uncle Billy."

Emily and Ruby kept a firm hand on the children, though Henry vowed he wasn't a toddle baby and didn't need "watching." He stuck by me like tar, day and night. I liked that well enough. I took to telling him about William Henry and the antics we used to pull, till Ruby got fed up and fussed, "Don't you be filling that child's head with your nonsense, Robert Glover. He has plenty of his own!"

But when I told Henry about Jeremiah, Ruby drank in every word, like every stunt Jeremiah had pulled was the funniest thing and pure gold. I can't say as I blamed her. She'd waited Jeremiah's lifetime to know him. We determined to contact William Still just as soon as we reached Laurelea. He'd have the latest news from Jeremiah. I was sure of it.

Emily and I talked about opening a school at Laurelea for Henry, Jubal, and Lizzie, for Jacob when he got older, and maybe for other freed children. I felt sure Mr. Heath would take to that idea, and that Mr. Garrett up in Wilmington might be persuaded to help with funds. The meeting house Mr. Heath had built for the colored church at Laurelea would be just the place. Our plans grew bigger every day, stretching our hope.

On those rare times Henry slept, Emily sat close to me, and I told her details about my life at Laurelea, about Mr. Heath and the Henrys, and especially about William Henry. I told her what his friendship had meant to me, how it walked with me still. By the time we reached the Maryland line I think she knew him pretty well, though she'd never laid eyes on him and never could this side of heaven.

The thing that worried me was Pa—how he'd take Ma's death and what it might do to him. I believed he'd made it through the war. I had to believe that, couldn't let my mind wander down any other path.

When we reached the Susquehanna River I breathed deeply of the summer morning. By the time we crossed the river and finally reached North East, the sun had stretched across the sky. It was all I could do not to push our team beyond their limits. When we crossed the narrow bridge over the Laurel Run, the setting sun had washed everything in rose and gold. I thought my heart might burst.

I glanced over my shoulder, glimpsed the small group huddled in the wagon bed. We were every shade of black and brown and tan—from Henry, whose skin was the sleek black of a raven's wing, like William Henry's had been, to my tan, like sand at the bottom of the run—every color I knew and loved. And we were nearly home.

We turned down the lane to Laurelea. There was Pa, walking slow beside Joseph Henry as he limped, coming in from the fields. I strained my eyes to see who walked beside them. It was a man, a young man about my age, about my size, white—or nearly—with chestnut hair and oval face. When he looked up and saw me, he stopped short, studied half a second, then tipped back his head and laughed out loud. Before Pa realized who I was, Jeremiah let out a whoop and tore like a deer across the field to meet me.

It was too good. I reined in Stargazer and Gus in the middle of the lane, jumped from the wagon, and charged into my friend. We pummeled each other, beat the living daylights out of each other's backs, and laughed till we both nearly choked. I had no idea how he got there. It must have had something to do with William Still. It didn't matter. As soon as I could talk I pulled Jeremiah round the back of the wagon and placed Ruby's hand in his. "Your ma" was all I said. Ruby gasped. Jeremiah gasped back. Tears flowed as Jeremiah pulled her from the wagon. We didn't see the two of them for hours.

Pa and I couldn't stop shaking hands, could barely hold back the dam behind our eyes. Joseph Henry slapped me on the back and picked me off the ground in a bear hug. I thought Aunt Sassy wouldn't stop touching me, wouldn't stop fussing over me, wouldn't stop feeding us all till we nearly burst our buttons. But she did. The minute little Henry decided he might adopt the mother of the famous William Henry, Aunt Sassy had eyes for none but him. She fed and helped clean and bed the others, but Henry was hers. I wondered if they'd call him Henry Henry. William Henry would've liked that.

My long absence had aged Mr. Heath. He was frail in a way I'd never seen, and I worried for him. He took a real shine to Emily and she to him, both gentle natures with big plans. It was good to see a light come in his eyes.

Pa took the news of Ma quieter than I'd expected, at least in front of me. That puzzled me at first, but I guessed he'd lost her a long time ago and had grieved that loss all those years. He asked me for the particulars. I held nothing back, though the telling was hard.

He sat a long time after the evening read that night, staring into the darkness, and every night that followed, for months. He took long walks, sometimes stayed out all night. I'd find him sitting in the rocker on the porch at dawn, long into the fall. I remembered Ruby's question the day we buried Nanny Sara, "Is there never any end to sadness?" For Ruby there was. I prayed that would be true for Pa.

A letter, much rejoiced over, came from Andrew and Katie Frances Goforth in early September. They were living near

Katie Frances's family outside Petersburg, expecting their first child in time for Christmas. Andrew had taken on a post of itinerant preacher with a four-church charge. Jeremiah hooted when I told him, remembering the time the O'Learys had hidden us in their coffins as we traveled the Underground Railroad. "That preaching fits in handy with the family coffin-making business! Folks can get a 'two-for-one!'" I laughed too, glad for the Goforths' happiness, still wondering if I'd ever know such.

Emily and I started the school within two weeks. She was a natural born teacher and a motherly sort besides. Pa and I both watched her, wondering how she'd adjust to this new life, fearful, not saying out loud what we were both thinking—*Will she be like Ma?*

I tried to hint at my worry, tried it in a dozen ways a dozen times. That exasperated Emily until one day she blew up at me.

"For heaven's sake, Robert, I don't have time for this nonsense! I've lived through a war. I've run a plantation, freed my slaves, taught them to read, cooked for an army, smuggled gold under the noses of barbarians, buried my dead, and nursed the living—sane and not. There are two dozen children in this school now and six adults all needing to learn to read and write and handle their own money in order to survive the present. You can worry all you want about the past repeating itself, but don't pester me with it!" She kicked me out of her classroom on my ear.

I took that as the Lord's answer to my question and stopped worrying. Emily was Emily. She had adapted time and time again, stepping up to do the thing that was needed and doing it with a grace that reminded me of Miz Laura. I think she reminded Mr. Heath of Miz Laura, too.

Once in a while Emily would talk about her father, about

how she loved him, how she missed him. Pa welcomed her talk, encouraged her, shared old memories. I thought well of him for it, but knew I had a ways to go when they did that. I never told Emily what Cousin Albert had done with the Testament she'd sent him. There was no need.

Summer ripened till our crop was full and fall started with a good harvest in plain view. One late September night, after the evening read and after the children were put to bed, Emily and I walked the dusky lane, down through Mr. Heath's orchard. A chill had set in two days before, and the air smelled of leaves, apples, and wood-burning fires. Frost was near. The russet apples had ripened. I reached up, pulled a beauty from the heavy branches, and offered it to Emily. She blushed in the early moonrise, pulling her shawl tight around her. My heart picked up a beat.

By way of making conversation I asked if she was happy at Laurelea and marveled that she didn't seem to overly grieve for Mitchell House.

"My family is no longer there," she said, and sighed. Emily cradled the apple against her cheek and looked up at me. "I guess I'm in need of a new family," she said, and waited. When I didn't answer she turned her back on me and mused, "I wonder where I'll find one."

"Well, I guess there's Henry and Jubal and Jacob and Lizzie," I considered, keeping my face straight. "They pretty much make up a family big enough for anybody."

Emily stood, waiting a little longer before she got fed up, turned again to face me, dug her fist into her hip, and set her mouth grim.

That was as long as I could hold. I pulled her into my arms and whispered in her ear, into her hair that smelled of cold and fall and apples just ripened, "'Course, I'm partial to families. Fact is, I'm needing a bigger family. I bet if we put our heads together we can come up with a plan that'll suit us both."

Her lips turned up into a half smile, just before they met mine, just before all her feistiness and prickles melted in my arms. Never again did I envy the love between Andrew and Katie Frances. Never again did I pine for a family other than the one I'd just set my feet to claim.

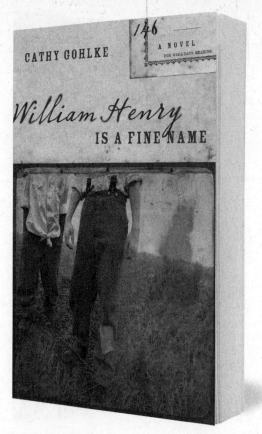

ISBN: 978-0-8024-9973-8

They told him his best friend wasn't human. Robert's father assisted the Underground Railroad. His mother adamantly opposed abolition. His best friend was a black boy named William Henry. As a nation neared its boiling point, Robert found himself in his own painful conflict. The one thing he couldn't do was nothing at all. William Henry is a coming-of-age story about a 13-year-old boy—and an entire country—that comes face to face with the evils of society, even within the walls of the church. In the safety of an uplifting friendship, he discovers the hope of a brighter day.

by Cathy Gohlke

Find it now at your favorite local or online bookstore.

Sign up for Moody Publishers' Book Club on our website.

www.MoodyPublishers.com

ISBN: 978-0-8024-8733-9

When Marty Winslow's daughter dies of a devastating genetic disease, she discovers the truth her child had been switched at birth. Her actual biological daughter was recently orphaned and is being raised by grandparents in a retirement community. Marty is awarded custody, but Andie refuses to fit into the family, adding one more challenge for this grieving single mom that pushes her toward the edge, and into the arms of a loving God.

For Andie, being forced to live with strangers is just one more reason not to trust God. Her soul is as tattered as the rundown Blue Moon movie drive-in the family owns. But Tuesday night is Family Night at the Blue Moon, and as her hopes grow dim, healing comes from an unexpected source—the hurting family and nurturing birth mom she fights so hard to resist.

by Debbie Fuller Thomas

Find it now at your favorite local or online bookstore.

Sign up for Moody Publishers' Book Club on our website.

www.MoodyPublishers.com

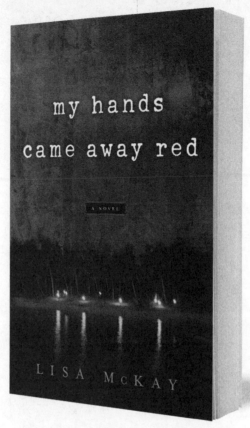

ISBN: 978-0-8024-8982-1

Cori signs up to take a mission trip to Indonesia during the summer after her senior year of high school. Inspired by happy visions of building churches and seeing beautiful beaches, she gladly escapes her complicated love life back home. Five weeks after their arrival, a sectarian and religious conflict that has been simmering for years flames to life with deadly results on the nearby island of Ambon. Within days, six terrified teenagers are stranded in the mountainous jungle with only the pastor's teenage son to guide them to safety. Ultimately, Cori's emotional quest to rediscover hope proves just as arduous as the physical journey home.

by Lisa McKay
Find it now at your favorite local or online bookstore.

Sign up for Moody Publishers' Book Club on our website.

www.MoodyPublishers.com